SEVERED

A NOVEL

VL TOWLER

INIMITABLE
PRESS

Dover, New Hampshire

Copyright © 2015 by VL Towler
Prior Copyright (*Right to Die*) © 2002 V.L. Towler

Towler, V. L. (Virginia L.), author.
    Severed : a novel / V.L. Towler.
    pages cm
    ISBN 978-0-9968772-1-3
    ISBN 978-0-9968772-0-6

    1. Women detectives--Fiction. 2. Criminal
    investigation--Fiction. 3. Homicide--Fiction.
    4. Louisiana--Fiction. 5. Detective and mystery fiction.
    6. Thrillers (Fiction)   I. Title.

PS3620.O942S48 2015   813'.6
                    QBI15-600230

COVER DESIGN: Anderson Newton Design
INTERIOR DESIGN: Marina Kirsch Design

inimitable.press@gmail.com

My words fly up, my thoughts remain below. Words without thoughts never to heaven go.

Hamlet, Act 3, Scene 3
William Shakespeare

Dedication

To my mother, Dr. Carmen Buford-Paige: your DNA is part of this story in more ways than anyone could ever understand. Your unwavering support and midwifery in all aspects of its lengthy birthing process has made this book a final reality. I could not have finished this novel without your always gentle but critical attention to detail.

You will always mean the world to me.

Acknowledgments

My deepest thanks to the following people who have been a part of this truly arduous process:

Phyllis Ring, my editor and guardian angel, who toiled through my original tome, using her editing skills to help me sustain my original voice while helping me recognize the need for major surgery to amplify it. You have elevated editing to a heavenly profession. Thanks for going the distance with me.

Dr. A. Midori Albert, Forensic Anthropologist and Professor at the University of North Carolina Wilmington, for suffering through my endless questions about forensic anthropology, and spending an afternoon with me in her campus lab.

Jeffery K. Tomberlin, PhD, D-ABFE, Associate Professor/ Departmental Internship/Research Coordinator and Associate Director, Texas A & M University Forensic & Investigative Sciences Program. He took up where Dr. Albert left off, and provided me with crucial information and entomological insights.

Both Professors Albert and Tomberlin were selfless in providing me with their scientific insights without ever knowing the plot of the story or reading the finished product. Therefore, nothing in the novel's plot contents, including any mistakes and errors of scientific principles, should be considered sanctioned by or attributed to them.

Carolyn R. Towler, MD, for digging into her well of knowledge to provide crucial information to assist me in telling my story, and my niece, Carmen Towler, for her hip-hop insights.

Jim Berger and his wife, my sister Jocelyn Towler, PhD, both of whom supported my television writing efforts by hosting me in their home in southern California for over a year. And Jim's mother, Elaine Berger, who read everything I ever asked her to read.

Valerie Cunningham, Founder of the Portsmouth Black Heritage Trail; both Dr. Kathleen Wheeler, Archeologist, and Ellen Marlatt, of Independent Archeology Consulting; and Vernis M. Jackson, Chair of the Mayor's Blue Ribbon African Burying Ground Committee: your work uncovering the bodies of the Africans buried under the streets of Portsmouth, New Hampshire (which inspired my protagonist Lula), and your passion in shepherding the dignified reburial, mirrors so adroitly my own quest in the fight for dignity of Black Americans still living in the diaspora.

JerriAnne Boggis, Chair of the Black New England Conference, for inviting me to publicly speak about my writing travails in two writing conferences. You believed when I still did not, and I am grateful.

John Gonzalez, for prefacing every email or text communication with the question: "Finish the book yet?"

Geraldine (Jeri) Palmer, my refuge on Friday nights, giving me an escape from both my writing and my life struggles.

Rebecca Hidalgo, Esq., an Assistant United States Attorney, who, decades ago, came to me in my hour of need in one of the darkest times of my life. I will never forget your charity to me, a stranger.

Sara Criscitelli, Esq., a former DOJ colleague, for letting me use her D.C. basement forever for storage.

Patty Hartwell, for introducing me to, and being my first follower, on Twitter.

Laurie Lemmlie-Leung; Antwine Chevalier; Donald Temple, Esq.; William Kummings, Esq.; and Gaylyn Boone, Esq.; for believing in my talents.

Posthumously, to the late satirist and author, Art Buchwald, of the Washington Post, for being the first to truly understand my plight and for counseling me in my hour of need.

Special Mention

My writing has endured many evolutions (and revolutions). Ultimately, I finished because my family propped me up by encouraging, cajoling, and suffering along with me. Their steadfastness could only be the product of love, and it worked: they wouldn't let me give up. And so I didn't.

Laurine, Jocelyn, Michael, Carolyn, Stephanie: my hope is that we will share an eternity together, but thanks, nonetheless, for your support during this round on Earth.

To Percy Eldridge Towler, my deceased father: your Shakespeare quote has rung in my ears my whole lifetime, and has provided me with much guidance and solace.

Contents

PART I

CONNECTED

1
POINTING FINGERS

A bomb squad should have been called. But this was Nakadee, not Manhattan. Anti-terrorist protocols were far removed in time and place for this parish. September 11th was an afterthought in the minds of this rural Louisiana police department.

So the police receptionist actually thought that the box with the green ribbon, sitting near the entrance, might be a St. Patrick's Day gift. She picked up the package and walked it into the foyer, eagerly unwrapping it in front of her receptionist station. She looked inside to see a cardboard wine caddy, which she opened. A wine-soaked finger corking a bottle of sherry fell out.

She couldn't stop screaming. Terrified, she shoved the bottle away, shrieking even louder when it toppled over and the pinkish-grey finger with its jagged tear and exposed entrails plopped onto her desk below the counter, the wine cascading like a small waterfall onto the forest-green carpet.

Her confusion about what body part she thought had been corked in the bottle revealed instantly that the 24-year-old had likely never even seen a penis in real life.

Hours later, unbeknownst to her, she would become the butt of many a joke at the police department breakfast meeting in the storage room at Mama Mary's Famous Eatery, where the monthly gathering usually took place. The detectives and police officers traded barbs about the finger's arrival at the station.

"I've got my finger on it." Ba-da-bum.

"It's pointing somewhere." Ba-da-bum.

"Put your hand in the hand of the man." That one didn't go over too well.

Captain Nate Padgett, Head of the Criminal Investigations Unit, shook his head as he popped another stick of cinnamon gum into his mouth and eyed the merrymaking at Mama Mary's lopsided banquet table. He had no Grecian beauty of chin, nose, or lips. His blue-grey eyes were just dull enough to escape notice. A full head of dark hair cropped at a respectably conservative length, and a certain ruggedness could make him seem macho or sexy, depending on the beholder. He was popular among the department's police and detectives alike.

The sounds of revelry were more like those of a fight than a monthly parish police breakfast meeting. Chief Allouicious Broussard nodded at Nate and motioned to a waitress to take his order, but Nate waved her away, politely. He was watching his weight. The chief raised his glass of orange juice toward Nate in a private toast. Nate lifted his mug of black coffee in return.

His junior detective, Devon Lemonde, jokingly voiced his misgivings about investigating the matter of the finger. "Aw, shit. Oh hell—no. Looka here. It don't take no weather man to tell you that the sun is shinin'. You follow me?"

Nate interjected. "Yeah, the sun is always shining, but we ain't gettin' the heat today, now, are we?" He reached in his pocket, pulled out a smartphone, and looked at it. "Sheesh. It'll be 44 degrees tonight! Besides, Devon, nobody looks at the sun anymore. They look at their smartphone to tell 'em if it's nighttime yet."

"Well, whatever." Devon clapped his hands. "Tell you what, Cap'n: ask that smartphone of yours whose finger it is and leave my girl out of it! Besides, what she gonna tell us 'cept what we already know: somebody is missin' a finger. I don't need to see a forensic anthropologist to tell me that!" He smirked. "Man, she been here a whole two years and you ain't needed no forensic anthropologist 'til now, so you all just pretend she ain't here. I ain't havin' it. I do not mix business with pleasure."

Devon's handsome looks and reputation as a "player," "Romeo," or "Mac Daddy," were in full effect as he savored the attention.

Nate snatched up a metal folding chair, turned it around, and sat down, resting his arms on its back. "We need to find the body that goes with that finger," he said.

Then he explained why Devon was assigned the case: Nate didn't want to match wits with "no female Yankee," and certainly not a forensic anthropologist.

"You can talk jive to her," he added, smile disappearing into his cup of coffee as he tried to avoid eye contact with Devon, who shook his head, laughing.

"See if she has any clues about the weapon. How long has that finger been dead, and is there a body, alive or dead, to go with it, in her professional estimation? See what she can tell us. Make sure it's checked out properly and tell her to take all necessary precautions, you know, to handle the evidence. Find out if it's a man or a woman, etcetera."

Devon snatched his keys from the table in mock anger. "So, no breakfast for the Creole. I get it."

"You just put your lunch on my tab, here, okay? I'll tell Mama," said the chief.

Someone yelled, "I thought you was givin' up eatin' for Lent, Devon?"

Everyone laughed as Nate added, "Take your jacket, boy. It's cold out there."

Devon grabbed his police-issue jacket hanging on a nearby nail, then raised his keys in the air, signaling that he was on his way.

He always did what he was told. That's how he had become the only nonwhite in three districts to hold a detective title. As he walked away from the group, he was eager to stop putting up a front. He had a feeling that he'd get more than answers about the specimen he was taking to his girlfriend. There were dark clouds on the horizon for them both, and the "fickle finger of fate" in the freezer box that he retrieved from the department on the way to Nakadee University was as good a fortune-teller as any gray clouds forming in the sky. Nate had been right about the weather forecast, and the thought of seeing Lula gave Devon an extra chill.

2
BREAKING UP

EXTERNAL EXAMINATION SUMMARY
The body will be presented in a black body bag. Severe burns will cover the full front part of the body, sides and back. The fire will appear to have terminated on the dorsal areas, possibly through extinguishment.

At the time of the official examination, conducted at the medical examiner's site, the body will be inspected first fully clothed as the remains suggest a shirt, pants, socks and shoes. From what will be visibly discerned, it appears that the body will not be wearing cotton khaki pants (of the JCPenney Dockers variety), a forest-green rugby shirt, and rubber-soled Cole Haan shoes.

The body will be that of a normally developed, well-nourished Caucasian male, conceivably measuring approximately 67 inches in length, with shrinkage, weighing an indiscernible amount, but not of any large or obese size. It will be difficult to discern his age, except that the hairs on the back of his head will appear to be brown, kept so with the aid of some coloring product. He will likely be between the ages of 37 and

50 years old. The body will be cold and unembalmed, with pronounced rigor and posterior fixed lividity.

DESCRIPTION OF INJURIES – SUMMARY

The body might or might not be burned over three-fourths of its circumference. There will be no evidence of any external blows to the body, except that certain fingers are missing from the corpse.

INTERNAL EXAMINATION - SUMMARY

All remaining organs are within normal limits, although the existence of a brain was always in doubt. No underlying pathological disease conditions for congenital anomalies can be observed due to extensive fragmentation, manipulation and dissection.

TOXICOLOGIC STUDIES

Blood Ethanol: No heart. No blood

Urine Drugs: Maybe

Clinicopathologic Correlation: pathological liar

EVIDENCE COLLECTED

1. Samples of Blood (type V), Tissue (no evidence of heart tissue, brain, kidney, liver, spleen).
2. Twenty-five autopsy photographs: you ought to be in pictures.
3. Six postmortem x-rays
4. Five golden rings
5. Four calling birds

Clothing transferred to private crime lab for more appropriate costuming.

CAUSE OF DEATH

1. Burn, shock, surprise, arrogance, sour disposition.

Manner of death: Trial by Fire, Sweet Revenge.

"Is this a joke?" Lula Logan asked after she finished reading the report. It was carefully and pristinely encased in wax paper, presumably to avoid leaving behind any trace evidence.

"Okay. So we see the same thing, then." Aggie touched her auburn shoulder-length hair and heaved a sigh. "Good. I thought I might be off my rocker."

The women laughed as Aggie sat in a rocking chair with her feet planted on the ground. The two women were in her living room. Aggie was dressed like an ad for Laura Ashley clothing: a flowered collarless blouse with short sleeves under a thin, sleeveless, denim-like cotton dress with oversized front pockets. She was on the tail end of her sick leave, recovering from fibroid surgery.

"Why do you think you received this?" Lula asked.

"No idea." She shook her head slowly. "Maybe because I'm the only forensic pathologist in this parish. Hell, I dunno. You know this town has no secrets and any one of us can be found, whether we like it or not."

Dr. Lula Logan and Dr. Aggie Sheaf had first met in Dallas at a course Lula taught for medical doctors called *The Bare Bones of Forensic Anthropology*. The always-popular lecture allowed Lula to travel to different cities every three months for a three-day stay in a luxury hotel and the opportunity to interact with other professionals.

After reading Lula's credentials during one of her lectures in Dallas, Aggie approached her during a break and the women exchanged business cards. They promised to meet in Nakadee for lunch one day, but never did. Instead, their paths would cross occasionally at one of the larger supermarket chains fifteen miles outside of town, where, again, they would make promises to get together soon, and, true to custom, never follow through.

Louisiana had only one crime lab, and Nakadee had no other forensic pathologist, so occasionally their lull in communication would be breached by Aggie, who needed Lula's help with periodic police inquiries about body parts that surfaced in the Kissadee forest.

The area's large scenic byways and trails were spacious enough for hikers, and the alligators living in the nearby marshes. Aggie had asked Lula, as a favor, with specific instructions to defer to the police, and to take their earnestness seriously so as not to make them feel stupid. She mentioned one occasion when the police had mistaken a wild boar's ribcage for that of an infant.

From what Lula could tell, Aggie led a typical Southern life of comfort and status in her white social circles. She belonged to a prominent Southern family of rice-growers (cotton had proven to be less cost-effective, post Emancipation). The family now owned only a small percentage of the company that was still known by the family name but its trust kept Aggie very comfortable, so much so that she had not asked for alimony when she divorced her husband of ten years.

Lula had to admit to a nagging feeling that tended to find refuge in attributing a white person's material success to having the right combination of "social circumstances," usually identified by the mere color of one's skin. However, in the South, the barometers of class were determined by your pedigree, the family to which you belonged, and the company you kept. No one talked race in Nakadee. You just knew where you fit.

So Lula was a fish out of water when it came to finding friends with her background and educational achievements in the town. Only now, after two years, was she beginning to call it home.

She lived alone, in a black neighborhood, and didn't belong to any of the organizations of the black bourgeoisie, such as Jack and Jill or the Links. Nor had she ever been a member of a black sorority. To make her feel even more lonesome, there weren't enough black forensic anthropologists nationwide to form a clique, let alone an organization.

Lula and Aggie were equals in nobody else's mind but Lula's. She was certain Aggie never even thought about Lula's circumstances, and if she did, they would be too mundane and desultory to mention: Lula was a single black woman, without prospects of finding an equal partner or professional of her own race. Her closest chance at a hint of a social life, with Devon, was about to end, also. She would have to get used to being truly alone again.

Lula was as much to blame as Aggie for not initiating a friendship. It was the environment, she justified to herself. Nakadee was different from Shreveport, Baton Rouge, or New Orleans, where the multitudes of cars, trucks, large buildings, civic centers and gala events spawned a more culturally diverse social lifestyle.

In Nakadee, there were no buildings more prodigious than the downtown courthouse and the Portuguese colonial edifices that had stood along the riverfront for more than a hundred years, later refurbished as university apartments.

Strolling in downtown Nakadee was no leisure walk, either. Where Nakadee denizens took walks downtown in the early evenings, Blacks stuck to their ghetto, separated by the train tracks, a constant reminder of the inequality of their environment.

The town of Nakadee had been very conscious of protecting its antebellum traditions until political expediency dictated otherwise. The biggest local uproar, secondary only to the polarizing War Between the States, as some Southerners still referred to the Civil War more than a century later, had been the decision to remove the statue of a smiling "darkie" tipping his hat, a once-enforceable requirement of any black male when meeting a white person.

Apparently, there was a sense of nostalgic delight in the white community that some old black men still upheld part of the tradition, but at least today they no longer had to get off the sidewalk completely to let Whites pass. The statue was an integral part of Nakadee's history, not only as part of an historical district, but in keeping with its status as a town trapped in a time gone by.

Blacks, however, except for one local Republican councilman, would just as soon have burned the statue in effigy.

Nakadee had been the intended capital of Louisiana until its neighbor, Natchitoches, twenty-five miles to the North, beat it out. Both places had been French settlements, river ports for trade between the settlers and the Spanish Texans. The town stood as a lesser bulwark against invasion by the Spanish-speaking dueños of the new and ripe Americas. Its sleepy hollow of small cobblestone streets and plantation-style buildings stretched the full length of downtown, facing a portion of the sinewy 32-mile Cane River.

Wooden benches lined one side of the main street. Facing inward instead of outward, their wrought-iron backs lined the river waters that flowed past, their seats facing the town sidewalks. Even the design of the streets reflected the townspeople, who faced inward, only, and did not go too far outside of their town's comfortable confines.

"So, this report came in your mail?" Lula asked Aggie.

"It was on my porch when my kids woke up, right on the door mat, in a manila envelope. I should call up Mr. Peoples and see if it's something he knows about."

"Mr. Peoples?"

"You don't know Mr. Peoples?" Aggie looked at her puzzled. "My diener, part-time, who stays there full time."

Lula did recall hearing about this man. A real character. His name, when uttered by Aggie, was usually accompanied by a roll of the eyes.

"He loves what he does. You might say he's obsessed with it. I don't think he has any family. Close anyway. He has a couple of male friends, or something to that effect. I don't wanna know and I don't really care. He does his job and reckons I work for him but that's fine by me."

He fancied himself in charge of the autopsy department merely because he'd been there longer than anybody else.

"How about you go down and look at things there, if you want," Aggie said, with a coy expression on her face. "I can call in advance."

Lula eyeballed her, sideways. "Have you told the police about the report yet?"

"Yep. Detective Nate will be coming by later to look around and take prints. Let's see what they come up with. Maybe he wrote up this report and wanted to get a comment out of me. I can't figure why anybody else would care to give it to me. Heck, it could have been copied from the Internet."

Somebody was having fun with her, Aggie added, asking Lula to sort Mr. Peoples out because she hadn't been able to do it after 10 years of working with him. She also warned that Mr. Peoples was kind of weird—ghoulish, she called it—but boy could he cut up a corpse. Mr. Peoples could eat his lunch off the cadaver's gurney while the corpse lay on it, like a centerpiece.

Aggie thanked Lula for playing sleuth on her behalf. Lula had an 11 a.m. class coming up, but would make a visit to Aggie's workplace immediately afterwards.

12:30 p.m.

Aggie's autopsy suite had its own entrance, adjacent to the hospital and parking. When Lula arrived, a tall, older, dark-skinned black man was waiting for her at the side entrance. He greeted her with a faint look of incredulity, and an accompanying interrogatory, as he tried to hide his surprise upon meeting her.

"Miss Lula?"

She was accustomed to people expecting someone who looked a lot different than she did, especially after speaking with her on the phone. Her ability to speak the King's or Queen's English and "Ebonics" made her bilingual, though she stuck to the more formal vernacular in her professional life.

She marveled that while the average white Southerner spoke some facsimile of "Ebonics," nobody seemed to take any notice, nor decide how articulate he or she sounded, the way they did when sizing up those of her race.

The slave masters who populated the South had left an indelible mark on half the population of a new country, giving them speech patterns that were warped in time, gradually to be replaced in popularity by a Northern form of the English language judged to be more pleasing to the ear. Today, the slave-holding fathers' mixed progeny showed barely any vestige of their vernacular, except for the old English "axe," which, among slave descendants, was still *au courant* as the word "ask."

"'Dr. Logan' is fine. I'm not from here," she told the man.

"I thought you might be a Yankee. I suspected right." He snapped his fingers in approval.

"Well, I'm not sure I had any say in those Civil-War classifications, sir."

"So I heard. You were running up North, hiding in the bushes, weren't you? While we stuck it out, like soldiers." He opened the white aluminum screen door, moving the wooden door behind him to let her inside.

"That's a novel way of looking at it." She smiled as she stepped inside.

The place was spotless and minimalist, a barren room with little in the way of furnishings, and bright fluorescent lights overhead. A faux granite beige-and-black-speckled countertop, half of the room's circumference, looked like a lunch counter at a diner. Large mirrors hung on the walls at an angle so that students could watch, backs turned away from the tables, as the diener assisted the pathologist in dismembering corpses. The shiny aluminum autopsy table was in the middle of the floor, waist-high, fitted with spigots, faucets, and pipes for washing away blood and bodily secretions.

The room had an industrial feel, aside from the golf-clubs bag sitting in a corner. Lula spied his makeshift putting green: a drain on the floor into which blood and the juices of human entrails drained.

"By the way, do you have a name?" Lula asked.

"My friends call me Giggles. My real name is Theofolus Eldridge Peoples."

He was dressed more like a maître d' in an expensive restaurant than a butcher of humans. He wore a white shirt with a silk tie design of oversized golf clubs. His effort at looking nonchalant was wholly ineffective as he asked, "So, how can I help you?" with a twinkle in his eye.

Lula had been present when Aggie explained to him over the phone that she would be bringing the report for his perusal and commentary, but it was obvious he wanted her to seek permission from him directly.

Negroes.

"Well, Mr. Peoples. As you know, I'm here to find out where this report originated from."

He barely glanced at it, waving it in his hands, gracefully.

"Well, it looks to me like a forensic pathologist wrote it up. Looks like it, anyway."

"Could you read the first paragraph, please?"

He did as instructed, then glanced up at her, knowingly.

"Okay. So it's written like it's about to happen, not like it happened already," he said.

"Any idea where it could have come from? Do you have any recall of a case like this? Recent deaths of finger amputees?"

"No."

"Accidental deaths?"

"Not a one." He leaned into her ever so slightly. "Now let me understand something. Are you interested in the report or what's written in the report? I'm not sure I get what this is about."

"How about both?"

He looked her straight in the eye, then a smile came across his face, displaying his gleaming teeth. He wore some form of dentures, she could tell, his perfectly lined teeth looking like the white keys of a piano.

He clapped his hands. "Well, okay, then. So, this looks to me to be a case about BIID, Doctor."

She watched as he opened drawers officiously, though he didn't appear to be inspecting anything.

"And that means ...?" She waited for his reply.

"Body Integrity Identity Disorder. Did you all talk about it?"

"No. I'm vaguely aware of it, honestly, but, please do tell. I'm all ears."

"It don't matter what body part. They'll cut it, whatever it is. They're cutters, but only in a more dramatic way, let's say. They cut their limbs off."

She studied him. He was smart, aware.

"Did anyone check the nearby hospitals for emergency-room cases?"

"We're starting out here, because Dr. Aggie said you might be able to help me. She spoke very highly of you."

Mr. Peoples' aspect changed immediately. Where he had first seemed full of haughty pride, now he relaxed a little.

"I won't find anything, but I'll do it just to be thorough," he told her. "We are a bit behind here, still have microfiche that needs scanning, but those records are old and ain't no never mind."

He had set the report on the counter, but returned to it with urgency now.

Lula watched, respectfully, then added, "The report was delivered to Dr. Sheaf's house."

Mr. Peoples kept his gaze fixed on his duties, picking up files and leafing through them mindlessly. He turned from her, setting the pages on the counter. "Is this a report that the police have?"

Her reservations about him changed to compassion as she realized that his hand was shaking slightly. He probably had a hell of a life story that had gotten him here, where he, no doubt, would be proud to work until his dying day, and rightfully so.

She surmised that he was a drinker, as he glanced at her quickly. He was a character, but seemed too self-conscious to do anything that might jeopardize his position. He likely lived for his job, which probably didn't pay enough. His white shirt was yellowing at the collar, and a string hung at the bottom seam of his polyester-blend pants, exposing the frayed edges of a hem. His Stacy Adams shoes were in need of new soles.

"By the way, this report was written by a man, not a lady," he said.

"How do you figure?"

He gazed up at an oil painting in a medium-sized wood frame showing a jaundiced-looking white man with a sandy-blond crew cut. He wore a brown tweed jacket and shoestring tie, and a beard but no mustache, a style Lula could never imagine enhancing any man's appearance.

"I was trained by the dean of all dieners, the legendary Robespierre Beauregard. I was his best pupil, which is why I have the honor of still working here." He lifted up the report. "My mentor taught me never to cut the testes off a man if it could be avoided, and there's no mention of them here. Penis, yeah, but no testicles. That's an old tradition. Dr. Aggie doesn't honor it, her being a feminist and all. She cuts those first, if you wanna know."

He continued examining the report, never meeting her gaze.

"The format isn't Dr. Aggie's, either. She uses a different font. This is a Times New Roman font. We don't use it here. We use an Arial or Helvetica. I likes pretty reports, if you must know."

"How do you know she didn't use a different font before you got here, and the records could still be here?"

His disapproving look stilled Lula. "I got here before her. She came here about ten years ago, with her New-Age medicine, talking about preserving all the knowledge of the life extinguished, including dissecting the balls. She wasn't having it. Those balls had to go. So this report is either from before she got here, or someone is copying something and writing it down. But whoever it is, it's someone who knows the real tradition: *Ne joue pas avec les boules.*"

3:00 p.m.

Startled by the pounding on her laboratory door, Lula almost dropped her skull specimen. She broke its fall by clutching the mandible, creating a comical scene of a skull trying to eat her hand.

Chuckling, she put the skull back on the white cloth covering the Formica table. She couldn't see who was at the door from her vantage point in the storage room, but the knock was classic police officer: loud and repetitive.

The force of Devon's rap equaled the degree to which she didn't want to see him. Not now, anyway. It was way too soon. She mentally raced through the apologies that she could use to curtail his visit.

She had warned Devon many times not to bang on the lab door this way, but until the university put a doorbell at her lab's entrance, he was going to stick to this method. Today, she could even hear it over the noise of the fans that provided air-conditioning in her laboratory-office. Devon, an alum of Nakadee University, was friends with the campus police and could walk anywhere on campus unescorted.

In her own Black-American circles, Lula would be deemed very attractive, maybe even "fine." She wore her healthy head of dark-brown hair permed and just below her shoulders, without the aid of a weave or other embellishments.

She had the kind of full lips lipstick commercials coveted for both their black and white models. Her skin was honey-colored, and her almond-shaped eyes sparkled a deep maroon in the sun (or so she had been told). She had heavy brows that she consciously controlled, and kept her nails unpolished and just long enough to pick up a bone shard.

Her curvaceous 5′ 5″ figure could provoke catcalls in the Oakland, California Bay Area neighborhood where she grew up.

However, here in Nakadee, in northwestern Louisiana, she was a mere mention of a woman, in a town of Whites, Creoles, and Cajuns, all of whom were higher up on the social scale than Blacks.

Lula trundled to the door to give the stern appearance of being in the middle of working on something, without time to entertain.

Devon breezed in carrying a beverage cooler, as if he didn't notice her demeanor. "Damn, I been trying to find you all day!"

"Well, Detective, you know my schedule. I'm usually here on time. Whatever it is you want to discuss can wait until later. I'm busy. We've talked enough."

"This is a professional visit, Dr. Logan." Devon lifted up the cooler's lid to reveal a severed finger. "We can't put a finger on how we got it." Devon's voice filled the room as he laughed. "We do know that we definitely have a finger. Can you do your magic thing and tell us the name, age, serial number, birthdate of its owner, and what instrument was used to cut it off, and when it happened? And why?" He was trying to be jovial and avoid the "situation" between them. "You see, it is possible for us to be professional, regardless of our personal circumstances."

"Some things are better left unsaid, Devon. I need no reminders." She cleared a space for the cooler on a nearby workbench. Devon set it down, then leaned against one of the immovable metal tables in the middle of the room. He smiled his apologies and gave her a remonstrative look. "Now, you know we're not finished—"

"Devon, as long as you carry on being married, there's not much we can do for each other."

"After everything I shared with you, you wanna insist that I'm still married? Wow. I thought you were intelligent."

"Not now, Devon. I have my own projects I gotta keep working on to keep my funding—this is not the time."

He raised his hand to ward off any more protestations.

She opened the cooler and lifted the container from its moorings, then set it back down again. Checking her watch, she picked up a notepad and started writing.

She reached for a sterile glove and put it on, then removed the finger from the cooler from where it lay nestled in a miniature glass drawer, an inch thick on each of its four sides.

It appeared to be a middle finger, pale in hue, but not the yellow, sallow tones of a Creole or Cajun, whose opaque colors were generally distinguishable from Whites. The mix of races in Louisiana would make identification difficult. It would take more than a first impression to influence her opinion.

The digit, stained with blood, showed straight lines slanting toward the right from knuckle to fingertip. It looked to be a relatively fresh cut from the right hand, with no signs of decomposition.

Somebody was smarting about now, Lula thought. She was also annoyed with Devon hovering around her. Truth be told, she was disgusted, and couldn't bear to look at him. She stepped back from the counter.

"Okay. So, I have my assignment. You can leave now."

"You're serious about this?" Devon stood, feet planted firmly on the white linoleum floor.

Wiggling her fingers, she pointed to her ring finger and grabbed a chair.

"You know what they say about pointing fingers. Sometimes they get cut off. You got the specimen there to prove it," Devon said with a smirk.

"Ooh … I'm scared. Guess I better call the police. They supposedly protect and serve."

"You said I made you feel safe. Once."

"Yeah, you did, but not good enough, obviously." She pointed to her ring finger again, then pointed her index finger at him, telling him to go, shaking her head to show her defiance.

"Fine. Okay. Whatever. But you need to know I was not trying to play you, Lula. I was just waiting for the right moment."

She grunted, involuntarily. "Yeah. In bed. After you got what you wanted. We've talked about that already. Chalk up our little time together as a mutual booty call. Your services were more than adequate and my body appreciated it, but my mind is under the distinct impression that you're an asshole. I'd like you to make

31

sure that someone else is assigned this case, if it ends up requiring investigation. I meant it when I said I didn't want to see you again. I've got a class to teach and some fieldwork to do this afternoon. You may go now."

"You're for real?"

"Yes. I can resist your charms. This is not a joke, Devon. I'm not smiling or laughing. I'm serious when I ask you to get someone else from your department to handle this case."

He shrugged, his expression incredulous.

"No can do. I was assigned this case because of our relationship. Nate specifically chose me because of our thing we got goin' on."

"Our thing we got going on is gone with the wind, now, Devon. We were supposed to have a discreet relationship, or didn't you notice the population of 50 people in this town?"

"Fifty? Try thirteen thousand." Devon scowled. "Even so, it's kind of hard to keep a secret if the guys see us at dinner a couple of times a month. I let them think what they want." His face softened as he spoke gently, taking a step toward her, his fingertips grazing the metal table. "Hey, Lula. I didn't wave a flag or anything about us. They just feel good for me, considering … you know, n'all. Can you fault them for that? They're glad to see me happy. Something positive has happened to me, for a change."

"I wish you continued happiness, Devon."

"So, you don't want company tonight." He looked at her sideways. "We can't get through this?" He grasped her arm with two fingers, stroking it gently, staring into her eyes. "After all this?" Slowly, she felt his fingers pressing between her forearm's tendons, as if wedging them apart. She felt pain but was more startled by Devon's demeanor. His dark eyes flashed, stoking his anger.

"Devon .... " She hissed.

Before she could utter another word, his fingers released her, slowly.

"Hey, Lula—okay," he said, coldly. "I'll have another detective pick up the finger when you're ready."

A whiff of his cologne lingered as he strode to the door. She rubbed her forearm to release the sting of his grip. On her life.

Had he just tried to hurt her? Was he being physically abusive? She cursed herself for getting involved with anyone in this small town, let alone a police officer who was married and had had no intention of ever telling her.

She was definitely ready to move on. Before he had begun spending time with her in her home, sharing her bed, and serving as her personal foot-warmer, she had lived a sedentary, solitary life. Fine. She would concentrate on her research; but this time, she was sticking around. She wasn't going anywhere. She had left the Bay Area to get away from one doomed relationship. If she kept running from each failure, she would run out of employment prospects.

Her research was a dream come true. She'd do what she could to avoid Devon, and go back to being the studious bookworm she had always been, which had brought her to Louisiana in the first place. She hadn't come to Nakadee University to acquire an M-R-S-Degree. She wasn't studying to be somebody's Miss-Tress, either.

"Fo'sho. Fo'sho." She chuckled to herself.

8:33 p.m.

It felt like forever, trying to finish her work to get home. Once there, she had a quick shower, then fell onto her bed wearing only her towel, letting the night air dry her as she lay looking at the ceiling.

She turned her head to gape at her alarm clock, placed far enough way that she had to get out of bed to turn it off. She'd have just enough time left to get in 7 hours' sleep, if she could remember to turn the television off. She nixed her thoughts about jogging tomorrow morning, and didn't feel guilty about it. She needed to sleep it off, "it" being her problems—namely Devon.

Lula felt vulnerable, something she hadn't felt when he was a part of her world. She missed Devon's physicality, his closeness, the smell of his after-shave, his aromatic musk scent, the things that made him who he was: a protector. During the night, while they were sleeping, his arms would envelop her body, hugging her tightly to him. She would have to pry them apart in order to make any move to get out of the bed, and when she returned, he would automatically assume the same position. He had been a welcome nighttime tonic.

She sat up in bed to prevent shedding tears over what could have been. They had welled up before she even knew for which pain she was crying. There were enough: her father's untimely death; her San Francisco boyfriend's betrayal when he inexplicably called off their wedding and disappeared; being told that she would never be able to bear children. All of the above.

The sound of a slam made her heart and body jump. Clutching the towel around her, she grabbed for her bathrobe, then raced around to turn off the lights. She stood frozen for several seconds, listening for sounds of retreating footsteps or a car driving away.

Nothing.

She craned her neck, peeking through the curtains to discover the source of the sound, and her fear: a clay pot, sitting on one side of her doorstep, where it had fallen to the ground with a thump. Luckily, it hadn't broken.

She released a sigh, putting her hand to her chest as she shook her head. She had lived alone before she met Devon, so knew she was trippin' now. She walked back to her bedroom, chastising herself. Here she was: little Miss Independent, succumbing to having a man around, letting him run the show while she let down her guard. Now, she simply felt stupid, dating a married man whose situation everyone knew, except her.

She wasn't ready, Devon had said, explaining his reticence in telling her. On her way back to her bed, she grabbed some body lotion and began smoothing it over her legs.

She had learned the truth at church, when she got a telltale glimpse of Devon's other life. He was holding the hand of a honey-colored little girl whose Negroid features rang out loud and clear against the backdrop of her gray and lime-green gingham dress. The girl's braided hair cascaded just below her shoulders.

Lula had watched him guide the girl to her seat. How had he managed to keep it from her that he was married until only last week, twelve months after they had started sleeping together?

When he had called to invite her to dine at Sparky's Cajun Restaurant that same evening of the revelation, she obliged him. He needed to talk to her face-to-face, he'd explained.

They sat quietly while a sullen waiter prepared the table for them, spreading large white napkins on the deep burgundy tablecloth. Devon's hands had fidgeted, rubbing the fabric, as if doing so might do the same to their relationship—smooth it out so they could continue being each other's comfort in the night.

Lula stared at his hand, then up to his creased brows and forehead, as if those features were speaking, finding words to salvage the relationship. He talked, without pause, as if he didn't want her to absorb the information any more than he wanted to tell it.

They had both ordered the Cajun catfish and mildly spicy red beans and rice, which arrived on colorful ceramic plates while sounds of R&B crooners wafted through the joint, occasional bass beats registering in its sound system. They had sat at a corner table, looking very much the forsaken pair.

"This shit" had worn him down, he said. Whenever there was a chance to get close to a girl—"a woman"—he corrected himself, "this shit," would come up.

Lula thought it disrespectful of all women that he used such language to convey his pique at having to explain that he had a wife and child.

He sat, slumped and tired, staring at his interlaced fingers resting on the table. He was talking more at them than to her. His anger was right on the surface. He pouted like a truculent little boy in the body of a man with sexual urges he was being told would be denied satisfaction, from here on. "This shit" wouldn't let him.

Lula said nothing. She looked at him from under her eyelashes, sideways, as her thumb and index finger anchored her chin and head, cocked ever so slightly.

His wife Trisha was the excessively jealous type who had never become accustomed to his irregular hours as a police officer. They would argue incessantly, as she believed that he was cheating on her, no matter what proof he provided to the contrary. After their only daughter was born, his wife's anxieties became manic, and her nagging turned into physical violence. She would hit and kick him. One night, her worries about her husband's infidelities had taken a very nasty turn.

Devon had called Trisha to say he'd be late coming home, arriving sometime after midnight. Rarely turning down an opportunity to make more money in a small town like Nakadee, he had jumped at the chance to volunteer overtime hours to replace another officer.

He could tell by the sound of his wife's voice that she had been on one of her drinking binges because she barely responded, and her speech was slurred enough for him to realize she had to have been at it for several hours. He suggested she get some sleep.

After his second shift, Devon arrived, at the appointed hour, at a barely-lit house. Believing that Trisha and their daughter were sleeping, he took his shoes off, tiptoeing toward the bedroom so as not to disturb them.

But Trisha was lying in wait behind the front door. She was nonsensical, yelling that this time she had proof he was sneaking around.

When he instinctively raised his arm to protect himself, she exposed her left arm, which she'd kept hidden, revealing a carving knife, which she plunged into his chest, right below his heart.

An unexpected adrenalin rush had helped him kick the weapon out of her hands before he fell. He grabbed a small pistol from his calf holster and shot her in the arm.

As they both lay bleeding, he gathered just enough strength to call 911, gasping, "Officer down," into a walkie-talkie sitting on its perch on an end table next to his front door. He recited his address before fainting.

During one memorable night, as she lay in the crook of Devon's arm, Lula had rubbed his chest, felt the raised, keloid skin and asked about his scar. Rather than answer, he had said he would tell her one day, when he felt she was ready.

Ready had come too soon, the hard way.

The knife could have ended everything for him had it been a centimeter higher and to the right. He had been at odds with the local prosecutor, who wanted to press charges, but Devon's support of his wife at trial didn't exonerate her. Trisha pled guilty and was sentenced to fifty years—seven of which she had served—for attempted murder. She'd been locked up in a women's detention facility, then transferred to a psychiatric hospital.

His situation made relationships hard to pursue, but Devon had sworn to himself that he would never divorce his wife so that there would be no custody battle over their daughter. He admitted to Lula that many opportunities to cheat had arisen before his wife's incarceration, but he had stayed devoted to his family. He wanted to provide his little Fiona with as much continuity as he could with her mother locked up.

Fiona lived with his wife's mother in the next town, but visited Devon every other weekend, when he tended to her every need, including her spiritual development, which is why they attended church, he'd explained.

Devon was the funny man on the force, who intentionally acquitted himself of the "bad guy" image expected of a cop. But when he was with Lula, he would refer to himself in the third person. "That dude is just an act. People want to see what they want to see. So I give it to 'em. They think I'm the Mack just because I got a Johnson," he harrumphed.

It all started to make sense, Lula thought: the weekends when he wasn't available were the ones he spent with his daughter. She and Devon led independent lives, so it didn't bother her that she couldn't see him all the time.

Don't sleep where you work, her mother had warned her.

She felt foolish, remembering her mother's sage advice when told that she and Devon were together: "You may be a Ph.D., but you can still be stuck on stupid."

And, truth be told, Lula liked his Johnson. But sitting in that restaurant, listening to the story about his wife, she heard enough to know that it was over between them.

3

A HOUSE DIVIDED

The police officer's rap on Lula's office door was a variation on Devon's: slower, but just as firm. Her instinct was affirmed when she opened her door to find Chief Detective Nate. But she didn't expect to see Devon, behind him, looking gloomy and detached. He was again carrying a cooler, and his eyes avoided hers.

Nate explained the discovery of a second finger, which, like the first one, showed jagged soft tissue and burn or acid marks where the fingerprint would normally be.

Someone—a man, Lula conjectured—was being tortured in the vicinity of Nakadee. The blood on the finger had barely congealed when the police found it in the early morning. An accompanying handwritten note ordered the finder to "Pick up the Pieces." The police had taken photos plus blood samples.

The men refused Lula's request to stop at home so she could change before accompanying them to the station. Nate, who was the only detective who spoke to her, warned that Chief Broussard was getting nervous, and the timing of this finger "caper," as he called it, could not be worse. The Hot Sauce Festival was tomorrow and the last thing any police chief on a political campaign wanted was to run on a theme of "Safe & Secure" while a chainsaw bandit was chopping off fingers. So, with Lula's guidance, they were ramping

38

up attention to this case and were there to escort her directly to talk to the chief.

Lula suggested that she follow them in her car.

Nate raised an eyebrow, glancing at Devon, who answered by opening the lab door for all three to go outside, down the three flights of stairs into the bright, mid-afternoon sun.

Their cars reached the outskirts of town with unusual speed, although Lula still had to push on the gas pedal to keep up with Devon, who loved driving fast—60 miles an hour on routes lined with 35-mile-per-hour signs.

"Bastard," she said, contemptuous.

Soon the highway was passing fenced-in farmland and desiccated dust beds where swamps once sat, now erased by the vagaries of time and climate change.

Devon slowed his vehicle until it was riding alongside her on the left, while Nate rolled down his window.

"Another finger," Nate announced, using his own to point forward. "124 Muir Street. After the two bridges, then three miles past the gas station, take a left, then right, past Magnolia Estates."

Lula nodded, then put on her blinker and moved behind Devon's car.

Seven minutes later, they had passed the second bridge and the gas station, a throwback to stations from the 1960s with slow-moving gas pumps and take-out greasy spoons selling liver, gizzards, hot wings, and chicken strips. These junky filling stations always had a line of patrons snaked outside the door. They made more money cooking meals and selling fish tackle than pumping gas, and nobody was inspecting for a food operator's license.

By now, the green cumulus-shaped foliage of pecan trees whizzed by in seamless repetition. This part of Nakadee revealed its abundance of lush acreage, punctuated by estates—some fenced in, others dotting the horizon. Quiet and expansive, the land was owned by old-moneyed interests, who still kept the wealthy landowner's tradition of being too rich to harvest pecan crops, but savvy enough to allow the local citizenry to do it for them for a fraction of the profit.

Devon's Buick coasted to a stop in front of a two-story mansion. Hesitant to block the driveway behind the leader of their two-car caravan, Lula inched her car forward tentatively, then turned off the ignition.

The front of the house was cast in partial shadow as three o'clock approached. Lula's location prevented her from having the same vantage point as Devon and Nate in the car ahead of her.

She was surprised to see them throw open their doors and dash out in pursuit of what, she couldn't see. Devon abruptly broke into a sprint, while Nate trotted a couple of steps behind him, then gave up, realizing the futility of trying to keep pace with a former All-American running back. Instead, Nate turned back toward her, winding his left arm as he motioned her to come along, before he turned a corner and disappeared around the side of the home.

Once Lula rounded the bend herself, she saw a black teenager running zigzag across a large green lawn. Devon's long strides were closing in on him, while a driverless lawn mower meandered around the grassy yard like a robotic vacuum, stopping, turning, stopping, turning, as if trying to penetrate an invisible force field.

Nate moved toward the mower while Devon yelled at the boy to stop running.

"Boy, you better stop. I ain't gonna do nothin' to you."

"Yeah, right."

The boy faked Devon and ran toward Lula, his billowing Afro trailing behind. As he slowed, Devon caught up and, with gusto, tackled the spindly youth while deftly protecting him from falling on a cement patio where two silent onlookers were standing.

It seemed wholly unnecessary to tackle the boy to the ground. Devon's overt physicality had a tinge of vindictiveness about it.

As if reading Lula's thoughts, Devon immediately pulled himself and the boy up as quickly as they had fallen. The boy's bony, dark-brown legs looked comical jutting in the air from his baggy knee-length shorts, their oversized pouches falling like a skirt around him, exposing his white cotton briefs. He wore white socks, dark Nike sneakers, and a basketball jersey of the Nakadee Cicadas.

Lula glanced at the house as Devon and his captive walked toward her. It was much more imposing than it appeared from the street. She couldn't tell whether the place was a redesign of an earlier structure or a newly built amalgam of the influences of every colonial power that had contributed to the state's architectural uniqueness. There were balconies on every side of the upper story, girded by iron lacework porch panels with the most intricate designs she had ever seen.

She squinted up to see a face looking down at her from behind a screen door but when it disappeared just as quickly, she thought it an apparition. She glanced at Nate to see his reaction, and saw that he was watching Devon and the boy, who both stood panting.

"Boy, if a man tells you to stop, you stop. I held out my identification," Devon admonished.

"Yeah, like I can trust that. You gotta take me down, 'cuz I ain't gonna stand around and get punked by you."

Nate pulled out his identification, putting it in the boy's face. "Well, how 'bout this one?"

"You the one I'm running from. He's just your slave. I know the deal," the boy said, head downcast. Then he looked up and stared at the detective.

Devon was glowering. "We ain't here to talk history with you, son. Does your momma know you're here?"

"Yes, sir," someone interjected.

Lula turned to the voice. The young man who spoke wore a beige crew shirt that seemed colored more by accident than design, and baggy jeans, held up by a belt. He moved closer, stroking his hand over rivulets of his close-cropped hair. His goatee and short mustache, moving in sync with his jaws as he chewed gum, momentarily mesmerized Lula. She guessed he was in his mid-twenties.

The goatee spoke: "He at his dad's when his mom come back late. I pick him up and run errands and the like for his dad. Drive him around ...'n stuff."

Devon stepped away from the boy, while Nate held his shoulder and addressed him.

"Why aren't you in school?"

"'Cuz I'm working. I mow the lawn here."

"So, you're truant," Devon conjectured.

"I ain't truant. I'm working. I mow the lawn here, or didn't you hear me, Grandpa?"

Ignorant of when enough was enough, the boy punctuated his jibe with a sputter on the last syllable.

His listeners silently smiled in sympathy. The boy probably reminded each man of himself at the ripe age of fourteen, when he'd believed he was smart enough to match wits with adults, but too naïve to know whether the adult was friend or foe.

The boy's caretaker spoke up with authority. "That's enough, Melvyn. You gonna lose this battle, any ways you look at it. I'd be respectful, I was you, man."

"Yeah, well, I'm gonna sue them for police brutality, for jackin' up my knee."

Devon chuckled. "Oh, so now I'm a cop."

Nate, visibly tiring of the small talk, spoke abruptly.

"Who are you, by the way?" he asked the goatee.

"Richard," the man answered.

"You made the call?" Nate asked Richard.

"I did." The reply came from the elusive man from upstairs that Lula had seen earlier. He stood at a screen door, now, facing them at eye level.

He opened the door and stepped out. "Blaine Dworkin." He shook hands with Nate, and nodded at Devon.

Blaine was a diminutive 5'7" and wore baggy khaki shorts that hung below the knee. His candy-apple-colored crew shirt with a horse logo had barely a wrinkle. His face was ruddy, and his nose, perfectly angular and smooth, bore the telltale signs of cosmetic work. His hands were almost too large for his thin frame, and although not quite a comb-over, wisps of hair hung like cobwebs over his skull. He looked like a boy stuck in a man's frame. To Lula, it wasn't endearing.

A Latino-looking man opened the screen door after Blaine. He was handsome, by anyone's estimation. His face was creamy-smooth, his chiseled chin like the Greek statues around the Shreveport museum. He had large eyes, with equally pronounced eyelashes, and dimpled cheeks.

"And who is this gentleman, here?" Nate asked.

Richard pointed to the handsome man who stood, crossing his arms, his muscles rippling under his tank top. "That's Juanito."

Juanito cast his accuser a defiant look. His full lips and piercing dark eyes made him look like a runway model.

"What do I have to do with this?" Juanito asked.

"I told him that you live here." Blaine countered.

Juanito's face turned ashen for an instant, his dark brows doubling up on each other as he turned away to spit on the ground.

Somebody somewhere was being tortured and someone in Nakadee knew who the victim was. The fact that fingers had surfaced at the police department twice and now a third time at a Nakadee resident's home, should have given the police a sense of urgency. Even with fingerprints, the investigation would require a morsel of sleuthing, something in which Nakadee police didn't seem to engage. How long was it going to take Nate or Devon to do any real detecting? They acted like time waited for them, a well-founded fact in places like Nakadee. These towns were mini-states, where the local police ruled communities of twenty thousand or so and were lords among their rural serf populations.

Nate was the Master of the Universe in this neck of the state. He set the pace for the detectives' collective laziness, except for Devon, who worked efficiently and took his job as a detective quite seriously.

Nate and Lula's first encounter was memorable for her precisely because of its insignificance to him. Introduced by Aggie Sheaf, Nate had greeted Lula with a curt nod, ignoring her immediately thereafter. Apparently, Lula was not worth the polite custom of a follow-up question, a repeat of her name, or even an idle segue into discussions about the weather.

There was no love-fest among these three, who would otherwise be detective, forensic pathologist, and forensic anthropologist, a proverbial trinity of professionals tasked with working together to solve the mystery of the circumstances of a human's death.

Lula wondered whether Nate's rudeness at their first meeting had been a personality flaw, or had he shown a preoccupation with

Aggie? Their flirtation was noticeable, almost palpable, its electricity making her feel slightly uncomfortable.

A year after first meeting Nate, when Lula had started seeing Devon, Nate had been introduced to her again when he approached the couple sitting at a booth in a restaurant. Unlike their first meeting, Nate had been obsequiously deferential to her, in the presence of his male colleague. He even repeated her name that time, and his next words, though spoken like a declarative statement, had actually been a question: "Kind of medicine."

When she answered, he said: "So you identify human remains."

Having forgotten that they had met a year earlier, he asked her whether she knew Aggie Sheaf and when she said yes, his interest was piqued.

"Wow. You better go find your seat next to that Maytag repairman. You're gonna be bored to death here."

Not eager to engage him in conversation while she was with Devon, who was very silent, she'd answered quickly, "As a matter of fact, I stay fairly busy at the university."

"Oh, you teach?" She couldn't decipher the nature of his question. Had it been genuine interest, or a put-down? She nodded, then looked at Devon, and asked if he was ready to order. Nate then excused himself.

Now that he was assigning his men to work with her, Nate remembered enough to call her "Dr. Lula." How far things had progressed, from an insignificant dot on a radar screen on campus, to infinitesimally smaller today, in this fraternity of men.

Where were the women of the house?

While Devon took down names, Nate unwrapped a stick of gum, ogling it intently. He put the gum in his mouth, then quickly took out a second stick, repeating the ritual even more quickly, slurping while he chewed. As the smell of cinnamon wafted under their noses, he turned to Lula and offered her a stick.

She politely declined, then spoke. "I'd like to see the specimen while we still have some natural light. Can I get to it, now?"

Blaine, the invisible one, looked at her as if seeing her for the first time.

Nate said, "She's a forensic anthropologist. She'll help determine the identity of the finger, male, female, you know. Name, rank, serial number. The *CSI* stuff."

"That's taking it a bit far. I'm not sure an inspection will reveal an identity, but I might be able to assist in figuring out what implement the victim was cut with, which could lead to other identifying clues. As for any comparisons to *CSI*, trust me, it's not that glamorous." She smiled, graciously.

The men were quiet now, staring at her as if she, herself, were the specimen. A black female cadaver-digger.

Devon excused himself to retrieve a camera while Nate motioned to Blaine, who was standing in front of Lula.

"I see you got a hotel here. You the owner?" Nate asked.

"We're a production company."

"Who is we?"

"Preston Pratt."

"Where is he?"

"Traveling."

"Lemme talk to you while we're waiting on them to take their pictures." Nate held out his arm for Blaine to step aside. He yelled after Devon, "Call Seng here to drop by and take more pictures, you hear?"

Devon nodded, pulling out his phone.

"Do I need an attorney?" Blaine asked.

"That depends. Did you chop off one finger or three?" Nate asked.

After Devon got directions from Blaine about the location of the finger, he led Lula, who was holding her toolkit, through the side-door entrance of a relatively narrow office with two desks in different corners of the room.

Devon turned left and up a couple of steps into what appeared to be a study, then through another door into a living room.

Lula walked toward the specimen, which was sitting on top of an ornate writing desk. The room was warm, and well-lit by the rays of the sun shining in from the western horizon.

Devon took photos, while Lula took out latex gloves. She and her ex were consummate professionals. Memories of their lovemaking were light-years distant, part of a shared past she would just as soon forget. She moved aside so he could get closer to the specimen.

"How many you need?" Devon asked, lengthening his arms to take a digital shot.

"Take 'em from different angles: close up and wide. Let's say, ten or so."

Devon aimed and pressed a button. The shutter opened and closed, repeatedly.

"Anything else?"

"Let's turn it over and see what's there." She walked up close, prodding the finger with a pencil. A burned finger pad was revealed, just like the other two, with a burnt marshmallow-like darkness.

"Damn." Devon lowered the camera to see for himself. "Was it burned by fire or something else?"

Lula muttered, almost talking to herself. "It could have been acid. Interesting."

"Was it burned before or after it was cut off?"

"I don't know. That's a decomposition question I'd have to mull over, Devon."

She looked up to see him staring at her, his eyes probing hers, looking for some sign that her views had changed.

She turned away when Nate walked into the room.

"Whadda we got here?" Nate bellowed.

Lula remained staring at the specimen while Devon moved toward Nate. "We got ourselves a sick bastard, who cuts and burns, or burns and cuts. Doubt we'll be able to identify this one either."

Nate sought clarification: "Burned? As in fire?"

"Burned as in dipping the fingers in sulfuric acid, maybe," Devon said.

"Maybe?" Nate was looking the finger over. "We'll take them to HQ, get them signed in and all, and Dr. Lula can come get 'em when she's ready." He spoke to Lula using a friendly tone. "Which should, hopefully, be after the festival. You goin'?"

"Yep, my neighbor roped me into it." Lula rolled her eyes.

"Good." Nate clapped his hands.

"So, we're done?" Devon asked his boss, abruptly. "We getting statements?"

"I got enough, but I wanna see the pretty boy on Monday. He got some tattoos on his neck worth checking into."

"What's his story?"

"Not sure. Claims he works with a Nakadee student here at the production company. Sherry. We might have to find out who she is and get some information from her, too. Says she stays here on weekends. Which is why I wanna see him."

Lula didn't show it but was surprised to hear mention of the name Sherry. It was likely that she was one of her students, with just the type of personality to be involved with people in the entertainment industry. She would find out soon enough. Sherry was a ubiquitous presence in her life as a professor at the small university, but she wasn't one of Lula's favorite students.

Her thoughts were interrupted by Nate, who gave instructions to Devon. "Get his info before he goes somewhere. I told them to stay out of this part of the house until after the crime-scene people get here. Seng will do his thing and we'll come a callin' after the weekend festivities."

"Now we're talkin'!" Devon exclaimed.

"And who is Seng?" Lula asked, with a puzzled expression.

"Our crime scene photographer. From Vietnam. Good guy."

Nate snapped his fingers. "Oh. Right. The boy's mom wants you to take him home, Dr. Lula, if you'd be so obliged. I talked to her. She asked you to call her at her number." Nate fished in his pants pockets and produced a notepad from which he tore a sheet of paper with a phone number written on it.

"What's the boy's name?" Lula asked.

"Melvyn. The know-it-all."

"And Richard?" she asked.

Nate nodded. "They're gonna finish the lawn, put the mower away, and the kid will wait outside for you."

"Why can't Richard take him home?"

"He's gonna clean up. He'll be here another half-hour, he said."

"And Juanito, the pretty boy?" Devon asked.

Nate rolled his eyes. "He went inside with the short guy." Nate shook his head. "We got all kinds of weird in this state. I stopped asking questions a long time ago. Tell him to come visit us on Monday to chat with us. But, hot damn, I'll be ready for my Hot Sauce Festival tomorrow. And it ain't gonna be made outta peppers, neither!"

"So much for Lent," Devon smirked.

"I can give up what I want. I'm saying goodbye to pork for forty days, not to drinking."

"All right. That's cool. But they gonna be sellin' pork at every stall. How you gonna go to a hot-sauce festival and not eat pork?"

Lula listened to the men talk, neither displaying any interest in the investigation. In small towns like Nakadee, where traveling three towns away was cause for putting on nice clothes, the parish citizens, including the police, were more interested in crowning their local "Hot Sauce Hottie" and parading her on a float than in caring about the plight of the owner of the dismembered digits. Life here was more about what was hot and alive—not cold and dead.

4

SPARE RIBS

7:30 p.m.

As much as she wanted to, Lula couldn't beg off helping Melvyn's mother and her impromptu telephone invitation to dine at her home, a show of her gratitude for looking after her son. There would be no imposition, Bebe said, and she would pick up dinner on her way home from work. It was "ribs night," and if pork was her fancy, she would buy Lula the whole pig.

As happens at most Creole restaurants, the black cooks were outdoing themselves this year, she told Lula. The ethnicity of the chefs and food-preparers was important in a state that prided itself on its cuisine. It wasn't an issue of whether only Blacks could cook in Louisiana, she said. The question was whether the white chefs would skimp on the seasonings, to save money, something no black chef would ever stomach.

Bebe knew the chef at this joint, and was aware that they had been turning the barbecue on skewers for almost 24 hours straight for days, in anticipation of tomorrow's festivities.

During the drive to Melvyn's home, Lula was trying to figure out where she had met him before. She supposed it might have been at a church, because Lula had visited all the black churches within a five-to-ten-mile radius when she first moved to Nakadee, to get the lay of the land and its people. Melvyn dispelled that notion, however, explaining that he and his mother rarely went to church nowadays. He called religion the "opiate" of the black masses, but added that it was okay to sing the Negro spirituals because they were testament to "our resilience in finding ways to communicate right under the overseers' noses." Contemporary gospel was cool, but it was mainly where the talented "R&B singers go now," he instructed her, with an air of authority.

Melvyn said that he and his mother had met her at a funeral for Hargrove Pettis, the oldest black reporter for the local weekly, The *Parish Parrot*. That had been more than a year ago, she remembered, as she and Devon had attended the funeral together.

Too old to walk the beat after thirty years, Mr. Pettis had held court in a corner near the restrooms of the local bakery, named "The Most Superior Beignets in Town." People would pop over to tell him a juicy tidbit, which was virtually guaranteed to make it into the paper, with the reporter's full name, or, according to his or her preference, "from an unnamed source." Naturally, he was a popular fellow because it had become a local competition to try to get one's name in the paper. It was only after he died that everybody learned he owned a quarter of the French pastry shop, and had staked his "office" at the back of the restaurant to help drum up business there.

His funeral had been fun, in traditional Louisiana style. A band played, while the so-called bereaved danced, scarves aloft, and liquor—his—poured. A good time was had by all present, doing their best not to mourn their loss, but rather to remember *les bonnes temps*.

Driving the speed limit on the same roads that she had been racing on earlier made the return toward town seem much longer. When Lula mentioned this, Melvyn seconded it, volunteering that driving home on his Dad's lawnmower took him forever, too.

Melvyn couldn't stop talking, so effusive was his need to display his intelligence and mental parity with her. He wanted to know where she was from, did she like the South, and why there were so many gangs in the North, like the Crips and the Bloods. He mentioned his bike-riding friends Boojay and Garrett, but the three of them weren't in any gang, he assured her.

She answered him directly as best she could. After thirty seconds of silence, he turned his head toward her and asked about her job as a forensic anthropologist.

"You see dead people?" he joked.

"Yes, and I carve them up, too," she offered, ghoulishly, leaning toward him while keeping her hands on the steering wheel and her eyes on the road.

"Oh, you ain't scurred?" he followed, chuckling over his hip-hop turn of phrase. "So, you gonna cut up the finger back there?"

"Well, first I'll study it."

"Like, what you gonna look for?" he asked, innocently. "It's a finger—that's obvious. And the owner isn't with it. What else do you need to know?"

"Is it the finger of a male or a female? What's the ethnicity of the wearer? Asian, Black, White?"

Lula kept her eyes on the road, still running through her thought processes. "How was it separated from the wearer? Was it torn, burned, chopped off, was acid used. These are broad questions that, if answered, might narrow the scope of the investigation."

"Right. I see. Up there at the railroad crossing, you take a right turn, but not a hard right. You see how the second road there goes? Go that way."

They drove in silence for several seconds, while Lula slowed down. Melvyn was gazing out of the window, his head moving up and down, quietly.

"What you gonna tell my momma when you see her?"

"What do you want or don't want me to tell her?"

"That sounds funny. You sound like my mom. She be giving me grammar lessons all the time." He clasped his hands around an Afro pick while looking out of his window, then continued, "Nothing. They gonna call her up, anyway." He grazed the metal tongs of his comb with his thumb and fingers and licked his lips, unconsciously. His eyebrows furrowed slightly.

"Will there be repercussions?" She chose the word to see if the precocious boy's intellect could truly handle the nuances of adult conversation.

"Aw ... naw. Not with my momma. She knows the black man is always a target. But my dad—man, that's another story. He won't be too happy if he finds out the police know who I am."

"Well, can you talk to your mother about it first? Maybe she won't tell him."

"I'm not worried about her telling my dad anything. They hate each other. The police will tell him. Or Richard might open his trap, like he always do."

"Richard?"

"My kinda sorta babysitter," he answered.

She nodded.

"I just hope the police get to Dad first." He sighed.

"You believe Richard's going to tattle? What about?"

"Just anything. Richard's always nosin' hisself in other people's business and likes to be the first one to tell the news."

They rode in silence until Melvyn told her to make a turn onto a wide street lined with large homes. The whole subdivision felt new, a Stepford Wives gloss of affluence, though the houses were unremarkable. The architecture made an attempt at a Japanese theme, an exotic enticement, of sorts, for the junior executives and other arrivals, all flush with money. They worked for the poultry, fertilizer, and farming corporations that were homesteading in Louisiana with the promise of renewable energy and shared profits.

After thirty yards, they turned into a driveway next to an emerald-green lawn, also mowed in a patchwork design in a similar, but smaller, pattern to the one at the bachelors' mansion.

When they walked up to the front door, Melvyn's mother was there to welcome them, holding out her hand to Lula and patting her son's head in quick succession.

"Glad I got here before you with the food." She called after her son: "Say goodbye to bad hair, honey, and hello to the barber."

"You said I could wear it for tomorrow! You said cut it next week," he called back while running up the stairs.

The women laughed as Melvyn's mother closed the door, but Melvyn's muffled expletive reached them.

"Boy, I heard that," she added, punctuating her comment with the door's closing.

Bebe Armstrong had the classic features of Negritude, with a burnt-sienna tone to her dark skin that matched the sienna-colored tips of her Korean hair extensions. She wore her hair and clothing well. She was, overall, an attractive woman.

She was dressed in an expensive purple-and-gold Louisiana State University jogging suit and looked athletic and chic in her gear. She carried her heftiness regally, a trademark of thick black women who knew that they still looked good, despite their excess poundage.

Judging by her attire, Melvyn's mother had likely gone to a gym in her heyday, before the trials of raising a son put stresses on her. She probably still had a decent figure underneath that could be pushed and tucked here and there with a good old-fashioned girdle or expensive pair of Spanx.

Many black women with large frames lived their sizes out loud and in full Technicolor, sans any self-inflicted stigma. Food was often the only balm against the pressures of the world weighing on the lonely shoulders of a single mother.

Lula also ascribed to the philosophy that there was no problem that couldn't be solved by putting warm, good-tasting food in one's stomach. Unlike her white colleagues in the Bay Area, who fixated on obsessive calorie-counting to stay razor thin, she and her black women friends could be found taking refuge in the love of food, sometimes more than in their desire to find a mate.

She glanced down at Bebe's fashionable Italian leather running shoes, a unique mustard-yellow suede, of a brand she didn't recognize, but which looked quite expensive.

Bebe motioned Lula into the kitchen, while calling Melvyn to come get his meal. After she had handed Lula a hard cider, she stepped to the stairwell and yelled again for him to come downstairs. Her hand pounded the handrail in time with her count.

"*Eins, zwei, drei, vier, fünf.* How many more before I get to *zehn*, boy?"

He vaulted down the stairs with his headphones on, which were connected to a smartphone attached to his belt.

"I was texting Daddy about an upgrade."

"What did he say?"

"If I up my grades, I'll get the upgrade. He got me on that one." He smiled. "Man, my heart was pounding."

"What did I tell you about texting him when he's away on business? The last thing he needs is a distraction. I'm counting on him to put you through college."

"I know, I know, I know," he replied, simultaneously glancing up at Lula while stepping back from the reach of his mother's airborne hand, which was aimed to lovingly scoop his chin. When Bebe turned around to go into the kitchen, Lula stood in the foyer, unsure whether she should follow. Her question of where to go next was solved as Bebe came back in a flash with plates and silverware, which she set down, then began opening foil bags with their steaming contents.

Lula watched mother and son as he picked out his ribs and chicken pieces, fighting his mother over a mutually coveted plump chicken thigh. She wasn't sure if this display was for her benefit, or if it was the usual communication between the two—a perpetual high-stakes game of bartering, but not spoiling, of desiring, but not begging. The fine line walked by a single mother who wanted to protect her son yet also fortify him to combat life's everyday hazards.

Melvyn heaved a large baked potato onto his plate and was piling on the coleslaw. "Can I be excused?" he asked, licking his fingers.

"Are we boring you, by chance?" Bebe nodded, with a sideways glance.

He carried his plate into the large family room that replaced the living room, where two large recliners sat in an alcove on the left side of the room, facing a 50-inch flat-screen television.

"Ear phones on, Melvyn."

"You don't gotta tell me. I know the deal, Mamasita."

"Mama huh? Let's untwist that."

"My Queen." He turned sideways, looking back at Lula, flashing a winsome smile. "That was whack, Mom. It's 'Don't get it twisted.'"

"Whatever."

The women smiled. No longer sidetracked by the youthful distraction of a teenager, it was their turn to find a level of comfort with each other. Usually, any social divide among mothers could be bridged in a mutual unity of purpose or clarity of vision on the rearing or teaching of children. But Lula had no children, and, therefore, no means of sharing meaningful pleasantries about them. They could discuss national affairs, and the Obama "post-racial" presidency, but she didn't know her host's politics.

Bebe seemed to be on the progressive side, but Lula decided to hold that thought until she knew more. The Republican party of Abraham Lincoln still had many Black Americans in its ranks. Lula played it safe by asking about the take-out barbecue they were eating.

Bebe chuckled. "I know they regard black folk as difficult, but the truth is that we just have standards, honestly. How am I gonna take some ribs from a white establishment and not be picky about what I'm gonna get? Now they tend ...." She scanned around the room dramatically, then continued, "Well, put it this way ... you gotta tell them from the get-go to give you the burnt ones."

She looked at Lula knowingly, sharing her secret: "Carcinogenic, my ass. You know how many pieces you'd have to eat to get cancer?"

She took a carnivorous bite, her pinkies extended, dramatically.

Lula laughed, encouraging her.

White people were great foils for conversations between Blacks with nothing else in common except living under majority-white rule.

Bebe continued talking. "Girl, I don't know why we can't do our own shit. We buy their food and their hair products that come from our old family recipes that we cooked in their kitchens. But what can I say—we just some lazy-ass sons-uh you-know-what."

Lula didn't dare engage with a Southerner in the politics behind Black Power where business was concerned. In the South, post Reconstruction, black communities had thrived, buying from and selling to each other, until Whites began to do the math. They created institutions, banks, societies, and other means of gaining a competitive edge so that black business became white business. She didn't want to go there, so she just laughed along with Bebe, listening.

While they chatted, picking at their food, they caught snippets of the news from the kitchen television that hung in a corner. After forty minutes, the women were full.

"Can I offer you a drink?" Bebe asked. Before Lula could answer, Bebe raised her voice. "Boy, you better wash those barbecue hands before you touch anything else in that room. Then go upstairs. You know what time it is."

"I thought you wanted me to tell you what happened?"

"Not now, Mr. Man. I want to talk to Miss Lula here. Now, do as I say." Bebe winked at Lula and smiled.

"You gonna tell her about the finger, Ms. Lula? She was investigating, Momma. She saw the finger. It's in her car."

"Come again?" Bebe stared at her son in disbelief.

"It's a finger ... in her car."

"That so?" Bebe looked at Lula.

"No, the police have the finger."

"It's not in the car?" Melvyn asked.

"It's in an ice chest in Captain Nate's car," said Lula.

Melvyn watched her, eyes bright with anticipation. "It's nothing to be afraid of, Mom."

"I'll just take your word for it, Melvyn." She laughed, putting her hand on his shoulder and guiding him upstairs. "It's been a long day, huh, Mr. Man? Go run your bath and relax and get your PJs on. I'll be up in a few."

His shoulders sagged.

"You get ten minutes on the computer, but don't let the tub get full. If I catch you on Twitter, you're gonna have to get to writing."

"Why I gotta go upstairs?"

"Because I want to talk with your friend, here. Say goodnight."

"Sho' you right. Okay. Goodnight. Do you Twitter, Dr. Lula?"

"No."

"It's easy. Look for me on Twitter. My name is Pud'n Tang."

"What?" Lula asked.

"She knows the rest," Bebe interrupted. "Boy, get outta here."

Lula laughed at the boy's ingenuity. "Ask me again, Melvyn," she offered.

"I'll tell you the same!" He hollered from upstairs. A door closed and the bath water started running.

"How about that drink?" Bebe asked again.

Lula spent another hour with Bebe, sitting in the alcove of the family room. Looking through the glass sliding doors, she saw a miniature desert of barren hills, several cacti, large granite boulders, and magenta, blue, and orange garden lights—Bebe's wildflower garden. Her host could not hide her pride. The back yard was more than 1500 square feet of walkways, greenery, and narrow irrigation waterways.

She described how she and Melvyn had cultivated the garden, digging up the soil to prevent it from growing weed seeds. She explained that wildflower gardens were not "wild" per se, as they required steady maintenance because the garden needed just the right amount of moisture to ensure germination. She and Melvyn had changed the sprinkler system to redirect the water flow and to bypass some wildflowers while providing saturation for others. She said that if the Red River could change course, and its name, too—as it was now called the Cane River—then she could do the same in her own backyard.

"Word to the wise: Don't lose your balance and fall on cacti. They don't business." She showed Lula her hand, with a large Band-Aid on the front. "Cacti can break your fall, but you'll be a walking acupuncture model afterwards." She chuckled, shaking her head, ruefully, saying. "I'm a hazard to my own self!"

They laughed together, as they relaxed, trading stories of stupid things each had done as both younger and more mature women. There were also stories about their exploits as single women—a late-night rendezvous, where putting clothes back on in the dark created challenges; walking around with smudged lipstick after their boyfriends kissed them.

Their laughter turned into cackles. Lula was feeling good, less a visitor and more like someone reminiscing with a friend.

Bebe excused herself to make sure her son was in bed, then returned to the room, smiling. She picked up her drink, taking another sip, then set it down again.

"That boy. Sometimes, I swear he was switched at birth, honestly, but we got the same birthmark to remind me he's all mine. I can tell you he's a product of his daddy in temperament, but that's it. He's a sucker for a pretty lady, and will do whatever it takes to get her attention. He told me if you were a bit younger, he'd date you."

They chuckled softly, trying to stifle their voices.

"I'm just glad no cougars live in the neighborhood. He'd be married by now."

Lula sensed that Bebe was cracking the door open just a little bit, trying to find out what had happened that afternoon, but, like the trait for which Southerners were stereotypically known, she was very politely beating around the bush before asking directly.

Lula took the initiative, stepping up her offensive to relieve the other woman of her politesse. It was eleven o'clock, and she had no idea where the time had gone.

"Well, let me brief you on what happened today," she said.

Bebe nodded her head, saying nothing. The women sat on their respective recliners, Bebe sitting with one leg underneath her. Maybe she did work out, Lula noted. She seemed younger than she dressed.

Lula listened to Bebe talk about her son with a softness that she might not have had but for his importance in her life. She wondered if Bebe did as many single mothers do: place too much emphasis on the child being her "man," to a degree that only put burdens on him, and which would only result in problems later.

"You might be the first parent I know whose son takes baths," Lula said.

"Girl, that's the only way I can get him to calm down. He's a bit hyperactive, so at least by evening, if he takes a bath and winds down on the computer for a bit, just to get it out of his system, then he's good to go for the next day. If he takes a shower, I can guarantee you he'll be bouncing off the walls. We're in the wildflower garden a lot, so I can teach him the value of being patient, looking long-term, not for the immediate gratification these kids are so used to nowadays. Did you know the average age for kids having sex now is eleven?"

Lula expressed her shock, then saw an opportunity, and asked, "What's his relationship to the men up the way?"

"He mows their lawn. He wants a smartphone-tablet-gizmo-whatever, you name it, so he has to learn the value of those items. I told him if he could find a way to make a living picking up money here and there, I would match the funds and he could save up and get whatever he wanted. I thought he'd do something simple like pick up trash or tutor somebody. No, not him. He's like his father. He hustled and got himself a job landscaping, mowing, watering lawns, pruning bushes for the white upper-crust up the way."

They shared a laugh, simultaneously sipping their drinks, which made them laugh even more.

"I guess I taught him something. When one can't, one learns to 'can'. So, we'd open the manuals, and follow directions. Go figure. Now, he can take stuff apart and put it back together. He's like a surgeon, that one. If something breaks, I'll call him. He figures it out. He likes picking up dead bugs and taking them apart. He won't kill them, but he'll definitely scoop up the dead ones if he sees them. He's got a little laboratory in the shed there." She pointed to the yard.

Lula tried to peer through the glass sliding doors, but at that hour all she saw was their torsos in silhouette and the glow from the ceiling lights, like a protective aureole above their reflections.

"He's quite smart," Lula said.

"Yeah, he's a smart boy, that one, just a bit too big for his britches."

They commiserated about the youth of today, contrasted with the way their own grandparents had taught them. In their grandparents' day, virginity was taken for granted as a natural consequence of being a teenager, something precious that you lost on your wedding day. Bebe and Lula had each learned some form of variation on that theme, but their time was the day of the "pill," the ingenious means for preventing pregnancy and allowing you to have sex with anyone who was likely straight. Now, teenagers could buy the morning-after pill.

"We don't wanna go there, do we?" asked Bebe.

They feted one another in a toast of drinks instead of high fives, believing theirs would be the last generation who could say they lived normal lives. Bebe added her insights about what it was like to raise a son in these perilous times, where a black man was a target for police and a black boy was a target for everyone but his absentee father.

Lula mentioned Melvyn's advisory to Nate and Devon that he would tell his father about the incident, and how each officer had reacted.

There was weight to what Melvyn warned, Bebe confirmed. Her ex-husband was working on a natural gas pipeline that ran from Brazil to Nakadee and would bring jobs to the area. The police chief had political aspirations, and was primed to be in politics for years to come if the deal went through.

"The SOB," she chuckled, referring to her ex-husband. "He's about to blow up big and his white-trash whore is gonna reap all the benefits. But she can have him. He caught prostate cancer, probably from her." Playing a mini-violin with her fingers, she showed a sad clown's face, then sucked her teeth. Lula didn't think to interrupt Bebe's diatribe to share the scientific odds that it wasn't contagion that inflicted the cancer on him. Instead, she opted for small talk.

"Does Melvyn like her?"

"What's not to like? He has a big-screen television in his bedroom, they eat out several times a week, and he doesn't have to clean. And his dad took him to Brazil a couple of weeks ago, so he's not complaining about the arrangement. But like he said to me earlier, he don't got it twisted. He knows the deal."

The women sat quietly for a spell, not regarding each other, as they took a couple of sips from their drinks.

"So what's the finger jazz all about?" Bebe asked.

"I'm not quite sure. You can't tell much if the fingerprints are gone."

"Wow. It's like that. So what are the police doing? I imagine they can get the hounds out and start sniffin'."

"Well, we have severed fingers, but no body."

"And no one's calling to say they are missing fingers, I suppose?"

"Right."

"I have a friend who works for *The Parish Parrot*. I can put you in touch with him."

"That's not really my area. I'm just on the sidelines. I'm not an investigator, and I have my other work literally cut out for me," Lula said.

"I heard that. Literally and figuratively. Right! Well, what's the figurative part of it? What do you do for a living?"

"I'll answer in a sec, but do you mind? I've been wondering all evening: Is Bebe your full name?"

"That's what my friends call me. My real name is Barbara."

"Great." Lula heaved a sigh. "I just wanted to get your name right."

"So, what's a Yankee sister doin' here in the dirty South, of all God-awful places?"

"I like it here, I guess."

"Girl, you must have a fever," Bebe joked, putting her ring-studded finger on Lula's forehead.

They laughed.

Bebe was engaging and affable. Lula loosened up a bit, answering Bebe's questions about her background, giving a Cliff Notes summary: her degrees, her grant research. Her whole professional life was an open book.

Bebe asked whether she was certified.

Lula answered that indeed she was, from the American Board of Forensic Anthropology.

Bebe listened attentively, absentmindedly fingering the dangling gold hoop on her left ear, while Lula recounted her trip to Africa that had started her on her journey to becoming a forensic anthropologist.

The group of students had seen the place a mile off the coast of Dakar, Senegal, where, after being housed in small, dank dungeons, millions of slaves first embarked upon their journey to the New World. The prisoners were walked through the narrow Gate of No Return, a small, white-walled waiting station, onto a ship, then into a darker world that would, centuries later, find their descendants still living in unfathomable social dungeons of prejudice and contempt in the United States.

The Gorée Island Slave House visit had been a haunting reminder of the savagery of nations like Portugal, whose marauders first set foot on the island to promote the slave trade. The country's claim to fame, five-hundred years later, would be delectable sardines, tourism, and the administration of the gambling haven of Macau, near China, along with a prolonged effect on the psyche of black peoples, particularly in the South-American country of Brazil.

The other co-conspirators, the Dutch, had built the slave houses in which family members were forcibly separated and sent off to different countries, never to see each other again. The Dutch would have a slaveholding domain in South Africa, with which the United States would have a deep and lasting camaraderie, like brothers in crime.

As the only Black among a group of ten college students on that journey to Africa, Lula had been unprepared for her reaction to the fortresses' remains. The spray of the ocean on her face as she looked through the door where some slaves had favored jumping and being eaten by sharks rather than leaving their homeland, blended with Lula's tears.

Her classmate, Bennett, a Canadian, was equally shaken, but, in typical Anglo-Saxon fashion, kept a stiff upper lip and took several deep breaths. His grip around her shoulder, which had almost cracked her back, had been as much to hold himself steady as to keep her standing. Both had their desperate need for comforting and salvation—he from a race of people who profited from free labor—and she, a descendant of an African people who had, some felt, unwittingly aided and abetted the decimation of their own brothers, sisters, and cousins in the world's most infamous, centuries-long genocide.

After the journey to West Africa, Lula fell ill with amoebic dysentery, although she believed she was viscerally struck down by what she had seen. She returned to UC Berkeley determined to study anthropology.

Putting her heart into her newfound studies, she earned a 3.87 grade-point average and a fellowship toward a Masters degree at Western Michigan University. Living there for three years solidified her interest in physical anthropology and she returned to California to attend UC Santa Cruz for her PhD in osteology, which qualified her to examine bones, teeth, human osteology, and dental anthropology.

She explained to Bebe how bones were like pieces of a puzzle, not just physically in how they interrelated, but metaphorically. A bone tells much more than is generally perceived. Bone analysis can divulge the whole lifestyle of a society.

Lula was determined to understand the lives of those Africans who had come before her, centuries ago, and explained that she was conducting her research at the university.

Bebe added liquor from a mixed-drink decanter to her own almost-empty glass, then motioned for Lula to extend hers so she could top it off, too. Lula held her glass out and sank into the couch.

"Girl, get comfortable. The sofa there folds out into a bed; or I can make a fresh bed for you in one of the bedrooms upstairs. Friends don't let friends drive drunk."

Lula sat up, with mock paranoia. "Oh my God, am I slurring?"

Both women laughed as Bebe stood up.

"I have an extra set of pajamas, compliments of T.J.Maxx. I should have bought stock in Joe Boxer. PJs are like purses. You wear them for different occasions. This is a Joe Boxer slumber party tonight. But I want to hear the rest of your story, first. I'll be back in a second."

Lula's eyes followed Bebe, hearing her voice trail off as she walked to a nearby bathroom. "I have lots of new toothbrushes. You know a girl's always gotta have those around."

Lula chuckled as she sipped her drink, dipping her finger into the iced elixir of brandy, crème de cacao, and milk. The color of her drink wasn't as appealing as its taste. Resting her head against the high back of the recliner, she let her eyelids close gently. She barely noticed Bebe's return.

As promised, pajamas, pressed and folded, were laid on the table in front of her, along with a toothbrush still in its package. A feather pillow with a crisp cotton case was placed behind her head. Lula was tired. Dead tired.

She smiled wanly and said, apologetically, "I'm a lightweight. I'll just rest my eyes a bit."

Smiling, Bebe placed a starched ironed sheet on her guest and put a down bedcover next to her on the couch. Lula relaxed, still upright, her glass held tightly in her hand. She barely registered Bebe's prying the glass out of her loosening grip and placing it on the table.

"Sleep tight," Bebe whispered.

"Thanks," Lula replied. "I'm more tired than I thought." Bebe put one hand up to her own mouth, yawning, the other one waving her goodnight.

Saturday, March 19th, 7:30 a.m.

Lula awakened to a glass of tomato juice and a bottle of Aleve sitting at eye level opposite her on a tray table. Alongside the hangover antidotes was a note:

> Make yourself at home. Danish and boiled eggs are on the kitchen table under the cake dish, and the coffee machine has assorted flavors you might like. Melvyn's performing at the festival so I have errands to run. Just lock the door on the way out.

Bebe's handwriting was a beautiful cursive that suggested training in calligraphy. What an interesting woman, Lula thought as she glanced at her watch.

Seven-thirty a.m.

The commute to and from her lab took a half-hour each way, not including the other thirteen miles away to the slave burial site where she was conducting her research. She could stop by the police station to pick up the finger specimens, drop them off at her lab, and still have enough time to shower and meet her neighbor, Pomona, at the fair, as she'd reluctantly promised.

Lula closed her eyes for a minute's catnap and awakened almost three hours later. Alarmed, she raced to the bathroom to brush her teeth and splash water on her face, drying with a plush hand-towel that was part of a fresh set Bebe had placed on the bathroom sink. She gathered her purse and bolted out the door, remembering to lock it, as Bebe had asked.

After she picked up the specimens at the police station, Lula assessed her task as she drove to the University lab. At this stage of the investigation, her job was merely to figure out what tool had been used to cut off the three fingers.

However, that narrow focus couldn't erase her nagging curiosity about what sort of individual would do such a thing in a town like Nakadee. Then again, this town's inhabitants were a different breed from what she was used to. She was still acclimating to this small-town, with its parochial, insular worldviews, steeped in antebellum social mores understood only by the somnambulant inhabitants.

When she'd asked the officer at the front desk of the police station whether any further mischief had been reported, his response was no, but that there would likely be a status change after the festival.

Ignorance was bliss in these places where petty domestic disputes instigated fistfights instead of fatal gang warfare. Cutting fingers was a pretty harrowing turn of events in a bucolic oasis like this, where the lore of slavery's savagery had nearly been erased from the collective conscience.

At her lab, Lula measured and examined the blood-soaked digits to see where they'd been severed. Whatever had been used to cut them, there had been a hiccup in the process.

The fingers were still soft, their pigmentation still pliable, even slightly oily. Though the blood had soaked inside the fingers' soft tissues, it had yet to attract the blowflies and other scavengers that usually showed up to feast on a newly dismembered body part.

The pads on each finger had been burned or singed, masking the grooves and indentations of the soft tissue, most likely to make fingerprints difficult to match in any state or federal database. Notwithstanding, there was enough adipose tissue to provide a unique insight into the health of the fingers' owner. Both the fingertips and nails were round, but the nails spread outward—signs of potential clubbing. Whoever owned the fingers possibly had a heart condition.

5

CORPORATE INTERESTS

Sherry dove into Preston's swimming pool, making the glass-like surface of the water disappear into waves. Her diving form was beautiful to behold, a fact she knew very well, as she had honed it to perfection. She glided through the water, feeling its protective embrace.

After relishing a lap or two, she began thinking about school and the assignments she had ahead of her that day.

She stretched her arm forward in the water, wishing she could just as easily fast forward to graduating. She was done with school, sick of going to classes, tired of homework, writing assignments for subjects she would never use in real life.

Forensic anthropology satisfied her science requirements, but she was interested in it like she was interested in becoming a midwife to starving babies in Africa. She could care less about Dr. Lula's homework. Her other assignments were beckoning her.

Sherry's calling was set. Her fortune would be working with Preston's production company. She was going to be in the movie business. She didn't care if she were in front of the camera or behind the scenes. She would figure that out. She was already an insider.

But had she doomed her prospects by bringing Juanito around? He was a game-changer, in more ways than one.

Sherry knew that women envied her, and men wanted her. But after meeting Juanito, her outlook on her desirability had changed. His arrival made life exciting in ways she could never have anticipated, but also made her feel less certain about her position in Preston's company.

She took a deep gasp of air as she flipped over to swim backstroke, and remembered how she had first spied him in the pool at the private gym.

Juanito had ignored Sherry, which meant that he had noticed her, too. As weeks wore on, she discovered that they had similar evening gym schedules and were often swimming laps a couple of lanes away from each other, sometimes in tandem, and at other times, from opposite ends. She started stealing glances at him, watching his sinewy biceps sparkle as he swam laps, patches of his dark hair clinging to his face as his head moved from side to side.

One day they found themselves in a lap competition, until Sherry gave up. She hung out, afterward, waiting for him to reach her end of the pool. He gripped the edge, and spat water onto the shiny tiles.

Sherry hoisted herself up out of the pool and stood looking down at him. "How many laps?" she asked.

"Two more than you," he replied, smiling.

"So we were competing? I wish I had known. I would have tried harder." She crinkled her nose at him, playfully. "So, do I buy the winner a beer, or do you buy for the loser?"

She eyed the soft-looking hairs of his armpits as he smoothed his hair back. His mane was full and thick, not long enough for a ponytail, but enough to caress his neck. He bathed his arms with the pool water.

"I'll own up to losing," she added.

"Well, of course, I must pay. You are the weaker of the two of us, so I must pay." He didn't have too thick an accent, but his words lingered over the vowel sounds in a way that was pleasing to her ears.

"Weaker? Dude, I knew that you would pay, so who is the stronger of the two of us? You, the macho, or me, who lets you be macho?"

That's when he told her that appearances were deceiving.

Sherry didn't bat an eyelash. "I don't make any assumptions nowadays, especially when it comes to pretty-boys like you."

As if to spite him, she bent over, her breasts almost spilling out of her bathing suit as she splashed pool water on her feet.

He reached up and cupped her right breast with his hand, retracting it, slowly.

"They real?" he asked.

She didn't flinch. "Yep."

"Well, are we still going for drinks?" He smiled, his eyes slanting sideways to look at her as he pushed himself back from the edge, treading his legs gently in the pool, causing slight ripples in the water.

"Sure. I'm already out of the pool. What's holding you up?"

He nodded. "You go ahead, I'll follow."

She started to walk away then stopped to turn around. "Are you okay?"

"Sure." He lingered in the pool.

"Are you disabled? Do you need some help?"

His hands covered his front, obscuring his dark trunks.

"I'll just hang back a bit."

"Should I wait?"

"No. You go ahead. Something came up, unexpectedly."

She opened her mouth wide in surprise. "Dude. Please tell me you're gay. It would be the highlight of my college experience to know that I could get a rise out of a gay man. Please."

He laughed, merely raising his eyebrows.

She turned around, letting him appreciate her walk to the women's locker room as she tugged her swimsuit free from her crevice. Gay or not, she knew that he, like the few black men on campus who didn't call her by name, appreciated "Ms. Black Booty."

After six months of hanging out with Juanito at the pool and palling around town for drinks, Sherry had decided to take a gamble and introduce Juanito to Preston. Her purpose had been to show off her handsome find to a man who appreciated a good-looking man. Finding Juanito was solid proof that she could spot talent.

The three of them drank beers poolside that day at Preston's. He'd invited them both to swim naked in the pool, something Sherry did regularly anyway.

When she'd returned with the towels, Sherry couldn't mask her surprise when Preston told her that she had a new co-worker. Juanito's de facto interview had lasted all of three minutes, as Preston hired him on the spot to become his personal assistant.

Preston arranged Juanito's schedule so that he worked on days when Sherry was in class. Even better for Juanito was that Preston gave him Fridays off.

Sherry recalled Preston's Cheshire-Cat smile, which seemed to suggest that he could manipulate anyone into the allure of Hollywood, like a mythical siren singing ships to the ocean depths.

After her begrudging acceptance of Juanito's newfound position in the company, she and Juanito became coconspirators in his voyeuristic game of letting her watch while he played the tease, just as he had done with her at the pool. He was a male coquette, using his looks to control Preston, winning him over with his toothy smile and deep dimples. She didn't dare ask if he and Preston were ever intimate.

Ultimately, she didn't care, because she could relax with Juanito. Her relationship with him blossomed once the prospect of having sex with him was off her radar. He was the girlfriend she'd always wanted, someone who didn't envy or try to compete with her. Her own beauty had become a financial liability, as it was burdensome trying to compete with some of the wealthier students and remain fashionably and stylishly *au courant*.

Sherry wasn't from a wealthy family, but had perfected the art of living well on a shoestring budget. She was part of the white minority of Affirmative Action recipients that had never been contemplated in the national debate about entitlements.

No one knew she was from a low-income background because she buffered that truth with a Scarlett-O'Hara-like pretense of wealth. She scouted all the best second-hand stores in Shreveport, where the takings were better. She declined most invitations to eat out with her few girlfriends, using the partially accurate excuse that she was watching her figure.

Before meeting Juanito, she would simply do without, especially when she couldn't get financial help from her father. His first wife still demanded money from him for herself and the four children they'd had together, which didn't leave much money to spend on Sherry and her mother.

Whatever Juanito may have gleaned about her financial status, he never let on. He simply had an instinctive way of helping her without seeming to do so, paying for drinks whenever they went clubbing, and splitting a meal with her that he paid for.

When she faced the prospect of her car failing inspection because of a cracked exhaust pipe, he advised her to get it repaired rather than buy a whole new one. He also helped alleviate her financial woes by enlisting her help to supply students with their all-important study aids: Adderall, Ritalin, Xanax, and Valium.

Juanito told Sherry that her job was merely to dispense the drugs, not advise anyone about their use. What the students did with them was not her concern. Whether they used them as stimulants during late-night studying, or recreationally to make 8-balls, or injecting crushed Ritalin into their veins, which the high flyers tended to do, the only warning she could give her customers was not to take any Benzodiazepines with alcohol, a potentially fatal combination.

He also warned her against pursuing black students as customers because they got too loud when they were angry and could draw attention to her. They weren't worth the effort, anyway, because they preferred reefer. Juanito wasn't into selling any drugs to black student athletes, either, because they were always being tested for drugs and steroids.

Juanito would come to the campus to pick her up, delivering the drugs that she sold to her friends, and splitting the take with her. She could make as much as five hundred dollars in a good week, and no one had a clue.

Sherry distributed to about fifteen students on campus, and used Professor Logan as her unwitting accomplice. She visited her professor once a week, making rounds to her buyers right outside the forensic lab, in the building that students called "the dungeon." It didn't get much traffic, so she could hang out or meet her customers on the third floor without drawing attention to herself.

After Juanito became part of Preston's production company—and social entourage—Sherry found ways to get out of reading scripts at Preston's on Friday nights so she could rendezvous with Juanito instead. After Preston retired for the night, she'd sneak out and walk the quarter-mile down to where the dimmed lights of Juanito's car were waiting.

Life was almost perfect for Sherry. She was attractive, fit, passing all of her classes, and, thanks to Juanito, had some extra cash in her pocket. Other than Richard's nagging jealousies, life was pretty good.

She had told Richard, repeatedly, that she wasn't involved with Juanito sexually, intentionally suggesting that there was some question about the Cuban's sexual preferences, to throw him off. Still, Richard wasn't having it, saying that no "gay dude" would play with her hair or rub her shoulders the way he'd seen Juanito do on occasion, when Richard picked up Melvyn some afternoons.

She explained that Juanito was from a different culture, one whose cues she didn't quite understand, so that what Richard saw as lust was nothing but appreciation of her as a friend, who just happened to be a woman.

Richard countered that the gestures were foreplay. There was no mistaking that Juanito wanted to bed her, and Richard reminded her that they had vowed to be monogamous so that he wouldn't have to wear condoms, and because nobody could do her like he did, anyway. She was wasting her time even thinking about being with someone else. She was his property and nobody else's.

Whatever Sherry's plans were with Juanito—and they were still unknown to her—the less Richard knew, the better.

10:30 a.m.

Blaine returned his desk phone to its cradle, with an audible sigh. Preston's wife, Miriam (nicknamed, "Mare"), had confirmed, a third time, in as many calls, that she'd arrive the next day. He had tried to be as cordial as he could, but she was the last person he needed to see, especially now, during Preston's absence.

He wasn't sure how he had ended up so ensconced in the company of women in his work, considering his overall belief in their unimportance. Short of having them in love scenes, he didn't see a need for women at all, especially behind the scenes.

Filmmaking was a male province, like composing classical music. The female sex weakened the storylines, or slowed the action, turning a man's heroism into a slobbery mush. He was aware that the women in the company, namely Mare and Sherry, knew that the balance of power had shifted, however, and they didn't hesitate to use their femininity like a weapon to remind him of who he was and who he would always be, as far as they were concerned: an inconsequential eunuch, an afterthought who was tolerated solely because of his financial connections.

Although industry insiders scoffed at Preston and Mare's union, their marital relationship seemed a legitimate one, much to Blaine's befuddlement.

The newlyweds had run counter to convention at first, spending lots of time apart, in separate homes, with no discussions about children--the traits of other hastily-arranged Hollywood mismatches.

But to Blaine's surprise, Mare and Preston had morphed into a traditional couple. They finished each other's sentences, had private jokes, and talked with each other on the phone regularly during the day.

His strategy of transferring their production offices to Louisiana had backfired. Mare had been livid when he'd suggested the move four years ago, seeing it as a desperate measure to sideline her and minimize her importance to the company. Blaine had insisted it was a necessary evil to get Preston to concentrate, if he was going to be the artistic leader he aspired to be.

Mare hadn't spoken to Blaine for weeks, afterward, until Preston had placated her, offering the olive branch that he and Blaine would have separate homes joined by an office, and would share only the office, pool, and tennis court. They'd even have separate garages. The two men had their Nakadee property built within 18 months, and moved in within another six.

Now that they'd lived here for more than two years, Mare jokingly labeled them the "Odd Couple." Even in Nakadee, away from her influence, Blaine felt he was losing his importance, even his relevance as a business partner.

Preston had begun teaching a beginner's screenwriting course at the university. It was popular and well-attended and this local recognition changed the dynamics of their relationship in the rural outpost. It became obvious to all that Blaine wasn't needed as much. After the successful first two seasons of their television series, Blaine was all but invisible to Preston, who basked in the limelight. As he travelled more, he even stopped sharing his itinerary with Blaine.

When Mare had last called to confirm her arrival, Blaine insisted that her husband wasn't there, and she asked why that mattered when she had the keys to her own home? She also said that she hadn't heard from him in weeks and thought it would be a good time to visit. She needed some records that were in his possession.

Blaine knew what she was looking for, but she'd never find it. Preston had told him he'd made sure of that.

Feigning ignorance, Blaine told Mare he was no closer to knowing where his business partner was than she, and wished her well in her search. He would order her a limousine. Her claim that she'd tried to text Preston raised Blaine's suspicions, because she should have known that he wasn't tech-savvy.

Months earlier, he and Preston had been preparing the invitation list for the private ball to be held at Preston's home. Although Preston could type on a keyboard, he couldn't do much else with one. Using the telephone was so much easier than communicating by email, he had said, though he didn't use a smartphone for tasks he felt were the purpose of unpaid interns like Sherry and Juanito. He hadn't learned now to read emails on the phone, or use the keypads to text. On his own computer he didn't even know how to change fonts or use bullets and numbering.

If Blaine ever received a text message from him, Preston had said, it should be perceived as a legitimate SOS that he was in danger.

They chuckled together at the time, but, two days ago, Blaine had received a text message from Preston's phone:

"43LP 43LP 4QPP9 54QRADFF PHACJ"

Whether it was a joke—as it likely was—or not, Blaine had lost his sense of humor where Preston was concerned. He was tired of being so easily dismissed after being the company's financial savior for so long. Whatever mess Preston was in, he'd have to solve his own problem.

And Mare could do whatever she damn well pleased—as she always did—but he'd avoid her as much as possible.

His hands hung over the arms of his chair, lifeless. Then fear shot throughout his body as he seized himself into a ball. He bent over, trying to breathe.

He looked up to see Sherry staring at him, a towel covering her bathing suit, her wet hair slicked back. Had he said anything aloud that could make him look suspicious?

"I'll be upstairs if you need me," she said, then hurried through the office into Preston's side of the house.

6

COLD SWEAT

1:00 p.m.

Second to Mardi Gras, the annual Hot Sauce Festival was the most anticipated event in Nakadee. Lula's neighbor, Pomona, persuaded Lula to attend, mainly by convincing her that she needed two pairs of eyes to keep track of her five rambunctious kids. Lula insisted, however, that they drive in separate cars.

After visiting animal stalls of emus, pigs, donkeys and sheep, the two women managed to get separated.

Lula scouted only half-heartedly for her neighbor, distracted by all the booths displaying their varieties of hot sauces. Before long, she felt qualified to teach a Masters-level course on this all-important Louisiana condiment.

Every table bore a variation on the theme, each claiming its own bragging rights. The cooks extolled the unique nature of their sauce and its historical relevance to the festival as a "truly Southern phenomenon."

A Mardi Gras krewe from weeks earlier had reassembled a float, a long cattle truck with an elevated stage where young girls and boys danced and gyrated in sequined bikinis and shorts to electric dance music. Teenagers and adults alike were following behind, holding out their hands for Mardi Gras beads and throws.

Lula found herself inching forward in the crowd that was surging toward a large tent with garlands of ribbons and balloons.

Pomona spied her as she used the stroller she was wheeling to move against the flow of the crowd. When she got close enough, she yelled to Lula that she would be at the face-painting booth.

Still swept up in the human current, Lula found herself in a tent and heard a male announcer's voice, although she couldn't see the stage.

"Okay. My program says that the SwampBoyz are going to be performing for us in the next 15 minutes, but they're running a little late, so this is the drill for the newcomers: write down your questions, and someone will collect them and send them up here to me."

Whoever was speaking wasn't on stage, so, like everyone else, Lula craned her neck to see who he was. She was pleasantly surprised to see a black man. She had believed that she'd met every one of them in town, but this one was a new face, and he appeared to be a looker, amber syrup in color, with a short-cropped haircut and a slim moustache. She became an instant fan, like the smiling audience hanging on his every word.

Silently, he read from a small piece of paper and, shaking his head slowly, smiled.

"Do you take ... brides?" he read aloud.

His voice was not quite Southern, but had a lovely resonance to it, a baritone warmth that smoothed over the air, gliding to Lula's ears.

The crowd yelped with laughter.

"Wow, that's pretty direct. Well, that all depends on the age of these young ladies, here. I'm not exactly a senior citizen yet. And, yes, I am single. I would take any one of these as my bride."

He had walked up three steps to the dais, pointing toward the women behind him, sitting on chairs.

If the judging were decided by the efficiency of the contestants' sweat glands, all five would be tied for first place. Makeup and sweat cascaded like tears down their faces as they flapped their royal fans to cool themselves. They were four Whites and one very dark-skinned Black, all smiling dutifully.

The crowd, on cue, murmured in anticipation, as the speaker considered the ladies with a questioning look.

"Oh. Let me read that again." He pretended to have poor eyesight, putting the paper up close against his eyes.

"Oh! Bribes? Hell, I don't have to be bribed to be with any one of these beautiful brides, even if I am old enough to be ... their big brother."

Lula was enjoying herself, and like everyone else, eagerly awaited his next words.

"The answer is yes, but there are legal bribes, as in within the law, versus outside the law. If you want a bill you support to pass, why you might make a deal, not as a bribe, but a 'Let's Make a Deal.' I'll support your bill if you'll support mine. That kind of bribe. How's that? I don't need money, so that doesn't faze me. But a quid pro quo deal, it's done all the time. Hell, that's called politics!"

Chuckles of awareness and murmurs of assent wafted through the tent.

Lula stretched her neck around the torso of a tall man to get a better glimpse of the speaker.

"Okay, two more questions."

The audience groaned.

"Two more, I'm being told, and we have a couple of acts, after which we crown one of these beautiful ladies 'Miss Hottie.' Y'all didn't come here to see me, and don't I know it. Okay. Another question: 'How many committees do you sit on?' I can tell you that. Too many."

His eyes scanned the audience. "There are committees and there are subcommittees, and every member wants the popular ones. I lucked out. I'm on the Judiciary Committee, which sounds boring enough, but someone's got to explain our state's Napoleonic Codes, right? Our law is unlike any other in the country. *Vive les pommes frites, n'est-ce pas?*"

Sporadic handclaps and comedic groans followed. "I'm proud to say I have been on that committee for six years now." He glanced around, nodding to someone whispering to him from stage left. "I see the proverbial cane coming out, so I'll just list the others: Environmental Affairs, Defense, Interior, and Transportation."

He looked down at the last paper handed him. "Last one, and I'll make it quick." Wiping his face with a handkerchief, he returned the paper he had just read to his jacket pocket, then took another paper handed him. His jaws tightened as he read it. Then he peered through the throng, hand at his brow, searching the audience. His face wore a knowing, quizzical smirk as he shook his head.

"Well, I'm not sure I want to read this one out loud. It's a bit more direct, and it has some choice words in it. Somebody knows about Markups—hot dog—that is quite commendable. So, I'll just pocket this one. And in case you want to talk to me directly, you're welcome to come to my local office. Make an appointment with my secretary."

He spread his arms wide. "Now, how's that for representation? Any of you are welcome to visit me. I'm not one of those stuffy types, you know. I'm no different than you."

"No, you're richer!" someone yelled.

The speaker's response was quick: "Ah, but for what shall it profit a man, if he shall gain the whole world, and lose his own soul? The day I become a sellout to fame and fortune is the day I can't look myself in the mirror, which I am known to do quite often."

He exaggerated a loosening of his tie, and skimmed his hand over his head. "And I wouldn't get a chance to meet all the beautiful ladies here, lest they take me for a scoundrel, rather than a compatriot from the party of Lincoln. That's highfalutin' talk for: 'I won't be able to rap to the ladies.'" He showed his fingers, free of rings or any adornment. He looked at Lula, directly, then winked.

She turned to look behind her and saw Pomona waving to her from the back of the tent.

Lula looked back at the speaker, who was being congratulated as a member of the U.S. House of Representatives as he handed his microphone to the emcee and walked off the stage.

"Okay," said the emcee. "Thank you, Congressman. Now, we've got two Nakadee minutes, which means ten, then we're ready for the SwampBoyz next! So let's synchronize our watches."

Lula took this as her cue to leave. She was no hater of rap music, but she didn't like it pounding in her eardrums.

She was turning toward the back of the tent to exit when Devon's stare stopped her in her tracks. His jaws were tight, his lips puckering in disapproval. Was that hatred in his eyes?

To break the spell, she raised her hand and nodded, politely, a gesture he seemed reluctant to return.

Instead, he gave her pursed lips and a mechanical nod, then pointed, signaling her to turn around, whereupon she saw Nate motioning them both toward him.

Dressed in a peach-colored Lacoste shirt and beige Dockers, Nate was smiling with his eyes, something Lula had rarely seen.

She walked over to him, reluctantly.

"Now before you start talking your forensic shit—excuse me, stuff—I'll let you know that I have been drinking, and it is also my day off. So no talking turkey, okay?"

He was now leaning on Devon, and emphasized his interrogatory with a slap on Devon's chest. "We're celebrating."

Devon stood erect, looking elsewhere.

"Oh? What are you celebrating?" Lula asked.

"Turns out our visit to the happy frat house up the road caused a chain of events to occur."

He didn't want to hear from her, she realized. He wanted her to hear him.

"I knew that one of them men is up to no good, and we reckon we know who it is. Turns out the pretty-boy is a Mariel Cuban with a questionable past. Gang ties, apparently. We're not quite sure what it's about, but the owner of the place, Preston Pratt, has been gone since Mardi Gras. Nowhere to be found. We're definitely calling the pretty-boy in for a little interview. You speak Spanish?"

"So much for not talking turkey," Lula muttered. "*Por supuesto*. You can't grow up in California without being semi-bilingual."

She asked Nate whether his impromptu "interview" could truly qualify her to serve as a Spanish translator.

Without missing a beat he replied that the interview would be recorded and properly transcribed, but, just in case the Marielito decided to slip into his mother tongue, they needed someone on board who could understand him to relay on the spot whatever he said. He assured her that she wouldn't be visible behind the one-way window.

"I'll have Devon pick you up. What time is it tomorrow, Devon?"

The chivalry of picking her up instead of allowing her to drive herself, though nettlesome, was police protocol for ensuring that their subject would arrive promptly. She could drive her own damn self to the police station. She didn't want to be alone with Devon. His stares were making it difficult to be civil with him.

Lula didn't have time to voice her opposition to their planned logistics, because Chief Broussard had interrupted as he guided the handsome Republican legislator into their midst.

"Well, here he is—I found him for you. Have you all met your Congressman Girabeaux? Well, meet him now."

Lula sized him up in an instant. He stood 5'11" but appeared several inches taller, his straight back likely a result of ballroom dancing, she thought, snidely. It was obvious that he came from wealth. She was from a middle-class upbringing, and her parents, careful spenders, put every extra cent into her education and a trust fund.

Although not a part of the black-bourgeoisie circles, Lula did know some wealthy people and guessed that a couple of them probably knew this man's friends in some remote six-degrees of separation amongst the moneyed lives of which she had only a peripheral view.

To her surprise, the legislator used both of his manicured hands to gather up her own, simultaneously bending to kiss them.

"*Enchanté.*"

"*De même,*" she replied, smiling demurely.

He raised his eyebrows, oblivious of any connection between Devon and Lula, and patted Devon on his shoulder: "Uh-oh, this is a smart one."

Still holding one of her hands, while Devon looked away, the congressman spoke to Lula.

"There are limitations to my French-speaking, you're forewarned."

Chief Broussard stood beaming. "Ah, you know French, Congressman, but it's only from a song—and if you sang it, I bet you five French-fries Dr. Lula would slap you into last place in your congressional run next year."

Nate laughed, taking out a pack of cinnamon chewing gum and waving it around. There were no takers, though he barely noticed.

"The prospect of any touch from this beauty would be worth the loss," replied the congressman.

His bearing genuinely unnerved Lula. After the dust settled in her brain, she spoke up.

"I'm not sure we're in the same district, Congressman."

"Never fear, my damsel. I can gerrymander your district to make sure you're within mine. You can fancy yourself voting for the Lincoln party, right?"

She was of two minds: of calling him out as the sexist he was in reducing her professionalism to that of a weak woman, or totally going with the flow and enjoying this raconteur. While she contemplated what to say, he placed his finger in front of his chiseled lips as he held her shoulder and guided her away from their onlookers. Still playful, he leaned in close to her ear to ask for the pleasure of her company that evening.

Had her heart just skipped? Before she could answer, he said, "You'll be safe in a crowd of three other people, myself included. At my home. I need a chaperone for a boring colleague of mine. You could add some balance and keep him awake. He likes beautiful women. I solemnly swear that you are in no danger."

He looked her in the eye, almost swaying to keep time with his silent clock of anticipation. Lula was caught in the headlights, as he continued. "Besides, I may be a stranger to you, but I'm known in these parts. If I take a piss in the woods, it'll be on the cover of every rag in the state. You're safe with me. Can I send a driver to pick you up?"

Before she had a chance to respond, Congressman Girabeaux was being hailed to join a barbershop quartet in full regalia of straw hats, white shirts with black armbands, and seersucker pants. Their cheeks were flushed, the beer jostling and spilling from their lifted steins.

He nodded, telling them he'd be right there, patting himself as if trying to find his cigarettes or wallet. He unearthed from his breast pocket a piece of paper on which he hurriedly penned his phone number and handed it to her.

"I'll be waiting by the phone. Don't disappoint me. I don't take no for an answer. I'm a Republican, remember. I'll send my army after you."

He winked at her, then turned to join his friends.

In the split second after he departed, her mind was spirited away in a kaleidoscope of future outings with him: operas, symphonies, and jazz festivals. She was almost ashamed of herself for falling so effortlessly under his spell, still feeling the softness of his palm and thumb that had caressed her hand.

She walked away, buoyantly, almost swinging her arms. Was she so gullibly drawn in by his political importance, or had she really felt a connection between them?

She glanced behind her quickly to see the legislator positioning himself on stage in the center of the barbershop quartet at what was almost the tail end of a doo-wop song that showed off their voices. Claps ushered the singers onto another song, by now, more faint as Lula walked away at a fast clip.

Then she heard a sonorous baritone voice singing, *"Carry me back to 'ol Virginny. There's where the cotton and the corn and 'taters grow...."*

She stopped in her tracks, turning around to witness a spectacle from a Norman Rockwell painting come to life, only now a black man was leading the red-cheeked barber-shop chorus. *Was that Negro reminiscing about slavery?* His voice rang out again.

"There's where this darkie's heart am longed to go."

Lula shook her head, unable to withstand the torment of seeing a black minstrel. *Darkies, my ass,* she thought. Who was this man, who seemed to hold so much contempt for his own race? On second thought, she would not be eating dinner at any Uncle Tom's home.

"Lula!"

Pomona was yelling for her, kids in tow, a jumble of intertwined plastic bags hanging from her stroller.

"Girl, I am really outta here, now." Her knife motion at her neck announced her fill of the festivities. She spun her stroller around toward a grassy area next to the parking lot. Her two oldest kids looked bedraggled, with Kool-Aid-stained lips. Cotton candy matted their hair.

Lula nodded and waved goodbye, then turned back to where the congressman was still singing.

That's a lot of verses. How many times is he gonna have to sing *"darkie?"* she wondered, glancing at her watch. She'd give herself a half-hour more of playing tourist before turning in to spend her evening grading papers and writing up a report on the three severed digits.

A sudden breeze brought a welcome coolness. As she walked to her car, she stopped to feel the reprieve it provided from the day's heat, grateful that it was still spring. In summer, the temperatures could reach as high as 114 degrees, sometimes even warmer in the southern part of the state.

Lula opened her car door to let the hot air escape. Leaning against the side of the car, she decided to dawdle a bit in the cool air.

When the SwampBoyz were announced, she remembered that Melvyn was a member of the group. From her vantage point, she could see Melvyn's Afro bouncing up and down as the boys strutted their stuff on stage. She couldn't follow what they were saying, but with all the signing, jumping, and pumping each other afterwards, they'd clearly performed to their satisfaction. If she ran into Melvyn's mother again, she'd honestly be able to say that she watched her son perform to an appreciative crowd.

Wally kept tabs on people that the police had no reason to follow except for a nagging suspicion that they were up to no good.

In a parish the size of Nakadee, there wasn't enough traffic for a police car to go undetected.

But furtive Wally was always on the ready, sometimes covering more than 200 miles in one day as he tailed his prey.

He particularly enjoyed wearing disguises: long hair, detachable mullet sideburns. He could even look partially bald if the situation required.

He wore casual clothing like that of a blue-collar handyman looking for work. Most people nodded to him, as he seemed so familiar, yet, he was enough of a threat to make them wary of getting too close to him.

He'd convinced himself that he wasn't a racist, but he did believe that people got along much better if they stuck to their own kind. He didn't hate black people or foreigners. He was just not interested in anyone who was not white.

At the Knights of Columbus meetings he attended, he felt he was doing what he could to keep law and order in the society in which he lived. He worked for God and his white country, the greatest on earth, even if it was being misled by European influences mucking up traditional American values. He had no problems with transgender people as long as the men looked like women. But he couldn't tolerate pedophiles and gays.

They reminded him of things he would rather forget. His uncle's hand rubbing on his thigh, too close to his genitals, while he was forcibly propped on the grown man's lap. The way his uncle would hang out with him in his room and pretend to look at his model toys. He always made Wally kiss him on the mouth when they said hello and goodbye, and Wally's face was always wet afterwards.

One day he would explain to his girlfriend why he didn't like to kiss. His routine excuse that he had mouth herpes and didn't want to pass it on to her was growing stale.

Grown men had no right to take advantage of young boys.

Children can't defend themselves. How is it a child can be prosecuted as an adult, when it's likely an adult that corrupted the kid's childhood? A child can't get his innocence back. Who was avenging the wrongs done to kids? He knew the cues, and could tag a pedophile quite easily. It was Wally's personal mission to avenge every child abused by an adult.

He would take care of each one of them in due time.

He had a lot of time to dwell on those things. He had seen enough weirdos to note their characteristics. He viewed the world through that lens, and had done enough surveillance to confirm his knowledge.

His instructions today were to follow some people at the Hot Sauce Festival—a Cuban gang-banger, some black congressman, and a black poultry engineer. Two were about to get stinking rich, and Wally had orders to track them and see whether either was cutting any deals with third parties of which those who needed to know (who were always nameless) should be aware.

It was tough tracking the engineer, Tyrell Armstrong, on weekends, because Tyrell was a weekend father who was always busy with work, driving to and fro, making different brief stops at stores and offices along the way. He had his kid with him much of the time. He picked the boy up at his ex-wife's home, where she barely registered her ex-husband's presence, and would stand like a statue, watch them leave, then shake her head and go back into the house.

Months earlier, he had watched Melvyn's dad push a riding lawnmower up a wooden plank onto his truck, then drop it off at the "Hollykook" house, that architectural eyesore. It was hard to do any reconnaissance there because there was no place to park and be inconspicuous, and those dudes owned the whole thirty acres behind and around their home.

Wally had watched the black kid's dad teach him how to use the mower properly, in a latticework pattern, and how to wipe it down after using it.

On another day, when he saw Tyrell drop Melvyn off at the house, he saw the boy's friends a half-mile down the road, popping wheelies on their bikes, waiting for Melvyn to join them. They were harmless, typically loud boys.

After tailing Tyrell's comings and goings, Wally figured out that Tyrell's wife was Richard's drug supplier because Richard routinely visited her when Tyrell was absent, once a week, usually in the afternoon before Tyrell's wife left for work on the second shift.

Richard would drive up or walk to the back of his cousin's house where the two black Rottweilers would bark their hellos. Leaving the side gate open, he'd throw a stick or roll a ball onto the driveway for them to retrieve. He would come out about five minutes later, with a brown lunch bag. It didn't look like it was food he was carrying, because he'd tuck it under his arm, and when he got in his van, he would bend over and push whatever it was underneath the driver's seat.

Wally reported his findings, which the Captain received casually, with slight annoyance. When Nate asked him to follow the black congressman during the Hot Sauce Festival, Wally voiced his displeasure with the assignment because that task was taking him to territory he didn't want to explore. Those were officers of the United States—legislators—and if the Nakadee Police Department had something up its sleeve ... Wally told the Captain that he needed to talk to the Capitol Police, or State Department, or whoever oversaw them. Besides, he didn't expect to learn anything except how boring all congressmen were, talking shop all the time.

At the festival, Wally leaned against a metal street lamp, tugging at his baseball cap as he watched Tyrell's kid and his posse get ready to rap on stage.

He liked rap, against his better judgment. The Beastie Boys. Kid Roc. Snoop. Ice Cube. Those black gangstas loved their bitches and hoes.

Wally pulled out his phone and filmed the boys, then panned over the enthusiastic crowd. Five minutes later, he watched the SwampBoyz leave the stage, where people had started to swarm. He began to walk away, then did a double take as those around him started running past in the opposite direction.

Wally's eyes widened as he saw that people were gathering around an argument between one of the pretty Nakadee U chicks, the stuck-up one with the body, one of his marks—the Marielito— and the local named Richard, who was dancing around him, like he wanted to fight.

Wally inched closer, but hung on the periphery, determined not to get involved unless things got nasty. He liked a good fight, like the rest of the audience, which was catcalling now, egging them on.

Richard wore an army-green shirt with a yellow star in the middle of his chest, his muscles bulging underneath. His jeans hung loosely from his hips as he danced slowly around Juanito.

"Oh, so this is one of your girls you say you be with?" he taunted Juanito.

"It's not your business, Richard. I don't owe you an explanation," Sherry said angrily.

"Yeah. I know. No strangs."

"Right. No strangs."

Juanito joined in. "You heard her, man. Just leave her alone. We ain't doin' nothing. I'm just holding her hand, man."

"Dude, I'm in her bed at least once a week, and she's tryin' to play me? You better get your Frito Bandito ass outta here 'fore I kick it to Mexico."

Juanito stopped to look at him while Sherry tried to gently pull his hand forward and away from their taunter.

Juanito didn't budge, only gripped her hand firmly, and prevented her from moving.

"So, you a bad dude, huh? Where's your little posse, Mr. Ponce de Leon? Or is it Raul Castro? Your gallantry shit is a little too late. I know what you two are up to, dude. You figure she can keep a secret from me?"

Sherry looked at Richard, imploringly.

"What I want to know is just who calls who 'baby girl' with the two of you?"

"Fuck you," Juanito growled.

"No. I'll leave that for you and your little man friend. You think you da man? You think you da man? Well, I think you not, Bitch!"

He circled Juanito slowly, fists balled like a boxer's, keeping his eye on Sherry.

"How you know he don't got AIDS, Sherry?" he asked her derisively.

Sherry walked away from him, but he trailed her, still mocking.

"You can call me the grim reaper, come to sow your seeds."

Wally moved forward, on the ready, now. It didn't look good. This would escalate.

———

"Hey!" Lula's yell was drowned out by the cacophonous handclaps and whoops of the crowd.

Wondering what was happening, she'd decided to check to see that Melvyn was all right as a crowd gathered where he had just left the stage.

By the time she reached the fracas, she saw Sherry spinning away from her with a look of terror on her face as she fell backwards.

The crowd gasped at the sound of her bone's brittle slam on the pavement.

A dark-skinned black man grabbed Richard. "Come on, man. That's enough. You puttin' on a show, man. Leave her alone." He spoke firmly, with a warning stare.

Richard raised his hands, turning on his messenger, menacingly. "Oh, so you doin' her, too?" Then he turned to his audience. "Anyone else?"

Lula knelt at Sherry's side, drawing her into her lap to support and calm her. It was a broken arm, nothing more, she assured her.

No sooner had she ordered an onlooker to call an ambulance than Nate and Devon arrived, each applying an immobilizing chokehold to drag the would-be combatants away from each other.

Devon's hold on Richard didn't keep Richard from talking.

"You need to arrest that girl, there, man ... messin' with my head." Richard wiped his face where a scratch had started oozing blood, then involuntarily looked up at Devon, compliments of the baton that pulled his head skyward. "Officer," he added.

Propped against Lula, Sherry cradled her injured right arm, its underside looking like the pale belly of a fish. "It's really broken? Oh my God," she cried.

"I didn't mean to do that, Sherry. I swear I didn't," Richard called out. "I've never put a hand on a lady, so help me God. Your little friend here was being a bit too proprietary." He turned to Nate. "It was an accident, man. You see the scratches? I swear. She tripped over my foot, but she was coming at me, not vice-versa."

"You must have said something." Nate countered. "We have lots of witnesses."

"And they'll tell you what I just told you. I called her a couple of names. It was a mutual altercation, man. She scratched me. And I bet her little girlfriend has AIDS."

Lula motioned to Wally and another man to help Sherry up without hurting her arm. Wally sat her on a nearby bench, and Lula urged her to avoid any movement until help arrived.

Richard was still talking. "I'll leave them both alone, okay? I ain't here to start no trouble. Lemme go. How about I just sit in my car and cool off?" He was throwing out all options, hoping one would stick.

Nate nodded to Devon, who stepped forward. "Yeah. You go sit a bit and get the alcohol out of your system, first. I want you sitting for an hour, before you start the engine, you hear me?"

"Yeah. Good idea. I'll go sit in my car." Richard repeated, but stood his ground, instead. Raising his voice to Sherry, he implored, "I'm sorry, Baby. Honest to God."

Devon ushered him forward. "No more scenes, man. Zip it."

This time Richard did as he was told.

"Hey, Miss Lula. I thought you were only a doctor for the dead."

Sherry and Lula both looked up to see Melvyn and his friends looking on. They held canned drinks, of a brand she couldn't decipher. Melvyn was acting more grown up now, like a real teenager around his boys.

"It'll get better, Sherry. You want, I can come by and help you feel better. Rub your toes like you like me to."

His friends were tittering.

"I am all that you need."

The boys laughed more, which made Melvyn show even more bravado.

"You just don't know it."

The boys swapped high fives, laughing at their inside joke.

Lula interrupted. "Are you here with your mother? Does she know where you are and what you're drinking?"

"Yes, ma'am. She knows what I'm drinking, but she's not here. She's supposed to pick us up in the next half-hour. It's a drink Dad brought me back from Brazil. Guaraná. It's not alcohol."

Suddenly, Melvyn jumped, startled, looking down at his pants. "That scared me." He fished in his pockets, retrieving a cell phone, shaking his head in relief. "I had it on vibrate."

His friends laughed good-naturedly.

"Hello?" Melvyn answered, pointing to Lula, then to the phone. "Okay. Dang, we gotta wait around for that long?" He listened, then interrupted, "Hey, Dr. Lula's here. She was asking about you ...." He nodded his assent to whatever his mother was saying. "All right."

He put the cell phone away and turned his gaze to Sherry. "Well, I'll be seeing you, Miss Lula. And I'll see you at the crib, Sherry."

Ambulance and police sirens were drowning out the sounds of the festival as the crowd began to thin, then part for the arrival of the paramedics. Two policemen accompanied the ambulance, nodding their salute to Nate.

"Take him in." Nate's head motioned to Richard.

"We just want to question you," he told him. "You're popping up like that doughboy, dude. Wherever you are, trouble seems to follow."

"Where? We just met!" Richard whined.

"I'll talk to you at the station." Then Nate looked at Lula imploringly. "Can you go with her? I'll be by to take a statement."

She nodded. What choice did she have?

The paramedics positioned the gurney and placed Sherry on it gently. Tears streamed down her face.

Nate addressed Richard. "Look, man. We got us a visitor from the United States Congress. We want to show him we're a city of law and order, got it? We gonna try not to make no arrests today, okay?"

Richard eyed him. "Yeah, man. I hear you." He looked at the ground, shaking his head. "Okay."

"How much beer you had?" Nate asked him.

"I'm under the limit, whatever it is, Mr. Officer. I'm not drunk. Just a bit inebriated, as they say. My girl there ... she didn't come home last night, and I was upset. And I said some bad things to her." He raised his voice, yelling to the heavens. "I apologize, Sherry! I apologize!"

Lula turned away from the crowd and began to follow the paramedics' path, then stopped, realizing that her car wasn't parked nearby. That's when Devon volunteered his services.

"We don't gotta talk," he urged.

True to his promise, Devon didn't say a word in the car, which only made Lula feel even more awkward.

She initiated a conversation herself by asking about Richard.

"Man, that one is a nuisance. He ain't about nothin'. But the Hispanic dude, we gonna keep tabs on him. He may be part of a Southern wing of some serious Marielito gang-bangers. Nate believes the fingers might have something to do with some ritual gang shit—I mean, excuse me—stuff."

He leaned his head toward her in apology, looking sideways at her.

She stared straight ahead.

"We're looking around to see if anybody else's digits have been turning up anyplace else, locally. We're supposed to get a report tomorrow."

She dared not ask more questions for fear that Devon would slip back into believing their relationship had returned to normal. They drove the rest of the way to the hospital in silence.

7

ARM TWISTING

6:30 p.m.

Lula hovered outside the hospital examination room observing as Sherry was tended to by a middle-aged nurse who lifted her injured arm, now in a plaster cast, and fastened the sling buckle near her hand.

Sherry winced, then raised her head and saw Lula standing near the door. The nurse spoke to Sherry briefly and opened the door, motioning for Lula to come into the room as she exited.

Even with disheveled hair and eyes puffy from crying, Sherry was a natural beauty. Her pink lips glowed. Both her height, just under 5'8," and her slightly turned-up nose, gave her an air of being above everyone else. Her steely blue-gray eyes looked relieved to see Lula, now a welcome friend.

Lula's history with Sherry was fraught with a recurring debate, both during and after class, about whether North or South had truly won the Civil War. Their latest discussions had taken place six days after Mardi Gras.

"I mean, aren't some things better left alone?" Sherry had whined, as she twirled her tresses in her fingers. She was referring to whether it was necessary to examine the mistreatment of slaves, after having voiced her opinion that some of the exhumations were better left undiscovered. "I just don't believe that people today want to relive those horrific stories."

Though Sherry was two inches taller, Lula's heels made them the same height. Lula had begun to pack her purse and a couple of books into her large duffle bag. Her home sofa was calling for her to order Chinese, spread out with her feet on her coffee table to channel-surf and simultaneously grade papers.

"Well, if you take another look-see at our textbook, Sherry, it's not titled, 'Forensics for Black People.' It is the science of forensics for the study of the dead. Whoever and wherever they may be. All I'm doing is applying my expertise to a neglected area of study."

Sherry had hugged her notebook to her chest, letting one of her arms hang free. "Well, my daddy says, if slavery was so bad, then why do so many Blacks still live in the South? I don't mean to challenge you, but I just don't understand why you all need to dig into the lives of the dead."

Lula took a breath and faced her student as two papers on the table fell to the floor while she arranged her backpack. She watched Sherry let them fall, not even thinking of coming to her aid to pick them up. Instead, Sherry was staring at the scalpel and glue sticks on a tray in front of her, fingering them, then, perhaps feeling ghoulish, placing them back on the table with a little shiver.

"Sherry, there's still lots to be learned about the savagery of humankind. The South is just another locale that I happen to be interested in, for obvious reasons. If people could do that then, they could do it now."

She then explained that colleagues of hers had dug or were digging at excavation sites in Bosnia, Israel, Argentina, and Cambodia, chronicling man's cruelty to man. It was only fair that American anthropologists be given the same opportunity to explore black slave burial sites. Wasn't it equally important to excavate America's heinous history of savagery in its own backyard?

"But we're not doing anything now!"

"I beg to differ, Sherry. That's not the point. Somebody's ancestors did, and we need to understand how, and, if possible, why. Why is killing the logical consequence when people are the same race, but share different religions? How much more insidious is the consequence of one race's domination and control over a different race, in the belief that the vanquished race was subhuman?"

Sherry stared at her as Lula proceeded. "In the 1920s, a white mob massacred over 400 Blacks in Tulsa, Oklahoma. If they did this in the 1920s, when Blacks were free, what could have happened when it was open season on black slaves? That is our country's history, and we need to understand it."

Sherry was averaging a B minus in her class, but was also a candidate for remedial tutoring in history, hence her after-class visits. Like the majority of Nakadee University students who hailed from the Southeast, the sins of their Confederate fathers lay heavily upon these children of the South. In Lula's class, students like Sherry always fell silent, chagrined that in their version of the Civil War, or the "War between the States," events were usually explained by books and mainstream media like a play-by-play of heroic battles in Mansfield (less than eighty miles away), Bull Run, Appomattox, and Gettysburg.

Lula's research supplemented this "history" with gruesome physical evidence of what had happened to those who lived enslaved, hoping that their progeny would one day live free. She wondered how a nation could be so enamored of its Civil War past, yet ignore the lives of its black victims, as if their histories were divorced from the very factors that made the Civil War necessary. So much American history was lost on Americans, because it conjured up too much fear in the white majority, ostensibly removed in time from that tumultuous period. Slaves had revolted in the 1700s and 1800s, each attempt aborted except for Nat Turner's, which succeeded in killing over fifty white men and their families.

Turner's wrath was specific, as it excluded Quakers and Native Americans. Almost all other rebellions, such as the one in Louisiana in 1811, where 500 slaves marched toward New Orleans, were aborted and the leaders killed. White retribution for rebellions was swift, and the cadavers of those slaves still lay in unknown graves.

"Nobody cares about the slaves, now. Even hip-hop," Sherry had protested, sighing and leaning on her hand, staring at Lula defiantly.

"I'm a scientist, Sherry. If my background can be used to solve mysteries, or to redress our collective ignorance about aspects of our own history, then I will offer my professional services to serve those ends."

Lula zipped up her duffle bag, then met her student's gaze directly. "Try looking at it this way. You've heard of the Holocaust, where Jews, homosexuals, and even some Germans were slaughtered like animals, and those who survived afterwards had to find each other again after years of being apart?"

Sherry nodded, her mouth parted expectantly.

"For Blacks, centuries later, we're still trying to find our families."

Overall, Lula didn't mind the opinions of her students, but she couldn't understand Sherry's motives in visiting her except to harangue her while sharpening her own dull debating skills. She wondered if Sherry had ever had discussions with a black professional before.

Or, was there some other purpose in Sherry's stalking of her comings and goings, timing her arrivals just as Lula was preparing to leave? She never asked questions about actual forensics. Instead, she engaged in dialectics about race and politics. Her student seemed to show an underlying antipathy toward the equality of both the sexes and the races, which manifested as a quiet but unrelenting attempt to chip away at Lula's authority.

Lula accepted her conferred roles at the University as forensic anthropologist, mini-ambassador, social commentator and advocate for the disadvantaged. What annoyed her, however, was that Sherry accepted Lula as a black ambassador, but not as a scientist.

Lula usually had the last word, anyway. Whatever Sherry thought, she would still have to face the music with every surprise pop quiz, which was what her investigatory visit with Lula was all about, Lula guessed.

Seeing Sherry now in the hospital's examining room, Lula felt a tinge of melancholy. It was so unlike Sherry to be beaten down, as she looked now, with her disheveled hair and bare feet. Defeated.

Lula approached her. "What's all this about, Sherry?"

"You got me, Dr. Logan. I went somewhere I wasn't supposed to, I guess, and it's all coming to a head."

"Boy troubles?" Lula cocked her head to one side.

"From boys to men. Not the group. It's too complicated."

"Well, do you wanna tell me what happened out there? Actually, no, you don't have to. Wait for the detective to show up. I'll just hang out with you until he gets here."

"I don't want to talk to him, Professor Logan."

"Why?" Lula asked, surprised.

"I just don't."

"I respect your privacy, Sherry, but I don't want it on my conscience if something happens to you. So, do you wanna give me a hint of what's going on? In confidence?"

She clasped her arms behind her back as Sherry looked her in the eye, then turned her head away.

Shrugging her shoulders, Lula said, "Okay. I'm not an officer. I don't need to know. I have enough on my plate as it is."

"Let's just say that I did something for fun that got out of hand. And now someone's mad at me."

"Who is *someone*? A he or a she?"

Sherry looked at her teacher. "I'm not using the pronoun for a reason."

"Well, then, it's a woman you're talking about."

"Let's just say, I messed with the wrong person." She tried to raise both arms until she remembered that the cast was on one of them. Using her free hand, she drew quotation marks around the invisible word "person" hanging between them.

"Should you be calling a lawyer, Sherry?"

Sherry sniffed. "A bodyguard is more like it."

"Oh."

"It's not what you think."

"Well, whatever it was, how did he or she find out?"

"I'm not sure."

"So what was that at the fair today?"

"Richard? He's just overly protective, you might say."

Lula spoke matter-of-factly. "He's so protective he pushes you to the ground?"

"He's harmless. He's got nothing to do with anything. He's just a pest half the time, and he doesn't like Juanito." She spoke quickly.

"I know you want to help, Professor Logan, but I'll have to figure out what to do on my own," she whispered, her eyes canvassing the floor. "That man is at the door. Don't say anything, please. I'm only speaking to you as a friend, okay?" She put her uninjured hand on Lula's arm. "Please," she entreated. "I'll be okay."

As Nate walked in, his masculine energy immediately changed the dynamic in the room. All three of them sensed it, Lula knew.

Standing with his hands on his hips, he said, "Why do I get the feeling that you two ladies are up to something?" He took two strides and plopped down onto a low revolving stool, while Lula headed toward the door.

"Women talk. We don't conspire," Lula replied jovially as she prepared to exit.

"Wait, Dr. Lula. Can you stay here?" Sherry smiled at her, meekly.

Nate motioned Lula forward, but didn't wait for her reply, instead looking at Sherry.

"So, you and your boyfriend got into a fight?"

"Friend." Sherry spoke, defensively. "It's nothing. He was drunk," she said, moving her hair out of her eyes.

Nate circled twice on the stool, lifting his feet off the ground. "I always wanted to do that." Using his long legs, he pushed himself back, looking at Sherry. "You and your boyfriend get in spats like this often?"

"He's not my boyfriend. I just say hello to him on campus. He has a crush, I guess."

"Well, I can see why, I can say that much. It's a kind of crush that you don't really mind, though, as I see it. I mean, he's not a stalker, right? We haven't gotten any emergency calls about him, have we?"

Sherry pursed her lips, pretending to be distracted by the floor. The paper sheet underneath her leg made a crackling sound.

"You like a little bit of local color to spice things up a bit—do I got it right?" he added.

Lula saw him checking out Sherry's smooth, tan legs. The rest of her was dwarfed by the pastel-blue hospital gown with its homely pattern. Her dirty-blonde hair, thick and flowing, cascaded below her shoulders.

"You strike me as somebody pretty smart underneath those good looks. You also been around the block once, but not twice, as I see it. So you're not talking because you kinda know'd what you was gettin' into, right? This isn't a surprise to you, that it happened, seems like, even though I'm ready to beat somebody's ass if they mess with a pretty little thing like you. We got a doctor here to take notes 'bout what I just said, but I'm not coming onto you, okay?"

Sherry studied her cast, tossing her hair out of her face with a quick jerk to the right, as if that gesture held her affirmative answer. She glanced around the room.

Nate was good. Very good. Lula watched as he spun Sherry into a web of his own design. He would ask questions to elicit the story that he expected to hear.

"You got a job here or does Daddy pay for everything?"

"Both." She smiled.

"What you wanna work for, then?"

"I work for a production company here."

He staged a dumbfounded look. "No way. We ain't got no film sets in this little hick town."

Sherry nodded with enthusiasm now, oblivious of her arm and her earlier despair. Her confidence reappeared as her chest swelled up proudly while she contemplated her answer.

For an instant, Nate looked at Lula, signaling with his wide eyes and raised eyebrows. Either Sherry knew nothing about their visit to the producers' house yesterday, or she was a damn good actor.

Lula watched Nate's interrogation with interest. He found Sherry's weak spots, massaged them, and after twenty minutes, had her story locked solid. She worked at the production company, but only on weekends. Her interest in the entertainment industry was whatever she could get her hands on. Right now, it was analyzing television manuscripts, plays, and screenplays of students taking film-related classes, who were given a yearlong assignment to work on one creative project. She was responsible for the coverage.

"Coverage?" Nate was lapping it up. Lula couldn't quite figure where he was going with his questioning.

"It's like an analysis." Sherry said. "I'm supposed to finish several tonight. I hope my computer microphone works so I can dictate."

"So, we got Hollywood right here in River City?"

"I never heard of River City, but Hollywood's wherever there's talent."

"Hmm. I think I'm beginning to get it," he said, as if light was dawning. "The studios are in Los Angeles, but the real creative stuff happens in places like this, right? The writers are here. You're gonna put Nakadee on the map," he said with patrician pride.

As she listened, Lula was surprised. Whatever Sherry was describing, it contradicted Lula's experience of Sherry as anything but literary.

"Wait—you tellin' me there's a whole pack of y'all settin' up shop here?" Nate asked.

Sherry giggled. "We're not invading, if that's what you mean. One of them is kinda sorta from here."

"I heard about him. He did movies in the '80s, right?"

"No, that's in Natchitoches. We got our own people here in Nakadee."

"You don't say!" Nate continued his own acting debut. "Would I know their names?"

Sherry perked up. "They're not like actors, where people recognize them, you know. Most of them are better heard than seen, you know?"

This was the superficial Sherry Lula knew. If something didn't fit her ideal of beauty, intelligence, or prowess, she just refused to accept it as viable.

Nate was looking at Sherry, shaking his head. "Let's see. The last movie I saw was ... let me see ...."

"That long ago?"

"Yeah. Before you were born, probably."

She shook her head. "I doubt I know, then, but I'll try."

He motioned with his hands for her to bring on the information. Sherry recited some titles.

Limited Imagination? The Sport of Hating?

Nate shook his head no.

Play Dough?

"I heard of that." Nate was now standing, using his girth to fill up the room.

The Bright North?

"Yeah, I heard of that one. That was a suspense movie, or something like that, right?" he said.

Sherry had forgotten about her arm. *"Words without Thought?"*

"I heard about that. It's a series, right? About the drug-dealing colored kid."

"Yep. It was a movie, first," Sherry explained.

"What color?" Lula felt moved to ask.

"Black. You ain't seen it? It got an Emmy last year for best new series. The mother's a crack head, but goes to school full-time, trying to raise her kid in the projects."

Lula rolled her eyes while they talked. She was invisible to them.

"Well, let me be the first to touch royalty, here." Nate said, beaming.

Sherry watched, grinning, as Nate deftly pushed his doctor's stool out of the way with his foot and sidled alongside her, rubbing his elbow against her uninjured arm. "I'm rubbing elbows with Hollywood, Dr. Lula."

Lula wondered what was taking him so long to cut to the chase about Preston and Blaine living in the frat house with no dogs.

"So is this location where you work where I suppose it is?" he asked.

Bingo. Here it came.

"At their homes," Sherry nodded.

Lula watched her student take Nate's bait as he asked, "They? There's two of them?"

Sherry nodded.

"That so?"

"Preston Pratt and Blaine Dworkin," Sherry announced.

Nate glanced at Lula, as if silently messaging her not to give away the knowledge he already had about the House of Men.

"Preston is from here. His people lived here a long time ago and left. But he came back. The other is a transplant. From New Hampshire. Are you from here?"

Sherry's interest in him caught Nate off guard. His head moved just a tad, as he furrowed his brow.

"Yep, but no. I'm an immigrant, by way of Mississippi. The food is better here."

Sherry barely heard him.

Lula knew she was up to something.

"You're not going to go talk to them, are you?" Sherry asked, looking at him out of the corner of her eye.

"Do you see any pen or paper on me, honey?"

She pleaded. "I don't wanna cause any trouble or make anybody think that I'm in trouble, either."

"Do they know about your B-F-F——what's his name?"

"Richard?"

Lula saw Sherry shrink into herself with the realization that she'd divulged revealing information. "He's no B-F-F of mine."

"What do those initials mean to you, Sherry? Boy Friend Forever? Or Best Friend Forever? Or are both of them Best Friends with Fringe Benefits?"

Sherry was tiring of the discussion. "You're the smart one. You figure it out."

"Well, I can guess, but it's so much easier if you tell me. Is he or isn't he? You decide. First you insisted he was your friend. Now he isn't. You want, I can file a report and bring him in."

She grunted. "Go ahead. He's a nuisance."

Nate removed a piece of nonexistent lint from his pants leg.

"Is he a *Fatal Attraction* case?"

"Never saw the movie, but I know about it. Not really." Sherry's energy was now subdued. She seemed just on the verge of divulging something as Nate and Lula sat quiet, looking at her bandaged arm. "He's just a nuisance."

"In what way?" Nate asked.

"I'd rather not say," she said, glancing at Lula briefly.

"I take that to mean that you don't want to file a report, then."

Sherry looked at her arm in the sling, then swung her legs back and forth over the edge of the chair. "I fell. That was it. He didn't do anything."

"Well, let's say if I wanted to give you some time to collect yourself and come talk to you later, where would I go? 'Cuz I wouldn't want to come on campus."

"Why?" She looked perplexed.

"That's not our jurisdiction. Y'all have your own cops."

Sherry paused, lips pouting with hesitation. "Preston and Blaine ... well ... they're ... away ... right now, anyway."

"That right? That's good for you, I guess. While the cat is away, n'all, right?" He laughed good-naturedly. "Can I reach either of them by cell phone?"

"I don't know their numbers by heart."

"Well, does your cell phone know them?"

Touché. Who remembers numbers anymore with the world at their fingertips? Lula smiled inwardly.

"Maybe. I got a call three days ago. He left it on my machine."

"And he is ...?"

"Oh. Preston."

"What did he tell you?"

"I'm not really sure. It was noisy in the background."

"And what is it you do for him again?"

"I'm a reader."

Nate looked at Sherry, while Lula watched him, wondering if he sensed, like she did, that Sherry was holding back information, even though she appeared to be cooperating.

"He asked me to look for a script for him, and finish reading another one by a certain date," Sherry added.

"Do you know where he is?"

"No. He could be with his wife."

"He's married?"

She looked vacant. "Yeah. He is. Miriam, but they call her 'Mare.'"

"Is that strange to you?"

"You've obviously never met him," she snickered.

"What? Is he the Hunchback of Notre Dame? King Kong?"

"No. He's regular looking."

"Like me?" Nate gave her his profile.

"You look way better," Sherry smirked. "Let's just say that money has a way of making the ugliest frog look like a prince."

Nate's hands were moving in his pockets, jingling either money or keys, as he looked down at her feet. "Where are your shoes?"

"I'm not sure."

"Do you care?"

"Not especially." She lifted up her arm in the cast, as if to show which body part was uppermost in her mind.

"So, you don't know where your boss is, but he called you up on the phone, left a message, and you haven't heard from him since, and that was three days ago, right?"

She nodded.

"Where did he call you from? Did he say?"

"Not sure."

Nate sat back down on the stool and asked if she could write down all the numbers she knew that Preston might call from to reach her. He imagined out loud that he'd give her a day to look up her records.

"My suspicion is that you ain't gonna hear from him again if he's getting his fingers chopped off." He mimed knuckles trying to dial a number.

Sherry laughed, politely. "He didn't say when he was coming back. You never know with him. They get on a plane to Europe to get their inspiration to write."

"Where can I sign up?" Nate laughed.

"Well, you'd be a good referral for the 'Words' series, so I'll keep you in mind. Do you have a card?"

Not missing a beat, still sitting on the stool, Nate spread his legs, leaned back, and patted both of his jacket pockets, as if fishing for cigarettes.

Lula couldn't interpret his reaction to Sherry's attempt at manipulation and assertion of her own power. He was quite an actor, though, and could surely see through Sherry's façade of friendliness, which no doubt aimed to get him out of her hair more quickly.

He handed her his business card. "Well, Ms. Sherry. I just wanted to follow up."

He stood. "Don't get up. I'll tell the nurse to come get you." He reached the door, then backed up, still holding it open. "I forgot my manners for a sec. Do you need a ride home?"

"I can walk."

"Barefoot?"

"It's only ten blocks away. I could use some cool air after being locked up here for three hours. Place is empty as hell, but I still had to wait," she muttered.

He walked toward her, then stood, not too close, but imperiously. "Well, it was good meeting you. Just so you know, we're the kind of police department that likes to preserve our way of life here, and I appreciate that your employers feel the same way. That's why your daddy and momma pay the big bucks for you to come here, right? To give you a genteel, quiet life, where you can have your quiet education before you go off to the big, noisy city of Hollywood." He rubbed his hands together. "You gonna be okay?"

"Are you going to talk to Richard today?" She licked her lips, which looked uncharacteristically parched.

"Not at this hour. You and your friendly nuisance. I'm starting to wonder which one you really like? Richard, or the Latin Lover? Which one is your frog? That is the question. Whoever it is, we can't have the likes of either of them getting our fair-haired little ladies upset, now, can we?"

"I'll be fine."

"Here's my personal cell number, okay?" He took out another card and wrote on it, then handed it to her.

"I have one, already." She lifted up the first card.

He took it from her and handed it to Lula, silently.

"*Personal*, I said." Nate pretended to be irked. "I'm here if you need me, okay? And if I'm not around, I'll send someone else instead. I am at your service, *mademoiselle*."

Lula watched Sherry lower her lashes with a coquettish smile as she gently pushed his hand aside. She extended her body forward, reaching to plant an awkward kiss on his cheek.

"Aw shucks, now. I'm about to blush." He smiled, winking at her before he left the room, a tad hastier than usual, Lula thought.

Once he'd disappeared down the hall, Sherry reverted to a sullen mood.

"He's trying to help you. You do realize that, right?" asked Lula.

"What do you mean?"

"Who are you trying to protect?" Sherry started to speak, but Lula spoke over her. "He asked about Richard, whether he knew your employers, and whether the person you spoke to was going to call you back. And if you do work there, how come you don't know about what's happening there? He asked where your employer lived and you didn't give him an address."

"I know. I'm not ready to talk yet. I need time to sort things out!"

"What things?"

"I've got my own troubles."

"Join the club, Sherry, but the trouble he wanted to know about was more than what shade of lipstick you'll wear tomorrow." Ignoring Sherry's eye-roll, Lula continued. "He was asking you, practically begging to know what should be done concerning your two friends."

"I told you, I need some time to sort it out."

"Is someone upset at you?"

Sherry nodded.

"Like, Sherry-you-didn't-turn-in-your-homework-upset, or something more dire?"

"I'm sorry, Dr. Logan, but I'm hurting and I'm not thinking straight." She slid off the examining table, her sling in the air. "I'll figure it out."

"What about a ride?"

"I'll be fine. My friend is on her way to pick me up."

"Well, do me a favor and call me at my office tomorrow, so I know you're okay. Will you do that much for me? The number's on the class syllabus, if you still have it."

"I have it." Sherry smiled, apologetically.

They walked together into the hallway. Shyly, Sherry looked at Lula, mouthing a thank you before stepping into a bathroom nearby.

When Lula left the hospital, Nate was standing near the entrance, popping a piece of gum into his mouth. Devon, thankfully, was nowhere to be seen.

"Someone is waiting for you at the police department, Dr. Lula."

She looked up at him, surprised. "Who?"

"The chief called the office to say the Congressman was asking for your ETA."

"ETA?"

"Estimated Time of ...."

"Arrival," she finished. "And you told him."

"He asked me a question that I happened to have the answer to, and I couldn't lie, now, could I?"

"Well, It's not your place to tell someone about my whereabouts. He could be a killer, for all you know. Am I a piece of property to be handed around?"

"Look. You and Devon aren't together, right?"

"What business is that of yours, Detective?"

"I know that that Congressman is going to get this region a billion-plus-billion-plus-billion-dollar natural gas pipeline, at this here little vegetable stand of a town, Dr. Lula, and if my chief wants me to, I'll hop on one foot and suck my thumb from now until next Tuesday." He walked forward, then back. "Look. The man's in a jam. He's a big-wig politician having a dinner with some political types and he needs a date for a meal at his house."

"And he saw me and ditched his first choice, right?"

"Come on. Do you know what we're likely to get if this natural gas deal pulls through? And what it will mean in a town like this?"

"Does Devon know you're lobbying me?"

"Look. Devon isn't in the picture right now, Dr. Lula. Tag, you're it. Sorry."

He shrugged his shoulders with the dejected look of a hobo, hands open-face, as if to reveal that there was nothing in his pockets. "I have orders to tell you that the Congressman's secretary went shopping for you. In Shreveport. The limo has everything in it you need; an outfit, a change of everything. And I hear she threw in a purse, makeup—you name it. You can change at the station, if you want."

8

DEAL CUTTING

8:07 p.m.

Lula was fatigued by the time they arrived at the police station. Cold and damp from the air-conditioned car, she wondered if the secretary had thought to give her a jacket of some sort. The sun was almost gone, promising a colder night.

How had fate taken her from a Hot Sauce Festival to a blind date with a Congressman in less than five hours? Because of her ex, she felt like some misfit mascot of the police department, and she didn't like it one bit. No matter how she tried to keep her private life private, Devon had somehow turned it into a soap opera for the department's voyeuristic pleasure.

At the station, she headed toward the waiting limousine and introduced herself to the driver. He pointed to the passenger seat, where a suit bag lay gently folded over to avoid any creases. Then he confirmed the evening's plan and told her that the Congressman had suggested that she could change at his place. The car would also have a police escort through the clogged traffic and single-lane highways that would take them the almost 40 miles to where the Congressman lived.

As the driver held the door for her, nodding, Lula was about to step inside when she glimpsed Devon's ebony Land Rover blocking the entrance to the parking lot. He honked.

Excusing herself, she walked toward him, casting a glimpse back at the limousine driver who had returned to the driver's seat.

She approached Devon's car and spoke firmly. "This is neither the time nor place for this conversation, Devon."

"I guess you're all the same, huh?" he asked, drumming his fingers on the steering wheel.

"Don't go there with me. You were supposed to drive me back to my car. Why did you disappear? Because your boss man told you to?"

He turned off the engine. "That one is not going to work, Lula. Face it. You took the bait. Being a good upstanding black man isn't enough. I get that. So to get you, do I gotta be blazin' too, in a limousine?"

He stared straight ahead, biting his lip gently. "Is Girabeaux in there?"

She shook her head slowly.

"I thought you were much deeper than that, baby girl. This was all a joke, huh ... but it's on me. You take care. In case he asks, just tell him ... tell him that I had a message for you that I had to personally deliver. And here it is: you were playing me all along. I do all the work to lay the pipe, now you go looking for a different plumber. Well, don't call me in your hour of distress." He turned back to gaze through the front windshield, then added, "There will be one, Lula. You best believe it."

She watched him turn on his engine and shift into drive. He flicked his head in the direction of the limousine and drove away, leaving a wisp of smoke beneath his screeching tires with the shiny rims.

10:30 p.m.

The dinner menu was Parmesan-crusted tilapia, rice pilaf, and a salad of shrimp *remoulade* on iceberg lettuce, followed by a small bowl of seafood gumbo. The house chef wore a crisply starched white jacket, white pants, and heavy-soled bright-red patent-leather Doc Martens. Speaking softly, he listed the desserts as gelato, sorbet, or a black-and-white-chocolate mousse, which was served in a glass.

The limousine driver, who was helping the sous chef, donned

white gloves with his black suit and tie and doubled as waiter, filling porcelain cups with tea or coffee. The servants disappeared as quickly and quietly as they had appeared, leaving only the gentle thud of the kitchen door.

The four diners were seated at the table in Ambrose Girabeaux's formal dining room. Their host pulled out two cigars, handing one to the man on his left. Judging by the ease with which each savored the aroma and studiously snipped his cigar tip with a quick snap of a hand-held guillotine, Lula figured that neither was a stranger to the proverbial good life.

Despite Ambrose's attempt at careful eating—he wore a blue sports jacket with an Italian silk tie slung over his shoulder—he left behind an unexpected injury of mousse parfait on his white dress shirt.

When he spoke to her, Lula had to prod herself not to hold his gaze for a longer time than necessary, as he was such a pleasure to behold. She did make an effort to participate in light banter with Mare, introduced by only her first name.

As they ate, the music over the sound system from an invisible quintet playing a jaunty scherzo made the dinner stuffier than it needed to be.

The other distinguished-looking man, Matt Killian, was also a Congressman, but wore traces of a reptilian coarseness just beneath his ruddy surface. He had big hands, speckled with freckles. There was no question of his power-broker status in this group as he cleared his throat to speak.

"This was a lovely dinner. I thank you for the invitation to taste a real Louisiana meal. I like steak just as much as the next guy, but this was a real adventure, tasty and spicy. Not too much, mind you, but just enough. You know, it doesn't hurt to branch out, taste food of other ethnicities."

For Lula, his condescension seemed almost theatrical.

Ambrose put his spoon down with a wry smile. "Where we're from, we call this down-home cooking, Matt. This isn't foreign food for us, and ethnicity isn't a bugaboo. Hell, the average Louisianan doesn't even know what race he is, to be honest. Our food is a mélange of French and Caribbean cuisine."

Matt patted his stomach and sides. "My friend, that sounds ethnic to me." He smiled, cocking his head, and nodding as if to congratulate himself.

"If taste is ethnic, well, join the human race." Ambrose declared. "Please, tell us, what kind of food do the Hollywood types serve at their soirees?"

"Well, I resent the appellation *Hollywood types*, but we do go for a wide culinary variety," Matt answered.

Mare interjected. "It's called Kraft Services." A joke Lula didn't quite understand, it made its speaker snort a quick laugh.

Killian looked at her, disapprovingly. "Not quite. California is the United Nations of the world, all in one state. We like our Asian cuisine. Not much French, though. I've never eaten frog's legs."

"Just how do you handle all the wining and dining in Hollywood and stay so fit, my friend?"

Lula sensed Girabeaux's first deception in calling Matt Killian a friend, because the gulf between them was not just at the table. Their positions belied any friendship. There was a veiled double entendre somewhere in their banter, but she couldn't put her finger on it.

Why did she feel protective of Ambrose? She admonished herself. This was not a battle in which she was involved, nor would she ever be. She didn't know the host any more than she did Matt and Mare, and wagered she'd probably never encounter them in any circle to which she did or ever would belong.

Why should she feel any sense of camaraderie with someone like Ambrose Girabeaux? Even if she did feel physically attracted to him, what could she do about it? He was a Republican.

Matt Killian's belly laugh brought her attention back to the room. He chuckled as he fingered his cigar.

"I ride bikes, about three times a week at the gym. I ride with a bike club along the Coast of Los Angeles County. Just to set the record straight, though, I pay for my meals and tickets, and it helps to know an agent." He pitched his head toward Mare. "Agents get invites everywhere, and if Mare needs an escort, I'm there for her."

Mare amended, "When my husband isn't."

"Well ... of course, Mare. Nobody's questioning that, least of all my wife. This isn't an ethics committee."

"Thank God for that. If that were the case, literary agents would be disciplined for the decisions they make on a daily basis."

Mare's joke lightened the mood a bit. Lula chuckled along with everyone else, stealing an appreciative glance at her for adding levity to a hidden competition that was becoming ever more visible.

Mare had no real eye-catching asset to draw the eye beyond her clothes. Her brown hair featured the different hues of her favorite hair colors, from auburn to red, with dark roots. Her lack of facial beauty was compensated by her figure. She likely wore a C cup, and looked like she worked out, with weights, notwithstanding her petite frame.

Her wardrobe was a parade of haute couture from head to toe: Jimmy Choo shoes and a Karl Lagerfeld off-white pantsuit, with a matching silken camisole underneath that made her look quite chic. Her Prada handbag was on her lap, and she smelled of Versace perfume.

Mare had "beaucoup bank," Lula decided, borrowing the slang of her Oakland neighborhood. Mare relished showing it, too.

"Can I count on you, Ambrose?" Matt was asking.

Ambrose looked down at his stained shirt and grimaced, then flipped his tie from his left shoulder to the front, letting it hang naturally.

"I don't quite know, Matt. This has been languishing forever—it's not like it's the immigration bill or something monumental like that. I don't feel very comfortable with tabling it yet again. To be honest, it should go up for a vote for the House to pass or not pass."

"I always want to be honest, my friend," Matt's tone was appeasing, "but we have constituents who want this bill to die, and we can facilitate that demise for a legitimate purpose. It simply isn't ready. That's the truth. We shouldn't rush to vote on it."

"Yawn, yawn," Mare interrupted. "It sounds like these men are getting ready to talk like they work for a living. I'll catch some fresh air while they attempt a grown-up conversation. Care to join?"

Lula was conflicted. She didn't know anyone but the Congressman, who was really a stranger. But she nodded her assent, excusing, and silently cursing, herself. She could be in her comfy bed about now, enjoying much-needed sleep.

Ambrose motioned them toward the curtains, where there were glass sliding doors that opened onto a spot-lit granite patio. Mosquito lamps hung from tall poles weighted down by stands filled with sand to keep them erect.

"Don't stray too far, ladies. Life gets pretty boring without you, you know," Killian quipped.

"Tell that to my husband, will you?" Mare shot back.

As they stepped outside, Mare rummaged through her purse for items she pulled out as they made their way toward a patio and pool.

"Where are those g-d fags?" Mare was impatient. "I thought I was going to die in there. When Ambrose and Matt pulled out cigars, I was so relieved, but then they never lit them, so, I was wondering what excuse I could give to get out of—Eureka!" She pulled out a thin box of *Gitanes* cigarettes. It figured that she'd smoke a French brand.

Lula declined Mare's offer to join her.

"Pot is so much more fun, but I daren't do that in front of a member of the House of Representatives. If each session started with smoking pot, the country would be in a much better state. They'd be nicer to one another and make decisions in a state of universal harmony." Mare lit her cigarette, holding it precariously between her lips, then tossing the cigarette pack and lighter back into her purse.

The cool air was crisp and fresh. The women breathed at the same time, one to fill her lungs, the other to expel smoke from them.

"Where do you know Ambrose from?"

"Well, we're really just acquaintants," Lula confessed.

"Handsome man. Republican, no less."

"What do you mean by that?" Lula looked at her.

"Well, he's got looks, political background, obvious wealth. He's Presidential material, I hear."

"Really?"

"Yep. I know he's looking at setting up a Political Action Committee to look into his prospects. He would be the Great Black Hope for the Republican party. A descendant of freedmen, who, if truth be told, owned slaves."

Lula looked straight ahead. "Wow. Who knew?"

"His conservative base. Obama is a great story, but it's not one that the average American can relate to—you know—growing up in Indonesia, madras education and all that. Ambrose is home-grown and a blue-blooded capitalist."

"What religion?"

"Scientology, of course. Would I have anything to do with him, otherwise?"

"Really?"

Mare looked contrite. "I shouldn't do that to you. He's Catholic, but if he keeps it up and shows an openness to other religions, it just might work. Trust me, this man is going places."

The night sky was bright, with barely discernible clouds.

"I need to spend more time here, really," Mare said. "Half the time, when my husband would tell me, 'I'm off to Louisiana,' I would shout, 'Where the fuck is Louisiana on a g-d map?' and he'd say, 'It's your second home, love. If you're looking for me, that's where you'll find me.'"

She stood still, staring into the distance. "And that was the beginning of our end. So here I am looking for him, and he's nowhere to be found."

The women were quiet until Mare asked, "Do you live around here?"

"Nakadee."

"Cool. Maybe we can do lunch?"

"How long are you here for?"

"Hell knows. I'm doing some house cleaning, scrounging through some of my husband's papers while he's away. Important shit. You know, the papers you don't leave home without ... as in D-I-V-O-R-C-E."

She threw her cigarette on the ground, smashing it gently with a twist and a push of her toe. "Said he got them notarized for filing. He was extorting me. Like I had his kind of money. He's a producer. I'm just a groveling agent who has to justify her ten percent. When we were negotiating the deal, as it were, Preston argued, 'Why go for the ten percent, when you can get the hundred?' He bribed me when he proposed marriage, and now he's extorting me over the divorce." She shook her head, smiling. "As if our marriage ever worked, anyway."

"Infidelity?" Lula was intrigued with the story now.

"That's not the half of it. Let's just say his little pecker had traveled the world in eighty days. That's the world he lives in. It's all about the sex. Free of charge. With beautiful people. Is there any better fantasy?"

She took a drag, leaning her head back, and continued. "Everyone in the industry is valued as a sexual being, no matter one's proclivity. Hollywood is a world of make-believe for the whole world, but for its inhabitants? A democratic free-for-all. For any perversion."

She pointed a remonstrative finger. "But, nobody judges."

Lula didn't say anything.

"It's not porn—just spanking good fun—as long as it's not on film. The private group sex parties at stately residences—you don't want to know."

"Well, I wasn't expecting a confession," Lula laughed.

"Hey, sister, I'm not confessing to anything." She laughed. "I was talking about my husband and where he likely is right now. My answer is he's likely cavorting with dark-skinned hunks; you know, the ones we can't have because we don't have the right equipment."

"Ah .... " Lula pieced it together. "How long have you been married?"

"Long enough to get fifty percent. One way or the other, if you know what I mean. Dead or alive. I'm joking, of course. I love him, like an ex-friend." She belted out a laugh.

"I should have killed him when I had the chance, honestly. I had the perfect murder all planned out—or it would have made a good film."

She glanced at Lula while flicking ashes.

"Here's a caveat. Thinking about murder isn't the same as doing it, so I can joke about it. I always had a nose for intrigue, from the time I was in high school. I had a crush on my best friend's Irish boyfriend. It was horrible. I don't even know why I liked him, honestly, but I was miffed that he was in love with her but sleeping with me. I got my revenge, though. I gave him an STD, and not the oil kind." She took a long drag on her cigarette. "Yep. They got married. DINKs."

"Excuse me?" Lula gazed at her face.

Mare was looking straight ahead, the moon catching a glint in her eye. "Double Income No Kids." She took another puff on her cigarette and released it, slowly, "No kids, thanks to me. Hey, talking to you is cathartic."

She paused and turned around, looking at Lula. "How do I reach you?" Before Lula could respond, she said, "I'll find you."

She flashed a phony smile. "I crack myself up. Don't mind me. It's the hallucinogens."

What a chatterbox. Lula was relieved that it was getting late, and hoped she could be on her way home soon. She took a seat on the soft striped cushions of a wrought-iron chair.

Mare looked at the chair nearest her, but resisted and remained standing.

"Where are you staying?" Lula asked her.

"At the bed and breakfast. The famous one." Mare hunted for the name.

"Little Missy?"

"That's the one." Mare snapped her fingers. "Can you leave a message for me there? I don't use Preston's last name. Mine is Miriam O'Hara." She clapped her hands. "How about lunch this week?"

Lula nodded.

"Call me." Mare mimed, pinky and thumb extended. Chuckling, she walked away toward the front of the house.

Lula relished being alone on Ambrose's patio, sans cigarette smoke. The night had only a faint dampness to it, just enough to force a shiver from the cold air. She wondered what she should do next. Leaning her head back in the chair, she wondered how in the hell she'd ended up dining at a black Republican Congressman's home, her belongings upstairs, in a mansion with ten bedrooms?

Too polite to follow Mare's lead, Lula stood up to enter the side door leading back into the dining room. The gossamer curtains were a deep burgundy—a bit romantic for a man, she thought. His nails were polished, his mustache trimmed to perfection. Was he a dandy?

Her question was answered when she reached the sliding door in time to see a brief skirmish between him and his guest. Neither man was smiling, and she saw Ambrose push the older congressman almost off balance.

"You don't want to push a black man, Republican or not. Politics won't keep me from going hood on you, Matt."

Matt pushed back, hissing. "I'll eat you for lunch, Ambrose. Do you hear me?" The point of his finger was two inches from Ambrose's nose. "I don't care who you think you are besides what I know: GOP window-dressing to make Democrats shut their traps about us being racists."

"Well, here I am, baby. Signed. Sealed. Delivered. I'm yours. That's your era, isn't it? Or is it 'Young at Heart'?"

"Whatever it is, you'll be singing it on your last day as a congressman. You're reneging on our agreement, Ambrose, and this must not stand! I told you how much this meant to me!"

"Yeah, well, let's just say my career depends on it, too."

"Tell that to my constituents. Do you have any clue of who they are, Ambrose? Do you think we're unique? We're fungible, my man. We can easily be replaced."

"I'm in service to my country, Congressman."

"They *are* the country, godammit."

"This little snafu is surmountable, then."

"Yeah, on my back."

"Well, on my dead back, then."

Lula stood motionless. The veil of curtains offered her only a silhouette of the men. The faint glow from the wall sconces gave the room an ominous feel.

Matt pointed at Ambrose, who deflected his finger with a karate-like swipe of his hands.

"Don't embarrass yourself, Congressman."

"Look, you promised—"

"No, I believe it was you who did the talking. Not once did I get my WIIFM answered."

"What?" Killian looked disgusted.

"Sorry, old man, the 'What's In It For Me?' WIIFM. Funny, I know everything about your proposed legislation, but you barely remember our conversation."

"Like hell, I don't. I remember. We talked about co-sponsoring an amendment."

"What's in a name? What topic? Do you think I'm that inconsequential, my man? I have to answer to people, too, and right now, they're much more frightening than a couple of Hollywood wheelers and dealers."

"Just remember, you called it off. Not me. So you give me no option, Ambrose, and I'm truly sorry to hear it."

Ambrose shrugged his shoulders. The men locked eyes until Matt looked away. "I'll visit your bathroom, first, if you don't mind."

"Down the hall to the right. My driver will take you back to your hotel."

"Much obliged," Matt muttered. He looked ready to point his finger again, then quickly retracted it. "A word to the wise, my friend. Rich people have friends in low places, as well as high."

He turned and strode out of the room.

Ambrose returned to his chair and took a sip of his coffee.

Lula waited a few more moments, then walked inside as if nothing had happened.

9

NO REST FOR THE WEARY

Sunday, March 20th, 9:00 a.m.

Lula's mood was already ruining her day, which had begun only an hour earlier. She longed to return to the rustic, converted A-frame shed, an abandoned shack desperately in need of paint, that stood alone near gnarled trees that lined a small creek in Natchitoches. But today, she needed to be at her lab, rather than out doing her research in the field.

Her fellowship work was far from glamorous, but the shack, the size of a poor efficiency apartment, was where she did her real work, and was her real home.

Prior to her moving in, the shack had been used for supply storage and as an informal watering hole for the park rangers. When it had been converted for Lula's research, the only luxury hung on a nail hammered into the side of the Formica table that served as her workbench: a key to a portable bathroom that the Park Service purchased on her behalf, so that she wouldn't have to share one with the general public.

Two days a month, a class of high-school volunteers helped sift through the dug-up earth looking for signs of a mass grave. There was always a festive atmosphere when they were present. Lula added drama by giving the bones names: Freddy Femur, Debbie Digit, and Herbert Humerus, inspiring the volunteers to divine what had happened to those body parts, the telltale evidence of the owner's last days and moments in life.

The students had seemed fascinated when she'd explained how DNA was like a truth serum, and that the staunchest white racists likely shared more genetic similarities with Black Americans than they did with their European ancestors. She'd also explained that mitochondrial DNA analysis was carried only through the mother, and, accordingly, each person in the world could be traced to common ancestors from Central Africa.

It was DNA that legitimized what Blacks knew to be more than rumor about Thomas Jefferson and Sally Hemings, a slave he owned and who had borne him children. There was also evidence that the dark-skinned Lemba tribe in southern Africa might have been the original Sephardic Jews.

Lula drew a comparison to the feuds of the Hatfields and the McCoys, who, like Blacks and Whites, were distant cousins who reached a social détente that allowed them to live together, but in separate societies, always on the precipice of war.

As a student herself, Lula had become increasingly perplexed by the human tendency to look for distinctions in appearance to classify worth or importance, especially considering the universality of the DNA pool that created the species.

That very phenomenon had led to her interest in forensic anthropology. She wanted to learn the individual story of each corpse she encountered, in as much detail as possible, and was known for her thoroughness in examining a skeleton and determining the manner of death.

In concentrating this kind of attention on the burying grounds of slaves, Lula wanted to know how they had died in captivity, an interest that drew scorn from some of her white peers who, like, Sherry, believed some exhumations were better left undisturbed.

She'd been admonished that her research could only reveal what everyone already knew—that slaves were mistreated—but she wanted there to be a record that verified the types of atrocities they'd suffered.

Her fellowship was an unusual one for a forensic anthropologist, because southern field sites were usually the territory of archeologists and physical anthropologists working with recovery teams to identify the war dead. Civil-War history was a source of great American pride, though the lives of the people over whom the North and the South had become divided in the first place remained shrouded in turmoil.

She wondered how a nation could be so enamored of its Civil-War past, but not in its victims, as though black people had been merely an afterthought in the growth of the new nation wholly dependent on their contributions.

Her research focused on an event rumored to have taken place in Nakadee in 1830, the year of the Nat Turner Rebellion. Turner, a slave with self-proclaimed visionary powers, led a group of slaves through the Virginia countryside, killing fifty-one white slave owners. Allegedly, as word spread throughout the South, other insurrections took place, Nakadee's among them. The word was that the Nakadee slaves had been massacred, with no record to confirm the event for fear that other slaves would get the same rebellious notions.

Lula's research sought to uncover the story of several slaves who, according to black oral history, had been beaten to death by a posse of Whites on a nearby plantation. Whether it was truth or fiction, Lula's research aimed to reveal the whole truth and nothing but the truth, and there were enough burial grounds on the still-barren land that might yield clues.

Even if the Nakadee rebellion was folklore, Lula could get a glimpse of the lives of the slaves. The Old Robert McAlpin Plantation, later renamed "Little Eva Plantation," was the fictitious setting for Harriet Beecher Stowe's novel, *Uncle Tom's Cabin*. It was rumored that, during a slave insurrection soon after Nat Turner's infamous rebellion, "difficult" slaves were killed and buried in mass graves, their executions forcibly witnessed by other slaves to serve as warning to any who might attempt to revolt against their enslavers.

The site of the graves had never been found, but children playing nearby had found a body buried near the setting where one of the rumored slaughters had taken place. The uprising and massacre in Nakadee might be fictitious, but since the Little Eva Plantation still stood, so might some evidence of a rebellion.

Lula wanted to give voice to the horrors of slavery not as a politician, but as a scientist. Her research had yielded a grant to study a cemetery in a historic site, which had brought her to Nakadee University and the burial site in Natchitoches.

Her findings would be a forensic challenge and of enormous scientific value, though the results would also be controversial. The Melrose, Oakland, Magnolia, Cherokee, and Beau Fort Plantations were national historic landmarks, living tributes to a bygone era that still managed, to this day, to divide the nation into entrenched pro-slavery versus pro-emancipation extremes.

But today, it was three dismembered fingers that required her attention. After taking their measurements, she lined them up closely to see if there were patterns in their appearances. Some sort of acid had disfigured the finger pads, but there was still enough of the dorsal nail beds to reveal the clubbing deformity she had noticed earlier.

People of African descent showed a higher propensity for clubbing, requiring more intense scrutiny for the familiar corresponding traces of lung or heart disease. However, the hues of these freshly shorn fingers suggested that they belonged to a White or mixed-race Creole. She would need to discuss with Aggie and Nate how to cull records of missing individuals with markers of lung or heart disease.

She next measured the nasty tears in the fingers' entrails that had caused the skin to string in some places, like thick spaghetti. The finger that had corked the bottle of sherry showed a wine mark, its insides congealed to a deep purple. The index finger had probably been severed and corked somewhere between two and five hours, and appeared to belong to the right hand. The palmar sides of the relatively small fingers were blistered and raw.

Under magnification, the index finger showed a razor-thin slash on its side, an injury that had probably preceded dismemberment. Moving the lens closer, Lula saw a white granule embedded in the slit. She removed the object with tweezers and placed it in a vial.

She planned to boil the flesh off the bone over the next two days, then study the striae left on the bones by whatever object had separated the fingers from their owner. Laying the fingers next to each other in the shape of a hand, she noted that the owner's right middle finger and thumb hadn't yet been discovered. Each finger belonged to the same hand, she realized, but in lining them up, she observed that their cuts were dissimilar.

What was obvious was that the skin on the dorsum of each finger was longer than the initial cut, as if the cutting object had slipped, dragging the skin with it. The implement used to amputate the fingers might have been makeshift, she deduced.

Sherry never showed up or called. Maybe she'd overslept, drugged and tired after yesterday's events. By tomorrow, she'd be ready to soak up the attention, something she tried and succeeded at more times than Lula wanted to admit.

Sherry was active in class, relished the spotlight, and almost fit the description of provocateur. She rarely bothered to be caught up on the latest assignments, which provoked Lula's ire, though that didn't faze the class hottie in the least. Whatever grade Sherry would eventually earn, it would have no effect upon her future. She would marry well; that was a sure bet.

When Lula finished examining the specimens, she locked the lab door behind her and left for her appointment at Aggie's. Outside, the white heat of the sun had dimmed slightly, and the clouds stretched languorously across the sky.

Aggie greeted Lula at her door and offered her a cold beverage. Thirsty, Lula immediately took a small sip.

"It's spiked," Aggie warned, smiling.

"Not enough," Lula joked.

They smiled at each other, then Aggie asked, "Did someone take crime-scene shots?"

"Not exactly crime-scene pics. Photos of the fingers? Yes. The police didn't see the one in either the front or back of the building until someone brought them in."

"No closed-circuit television at the police department?"

"I have no idea," said Lula.

Aggie pursed her lips, then said, tartly, "Even after 9/11, they haven't done squat. What have they done so far on the case?"

Lula told her about the condition of the fingers and discussed her perceptions of the case so far, providing a laundry list of questions the police still hadn't answered. She added that there'd barely been any time put into the case because of the Hot Sauce Festival. As far as she knew, Nate hadn't yet organized a search for the owner of the fingers. Maybe he was waiting for them to point to someone through another cryptic delivery. "I let him know that my students could help out in any search. It would be a great exercise for them, and get them out of the classroom."

The women agreed that it would help if they knew just where Nate was with the case, but Aggie didn't dare question a police officer about procedure, knowing the eggshell egos of some of the most macho among them. For the police in this rural town, theft, endangerment, or abuse of animals was more prevalent than crimes involving the parish inhabitants. Everything was fine here in Nakadee, according to them. Everybody got along. They did like their occasional car chases, however,

Lula finished her drink, but didn't stay long, telling Aggie she needed to get ready for the upcoming week's classes.

2:15 p.m.

Every nook and cranny in the country has an underground system of unseen, unheard men who tirelessly maintain the status quo for the true power players. Wally was their man in Nakadee.

As long as no news was ever reported about him, Wally was given free rein to do what he had to—whatever he had to—no questions asked. Only two people knew Wally's importance to the Nakadee police: the chief, and Nate. He was what they called their "roving seeing-eye dog," who could roam in any community and make his home there.

After surviving the Kush Mountains, he could live anywhere, under any conditions. That lowest standard of living became his norm, and anything above those chilly winters was downright comfortable. He trained himself never to grow too accustomed to the luxury of Western living.

In Afghanistan the troops lived for anonymous care packages from grateful patriotic citizens, but he always declined, giving his portion away. He would rather not feel the letdown after the toiletries and souvenirs were used up, though he did take the wool socks and protein bars.

After the war, he didn't know what to do with a refrigerator, cable television, or flushing toilets with seats. He had become accustomed to squatting and cleaning up with water (he even did it left-handed, like the natives). American life had become unreal to him.

The local Masons had brought him to the chief's attention. When something needed to get done, he could do it, as long as he stayed below the radar.

He had an older, divorced woman friend he slept with periodically, but didn't have time for a serious relationship with a woman his age. Things always got too messy with younger girls. They would nag about why he was always out, start to resent his late-night visits, and bemoan his disappearance in the early morning. None of his girlfriends had a chance to display her cooking prowess, as he was never available during mealtime, and they tired of going to the movies with him because his restless leg was a distraction. Worse yet, he often slept through the films. He had no complaints about the arrangement with the older woman friend.

At first, he kept an eye on the Nakadee Mafia, a small cadre of cash-only pizzeria owners who had their own underground gigs. They were small-time, but every now and then someone might end up beaten and deposited by the side of the road. The police chief would take no action, formally, but would put Wally on the case.

Since learning about the missing fingers, Wally was glued to his task of hunting down what the crime was all about. He was no stranger to this "payback" gesture. Violent gangs used it, like the Yakuza, the Marielitos, and some of the Neo-Nazis while on their drugs of choice. Black gang-bangers were too squeamish for that kind of mayhem. Instead, they had an overwhelming tendency to participate in drive-bys. *Cowards*.

When on an assignment, Wally first scouted in the usual haunts, like beer barns, where moonshine tastings were held on a daily basis. Or he'd hang out at the bowling alley diners, watching people bowl, listening to the sounds of the strikes while eating a large plate of steaming sweet potato fries.

His other place was Denny's, where he'd get a decent rib-eye steak with potatoes, without all the spicy shit in it. Sometimes a man just wants American food: a nice, juicy steak with Worcestershire sauce and bubbling fat.

He made the rounds to places where there was likely to be some buzz. He'd put a cigarette in his mouth, don a Clint Eastwood squint, and chat to elicit more talkback. He'd sit for hours in order to get some dirt on somebody. He understood the human need to be seen as intelligent, worth talking to. If you just plunked 'yerself' down or 'jess set' there, even an idiot would eventually tell you something of note.

Today he stopped by a barbecue stand, where meats were cooked on a large, open grill made out of empty oil drums cut in half. He watched the cook slop the barbecue on the meats, pour on some hot sauce, and hear the meat pop and sizzle.

It was there that he'd learned what was behind the altercation between Sherry and Richard.

The man tending the meats was the one who had told Richard to leave well enough alone at the festival yesterday, calling him by name. Wally asked him what he knew about Richard and Sherry.

"I knew his momma," said the black man. He was short and stocky, 'Geechee' dark, with pearly white teeth. "Fine lady. Librarian. Her name was... Desdemona... Desiree, some kinda ancient name ... Delilah!"

As he remembered the name, he punctured the air with the long barbecue brush he was using to slowly slather sauce on the smoldering chickens on the right side of the grill.

"Yeah, Delilah. He's Delilah's kid."

He chuckled. "Yeah, he was a smart one, that one. I axed her son once why he didn't use the nickname, 'Rick' or 'Ricky,' seein' as that's what most people do. They shorten the given name, like

William, to Bill, and Michael to Mike. He said his momma wanted him to have a name people could pronounce. Cain't nobody mess up Richard. 'If my momma woulda wanted me to have the name Ricky, she woulda named me that. It's Richard. Like the Third,' he'd say. I know that got somethin' to do with Shakespeare or somethin'. Yeah, he was readin' all the time comin' up, just like his momma."

The cook took a whiff of the smells emanating from the grill, set down his tools and started sprinkling the spare ribs with shots of hot sauce. "He ain't been the same since his momma left 'em alone with his daddy. His daddy is gone now. Richard got the house to his self." He stopped talking to sop up some sauce to keep it from falling between the grate spaces.

"Where's he work?" Wally asked.

"Everywhere and nowhere, man. They got no union at Nakadee— and he got a truck. So he'll do pick ups, deliveries, and can find pretty much anything you're lookin' for, includin' weed, or other recreational drugs, if that's your fancy. That's one resourceful dude."

The cook's face was sweating rivulets of water from the heat of the flames. Standing away from the grill, he wiped his long apron across and down both sides of his face while he continued to talk.

The cook was stirring a red sauce for pasta on another grill while he talked about how his son had known Richard when they were in middle school. Richard didn't quite fit in. He hailed from an isolated rag-tag community of nondescript do-it-yourself dilapidated homes clustered together between Nakadee and Natchitoches, a place where the streets didn't have names, but the postman still managed to match the mail with the right non-numbered mailboxes.

Richard had been home-schooled until he was thirteen. A new arrival to the incivility of the public school system, he wasn't wise to the ways of its "social etiquette" and was immediately ostracized by his white classmates, who called him "Cracker Boy." Contrastingly, the black kids accepted him, bestowing on him the honor of being a "brother." He was welcomed into a self-declared gang of misfits, who christened themselves "The Nakadee Blood Boys," and fancied themselves a splinter group of the notorious Los Angeles gang, the Bloods.

Over time he grew into their disfavor because, against his better judgment, he couldn't help but display signs of overt intelligence. Richard knew the topography of the area like the back of his hand, as he'd traveled it all of his life. The outdoors had been his lesson book. As happens with many teenagers, their innocent escapades grew increasingly more risky, if not dangerous. Richard took the bait, sharing his knowledge of chemistry, teaching the cook's son, and others, how to make miniature explosives and Molotov cocktails, taking his role of hoodlum to a new level. He got into increasing trouble at school.

"I didn't let my son run with him anymore. I told him that with Richard being Cajun, n'all, he could get away with more than my black son could."

After his mother died, his father put Richard in foster homes, using the excuse that he was a trucker. Richard ran away, quit high school, and moved back into his father's home, to which his daddy never returned.

"He's kinda tragic, tell you the truth." The cook looked at Wally sideways. "You know that man, 'They?'"

Wally shook his head.

"I didn't 'thank' so. I don't know 'em either, but *they* say he killed his pappy for cheatin' on his momma."

"That right?"

"I don't believe it, but you know most of us are half-cocked as it is in this country. Too big, too much of everything, and not enough time to do it in. Some ma' buddies said he done did it. Buried him in the fields somewhere. Who gonna look? And who cares 'cept the funeral parlor wants to get paid eight thousand dollars to put a damn hole in the ground. The bugs are gonna eat 'em up anyway. Who cares, man? We live, we die. Sometimes we do it before our time is up, but we know about time, don't we? Who it wait for?"

Wally nodded, taking out his flask to share with the cook, who looked at him quizzically, nodded, then took it from him gently.

"Ashes to ashes, brother." Wally looked him in the eye.

"My wife gonna kill me, drinking on the job." The cook took a furtive sip. "You ain't lyin'. Let me throw a bit uh likka on these

127

two ribs here, and we gonna have us a little snack. If my wife says something, I'll tell her you're a taste-tester, helpin' me with a recipe, okay?"

3:00 p.m.

Arriving home from Aggie's, Lula made a beeline for her bedroom, flinging her limp body onto the bed. She splayed her legs and arms wide, bare feet resting on the floor. Her open windows let in just enough air to make the curtains billow slightly. She watched them, breathing quietly.

So much had transpired in the last twenty-four hours. She was drained, both physically and emotionally. Was she still the same person, or had someone put a spell on her?

She unbuttoned her blouse, slowly revealing her lace bra and bare midriff. She turned to look at her reflection in the mirror beside the bed.

Who was that person last night? She closed her eyes, to see if she felt like the woman she was yesterday with Ambrose Girabeaux. She could still hear the music that had played on his stereo. After Matt and Mare had left, she and Ambrose looked at each other. There had been an odd pause.

"Nightcap? In the living room?" he asked.

"From your servants?" she'd mocked.

"I can make a mean drink without their help, thank you." He playfully stuck his tongue out at her, his eyes briefly meeting hers as they shared the laugh.

Then he excused himself and left the room. She had been bone-tired by then. Unsure of how formal she should be, she took her shoes off then put them on again.

She knew that she was out of control, operating in alien territory, her common sense left abandoned somewhere, a dramatic current sweeping her feelings along.

Ambrose returned with chilled glasses, went to the bar, and bent to look into the hidden refrigerator. He mixed two drinks, handed her one, then sat down beside her.

The dark Kahlua that settled at the bottom of her glass began to swirl with chips of ice and milk, slowly turning the drink a muddy brown.

Ambrose sat, his legs extended, feet crossed, and took a sip of whiskey. Its amber color sparkled from the light of the sconces.

One sip of her drink emboldened Lula: "This argument between you and the Congressman—what was it about?"

"What argument?" His eyes darted back and forth as he sipped from his glass.

"You two were fighting—what could be that important to go to physical battle over?"

"Let's just say that Matt has Mafia ties in Hollywood."

Lula looked surprised.

"Not really, but his Hollywood friends are as close to the Mafia as one can get, only they don't snuff people out. Instead, they ignore them. Forever. No funds for his future campaigns. No special invitations to events like the Oscars. No special parties."

He coughed, clearing his throat.

"We're talking about the people we're excited to meet, the constituents who have millions of dollars, chalets, cabins, private jets, and other untold wealth, who can put some of that money into our pockets. Yes, *those* constituents."

Ambrose's demeanor changed. He leaned back in his seat.

"What if I told you that those constituents serially raped people? What if I told you they sequestered someone in a room, pulled his or her hair back and raped them until they bled? Would you want to be around them? Would you want to go on a yacht with them? What if I told you that they gang-raped people, then cast them aside, and pretended not to know them?"

"I get it."

"No offense, but I'm speaking in metaphors. The rape isn't literal. It's literary."

She looked at him, questioningly,

"We're congressional representatives, in a country of three-hundred fourteen million people, and only 435 of us have the privilege of being called a United States Congressman. We work for adulation. We want to achieve, have a bill named after us—maybe obtain a higher position—like senator, cabinet member. Nobody wants to be left in the proverbial dustbin of history.

"I've got some deciding to do. Do I champion the rights of the individual writer, or the corporation that takes ownership of the writing? Do I promote free enterprise, even if it's corporate fraud? Do we disable a writer from making millions in the future in order to sustain the corporate status quo, no matter what?"

He returned his gaze to Lula. "But I'd much prefer to learn more about you. You're such a good sport to come here on a moment's notice to help a brother out."

"A brother? Aren't you a Republican?" She smirked.

He laughed. "Yes, and there are many of us! We're everywhere, like the air you breathe." He cleared his throat, then took a sip of his drink, registering a slight grimace as the alcohol moved down his throat.

Her eyes rested on his large Adam's apple. Moving upward to his chin, she noticed his smooth skin, with only a slight hint of shaving bumps near his collar. His top shirt button was open, as relaxed as he was likely to get. Boy, was he handsome.

"I'll know to stop when you're snoring." He pushed on her gently, ribbing her.

She told him that she was all ears, hanging on his every word.

So he talked, and she leaned her head back and listened.

He was much deeper, more knowledgeable than she had imagined in her admitted prejudice about his being a black Republican. His words flowed over her soothingly, giving an insider's look at what it really meant to be a congressional leader in Washington.

She asked him lots of questions, often requesting clarification. Their voices were low and quiet as the household settled down, the cook having stopped in to nod goodnight.

By the time Ambrose was through, she had a fuller understanding of the man and his motivations for belonging to his political party.

He wasn't like the black professors and so-called journalists who railed against their own people in the belief that somehow they were better, and that they could lead the toiling plebeian masses to support the status quo. Their allegiance to conservative values positioned them in juxtaposition to their own race, of which they really wanted no part. They would disparage their mother if she were darker-skinned than they, and lived every day of their lives ashamed of their color, which Ambrose wore as a badge of honor.

Those traitors were trying to be something they weren't: authentic. However, unbeknownst to them, everybody could see through the charade, he said, because as much as black conservatives wanted to belong, they never could: they would forever be tokens, the ones who were let in not because they were liked, but because they served the purpose of showing that his party's colorless flat-line could be inclusive.

"So why remain in Congress?" Lula asked.

Ambrose sat back, looking up at the ceiling, then stretched his arms against the back of the sofa, his right arm just grazing Lula's head, the other still holding his drink.

He was a rising star in his party, a counterweight to the Democratic Party's darling. The Grand Old Party in his district respected Girabeaux because he knew how to bring jobs to them. He knew how to make the elephants sweat, too, as they anxiously awaited the promised financial rewards. Republicans were hungry SOBs.

In spite of his large projects and corporate largesse, Ambrose always kept his focus on the plight of his rural district's poor, and worked tirelessly to end the region's economic drought. His voters lived in farming country inherited from their slaveholding ancestors, and were selling off their land, bit by bit, to new business concerns like the poultry industry.

His family had owned slaves without any sense of guilt, because their human property were treated well, and also permitted to learn to read and write. Most had stayed on after Emancipation, but later many had felt the call to go North to better jobs and living environments, or so they were promised.

Like the young citizenry of many of Louisiana's rural parishes, Nakadee's restless, idle youth had no prospects for a future. The best jobs—at the local poultry plants, or in grocery stores or day-labor construction—were highly competitive, and more responsible and employable adults usually won out.

The young people's only solution was to migrate to New Orleans and Baton Rouge, where it was much more expensive to live. Invariably, the rural poor would thrust themselves into the underbelly of society in those cities, committing petty crimes that became increasingly serious, hiking the jailbird rolls in the state prisons, or becoming part of the human debris like those left languishing at the New Orleans Superdome during Hurricane Katrina.

Girabeaux wanted to bring jobs to his community, which was a good enough reason to dine with Congressman Matt Killian.

He wasn't black enough for some of his peers in the Congressional Black Caucus, and he wasn't "Black" enough for some of the Whites in Congress, either. As long as he stayed in office he would have to deflect the daggers, knives, and chain saws that might be thrown at him during the current presidency while the nation was reeling over his party's dastardly desire to throw America into turmoil over the perennial theme of race.

In order to remain relevant and therefore "electable" as a minority, he had to appease his white constituency as much as he did his black one, which meant that he would always be adrift in midair in a non-stop political whirlwind.

"So where does Matt fit in?" Lula asked, leaning away from him to get a fuller look at his face. His eyes sparkled and his lips looked supple. His smooth skin had a soft glow. His brow furrowed as he lost himself in thought, clicking his tongue and shaking his head.

Leaning forward, he studied the wall as if reading it for clues. "He's always up to something, Matt Killian. He comes from Hollywood, and has been there forever, and can pretty much call all the shots. He's also the Chairman of the Judiciary Committee."

"Isn't he from your party?"

"He is. But you should know by now, since the new presidency, there's the legitimate Republican Party and the marauders, I call them, who have hijacked our platform. He's one of those. He wasn't, before the current presidency, but he sure is now. He wields enormous power."

"Why are you beholden to him?"

Ambrose slumped in his seat, rubbing his hand against the plush sofa. "I have my reasons."

"Ah. Top secret stuff."

"Well, no and yes. No national security's at stake, but let's just say my political currency is in jeopardy because I have a big IOU to pay back."

"So, tonight's dinner was to talk about how much you owe?"

"Hey, what are you—a reporter?" He leaned forward, peering at her with an exaggerated look of curiosity. "Because a good friend of mine is, and he could use a super sleuth like you. Remind me later. You'll love him."

Lula was feeling pretty mellow, in no hurry to end her conversation with this man whose politics took a back seat to his character. Finally, here was someone who spoke her language, and didn't mutter. He and Devon were worlds apart.

"So, back to the payback," Lula urged him to continue, adding, "What does Hollywood have to do with anything?" she asked.

He cleared his throat. "Pardon me while I search for listening devices." He faked getting to his feet, then sat back down, straightening his suit jacket.

He explained his dilemma of being accountable both to his constituents and his wealthy allies. Contrary to popular belief, he voted with Democrats on some issues, and with the Party of Reagan on others. His decisions were predicated on the belief that voting one's conscience wasn't as important as voting for the needs of your constituency.

"What could you two men possibly have in common that would fuel that level of passion?" Lula asked.

Ambrose pulled the knot of his tie from side to side, took a sip of whiskey, and lay his head back, deep in thought.

"We have faced pressure from the Hollywood lobby to protect their copyrights in music and other media for some time now."

"You mean like sharing digital music?" she asked.

"Not that kind of copying."

He explained how the studios won the battle against digital music file-sharing by creating paying sites for listening to music or watching movies online.

"This is creative copying. I was taking the position that there were certain types of copying that should be thwarted because of the very nature of their threat to the rights of original copyright holders. The more research we did, the more concerned we were about how pervasive the problem is.

"Let me put it this way: it's like someone kidnapping your child, then parading him in front of you every day. You know that that kid looks familiar, but you're not quite sure." He set his drink down on the end table next to him, yawned, stretched, then leaned back, draping his arm on the sofa behind her. "I was sponsoring a change in the legislation to make it a crime to perform comprehensive non-literal copyright infringement, to deter copying."

He seemed lost in thought, elbows on his knees as he gazed at the floor.

"Did you forget I was here?" Lula asked.

He sat upright and leaned back to drape his hand behind her, rubbing her shoulder gently, absentmindedly.

She tried not to register her surprise at his touch. Then, as if realizing a faux pas, he moved away from her, his hand brushing her cheek. He held it there.

His kiss was as soft as warm Belgian chocolate and she felt an instant appetite for his sweetness. When their lips met his tongue parted her mouth with coaxing persuasion. He held her face in his hands, tilting it up toward him. The room was silent, save for the rustle of their clothes.

He pulled away from her.

She looked at him. "Whatever you do, don't apologize. Please."

He looked at the wall. "It's your call. You know I'd like you to stay."

Lula whispered, "I know."

"I'll get the lights."

He moved toward his stereo. As she watched, Lula knew that when he returned, whatever step she decided to take that night, there'd be no turning back.

5:35 p.m.

After she'd showered, powdered her body, and put her hair in a ponytail, Lula strode toward the thumping sound at her door to find her neighbor urging her to come have a drink on the porch. Lula obliged, after turning on the sprinkler to water her yard.

As the women settled into Pomona's lounge chairs, her neighbor began to talk about the latest reality TV drama. It had become her running joke to give Lula updates, with the hope that she might catch the bug, even though she knew Lula wasn't interested.

"Yeah, girl, everything came to a head today. I told you about Shantay, right? Well, the bitch went off her rocker, girl, and they duked it out on the floor!"

Lula barely heard her as she looked over at her own property. The streetlights were coming on.

"I need some better curtains," Lula said.

"Oh. Okay, I get it. Change the subject."

"No, really. You can see inside my windows from here, can't you?"

"Only somebody who cares to. Guess what? I live smack dab across the street from you. If I want to see you I can just call or come over. Ain't no dirty 'ol man up in my place, and if he was, I'd be keeping the homie busy takin' care of me, you hear me?"

The women laughed as Pomona stretched out her hand for Lula to slap. "Don't leave me hanging, girl."

Lula obliged. Her friend's tennis bracelet clinked against the chair's armrest.

Pomona was dressed in matching white sweat pants, T-shirt, and white tennis shoes, which she was unlacing with French-tipped designer nails. She wore her hair in two large ponytails with white ribbons, which took ten more years off her already youthful appearance. The contrast of her skin, as shiny as a copper teakettle, was striking.

The women were silent for a while, until Lula's voice broke the slap and swish of Pomona's applying grapefruit-scented lotion to her naked feet.

"I met someone." Lula spoke quietly.

"Bitch. I knew you was up to something, sittin' there all smug and shit. Why didn't you just cut to the chase? You had me up here

135

talkin' about goddamned housewives I don't even know, and you denyin' me some real gossip?"

Lula shook her head, chuckling under her breath. She wondered how this single mother who worked part-time at the local supermarket, and had plenty of baby-daddy drama, managed to stay so upbeat. Had she been holding back her friendship because of the educational chasm between them?

She leaned back in her chair, realizing that she had a good friend in Pomona, who was now fixing a comic gaze upon her.

"Okay. Spill it."

Lula began, setting the stage for the Congressman's flirtation until Pomona interrupted her.

"But did he get your digits? That's all I want to know."

Lula sighed and clasped her hands in front of her, looking down.

"No?" Pomona's mouth hung open. "What the ...." She accentuated her disapproval by standing up, hefting up her chair and loudly setting it down again, crossing her arms as she sat, while Lula laughed. "Do I gotta take you to dating school? If he ain't got your number, you ain't got no relationship, honey! Is you crazy? Now, how we gonna handle this 'sitiation'?"

"Pomona. I know you graduated from high school. I know you took some courses at Nakadee Trade Tech. And I know that you know that there is no such word as sitiation."

Her friend barely acknowledged her, instead speaking with a devilish gleam in her eyes. "Is you or isn't you planning on giving him your number to remedy this sitiation?"

Lula burst out laughing.

Pomona smiled, mockingly. "Oh, so now you're laughing at me?"

They were both laughing from their bellies.

"Okay. I'll speak in English." Pomona paused, taking on a British accent: "Are you not planning on giving him your seven numerical digits that—shit, let me think, here—the punching ... of which ... allows him access to the device that permits you to talk to each other simultaneously?"

Her words were funny enough, but Lula was laughing at her friend's pantomime of using her pinky finger, drinking tea while talking on the phone. Lula hadn't had such a good laugh in a long while.

So you do speak English?" She smiled at her friend.

"Yes. But let me tell you something. That kind of English is what you speak when you're passing a cup of Earl Grey. Now, when I say, 'is you or is you ain't gonna let the mother-you-know-what contact you on your damned phone, well that's for conversations like what *weez* about to have, sister. It's the difference between ...." She paused, placing her hand on her chin. "Who was that bitch who wrote *Jane Eyre*?"

Lula guffawed, shaking her head. "Now you know that ain't right ... one of the Bronte sisters."

"Yeah. Charlotte. Well, it's the difference between Jane Eyre and a Ray-Ray Thomas novel?"

"Who?"

"Yeah, I figured uppity types like you don't know about him. Well, I like talking like Ray-Ray. He cuts through all the 'thees' and 'thous' and 'he tasted her delicacy' to getting-down-to-business-now-tell-me-what-he-did-he-plucked-her. That's what talking like this is ... and I likes it that way."

Lula had never heard colloquial Black English explained in such a manner, but her friend raised a good point.

"So, let's keep it real, and tell me—please tell me—that you was lying about not giving the brother your digits."

Lula looked at her blankly.

"I done had it with you." Pomona pounded her chest and bowed her head before bolting up to open the screen door. Hanging her 115-pound frame on the creaky doorknob, she yelled inside, "Who wants ice cream? Time for beddy-bye!"

The patter of kids running toward their mother's voice, high-pitched sounds calling back in response, ended the evening quiet.

"I do! I do!"

"Ice cream! I want chocolate!"

Lula saw small hands and feet wriggling through the door as they were ushered back inside.

"You'll get what we gots. Now turn back around. You know the porch is off limits when I'm talking to grown-ups."

Pomona winked at her friend, muttering under her breath. "I met somebody." She walked away clucking, as she scooted her kids back into the house.

Lula smiled as Pomona reprimanded her son, "Boy, what did I tell you about touching Mommy when she's wearing white?"

Lula gazed across the wide street at her lonely abode, comforted by the sounds of life inside her friend's home. She watched her sprinkler spin, spewing water ineffectively as it cascaded onto the sidewalk and down the street. It had already saturated her lawn.

She walked down the steps of Pomona's porch to make a closer visual inspection. Her home was quite plain. There were no two ways about it.

Most houses in her neighborhood were highly individual creations, born of the piggy-bank savings and mattress accounts of hardworking, enterprising black folk whose life dream was to own a home, ornate or not.

Her three-bedroom, two-bath was one of the nicer houses in the neighborhood, though it, too, was stuck in the Rock Hudson and Doris Day 1950s era of brick and plank. Hers had a red brick foundation and a wooden façade all around.

She crossed the street to turn off the spigot. Her windows didn't have the black wrought-iron bars that were a staple of her neighbors' houses and low-income ethnic neighborhoods. Lula had ignored her mother's insistence that she put them up when she moved in.

She gathered up the hose and coiled it like a snake into its ceramic holder.

On her first visit to this black neighborhood, she'd been struck by what was lacking compared to what she'd grown up with in California. There were no sidewalks, the street had no consistent surface. Its variations created unofficial property boundaries of sorts. On any given street in her neighborhood, black asphalt shared space with yellow asphalt, the only integration this city could muster up. But even these were in a state of disrepair. When Lula had to decide what color to put in her driveway, in solidarity with her segregated lifestyle, she'd opted for the symbolism of black asphalt.

When she returned to her friend's porch, Pomona, dressed in a full-length multicolored caftan, was carrying two tall glass steins of vanilla ice cream with Kahlua. They sat talking and listening to Pomona's radio that piped soulful sounds onto the screened-in porch.

Three hours later, as both of them fought off sleep, Pomona asked Lula if she wanted to sleep over and watch the Comedy Channel.

Lula said that she'd spare her friend her snores. Her own bed was calling her. She hugged Pomona goodnight.

10
UNWILLING WITNESSES

Monday, March 21ˢᵗ, 10:00 a.m.

Devon stood like a guard beside the door while Nate sat opposite Juanito. Dressed in a tight-fitting blue mesh shirt and bulge-revealing Levis, Juanito looked like a rock star.

The receptionist had quietly sounded the alarm that a hunk was in the police station, and now a little crowd was milling around the interrogation room trying to get a glimpse of the handsome man.

Juanito wore one earring. Clean-shaven, with long eyelashes, he looked like a mature altar boy, the picture of innocence, except for the tattoo on his neck and shoulder: a raft with some Mexican-style gang-lettering in the shape of ocean waves beneath it.

Nate decided to treat him gingerly. Juanito had shown up voluntarily without the need for a subpoena—a daring gesture for someone who could be in trouble—and he hadn't brought an attorney.

"How is it that I don't have to subpoena you? You're a bit eager, aren't you? You ready to tell us something about the Hollykook house?" Nate asked.

"I'm eager to tell you I know nothing."

"That so?"

Juanito, staring forward, as though hanging on Nate's every word, answered perfunctorily, "Yes. I got nothing to do with those fingers."

"So, we shouldn't be looking at you as a suspect?" Nate raised his eyebrows.

"For what?"

"I'll let you tell me that one. You know more than you're letting on." Nate nodded knowingly at Devon, who walked a couple of paces, then returned to stand behind Juanito, who was brushing dust from his jeans.

"So, tell us what you know, or what we should know about Preston and Blaine, and the last time you heard from Preston." Nate said, quietly.

"Whatever. Let me explain it this way. I'm an aspiring actor. I work for him."

"And live with him, too, correct?"

"In a manner of speaking. I have a key to the place, but I also have my own apartment in town."

"Does he have any enemies?"

"Well, I imagine. Why not? He's rich. Everybody wanted something from him."

"Including you."

Juanito ignored him.

"Does he always come and go as he pleases, without telling anybody?" Nate wondered.

"He's a grown man."

"So much so that he could disappear for a week and you wouldn't even wonder where he was."

Juanito leaned back in his chair, one hand on his belt, the other gesticulating as he spoke. "He went to Los Angeles. He went to film festivals, visited his friends in Aspen and Paris. If I had to keep track of how much he traveled, I might as well be an air-traffic controller."

Nate shifted in his seat. "Where was his wife during all of this?"

"I'm not her keeper, either, man."

"What do you know about the kid named Melvyn?"

"The smart-aleck nerd who thinks he's a gangster?"

"That one."

"Harmless." He gaped at Nate. "You lookin' at him, too?" He started laughing. "He and his rapper posse. Little punks." Still chuckling, he hid his face, shaking his head.

"How frequently did you see him?"

"He mowed the lawn and hung out. A lot."

"Who was he visiting?"

"He was like the house pet, man. He just came around when he wanted. They liked his company."

"Who is they?"

"Preston and Blaine."

"And Blaine is ... who, to you?"

Juanito looked defiant. "You gonna have to ask me a question. I ain't volunteerin' nothin', man. I'm no snitch."

"Even when kids are involved, right?" Nate looked away, casually.

Juanito's gaze hardened. "What's that supposed to mean?"

Nate pounded his fist on the table. "Hey, I'm asking the questions! You're wasting my time. You got nothing to tell me except you live in a house where a cut-off finger was found and you got no idea who put it there? And I seen you men with a kid hangin' around who don't belong to none of you? How about I hold you overnight, so you can think all this over?"

"Hold me for what?"

"I'm not sure, but you could be a danger to society, or something. At best a danger to a little colored kid."

"It ain't me you need to be talking to, it's the other dude owns the house."

"Ah, so now you're ready to talk?"

Juanito nodded, looking reluctant. He described how Blaine creeped him out, how he always felt that he had to stick around when Melvyn was there, because something didn't feel right.

Nate slanted his eyes at Juanito. "Did you ever tell his mother or father? Grown men, interested in a little black boy."

Juanito corrected, "Grown important men—writers. Producers. I don't know anything, really. I just felt like I had to protect the punk."

"And you were hired as what ... an actor?" Nate asked.

"No. Personal Assistant."

"What is that? Like a butler? You help him put on his clothes or something?"

"Personal stuff. Preston had a lot on his plate. He was writing, teaching, grading papers. You name it, he did it. A novel. A play. A movie. A television series. The arrangement was that I would keep the place tidy and drive him places, and I had a room there whenever I needed it."

"Okay, so he had his hands everywhere. Were they ever on you? Which one was his bitch. You or Sherry?"

Although Nate's elbows were on the table, he was fast enough to evade Juanito's swipe, right before Devon's chokehold restrained him.

"Hey, you've got quite a temper there, haven't you? Note to self, Nate. Temper, temper. That's the kind of anger that can snap and kill someone, then get rid of the body."

Juanito looked Nate straight in the eye.

Nate glanced at Devon. "Let's step outside for a sec. Let him calm down."

As the two men left the room, Juanito slumped in his chair, rubbing his forehead slowly, speaking in Spanish:

"No hice nada, cuño. No me vas a pegar con esta mierda, te digo. No me jodes, maricón. No hice nada. Que te dije, cavrón."

It was obvious to Lula, sitting behind the one-way window, that English was his first language. Cubans tended to speak quickly, but his pace was slower and she had no problem understanding him.

As Nate and Devon joined her at the wall behind the one-way glass, she told them what Juanito had just said about pinning something on him when he hadn't done anything.

Nate asked Lula what she thought.

"You asked me to translate. That's all I can give you." Nate looked at Devon, shaking his head.

"Don't tell me you don't have a woman's intuition about this guy. Is he good, bad, or ugly?"

"Well, he's not ugly. In fact, he's good looking, which isn't too bad, is it?" Lula smiled.

Devon and Nate sarcastically nodded to each other.

"He's not as dumb as he looks. You see him bringing up everybody else as a potential suspect?" Nate asked Devon.

"Yep. He's pretty calculating. He didn't snitch, but he snatched names out of thin air when he needed to, didn't he? He dropped the dime without actually dropping it, saying, 'I'm not gonna tell you about whatever ....'"

"Which was telling us just the same." Nate huffed. The men looked at each other. They had their man. "Watch us bust him. We'll tangle him up in his own web." Nate snarled.

Devon spoke up. "Who's talking about more than one finger around here? We've told everyone to keep it on the down low."

They looked at each other, then at Lula.

"I'm not saying I did, but I could have told Melvyn's mother after I took him home. I might have, accidentally. I know we talked about the one found at the house. I do recall that. I apologize, but his mother wanted answers about what was going on. I didn't think I could just ignore the subject altogether."

She felt like an amateur. What had she said at Bebe's house? Had she divulged something she shouldn't have? And what was Melvyn's relationship to Juanito, that they would be discussing the matter, anyway?

"Let's wrap this up," Nate said, as he and Devon headed back inside the interrogation room.

Sitting at the one-way window, Lula watched the men weave a web of intrigue around Juanito. Initially, Nate put him on the defensive.

Nate asked him about his gang ties and whether cutting fingers was something with which he was familiar. Was it some kind of signal, or a warning?

"The only finger symbol I know is the middle finger," snapped Juanito.

Nate smiled, nodding. Then he asked what kind of drugs Juanito used recreationally.

"Viagra works for me." Juanito added that he could go for hours on that, get all the sex he wanted.

"Except Sherry, right?"

"You asking for me, or for yourself? She doesn't like old men, just so you know."

Nate's face registered a tinge of honest surprise, even regret, at Juanito's words. He recovered quickly.

"'Cuz she's into Richard, right? Did you know they were seeing each other?"

"Seeing isn't ... you know," muttered Juanito.

"Believing?" Nate and Devon looked at each other. "So, even though you and Sherry aren't into each other, you look a little jealous of her relationship with Richard."

Juanito shook his head, saying that she could do what or who she wanted to.

"Because you're doing someone else, too, right? Presumably a woman."

"Why are you sniffin' at my crotch, man?"

Nate smiled, looking at Devon for support.

"I'm a detective. Trying to understand who you are in relation to what's been going on. Just trying to figure out if you discriminate in who you associate with, that's all."

"Look. I'm a pretty boy, but I'm not into men. I don't sleep around, either. I got my pick of women. But I know each of their situations. I don't dip my stick just anywhere, you know what I mean?"

"Well, that's good to hear. So, you're not gay. You don't sleep around. You don't cut off people's fingers and you don't do drugs, or sell them, I presume."

"You presume all the above, or that I don't sell drugs?" Juanito leaned back in his chair, looking up at Nate.

"Well, I was listing the different crimes you'd be involved in if you lived a Marielito life—you know, the imaginary one that I've created for you."

"Right. Imaginary. So dream on, Mr. Dick." Juanito folded his arms and looked bored.

When asked about his tattoos, he explained that he had been young and dumb. As his posse had started thinning out due to killings and incarcerations, he'd backed out, gracefully, and come to Louisiana, where he couldn't be found.

"So, you're hiding out in Nakadee. You know how to hide money, too, right?"

Juanito's face registered just a trace of alarm.

"We did some forensic snooping after we met him at the house and we came up with some interesting bank records showing transfers, *after* Mardi Gras, when Preston was seen for the last time." Nate spoke to Devon, as if Juanito weren't in the room.

"Well, he claims to be his personal assistant." Devon responded.

"I'm not sure daily transfers are part of the duties of a valet. Plus they're going to one account. In the Seychelles."

"Say what?" Devon mocked.

"One of those off-the-beaten-track island countries with ten people but 100,000 bank accounts."

Juanito declared that he had no knowledge of any transfers.

"So, is that what you and the Missy were doing? Working for Preston, living at his home, playing house, with him as the daddy?"

Juanito said he knew nothing.

Nate smiled, crossing his arms smugly.

"Well, well, what do we have here? A little bit of sweat? Devon, go turn up the air conditioning. Our guest is hot."

"No hice nada, cuño."

"Yeah, whatever. You're in America now, wetback. You've got a lot of nerve." Nate grabbed Juanito by his shirt, and put his face close to his, spitting in his face. "We didn't ask you to come here and peddle your gang shit in this neck of the woods."

He pushed Juanito back into his chair, then walked around slowly, drumming his fingers along the table.

"We're a small town, and we like it that way. Why, here in our town, our bankers know their customers, and they know the police, too, and it doesn't take much to get information from them. So, what were those five transfers about, the day after Fat Tuesday? Or should I ask Sherry more questions?"

Juanito glared at Nate. "Do what you need to do, Mr. Dick."

"What? You're not surprised how quickly Sherry 'fessed up?" Nate let that sink in before he continued, blithely, "It's amazing what people tell you when they're in pain. We had a visit together at the hospital. She said you two had the run of the place. Blaine was always in his section of the house. Y'all barely saw him. It was like y'all had the whole place to yourselves. Naturally, you had access to your boss's computers. After all, you were working for him."

Juanito looked perplexed, though still defiant.

"Are you a green-card holder, or are you privileged enough to be a United States citizen?"

"You askin' to be racist, or you got a point to make?" Juanito shot back.

"Racist? Me? When I got Black Charlie here as my ace detective?"

"He don't look black to me."

"Creole. Mutt. Whatever. Do he look like a white boy to you?" Nate rolled his eyes. "Do you know what a good 'ol boy network is, in these here parts of the country? We got ourselves some gangs, too. Only they wear hoods. You messin' with a pretty thing like Sherry. She's no match for you, *hombre*. You know where she comes from?"

Juanito then surprised them all with his revelations about Sherry and her drug addictions. Even Lula's eyes widened as she listened.

"That so?" Nate's eyes hardened for an instant, though his smile didn't leave his face. "Who doesn't toke a bit uh weed, every now and then?"

Crossing his arms, Nate had the upper hand in this chess game of wits. "If that's all she's taking."

Juanito stared ahead.

"And you're the supplier." Nate added.

"No, man."

"That right? Who is he, then?"

"Snitchin' ain't my style, and I'm not even sure that Richard dude is her supplier, anyway, so I can't say nothin'."

Picking up the reference, Nate asked, "Why do you know so much about him?"

"Do I need to get a lawyer, so he can listen to your *mierda*? You're wasting my time. You got nothing on me except that I worked for a gay dude. And they can marry now, so get over it."

"We'll stop it here, then, Mr. Marielito. So where will you be over the next couple of weeks, in case we want to call you in for another friendly chat?"

"Here and there, maybe everywhere."

"Don't you venture too far, unless it's to a place where you'll be staying permanently. In other words, let us know if you're leaving town."

"That an order?"

"A request."

"Well, then. I'll see if I can remember it." Juanito stood and smoothed out his shirt and jeans.

"We'll be checking your accounts. Bet on it," Nate volleyed back. "Oh, yeah. Another thing: please buy a car that we like, okay? So when we seize it, I can drive it."

He motioned with his head for Juanito to leave.

Juanito did as instructed, slowly, with deliberation, as if making a statement.

Lula watched Nate and Devon leave the interrogation room and stood up, ready to leave her post.

Devon stepped in front of her, blocking her path.

"How's your new man?" he quipped, looking down at her.

"He's fine."

"You didn't waste any time."

Devon wanted a confrontation. Thankfully, Nate called him over the public address system.

"Devon. I need your help, here."

"To be continued," Devon threatened. "I'm not gonna let you off so easily."

Startled by the comment, Lula was holding back to let him get out of the door first when Nate entered, pushing him backwards gently, closing all three of them in the small viewing room.

"The lawn mower kid has two mommies, and both want to be present during the interview," Nate told Devon.

"Where's their attorney?" Devon asked.

"AWOL. They were told not to worry, and that he didn't need to be there because the boy's not a suspect. I spoke to his mother earlier today."

"So this is in *my* lap, now? Gee. Thanks, Nate."

"That's why you get paid the big bucks." Nate joked. "One more thing. Remember, the chief knows this boy's father, Tyrell, who is out there somewhere bringing big money to this town. The chief wants to remain neutral, and out of the picture as much as possible, you hear?"

Lula watched Devon trot toward the high-pitched voice that was ringing through the halls.

As Lula rounded the corner, trailing Devon and Nate, she saw an exchange between a short white woman wagging her finger, and Melvyn's mother, who looked down at her, smiling.

"I got just as much a right as you to be here," the shorter woman said.

Nate glanced at Devon as if to say, "You see?"

Tyrell, who stood between the women, was 5′ 10," dark-skinned, with chiseled features: thick lips, cleft chin, and large, soft, doe-like eyes that were now flashing with anger. He wore a short-cropped Afro, rounded on all sides. His pressed jeans and blue-and-white flowered shirt gave him the look of a Caribbean visitor rather than someone from rural Nakadee.

He stepped between the two women and said to the shorter one, "Olive, why don't you go wait over there, and let me talk to my man, Nate, here, and we'll settle this."

Olive backed up two paces, while Devon stood in front of her. She was youthful, about 5′ 3," her skin the same color as her name. She had wide-set eyes and dyed brunette hair that showed hints of flashy red, all of it held in a tight bun. Her eyebrows were painted in broad arches that gave her a look of constant surprise. The lip liner, penciled just outside the line of her lips, gave her a Kabuki theater look. Her hips and thighs were encased in white pants, taut against her smock with its two large pockets and playful design of panda bears, a uniform that seemed out of place, given the havoc she was causing.

"Now you know the setting we're in, right ladies? So, let's talk this through like friends," Devon interjected.

"Friends?" Olive looked comical as she swished her head from side to side in denial, as if bobbing for something dangled in front of her.

"I will not have this woman thinking she has any authority over me. I am just as much a mother to her son as she is, and I damned sure won't be treated differently. I have the right to sit in on the interrogation with my husband."

Bebe turned to Devon, speaking firmly but quietly. "She may be his stepmother, but that does not a mother make, sir. She can remonstrate all she wants, but as long as I am alive, she will have no rights at all where my son is concerned, except to have him on the weekends when her husband is present."

She looked at the other woman, emphatically. "Yes, Olive. *Your* husband. You can have him. I do not know the man that you're married to, honestly, so don't you fret. The minute you wheeled and dealed to steal him from me on his hospital bed I figured it was not only his prostate that needed rehabilitating, but his mind. You two deserve each other." She laughed, her hand waving gently in the air. "You can be his wife all you want to. I have no interest in him except for the role he plays in raising our son."

She looked at Tyrell, then back at Olive. "*Our* son. Not *your* son. This is an interview where only his natural parents should be present."

"I don't care what you figure about nothin'." Olive said.

"But you do, Olive, and that's the problem. You want to be my stand-in to my son, but guess what? I'm standing. Right here, and if I'm not, he has a grandmother in New Orleans."

Olive looked to Tyrell for help, taking a step back.

"I got a mind ...."

"Then stop there, because no—you don't," Bebe interrupted.

Tyrell jumped toward Olive to restrain her, while Bebe held her own elbows, her shoulders bouncing with laughter.

"Olive. You will not behave this way."

"Whose side are you on, Tyrell?" Olive was raising her voice. "You're going to let her disrespect your wife?"

Nodding her head, Bebe proclaimed, "The way you disrespected *his* wife three years ago?"

Tyrell spoke up. "Look, we're not going to waste the officers' time here to debate this any further." He looked at Olive. "Take a little walk. Go say hi to Melvyn outside."

He craned his neck to look out the door.

Lula followed his gaze and saw Melvyn outside talking and slapping hands with Juanito.

Olive started to leave, firing back at Bebe, "I have better values in my pinky than you do in your whole body."

"That's *your* pink color, not mine." Bebe retorted.

Olive walked out, the whole lobby transfixed as she raised her middle finger high in the air.

Next, Nate dropped a bombshell when he announced that neither woman would be allowed inside the room with Melvyn while he was being questioned.

"Excuse me?" Bebe looked at Nate, cocking her head.

Tyrell pleaded with her. "Look, Bebe, let's just let the police do their work."

"So you gonna feed him to the wolves here? Just how is he going to feel with a bunch of men in the room?"

Tyrell looked at her. "We need Melvyn to feel comfortable, and he doesn't need to have to choose between his two mothers, and be scared of making Olive or me feel bad because he might choose you, and we don't need any outbursts or cat fights."

"Why don't we ask Dr. Logan here to sit with him?" Bebe asked Nate.

"Let me ask the chief," Nate muttered. "It's a bit unusual."

"Yeah, well, so are the circumstances," Tyrell said. "Our son might have information about a potential murder, and, truthfully, I just want to get this over with. So, how about it? We can listen in from the other room. It will make things easier all around."

Bebe looked to Nate. "How can I protect his interests if I'm not in the room with him? They already told the attorney not to come, against my wishes. Sure looks like a setup to me."

Tyrell shook his head in disagreement, and pointed to Lula. "Nate tells me this woman here is a forensic anthropologist, Bebe. She got no beef with nobody. She'll be there in the room, to make him feel calm n'all."

Lula stared at the group, confounded as to how she had become ensnared in a family drama like this. Bebe's once-friendly face looked very stern, now.

"Are you suggesting that just because she's black and I'm black that somehow she can stand in my shoes? Because, no disrespect to her, that's absurd. She can't stand in my shoes any more than that wife of yours can."

Tyrell looked at Bebe imploringly.

The station's double doors slid open, heralding Olive's return. She was rubbing her nose with the back of her hand, then said defiantly, "What web is she spinning now, Tyrell?" She sniffed.

Tyrell snapped his fingers, telling her to stop.

Olive did as she was told.

He turned to his ex-wife. "Let's get this over with, right, Bebe? Let's just get this over so we can move on. So our son can move on."

"This won't be over, Tyrell, until our son is eighteen years old," Bebe snarled. "When he doesn't have to be nice to *that one there*, out of respect for you."

Tyrell moved a step closer, trying to reason with her, but was stopped by Bebe's hand.

"Look. There's nothing you need to say to me. At all. You said it when you picked up that virus over there from the hospital."

Bebe looked at Lula, shook her head and chuckled. "Lord, have mercy. Don't leave your man in a hospital where female nurses have to wait on him. Don't let him have money, either. He went in for prostate cancer, and come out with a different disease. No tellin' what kinda 'recovery' process she put him through. Just look at her."

The room did as she commanded, and Bebe laid it on even thicker. "He'll throw his money at you, for a time. But it ain't gonna last. He'll get homesick for a real woman. Someone with more *savoir faire* in one nappy hair follicle than you have in all your DNA. You're a little Barbie wind-up toy to him—well, I'd say more like a Cabbage Patch doll, or a Smurf: country and dumb."

Bebe turned toward Lula and Nate. "You go ahead. Just record it for me. I'll listen to it later. I would just as soon not be in the same room with her."

"*Bitch.*" Olive uttered in staccato.

Bebe turned to Olive. "That's a fine piece of vocabulary, there, Ms. Turrets. That puts you at about elementary-school level. Did you learn it as a Candy-Stripper—I mean, Striper?"

"I'm a fully licensed registered nurse."

"Clap, clap, good for you. You rehabilitated one patient, at least. Besides, I know all I need to know about you, just by looking at you." Bebe looked her up and down. "And it takes all of a millisecond to define what you are."

Lula could see that Nate was sympathetic toward Melvyn's mother, though he didn't back down on his decision.

"Ms. Armstrong, if you'd like to, I can get a transcript or a recording of the interview. You can read or hear whatever he says down the road, and we do have Ms. Logan here as a witness."

"Dr. Logan, Detective. Doctor," Bebe corrected him.

Bebe looked over at Lula, who smiled wanly, their eyes holding each other for an instant. Lula felt Bebe's silent entreaty to watch over her son, and understood the implications of her gaze. These white men in their blue suits, in this neck of the woods, would not protect their people—*black* people. That much was sure.

Lula looked down as Bebe said, "I'll go get my son. I'll be waiting in my car."

"I'll drop him off!" Tyrell yelled after her. "No need to wait. I'll bring him to you."

Bebe stopped, turning to look at her ex-husband with a tired smile on her face. "Thanks."

Tyrell and Olive followed Nate.

Lula moved along the station's hallway to find people already arranging the chairs in the interrogation room.

"Let's see them interviewing skills, Devon," Nate said.

Devon's eyes widened. "You want *me* to do the interview?" His fingertips lightly touched his chest.

Nate grimaced, theatrically. "Well, you think *I'm* going to, after that out there?"

11
CROSS PURPOSES

Tuesday, March 22nd, 2:00 p.m.

It had been four days since the Hot Sauce Festival. Although Richard had had three bouquets of flowers delivered, one yesterday and two today, Sherry hadn't made any effort to thank him, or even acknowledge their receipt.

Back when things had been going well between them, Richard and Sherry would try to find movie characters that personified their relationship. Rhett and Scarlett were too conventional and old-fashioned. Richard suggested Spencer Tracy and Katherine Hepburn, but Sherry didn't know who they were. Bella and Edward, of the vampire love saga, were closer—full of danger—but Richard didn't like that Bella had another love interest. When Richard suggested Sid and Nancy, the ill-fated punk-druggie duo, Sherry took offense.

"Did Nancy go to college? I'm in college. I don't know about you. They were musicians, and I don't play an instrument."

"Not true." Richard smiled. "You play the one that matters. And I could hear that song over and over and over again."

They loved to wrestle to solve their disputes. She would try to wriggle out of his clutches when his head, arms, hands, calves, and thighs held her by any means necessary, and, inevitably, they would end up naked. As they continued their game, instead of pulling away, their bodies would find each other with a ferocity that left them both exhausted and sweaty. Sex with Richard beat going to the gym, Sherry would often remark.

Their sex was dangerous. Addictive. No matter how much she wanted to stay away from him, she always came back for more. They usually met each other one weekday and on the weekend, if her schedule allowed. Nobody knew they were lovers—not even her closest friends, who knew only that the couple liked to dance together at the club.

If Richard didn't see or talk with her for more than three days, he would go crazy with worry. Manic. Like now. When things had started to go sour, even before Mardi Gras, Sherry had started putting restrictions on seeing him at school or in town. When she learned that he'd been following her, she called and told him to stop, adding that he could text her, but not phone.

After Sherry's public repudiation of him at the fair, Richard seemed to be wandering through life. He drove everywhere and nowhere, confusing dates, times, and places that he was scheduled to pick up and deliver various and sundry items. The Go-Lo Chinese Restaurant owner warned him that he was skating on thin ice. If he continued to miss pickups of their used cooking oil and butcher scraps, they'd find somebody else to dispose of them. That threat was worth heeding, because Richard always received a free meal to go whenever he dropped by for a pickup.

His rendering business paid the most amount of money for the least work, as it combined two jobs. He made his rounds, loading up carcasses from the different independent butchers and poultry businesses looking to dispose of their animal waste, and dumped the debris in the dung piles at the poultry plant: dessert for the flies.

He had met Sherry at Club Bayou, a local Nakadee hangout, where she'd been slumming with her classmates. Like most of the college girls there, she and her friends danced in packs under gaudy strobe and neon lights with music so loud that it made your body quiver. The girls' dresses clung to their contours, ending just a quarter-inch below the buttocks, thighs in full view of their furtively captive audience.

Sherry and her coterie of nineteen- and twenty-year olds danced on an imaginary catwalk, their fists accenting their gyrations to the music. This was one of the best times to be young, and Richard, ten years older, wanted a piece of it—especially Sherry.

He frequented Club Bayou alone, wondering why guys went together to scout for women when it reduced the odds of each hooking up with someone. Usually he ordered a shot of Dewar's Scotch or a Hurricane, then sat on the periphery, or stood against the wall, where the lights barely reached, obscuring the voyeurs' and wallflowers' faces. Sherry had caught his eye a couple of times, and he would inch closer to her group whenever they showed up.

He had figured out when she went to the club, predicting her arrival within a seven-minute margin. He dressed for the occasion the night he decided to approach her to dance. He wore a silk T-shirt that showed his muscles, black designer pants, and blond cowboy boots. He'd doused himself with cologne, knowing that its scent would disappear with the streams of sweat he'd shed dancing that night. For extra measure, he pumped two sprays of cologne on his hands, rubbing them together and running them through his short-cropped curly hair.

On the night they met, he downed three shots of tequila to give him the courage to ask her to dance. She was standing near the dance floor with her friends when he approached to ask whether she was in the market for a better dance partner.

They hit if off immediately, in a nice way (or so he thought). They danced together for the rest of the night, with great physicality, each mimicking the other, so much so that people started to circle around them, watching, whooping, and clapping.

The performers had been given a hero's welcome afterwards. Richard felt like a king, buying everyone in her clique two rounds of drinks. He was ecstatic, feeling like the luckiest man in the world.

The magnetism they had on the dance floor spilled over into her bedroom. Richard adored her body, her scent, her sweat, the firmness of her legs. However well-mannered she was in school, her decorum disappeared when she was with him. He was astounded at how much she yielded control to him in the bedroom, considering he was a mere laborer and she was a future university graduate.

Had he been a braggart, Richard would have boasted that he needed to be with a woman only once before she was stuck on him for life. He wasn't a selfish lover, as he believed he could always be guaranteed a bedmate if he pleased his woman. The effort was worth it, as his happiness was dependent upon being in a woman's company. He subscribed to the belief that men really were *asshats*. They spent their time harassing, competing, and challenging each other to do the stupidest things to prove a senseless point. That macho shit that he was so good at wasn't really all that much fun.

After their sleeping together had become a habit, so had his dependence on Sherry for his happiness. She'd been the most decent thing in his life since his mother's death. Sure, they had some growing to do, together, but his mind was pretty set on doing whatever it took to win her over.

Like doing her assignments for her.

He helped her study for exams, edited her essays, and wrote coverage for her script-reading assignments. He joked that he was practically earning her degree. She would meet him at the Club Bayou, where she'd give him money. Afterwards, he would email her the completed assignments and give her the recreational drugs that she couldn't get from Juanito. Nobody cared about getting caught for making drug transactions at Club Bayou. The police chief's brother owned it.

Right now, Richard knew his momma must be scolding him for his behavior toward Sherry, and it was justified. He had grown increasingly frustrated with her, beginning to feel like her lackey, or her "slave-boy," as she called him.

Taking a deep breath and releasing the air slowly, he picked up the phone to call her. He wanted to see how she was doing.

How was her arm?

"Itchy," she replied.

How long would she have to wear her arm cast?

"I would never do anything to hurt you, you know that, right?"

"I suppose."

"I don't hit women."

"Don't I know it, even when she wants you to," she chuckled softly.

Unsure as to where Sherry had developed an appetite for borderline-kinky sex, Richard would indulge her fantasies (if he could keep a straight face). He thought the games were stupid, and would laugh uncontrollably, cupping his hands over his privates and flinching while accepting her riding stick's light blows.

When they reversed roles, she was always disappointed that he didn't reciprocate the pain she meted out to him. He thought it was silly. She would get annoyed, while he justified his unwillingness to take the games seriously.

Today, a couple minutes of suggestive phone talk had opened the door for Richard to visit. When Sherry invited him into her house later that afternoon, no one would have guessed that the couple had seemed sworn enemies the last time they'd been seen together in public.

He scooped her up in his arms and swung her around, careful not to jostle her injured arm. He kissed her all over, his tongue licking her skin, hungry for her. Setting her on the sofa, he sat on his knees, burrowing his head in her breasts until she pushed him off gently.

"Do you have ...."

"Girl, course I got it. I thought you liked foreplay. I know when the time is right."

She straightened her good arm and locked it, holding him at bay. "Not that. The work."

He was motioning to kiss her, until she blocked him again.

"Work? What you mean by work?"

"The coverage?" she snapped.

"Oh. I thought I'd never see you again."

Sherry looked annoyed.

"You're kidding, right? Not one of them?"

"Not a one."

"Richard, you promised! You promised! Why didn't you call and tell me you weren't going to help me? Now, I'll have to ask for another week."

"Well, baby, your arm is broken, so I'm figuring they're gonna cut you some slack."

She pounded her fist into the couch.

They both watched it spring back gently.

"Hey, wait a sec. It was you who wouldn't pick up the phone," he said defensively. He leaned back, balancing on his haunches. "I figured your boy would help you, seein' as you chose him over me. I figured he was smarter. Hell, he had to be. He's educated, right? Unlike me. I can write your essays for forensic anthropology and literature, although I'm not sure that Tolstoy really was Anna Karenina, but that ain't here nor there. Go to your man and see if his pretty-boy looks can help him think pretty for you, too."

The standoff lasted an eternity, as each combatant's hopes took a turn for the worse.

For Sherry, completing the assignments would gain her Blaine's respect for her skills.

As for Richard, he wanted Sherry to respect him. He was as bright as any student at the university, and he wanted her to see it. Recognize it.

This was a slow process, gaining her trust in his intellect. He'd ruminated over their future together, resolving to find a full-time job at the poultry factory and take care of her and their three babies (two boys, one girl). They would write movies together. He knew way more than Sherry did about them. His momma said he could be anything he wanted to if he put his mind to it. He was going to put his mind to "wifing" Sherry.

His mother had been his best friend, teacher, and fellow explorer, who gave him hands-on instruction about biology, plant life, and the healing qualities of herbs that grew wild in the forest that surrounded them. Sometimes, when his daddy was gone on the road, and the night was clear, he and his mom would sleep under the stars and she'd teach him astronomy. He could find Orion's belt and Pegasus, his favorites, and became intimately familiar with the Greek and Babylonian fables for which the images in the sky were named.

Those were the happiest years of his life. His dearly departed mother, obsessed with learning, taught him subjects that he would never have learned in a regular class. They would pore over all kinds of subject matter together: science, animal husbandry, American literature, Western European history, and politics.

With his mother gone, and no one looking after him, he realized how much he sought affirmation that he had something of value to offer. He needed only one person to accept him, and had thought it just might be Sherry. Until now.

"I can't believe you're doing this!"

"What? Asserting myself? What the hell! Am I your slave boy?"

"No, but you *are* a drug dealer."

He wasn't sure where she was going with this conversation, but he wasn't finding it humorous.

"That's a great yarn you're spinning. Better hope it doesn't tie you up and choke you." He had put his pants back on and was tying his tennis shoes.

"Do you think you're the only person in Nakadee with shit? You just made it a lot easier to get my stuff from Juanito."

Juanito.

"By the way, Richard: news alert. I'm seeing Juanito now. Yeah, the wetback. You and I stand no chance together, because you're going nowhere. You'll spend your life here at Nakadee, getting old and fat, but still lusting after college students. There's a word for people like you. It's *loser*."

His eyes looked vacant as he stared at her.

"I will yell rape in five seconds if you don't get the hell out." Scooting to the edge of the sofa, her injured arm hanging in the air, Sherry grabbed his shirt and threw it toward the door.

He crawled after it on his knees, shook it out, and stuck one arm into a shirtsleeve.

"If you dare call me, approach me, or even look at me, I'll be calling campus security and will get you fired. Then you can go back to your family business, shoveling chicken shit all day long. I used you. That's about all you can brag about, Richard, 'cuz that's all I got from you. You're a friggin' low-life, dude."

"You're not the only one with stories to tell, Missy. Your threats mean nothing to me." He shrugged on his shirt, smiling. "I suspect you're upset about something I caught onto, right? In fact, how the hell did you even get into college? From the likes of your writing, you barely passed middle school."

She stood up, pointing with her free finger toward the door, like the ghost from Christmas past. Silent.

"Okay," Richard said. "I'll go now and leave you to run with your little criminal friends. I'll be watching you, and at the drop of a dime, I'll do me some talkin', too. You go 'head. You try to spin your yarn. Somehow I got the feelin' that *I* might be the one they'll believe."

She glowered defensively, her trembling lips betraying her. Pulling her blouse over her injured arm, she walked toward him.

"You're knee deep into it, baby, but you're not smart enough to know it." Richard backed out the door, facing her as he spoke.

"Out." She put all of her weight into her uninjured arm and pushed him hard, making him stumble backwards.

He recovered, grabbing the wrought-iron rail on her small landing.

"How about I push you in *your* chest?" he challenged, showing his own pique. "You think you can just push any man because you're a woman? Women get their asses whipped, too, and some of them—like you—deserve it. This is equal opportunity America, now, Sherry. You can't go touching people like they're your property."

She looked more formidable in her rage, taunting him from her porch. "Yeah, right. I'll miss your broken-down truck. By the way, did I tell you that you stink? You always liked my perfume, right? I didn't wear it for you. That was for me, to mask your stench. I only use Irish Spring soap when you're around. You taught me a new word. Fecund. That's you. Well, here's a rhyme, Mister MC Rapper. You're not only fecund. You're my sloppy seconds. Besides, you're not even a rapper. You might have written the rap for the SwampBoyz, but it was pretty sorry. You're not really good at being original."

"You're going to lecture *me* about being original? Bitch, you better step back into your house—"

"—before you what? What? Finish it, you cretin."

Richard's smile disappeared. His temple was throbbing as she lay into him, her voice growing louder.

"I was only slumming, being with you. You're not my property. You're nobody's property. You could die in a ditch and no one would miss you."

The stares they exchanged were silent salvos of war.

"How about we continue where I left off?" He bolted up the steps. "Come here," he coaxed, grabbing Sherry. "How 'bout I break your other arm, you stupid, idiotic witch."

Sherry was backing up into her open door, but Richard jammed his shoulder against it, using his body as a doorstop, preventing her from getting inside.

She spoke in a low voice, grunting. "I will yell so loud your mother will come outta hell to kick your ass! Now you get out of here! Now!" She stamped her feet. "You bastard! Who do you think you are! Get the hell outta here! Don't step foot on my doorstep again. You're dead to me. I'm gonna call the police if you don't leave! Now! Do you hear me? DEAD!"

"D-E-D Dead?" Richard taunted her.

Windows started opening in her apartment building.

"You okay, Sher?" a young woman's voice called from above.

"I'm just getting rid of a stray dog. I'm fine." Sherry shouted into the heavens toward her neighbor.

Richard strode down her walkway to the sidewalk, then turned back, speaking softly, still smirking.

"Oh yeah, if you're looking for your homework, Melvyn's mom has it. I had it in my car, and gave it to her when she picked him up." He leaned toward her. "I knew we was comin' to this. The beginning of your end."

Sherry shut the door loudly, while he walked back toward it, speaking audibly so she could hear behind it: "You watch that pretty back of yours—I see it in crosshairs. Mark of the beast." He walked away, laughing. "We'll see who the criminal is, won't we, Sherry!"

Richard suddenly felt satisfied that he was stronger than Sherry realized. He'd been alone before. Most of his life. He could handle it. Sherry was a whore, who would give her body to anyone if it could help her. What was he thinking, to want to be with her? He had proven to himself that he could have done well in college without the burden of having to fraternize with kids whose only pastime was getting women drunk enough to have sex with them.

Sherry needed to learn a thing or two. And he would be her teacher, whether she liked it or not.

Bet on that. Smell, my ass. He laughed, and strode away whistling a ditty only he knew.

4:00 p.m.

The chief had copies made of the keys to Preston's place and gave them to Wally to do some snooping. Nate had pointed out the house, shared photos and backgrounds of the people who lived there, and told him to keep an eye on them.

It had been the perfect storm when Sherry had broken her arm at the festival and Wally had the chance to see all the players. Something was up, and his job was to figure out what. He looked for cars in the garage. Empty.

Blaine. Where'd he get a name like that? Wally had done a little research.

Blaine Dworkin wasn't a celebrity, but there was enough information about him in the middle pages of the *Daily Variety* and the *Hollywood Reporter* to make him appear to be legit. He'd been born in Rochester, New Hampshire, with a French-Canadian mother and a father who was a blue-collar worker.

He'd attended the University of New Hampshire as an undergraduate, and received a Masters in Literature at the University of Massachusetts. After graduating, he moved to the Fairfax area of Los Angeles and had been the only tenant in a nice bungalow. He'd worked on a then hugely popular children's television series that spawned the next generation of film stars. Four years ago he had posted on a blog that he was tired of the politics of filmmaking and just wanted to write. Shortly after, he moved to Nakadee for a quieter life.

Wally doubted Nate's story about the black kid, Melvyn, who, allegedly had keys to Preston's home to water the plants when Preston was away. Nate said that it didn't make sense for people like Sherry and her Latin lover to also have keys to come and go as they pleased.

Inside, Wally noticed an Oakland A's baseball cap at the foot of the stairs. He picked up the green-and-yellow cap and placed it on his head. Perfect fit.

He walked over to the refrigerator, retrieved a plastic container, and looked inside to find salsa waiting for him to devour. Smelling it, he set it down and opened every cabinet before he found tortilla chips. He sat on the counter next to the refrigerator, his eyes scanning the kitchen as he finished the salsa.

Twenty minutes later, he meandered upstairs, opened a door in the hallway, and found himself in a bedroom, obviously inhabited by a female. Pondering the propensity of women to make things pretty, he inhaled the feminine aromas that permeated the room. His eyes were drawn to the canopy bed, whose frilly, flowered duvet matched the curtains.

Inside an expansive closet, he found clothes hanging in dry-cleaning bags and stacks of shoeboxes lined up in a row. Standing on his toes, he carefully pulled out a box from the middle of one stack, which tumbled to the ground, emptying its contents: two-dozen micro-cassettes. The small surface area on the face of the cassettes had cursive writing: Melvyn 15, Melvyn 22, Melvyn 3, Melvyn 4, and the like.

He pulled a step stool from a dark corner of the closet, placed it solidly on the floor, and stood on it to retrieve other shoeboxes. DVDs. Labeled in the same numbering system: Melvyn 3, Melvyn 4, Melvyn 22, Melvyn 15, etc. The two boxes were companions to each other: one visual, one audio.

DVDs in hand, Wally moved through Preston's study and found a computer. He took a handkerchief out of his pocket, touched the space bar, and inserted a DVD. As he watched, the screen showed videos of black children speaking excitedly, simultaneously, practicing a rap tune, stumbling over it, and laughing. It was a Jon-P rap, and the boys were arguing about the proper way to say "nigger."

An adult voice could be heard in the background.

"It's 'nigga', like—"

Melvyn's voice overpowered the cacophony of sounds: "No, it's like 'liga,' in ligament. Boojay don't know jack. Nigga. Liga-ment. Ligga-nigga, but the first has *one g*, not two."

No faces were visible. Just chests and gangly torsos.

Nubile.

Innocent.

On film.

PART II

THE DISCONNECTED

12

BEBE

Tuesday, March 22nd, 7:00 p.m.

The last thing Lula needed was a night out on the town. She was tired, depressed, and wanted some time alone. Her emotions were all over the place.

When Melvyn's mother called to invite her to dinner, she wanted to beg off, but knew it might be perceived poorly. She needed all the friends she could get, so she agreed to meet Bebe at one of the Louisiana French restaurants, where couples ate in secluded booths.

The women settled at a table for two in the middle of the floor, where there was more light.

A white bus boy set two cold glasses of water on the table, while a waiter hurried by, tossing out, "I'll be back with your drink order and the menus in a sec, ladies."

Bebe smiled at Lula as they sat down. "Perfect. We can get to know each other better."

They began by talking about fraternities and sororities, a Black-American tradition, particularly at historic black colleges.

Bebe shook her head. "I thought of pledging Eta Kappa, at LSU, but I just didn't really feel it, you know? It's a great social networking organization, but I just didn't have the muscle for that and my studies. I was hell-bent on getting out of there, honestly. I did join the Sorority of Jilted Wives—but you know that already."

Lula looked at her, confused, and Bebe added, "You know—my story with my ex."

Lula looked down at the table. "Oh, that."

"Yes. That." Leaning forward, Bebe clasped her hands as she put her elbows on the table. "I want you to know that I do not believe in making a spectacle of myself. I usually hold my cards real close, but I'll be damned if I'm gonna let a piece of white trash dictate my affairs. If I wanted to take dictation, I'd be a secretary, you know?"

Lula smiled. "I heard that," she voiced in agreement.

"It's all water under the bridge. But she's still playing the game. I got out of the game the minute I realized I was married to a dick, not a man." Bebe leaned across the table toward Lula. "I was devastated for all of ten minutes, mainly for my boy's sake."

Lula shared how she was looking to settle down, but that her prospect would have to be quite special. This caused both women to laugh out loud. By the time a man was ready to settle down, Bebe pointed out, he was usually looking for a nurse, not a companion.

"You ever date outside your race?" she asked Lula.

"In college, when it was a novelty. Sure, I went on a date or two."

"White?"

"One was Armenian. He thought he was black. The other was a man ashamed of being black. So I include him, too."

"Let's face it. Most men don't really give a damn about race, as long as you got a red cherry." Bebe laughed. "Yeah, well, that little Olive, part-time nurse, full-time whore, she can have him. I guess there comes a time when a man loses his marbles and maybe they need to have lots of sex before that time arrives, so the craziness isn't passed on in his genes, or something. I don't know, but I'd like to know the ethics class she took as a nurse to learn her bedside manners. Bed-top manners, I should say. But enough about her."

Lula helped change the subject, asking, "Is Melvyn's father okay now? Why was he in the hospital, if I may ask?"

Bebe pursed her lips and reared back to tell the story. "Girl, he's fine. He just got back from Brazil, working on some venture to get natural gas here to Nakadee. There's only one pipeline in the whole area, and several factories need it. Like his father's poultry plant."

"His father owns one?"

Bebe nodded. "Well, it got bought out, but he's still in charge. Yeah. Tyrell's a chemical engineer. That's how we met."

"Have you been there? Brazil, I mean?"

"No. Carnival is too crazy for me. I can barely stand our Mardi Gras." She shook her head. "Can't handle the crowds. Melvyn loved it. His dad stayed a day or two later, and Melvyn and the bitch came back in time for Fat Tuesday."

The women sipped their drinks. Lula steered the conversation back to Bebe's husband. "So I take it you and your ex-husband are on speaking terms."

"We're both educated. Let's leave it at that. We can be civil, for Melvyn's sake."

"I hear you."

"It's his ignorant wife I don't get along with. You saw that. I just don't want her imposing herself in my affairs, that's all. Melvyn doesn't need any counsel from an ignoramus like her. She got Tyrell's thingy back working, so he's happy. Prostate cancer is no joke, apparently. I guess he was scared of death."

"I guess we all are, on some level."

Bebe took a sip of her drink. "So when he had the affair, the only thing I thought was—you'll be dead in no time, anyway, mo-fo. Have your fun. And I moved on. I said, 'Bebe, don't look back. Move forward. Move on.'"

"Yep." Lula waited for her to continue.

"You live in Nakadee?"

Lula nodded.

"Whereabouts? South or North uh the tracks?"

"North. The hood," Lula laughed.

"Girl, that ain't no hood."

"I don't mind it. I'm fine for now."

The women continued to talk, agreeing that they were both in a particular minority as black female scientists. Neither liked the prospect of working with people, preferring the clinical side of their work. Bebe agreed that she liked to use her brain more than her mouth, and wasn't quite a people person.

"I find that hard to believe," Lula said, then asked where she worked.

Their conversation was interrupted by the arrival of the food. The deep-brown barbecued ribs, packed high on the serving plate, looked enticing. Smoke emanated from the meat still bubbling with heat.

They ate quietly until Bebe looked at Lula awkwardly, hesitating a little while wiping her hands on a dry napkin. "Can I ask you a question, Miss Lula?"

"Sure."

Bebe gave her a half smile, contrite, yet demanding. "I'm concerned about my son and the police. You know."

"How's that?"

"Well, I'm just a bit afraid for him. If they aren't close to finding the killer, they might turn on him. I'd die if he ended up in a prison. Do you know how the investigation is going?"

"I don't know. You know I'm not really in on the investigation, right?"

"You sat in on Melvyn's interrogations, though."

"Well, actually, both Melvyn's and Juanito's—the Cuban—but I wasn't in the room for that one. The police invited me because I could translate if he spoke Spanish."

"Right." Bebe nodded, rolling her eyes as Lula rummaged for words.

"There's ... security in numbers, I guess, was the logic."

Bebe nodded again, meeting Lula's gaze. "Will they let us get our things back, or is the director's place sealed off?"

"I'm not sure. You'll have to call Captain Nate."

"Will do. Melvyn's father let him use his lawnmower and Melvyn wanted to drive it back home."

"Drive?" Lula raised her eyebrows.

"It doesn't go fast enough for Melvyn to imagine that he's really going anywhere. But he's anxious to get behind any wheel." Bebe chuckled. "Girl, you just don't know what it's like raising a boy in today's world. As a single mother, I have to let him grow up right, into a man. His dad's too busy being a muckety-muck with the pipeline project. There's a lot of pressure on him to deliver the goods."

"Do you even talk to each other?"

"Yeah. When we have to. I try to speak to him as little as possible. He's walking around like a white man, nowadays. They get that attitude, like they're the cock of the walk. But I also know that if he's successful, Melvyn will be set for life, so, contrary to appearances, I ain't mad at him."

"What does your husband have to do with the project?"

"Please." Lowering her head, Bebe leaned toward her, reaching across the table for dramatic effect. "My ex."

"Oops."

"Girl, don't pay it no mind. Well, he kinda thought of it. He was part of a group called *Les Bons Temps*—the Good Times. They own minority businesses."

Lula raised her eyebrows, nodding, her lips forming a congratulatory smile.

"Yeah ... the bastard started dreaming big after divorcing me, even though I told him he should try to get the certification. The poultry plant has been doing very well and it's grown in spades." Bebe grabbed a roll, tearing off a piece, picked up a knife and proceeded to butter the morsel.

"Now there are people who want to take it over from him. The police chief is rooting for his people to run with it, so things are pretty tense right now. The Congressman from Shreveport, the one at the festival, is trying to mediate. He understands that the money has to be shared, but last I heard, he wasn't of any help to Tyrell. He was giving in to the Mayor.

"Heads will roll if they get in his way," she laughed. "He wasn't a violent man, but most quiet black men harbor some form of rage inside that manifests in different ways."

"If Tyrell were gonna do it, he'd be smart about it, like he was in cheating on me." Bebe noshed on her roll, enjoying it.

"I hope you're joking," Lula said.

Bebe smiled. "His whore of a wife better pray I am, you mean. The trick is how he would do it. I guess he could throw some eggs at his enemies?"

Bebe laughed, then voiced her belief that white folk weren't going to let a black man be in charge of a multi-billion-dollar project anymore than the Republicans accepted the first Black President's post-inaugural invitation to the White House during his first term.

Bebe buttered another piece of bread and talked about the irony of black men jumping the broom "to ride a broomstick" at the direction of their new witchy white wives, "and, when it doesn't go right, the men can't handle it. Somehow they believe they're supposed to be accepted as white men, since they have their white women. They lose it when they see, time and time again, the white man still squashes their dreams. They get canned before retirement, or demoted.

"Melvyn's mess isn't helping things, either." Bebe shook her head as she reached for the bread basket, then looked at Lula. "Girl, now you gotta stop me, 'cuz do you know that I will get on a roll *and* a roll?"

They both burst into laughter.

"I have seriously been hogging the show—and the bread. I apologize. I guess I had a lot on my chest. Your turn. How is your week going?" she invited.

Although Lula was more than grateful for her neighbor Pomona's easygoing friendship, she had to admit that she enjoyed Bebe's company. They could communicate at the same level. But these were Southerners, she reminded herself, and she couldn't even begin to think about analyzing them.

13

MIRIAM

Three days earlier

After the dinner at Ambrose's house, his driver dropped off Mare and Matt at the downtown hotel where they were staying. She said goodnight to Matt and went to her room to call a taxi.

When she reached the house, she let herself out, unassisted, gave the driver a crisp hundred-dollar bill, and told him to return in 75 minutes, then waved him away.

The moon's glow lit her way like a spotlight as she hurried along the winding mosaic sidewalk to the side entrance of her husband's home. Or was he her ex-husband?

She was trying hard to maintain her cool, especially where her relationship with Matt was concerned. How much longer would Preston be alive before she could play the grieving widow and walk away with his millions? Boy, did that sound callous. But he deserved it.

Preston worked, churning out entertainment episode after episode in a frenzy of universally recognized creative genius. She was his partner in business, and a presumed heir to his estate, yet had been humiliated when he left her to live with a man in Louisiana.

She fumbled through her purse at the front door. Preston would be amused by her visit. She usually had to invite herself, as he had become a Southerner again, formal, and always busy, requiring that she schedule her visits.

Blaine's and Preston's home was a bastardization of a duplex. The business partners shared an office and a pool, but each had a separate walkway, with entrances on opposite sides of the house.

In keeping with the oddity of their arrangement, Preston's Portuguese-style abode faced East, while Blaine's "Tara"-like façade faced West. Each side had its own personality, merging into the infamous "Hollykook House."

Mare stepped inside, gently closing the door behind her, then stood still.

No floorboards creaked. No toilet gurgled. There were no signs of life. The house felt dead, all over.

Preston was dead. She knew it now.

She'd only been inside the house on three other visits to Nakadee, but this one was different.

When she turned on a table lamp, the light illuminated only the small area around it. She squinted, her eyes adjusting to the light. The living room furniture appeared to have been moved toward the center of the room. She knew that the police had searched for fingerprints. Someone must have cleaned up afterwards, without knowing where the furniture belonged.

She looked up at the large, sloping skylight through which the moon was shining down. During the day, the skylight cast the afternoon sunlight against the stained-glass windows of Preston's favorite room, the study adjacent to the office he shared with Blaine where he spent the most time.

She walked through the wooden doors into the study, turned on another lamp, and pulled a handkerchief out of her purse.

Startled by her reflection in a mirror with gargoyles on its frame, she knocked the mirror off the wall in her panic. The glass cracked into two large pieces as splinters of the frame's handcrafted wood crashed onto the hardwood floors and Persian carpets.

It was an omen, as though Preston were mocking her.

"Looks aren't everything," he would often say. Mare was not beautiful. Preston referred to her as "handsome." She had long suffered from acne and generally hid her two large scars under caked foundation.

Preston reminded her that it was a curse to be beautiful. The stories of the beautiful people all ended in tragedy: Marilyn, Rita Hayworth, Greta Garbo, Ava Gardner—goddesses who spent their lives adrift in a purgatory of being lifted too high to commune with humans, while being too human not to feel lonely.

Preston claimed that only certain of the "female species" had to wear makeup, and those were the ones who belonged on a large screen. He didn't like to see screen stars out of character, preferring them in makeup, with no imperfections, because they were gods and goddesses who must be put on a pedestal for all to admire.

When they'd first started spending time together he'd been enthralled with her friends who, like her, were mostly literary agents from boutique agencies of no renown. Some had one or two clients who ranked within the second-tier of bestseller lists for more than two weeks.

Mare wasn't a celebrity, but she wasn't a nobody, either. Her name carried weight. She didn't get calls returned as fast as some agents, but the receptionists showed her respect. Her calls might not be returned for a week, but at least they were returned. That was as high as it got in the honorable-mentions category from which she'd believed she would never emerge.

But then came Preston—her ticket to legitimacy. After her employer was named in a class action for discriminating against older writers, the firm had salvaged its reputation by picking up Preston as a client.

He had failed at a sitcom about two gay black brothers. It had been so over-the-top that even black gay actors hungering for acting opportunities hadn't wanted to be in it. After two mishaps, he decided to stay firmly rooted in his league, vowing to be the best B-series writer he could. That's when the magic had begun.

Everything was in sync once he gave up his quest to be a part of A-list Hollywood. It took the pressure off him. He had the pick of the B-movie litter: handsome men and women easy to get along with, user-friendly character actors whose faces would be familiar but wouldn't draw a crowd if seen on the street.

Preston was everybody's godsend, which made almost all of his productions happy affairs. Everyone in his company was delighted to be there, had enormous versatility, and was beholden to him, knowing he was the best alternative to playing dinner theater in empty restaurants in suburban America. Mare was envied for her good luck in picking a winner, and marrying him, too.

Although she had realized it only in retrospect, like many "public" marriages made in Hollywood, hers disintegrated once her partner's star began to rise. When his series had started to get some traction, Preston changed. His chest swelled when he walked, and he began wearing sunglasses everywhere he went. He attended meetings without her, and didn't report back what had transpired. Apparently, he had become a member of the elite cognoscenti and figured she no longer needed to know what was going on, as if she had no role in his success.

Mare knew she was alone in the house, now, but that didn't stop her heart from beating wildly. When she walked into the huge dining room to look around, she felt anxiety, a sense of impending doom, as if her husband might flamboyantly burst in, as he had last year, carrying a King Cake, inviting her and the two hundred or so other guests to partake of the delectable Mardi Gras pastry.

It was a running joke that Preston—and no one else—always discovered the trinket inside the cinnamon-roll pastry festooned with green, yellow, and purple drizzles: the coveted sign that heralded his anointment, for a third time, to throw the next year's Mardi Gras ball.

Last year this room had been full of the gold-painted faces of revelers in wild states of dress and undress, togas enveloping their otherwise naked torsos. She recalled how her husband had stood several feet away from where she now stood—in the center of the room—dressed in drag with a blonde Marilyn Monroe wig, his dark chest hairs tufting around the V of Marilyn's replica famous subway-grate dress.

Everybody had clapped, encouraging his feminine antics even more, which disgusted her, though she'd tried to appear jovial.

She realized that his insistence on her being at the Mardi Gras telegraphed what he dared not tell her face-to-face. Watching his escapades that night, as he paraded with barely clad muscular men hugging and cavorting with each other, she felt sadness—mixed with revulsion—that he had made his choice to act like a woman, rather than be with one.

Few at the crowded party had even known her relationship to Preston, but that didn't keep her from feeling humiliated and betrayed. If she'd had a pistol, she might have used it, then simply set it down and waited for the police. Preston did have a handgun or two, but she had no idea where he kept them.

She'd left the party and spent the rest of the evening in her room getting drunk. She would confront him when they had a chance to be alone.

Prior to meeting Preston, Mare had been a serial bedder. But her need for financial stability had forced her to look for something more permanent. Until then, everything had been up for grabs. She loved sex. Her men were always drop-dead gorgeous, on their way to fame as models or actors, and they needed an agent who could introduce them to the people they needed to know, through the back door, rather than having to suffer through auditions.

There was the unspoken understanding in her industry that sex was a bartering commodity, as long as it was discreet. It was part of the game played by an industry that had been given a license to both create and live in imaginary worlds. Although she wasn't a knockout, she dressed in a way that displayed her financial status, sexy enough for most men, especially the young ones.

By the time Juanito had come along, she was married and faithful. That meant she chose her bed partners carefully, in case an upstart ever blackmailed her.

She'd had sex with Juanito on many occasions after they met at a cocktail event held by a larger boutique agency. She liked his nonchalance. He didn't salivate at being in the business. He had rough edges, and didn't speak much, but when he did, real words came out. He was a thoughtful man, not bored by his surroundings. He was always processing the experience.

In bed, he would talk about his exploits as a Marielito, never apologizing for his affiliations. The Mariel Cubans had helped each other survive. When he was coming up in America they also protected each other against the Blacks they feared so virulently. It was better to belong to something.

Mare had sent Juanito away because she was growing fond of him, looked forward to his visits and always begged him to stay the night. He could not be pinned down, however, and when he started talking about heading back to Florida, she suggested Louisiana, instead. She told him she would introduce him to her husband and ask him to give Juanito a job. Preston would be very receptive, as he owed her a lot, she'd said.

Juanito had been grateful, and said he'd get the lay of the land before deciding whether he wanted to move to Louisiana. He'd asked for Preston's address and telephone number, but that was it. When she offered an expense account, he refused it, with thanks. He was his own man. That's what she liked about him. It was during that conversation that she mentioned the beautiful intern Sherry, who attended Nakadee U.

As Mare reached her bathroom, she saw that its Italian marble floors were polished and gleaming. Her flip-flops were where she'd left them. It was obvious that no one had used her bathroom, per her instructions.

When Preston had sent pictures of her room, designed to her specifications, she had held out the hope that there might be a future for them. That was before the series took off—when Preston was a mere mortal.

She had helped him with casting—without credit, of course. She'd also been the one able to convince the lead actor, Lamont, a bookish seventeen-year-old more likely to be reading history texts than perpetuating the drug-dealer stereotype, to play the critical lead. Lamont had come with an overly protective mother who had problems with the part for which he was cast.

Mare had taken her out to dinner at a popular seafood restaurant in Marina del Rey in order to discuss his character. His mother insisted her son be paid top dollar to perpetuate a negative image that she was doing her best to keep him from fulfilling in real life. He was college-bound, like the rest of her children, she'd insisted.

Mare had redeemed the production company in her eyes by explaining that Lamont's character, Alvin, was a paean to Jesus Christ. That had calmed his mother down, and they'd started to talk money, whereupon all of his mother's defenses had disappeared.

The series, *Words without Thought*, was in the top twenty Nielsen ratings almost every week during its first year. The writing accolades came rapidly, and Preston was feted as an auteur, a dynamic writer and director, in addition to producer.

Mare closed the door to the bathroom and locked it. She slipped off her high heels, kicking them aside.

Underneath the sink was a metal door painted the same color as the wall. The door opened after she pressed a code sequence on a hidden keypad. Taking a quick inventory of the safe's contents, she saw her Treasury bonds, several thousand dollars in fifties, and several gold and diamond necklaces, worth thousands of dollars, that lay where she had left them.

She unloosened her pants at the back and fished for an envelope she had taped inside them. Sitting down, she slid her pants off and took out the envelope. She'd already opened it, but wanted to look at it closely a second time. Sitting on the edge of her Jacuzzi tub, her legs extended, she opened the typewritten letter:

> *That heart of yours is dead*
> *But I know that you don't know it*
> *Your whole life is one big fat con*
> *I'll make sure it's in your obit*

> *But you won't be feelin' pain*
> *'cuz your heart is too damn empty*
> *Filled with so many misdeeds*
> *and all your falsehoods good and plenty*

She placed the letter on top of her cash and other valuables, then shut the safe door, giving a nod of approval to her surroundings.

Then she walked into her bedroom and opened the drawers and closets to inspect her belongings. Her lingerie drawers were untouched. The closet-full of clothing, which she had sorely missed while in California, hung on display, and shoeboxes were stacked perfectly, the way she had left them.

Everything was where it was supposed to be, yet everything had changed. She wasn't wanted here anymore, and she was ready to accept it. Once she could confirm her legal status.

Sherry

Lula awakened with a feeling she couldn't quite decipher. She looked around, then sighed with relief. She was in her bed, in her home, where the animals were making their familiar morning sounds as light in the sky heralded dawn. She heard the thump of the *Town Crier* as it hit the door, thrown from the oversized bed of the delivery man's Ford pickup, with its elevated chassis and monster wheels.

Her heart was beating faster than normal, and her body was warm and tingly, as though she'd had a good romp in the hay the night before.

She glanced over at the taut sheets on the bed, pristine as ever. Once she felt reassured that she'd been alone last night, she smiled at her fleeting panic that she had slept with Devon, betraying Ambrose.

She pondered the difference between the two men. Devon's essence would still be wafting through her place, with its powerful mix of cologne and testosterone. Her thoughts soothed her back to sleep.

Two hours later, she was surprised to still be in bed, startled by the ringing of her telephone.

"Hello?" she whispered hoarsely.

"Lula, this is Detective Devon."

"Look, Devon. I am exhausted. Can we talk another time?"

"Can you come down to the gym on Peachtree Lane?"

"What's going on?"

"You'll find out when you get here. Just get here quickly, if you can. We need you to identify a body."

Death will welcome each of us at its appointed time, but no matter how much we might accept it, we're rarely prepared to receive it.

Death embraced Sherry in the sauna of her gym. The janitor who found her was a muscular, round-faced black woman with hazel eyes, skin the color of oak, and a short Afro. Her oversized earrings, which dangled and bounced as she shook her head, sniffling and wiping her tears, distracted Lula.

"I seen some dead bodies in Iraq, but none like this. I don't know how it coulda happened. They tell us all the time, check the sauna, check the Jacuzzi, check the pool, and check each stall in the bathroom. There's no lock on the door. How could she burn to death like that?"

Everyone within earshot was listening.

"You never get used to it. No siree. It's too soon for a girl like that. Breaks your heart."

Nate nodded at Devon, who gently put his hand on her shoulder and slowly walked her away from the shower area. Everyone was as transfixed by the janitor as they were by the corpse in the sauna. One talked volumes. The other was silenced for eternity.

Nate looked at the burned body, the remains of a woman he had fantasized about dating.

"It's all so fleeting," he whispered.

He pulled out a handkerchief and blew his nose. "That pretty skin all burned like that." He looked around. "Seng, how much more time you need?" he asked the crime-scene photographer.

Seng stepped back out of the sauna to talk to him. "Not much, but I need the lights off to spray the luminol. I'm just glad this is a digital camera. It's hot in there."

"Be sure to get a picture of the control panel. We might need to check the breaker switch to see if there was some funny business." Nate paused. "Though it don't take a detective to ask questions about this scenario, ain't that right, Seng?"

"Third-degree burns can kill, I tell you that much." Seng agreed.

"That pretty face—now it's one big peel of skin off her bones. This'll be a closed-casket funeral, whadda ya say, Seng? Can she be prettied up?" He muttered under his breath. "Did you get under the benches there?"

"I'm fresh off the boat, huh, Nate?" Seng politely admonished him. "I took hundreds of photographs of bodies in my own country, Cambodia. Burned, shot, hosed with water until they drowned. But I think I know what I'm doing. Now, if you could just learn the difference between Cambodians and Vietnamese, we'd get somewhere."

He winked at Nate, who smirked in return.

Devon walked in and told Nate, "Hey, Chief—the cleaning lady said there were no cars in the lot when she got here. The gym doesn't open until six. She was surprised to find anybody in the gym, because there weren't any keys in the basket out front where they leave 'em."

"So how did she get here?"

"The janitor?"

"Sherry."

"The janitor thought she was here alone. She was bleaching the shower floors and checking the sauna's heat when she saw the body."

More specifically, she had glimpsed bloated, lightly browned fingers through the vertical slat of the door, then opened the door to find Sherry's body, charred and exposed. Sherry's eyes were closed, as if she were leaning against the wall, taking a nap.

Several police officers were walking around trying to take a peek.

Nate asked, loudly, "What are the chances of someone with a broken arm being in a sauna? Wouldn't the cast itch enough as it is?"

He looked around the shower room of curtained cubicles. "I need most of you to leave, for now. We need to have a look-see around the gym. And we need all lockers opened."

As Lula started to leave, Nate motioned for her to stay.

"Can you stick around? I'd like you here, as a witness for her parents, so they know their little angel was given top-drawer treatment, at every stage, okay?"

Lula was too tired to respond. There was no fight left in her. She opened her purse and pulled out a tissue. Leaning her head against the wall, she felt her tears fall like small drops of rain as she dabbed her eyes.

Seng worked quickly, graceful as a dancer, using his instruments as if they were extensions of his own being. The room fell quiet as he steadied his low-angle lamps in the direction of the corpse.

Dragging a small tarp from his carrying case, he laid it out like a picnic blanket. Next, he grabbed a lamp tripod and lowered it as best he could, taking care to put it at just the right angle. Then he did something few crime-scene photographers ever do: lowered himself onto his stomach to lie on the ground, four feet from the corpse. He turned his body at different angles, like a snake, as he snapped off his shots. Fifteen minutes later, he nodded to Nate and said, "Okay, we need a gurney."

Lula took a couple of steps forward toward the sauna door, then stood aside to witness the transfer. Although her heart felt heavy, it wasn't because of the sight of her student's charred body. It was a sickness felt at how often white Americans' actions arose from their sense of power over other ethnic groups. When it's all said and done, however, their skin color, hair texture, and body parts become dust, bones, and ashes. Sherry had no white power now.

Seng moved back so that the two forensic technicians could move Sherry's body. Her one-piece bathing suit was burned into her skin, making her look like a mannequin. The technicians lifted the gurney, on top of which lay the open body bag, ready to receive the corpse.

After the men wheeled out the gurney, Lula stepped forward to where the sauna door was now open wide. Seng snapped the camera shutter again, then turned to take pictures of the dials on the sauna door and the coals used to heat the room. When Seng walked away, Nate moved closer.

"What the ... shit." He looked at Lula.

On the seat where Sherry had sat lay a desiccated human finger, jutting out of the corner of the slatted wooden benches.

Nate's eyes glazed, his lips pressed tight.

Devon moved to his side.

When Nate finally spoke, his voice croaked. "We're on a manhunt, now. Call out all off-duty cops. Have them meet here in the next twenty minutes. No sirens. Just get here, fast, and bring the hounds. And no mosquito repellant, unless it's fragrance-free. Let's call the neighboring departments and see if they can send us extra men to scour the countryside. Devon, go swear out a search warrant to get access to Sherry's apartment."

"She's in a university apartment. I can get in without a warrant. Being a jock has its privileges." Devon winked.

"Do what you gotta do." Nate looked at Lula. "Can you travel with one of our men to register this at HQ, then do your workup? We'll need it ASAP. Help us figure out how old the finger is. It's in worse shape than Sherry."

"Not quite, Nate."

He stopped himself, realizing his faux pas. The finger's owner could still be alive.

"What have you come up with so far?" Devon asked Lula.

"I wish I had more. Whoever is doing this is using a rather large object. The slant of the cuts on all the fingers is upward, from left to right, like they were cut at the same time. But this one isn't as fresh as the other ones, which is a bit odd."

"How's that?" Nate asked.

"Well, we're getting this after how many days?" She didn't wait for him to respond. "Somebody's extremities are being cut, kept in a freezer, then placed wherever the culprit wants them to be found."

"That being the operative word," Devon said.

"Which one?" asked Lula.

"Found. The culprit definitely is trying to tell us something. He leaves the fingers right out in the open for us, to be discovered."

Nate's face lit up in animation. "You gotta wonder what kind of nutcase this is. A med student who's upset with someone? What beef does someone have that they'll chop off fingers, burn the digits and put them right out in the open for the police to find? We're how many miles away from downtown and this thing ends up here? And at the Hollywood frat house?"

"I guess somebody didn't like the company she kept," Devon muttered under his breath.

Nate sniffed. "Yeah. Including me. The problem is that most people snuff out someone they know, or they are professional killers. These people are a different breed altogether. It's hard to know what to do next."

His emotions were making an unexpected visit. He pulled out a big pack of cinnamon chewing gum, waving it among them. When no one budged, he opened one himself and took a deep breath.

"We gotta take a ride. Let's go, Devon."

Then Nate charged out, stopping at the entrance to the ladies' room to speak with an officer overseeing the crime scene.

Devon looked at Lula, winked a goodbye, and balled his fist and clenched his shoulder, pantomiming a gesture to stay strong.

Lula replied with a minuscule nod and sad eyes. She felt weaker than ever.

8:30 a.m.

When Richard's old scanner cackled, asking the police dispatcher for an estimated time of arrival for a crime-scene van, he spun his vehicle around to get to the location identified on the radio. Thank God the computerized trunking police scanners hadn't come to Nakadee yet. That would make it more challenging to trace conversations.

He pulled over to the roadside, about six hundred feet from the parked police cars up ahead that lined the side of the road. Turning down his scanner, he leaned his chest against the steering wheel for a glimpse of the long asphalt driveway that led to the gym in a forest clearing across the street.

He opened his door and bounded out, then slowed to a trot on the paved road, ambling with confidence, his hands in his pockets, as he approached the police cars. Slapping a gnat flying at his face, he wiped it on his green Nakadee U crew shirt.

There was nobody in sight. Hands behind his back, Richard looked inside one of the cars, peering through the glass at the police radio.

"Kenwood." He smiled, nodding in approval, and turned to walk into the light forest thicket that surrounded the gym on three sides.

"This little piggy went to the gym! Whatcha lookin' fer, little piggies?" Richard whispered to himself in a high falsetto.

He jogged forward several paces until he stopped to spy on a phalanx of six police officers walking up the driveway, hunched over, staring at the ground.

A plainclothes officer walked past them and up to where Richard was standing.

Quickly, Richard unzipped his pants, taking out his penis to sprinkle against a nearby tree trunk.

"Hey, what y'all looking for, Mr. Officer?"

Seng stopped, then looked away before starting to walk past him. "Excuse me," he said.

Richard continued his business. "Okeydokey, my man. Just watering where it's safe, what with y'alls' cars out there. What y'all lookin' fer?"

"We're searching."

"Somebody lose some gold, I hope? Is this a finders-keepers kinda search? Shit! I'll sign up."

"That's okay. Thanks." Seng was looking in the opposite direction.

Richard laughed, shaking off the remaining droplets and slowly zipping up his pants.

"Okay, then. You waiting for me?"

"I'll walk you back."

"Sure. This private property?"

"It's a crime scene."

"I know. I heard it on the scanner." Richard walked beside Seng out to the street, then began jogging to his van before he turned around and called. "Hey, man. Was this a 10-78? Or a 10-23?"

Seng looked at him with suspicion. "How you know radio codes?"

"Just a hobby." Richard smiled. "Was it 78?"

Seng set his kit down. "Depends on who was calling it in, right? If someone wanted help, it'd be a 78. If someone got here, it'd be a 23," he said, demonstrating with his fingers.

Richard touched his forehead while pondering his newly acquired information. "Right. Well, I'll be goin'. Over and out," he said, jovially.

Seconds later, he drove off, repositioning the driver-side rear-view mirror while accelerating, training his eyes on it as the man got smaller in the distance. He was still close enough to see the Asian guy writing down something on his hand.

Richard slowed his car and squinted at his rearview mirror again, seeing what appeared to be an apparition: a white man with a scraggly beard and hair to his shoulders, standing on the opposite side of the road. He waved to Richard, who put on his brakes, not quite remembering whether he had seen the man before.

The man was walking toward him now.

Richard accelerated, keeping his eyes on the road.

1:00 p.m.

Lula watched her students come through the classroom in small bunches, taking their seats quietly, foregoing the usual slamming of books and belongings on desks and tables.

There was a collective sadness about them today. They settled down more quickly than usual, some slumped in their seats; a couple were red-eyed. They all stared straight ahead. Eventually, the tick of the clock on the wall was the only sound. Word had spread like wildfire.

Watching her expectantly, in a way they never did when the subject was forensics and osteology, the students' faces begged for instruction—on how to grieve. She cradled her elbows as she spoke.

"I don't want to speculate about the news we've just received regarding Sherry's death. We don't know the official cause, so, as scientists, we can't jump to conclusions about how she died. The medical examiner has that task."

She scanned their faces, many of which were looking down at their desks, avoiding her gaze.

"Out of respect for her, we should not dwell on the circumstances of Sherry's death, but honor her life. For everyone who knew her, and even for people who didn't, this is a tragic loss. Her future was cut short, but her short life wasn't wasted. She was learning, and asking questions—yes, sometimes provocative ones. She was searching. She was trying to understand our country and society, and her place in it. She visited me often to debate things that we discussed here in class."

From the back of the class, a male student interrupted, raising his hand. "Yeah, like white power."

The class tittered, while Lula nodded, smiling.

"Yes, her politics were certainly different from mine, and maybe some of yours, I would hope. But I had to hand it to her: she said what she believed in her heart, which is more than I can say for all of the politicians who say one thing, then do another."

"Yeah, preachers, too," a female student chimed in.

Lula stopped her with a wave of her hand. "I'll stay out of religious questioning. Everyone here is entitled to his or her own beliefs. Education isn't just about books. It's about broadening your experience so you'll be able to navigate through the world."

"Did you like her, Dr. Logan?"

Lula couldn't see which of her female students had asked the question. She looked down. "I like all of you who come to class."

"Can we all get an A grade then?" a male student challenged as the class loosened up, snickering.

Lula smirked. "I am not here to like any of you, personally, any more than you're obligated to like me. However, I will say this: speak your mind, and you'll get respect. Speak your mind in a gentle tone and you'll get admiration. So I guess, in my own way, I admired Sherry. I'll miss her. She did speak a lot in class, but, judging by your reaction, it would appear that she had an affect on all of us."

Lula began to pace back and forth slowly. "There are things I wish I could have told her. I regret that I'll never be able to, now. So from here on, I want you all to do like Sherry. Speak up and be heard, whether you offend or not."

"Dr. Logan. I hate forensic science. How's that?" the student at the back, who had raised his hand earlier, professed.

"I second!" another male voice rebuffed.

"Me, three," said one girl. The class laughed, accompanied by lethargic claps.

"Read pages 260 through 295 of the text, and be prepared for a multiple-choice test on extremities. You're all free to go, whether you hate my class or not."

The class erupted in claps and whoops.

"You will forget Sherry soon enough. But today, give her the respect of honoring her short life."

The class became still again, as students slowly waited for prompting from Lula to determine if it was a joke or not that they could leave.

Quietly, the class streamed out, many nodding their silent thanks.

Lula picked up a tissue near her desk where she usually hovered while lecturing, then reached for her cell phone as she looked at the clock. She'd better leave for the police department soon. Devon wasn't escorting her this time, and Nate had a fire in his belly. This was personal now.

16

MELVYN

Aggie didn't ask where Lula was when the meeting in the police chief's office was called. No one asked where Lula or Devon were, or whether the group should await their arrival, because they hadn't been invited.

In meetings throughout the U.S. where only those with a need to know are called, impromptu meetings are held behind a locked door with an invisible "Whites only" sign. The others, conspicuously absent, will likely never learn that a meeting ever took place. If those who attend are ever confronted by those absentees, the meeting would be explained as hastily arranged.

The people in the chief's office were important, and special. Each had something to show and tell, but only Dr. Aggie could feel guiltless. She had invited Lula to her home to read the pathology report about the first severed finger the minute she got it, and only after her discussions with Lula had she mentioned it to Nate.

The crime-scene technicians had been little help to the investigation, informing Nate that the holder, if not the author, of the report knew how to safely create a document without any trace evidence. They could find no telltale saliva, sweat, or oil from fingerprints for mitochondrial DNA testing. The Southworth stationery watermark was visible, as was the typeface from a laser printer, facts which were of no use to the investigation. Southworth stationery was available at Big Box stores in every major city, and even small office stores in hidden locales like Nakadee. The technician suggested to Nate that the culprit who sent the report could have a law-enforcement or other related background.

"Or they copied it from a book somewhere, or the Internet," Chief Broussard guessed.

"Did you do any searches for similar reports online?" Aggie asked.

Nate sat quietly, his fingers touching as he slowly moved them back and forth.

"What about that diener of yours? The weird one?" he asked.

"Mr. Peoples?"

"Well, he first came to your mind, you said?"

"No, I mentioned him in passing because Dr. Logan visited him. He didn't sound off any alarms, she said. He just liked to talk about himself. She wondered if he had an axe to grind with me or something, but he knows that I let him do whatever he wants, as long as it's well documented. He wasn't coming up with any ideas when I spoke with him. He did an inventory of our records on the computer, to see if the amputations were registered in the hospital consortium databases, and came up empty—no missing fingers."

Nate switched the subject. "Let's go to the tape. We have a couple of minutes to watch. I'll get all your opinions afterwards."

Wally used a smartphone to start the CD-ROM. The screen immediately switched to a camera lens perspective and a view of a crowd. Someone was announcing the next act on the raised stage. The boys, all black, bounded onto the stage, arms waving, jumping, with microphones in the air; playing at being rock stars.

"The SwampBoyz!" yelled the announcer.

"Fast forward a bit." The chief instructed. "Here, please."

> *While your words may fly up*
> *All your thoughts remain below*
> *That's 'cuz words without thought*
> *Do not ever-to-heaven go*

You're as vile as a cockroach
and I'll stomp on you, I will
I will kick you up and down the block
Like-a-dog I'll make you heel

You may bling, and you may floss,
Toss that money to the sky
I know you know I know what's up,
You can't keep living lies

Your time is almost finished
You can't look me in the eye
You a perv, a fake, a bad mistake
Yep, you about to die

Refrain:
So------Never-to-Heaven Go
So------Never-to-Heaven Go
So------Never-to-Heaven Go

While you go livin' it up
I lie so deep, so deep in wait
Knowing every time you talk that talk
You closer to your fate

Soon you'll be struggling for air
From the low depths of the sewer
You'll be poked in your weak flesh
Like a shish-kabob on skewers

But you won't be feelin' pain
'cuz your heart is too damn empty
Filled with so many misdeeds
and all your falsehoods good and plenty

Now life imitates that art
and you about to deep-fish-fry
Drink up, take your last breath
As I said: you 'bout to die

Refrain:
So------Never-to-Heaven Go
So------Never-to-Heaven Go
So------Never-to-Heaven Go

How long you got before time's up
Till you be pushing daisies
You stuck on stupid cuz you can't
Originate, you're lazy

Try you might escape my hype
My bite's worse than my bark
You punk, you perv
Worse yet you serve
That devil in your heart

That heart of yours is dead, though
But I know that you don't know it
Your whole life is one big fat con
I'll make sure it's in your obit

Let me tell you this much,
You have yet to feel my power
Live it up right now, 'cuz God done told me—
You got 12 more last hours

Refrain:
So------Never-to-Heaven Go
So------Never-to-Heaven Go
So------Never-to-Heaven Go

The room was silent.

Nate offered his opinion. "I could barely understand it. I don't talk jive."

Aggie looked at him, smirking.

"It's a joke. From a movie." Nate offered, but no one seemed to be listening. He shrugged his shoulders.

"Here are the lyrics, if that's what they call 'em." The chief grabbed a small stack of papers and passed them around. "Take a look see, then let me hear your thoughts."

Aggie spoke first. "Well, it sounds like typical rap music—violent, frightening, and—"

"Full of shit?" Nate volunteered. "Those punks stand up talking about their Glocks and killing and gang-banging—in rhyme? Those aren't killers, if that's what you're getting at. They're too busy putting lyrics together. I don't get rap."

"I know the kid's daddy. He is a very important man. I sure as hell hope he's got nothing to do with this. I'll call him in for a visit," the chief said, rubbing his hands on the paper.

Aggie was staring at the lyrics. "Well, the vocabulary is pretty sophisticated. I'm not a fan, but, I dunno. What does Dr. Lula think?" she asked innocently. "Have you asked her?"

Nate was chewing his gum, steadily. "Is she our resident expert on all things black?"

"Last time I checked, some guy named Eminem, and even Hassidic Jewish guys are rappers, now. It's not a black thing anymore," Aggie said.

The chief interjected, "Call me crazy, but I see a threat in this song. He's telling someone that they're going to die."

"Isn't that what gangster rap is all about?" Aggie asked.

"Let's keep looking at the videotape," the chief ordered.

Wally pushed the play button. The camera surveyed the swaying and head-bopping crowd, closing in on a couple of interesting-looking characters, including Richard, who was seen dancing, rhythmically, walking around like a rapper himself, mouthing the words, pointing while slouching, and punctuating with his arms.

"Doesn't it look like he's mouthing the words to the song?" The chief told Wally to rewind a bit. "Watch his lips. When he comes around and faces the lens. There. He's mouthing the words."

At one point, Sherry stepped into the frame with Juanito, who could be seen nodding his head to the music, his knapsack on his back.

"Richard was at the crime scene today," the chief mentioned.

"Really." Nate sounded perturbed. "Who saw him?"

"Seng. He was taking photos and when he went out to his car, he saw him taking a leak."

"Why didn't he tell me?" Nate demanded.

"He said he'd forgotten all about it, figured the guy was just another loser, hanging around crime scenes." The chief leaned forward, his finger punctuating the air. "This is a murder investigation, everyone. This isn't some small-town incident anymore. We gotta get the guys who did it. We got big money coming into this town soon, and the last thing we need is some low-lifers messing it up."

"When will you get the warrants, Chief?" Nate asked.

"I'll be working on that. You go scouting and keep me posted on what you learn."

3:30 p.m.

Mare walked straight to the wet bar in her hotel room, poured herself two shots of whiskey and belted each down, followed by a slam of each glass against the wall.

One broke, while the other hit the floor with a thud, cushioned by the carpet.

She placed her Bluetooth ear set on and pushed a speed-dial button linked to Congressman Killian's cell phone. He picked up immediately.

"Preston's assistant, Sherry, is dead!"

Silence was his response.

"Well, that's not good news, is it?" he said, softly.

She heard him excuse himself from the table and walk away from the noise.

"Well, you can calm down, first," he continued.

"Matt. I'm next. I'm certain of it."

"What are you talking about? What do you have to fear? You're in California most of the time, aren't you?"

"I got a letter. A poem. Directed at me, sent to my hotel room."

Each listened for the other.

"Why don't I call the police and put a patrol car to guard you? I'm sure they'd accommodate you."

"So, it's 'you' now, is it?"

"Mare, don't get hysterical. I'm talking about protecting you. Isn't that what this call is about?"

She heard his heavy breathing. He was nervous. For whom, she wondered?

"Look. You just get here. ASAP. Then we'll decide what to do."

His voice was barely audible. "Unfortunately, I have to stay in Washington for the upcoming Markup."

"So you'll let them work me over while you redline a bunch of legal mumbo jumbo? You better hope I'm not murdered before you get here!"

"Come now, Miriam. Where's Blaine?"

"He's nowhere to be found. Typical. I'm sure he skipped town the minute he found out. Unless he's the one killing people."

She hung up. What a tangled web.

Lula's phone conversation with Melvyn's mother was unexpected, but before she had a chance to think about it, Lula was volunteering to help her locate him.

"My son's not picking up the phone and he's not at his father's either," Bebe explained. "He called me earlier today to tell me about Sherry, and now I have no idea where he is."

Lula listened intently.

"You never want your kids to 'know' the police in the South. It's bad all around. What with the last couple of weeks, I'll be damned if they haven't made him a junior officer with all the questions they had for him and those film nuts. It'll quiet down eventually, I hope. I don't know what possessed me to let him work for those people."

Indeed, Lula thought. *One dead, the other one nowhere to be found—and Bebe's boy knew both of them.*

"My work takes me out of state twice a month, of course during the craziest time of my boy's life." Bebe said.

"Do you have any idea where he's hanging out?" Lula asked. Bebe explained that his friends lived south of the tracks, but the streets were smaller, so they were likely riding their bikes around her home.

"I hate to impose on you. Are you out of class now? I'll be back tomorrow evening. He's a latchkey kid half the time, or at least until

Tyrell picks him up. And Tyrell will call the police. That boy has seen enough of cops for a long while. I just need someone I can rely on to do right by my son."

Lula told Bebe she'd do what she could, but asked if she could mention Melvyn's disappearance to Devon, so he could scout around, too.

"Only if it starts getting late and you don't find him."

"I'll do what I can," Lula said, softly.

"I can't thank you enough, Dr. Lula. Really. I owe you, now, for a second rescue."

"When was the first?" Lula asked, puzzled.

"At the police station. And now."

After they said goodbye, Lula called Devon but was greeted by his voice mail. She left a message, telling him that Richard might know where Melvyn was because he picked him up sometimes from school. If Devon did find him, she asked that he bring him to her to wait for the boy's father to pick him up.

Lula snatched her car keys off the kitchen counter and set off to look for Melvyn.

It might be time to change her perception of her Sleepy-Hollow town, now that it was rapidly turning into Grand Central Station for both the living and the dead.

4:00 p.m.

Friends since childhood, Melvyn, Boojay, and Garrett spent at least three days a week together. Today, while exploring the local wildlife along the lake, they'd ignored the No Trespassing and Private Property signs posted along the two-mile stretch of highway.

A half hour earlier, they had leaned their bicycles up against longleaf pine trees and had begun their foray into Louisiana's forest wilderness. Generally, federal forest rangers weren't present, which heightened their sense of adventure and discovery.

Led by Melvyn, and staying off the federal lands, they gravitated toward a little clearing where they took out a bottle of Scotch whiskey and a bag of potato chips. They poured some whiskey on the ground, for Sherry and Preston, then each took a swig. Before they could register their disgust, the landowner's shotgun startled them.

Now, however, Melvyn was standing at attention with his friends, holding his silence as he had been told to do by the white plain-clothes detective who smelled of cinnamon. Melvyn was keeping his eye on the white men standing in the distance.

Ordinarily, he was a confident boy for his age. His mother often joked that he was a "two-fer:" not only was he the man in his household, but its only child, too. Since his parents' divorce, he had proudly sat opposite his mother at the other end of the dining room table, fancying himself an adult.

His worries about his likely change in status struck panic in him. He rubbed his supple lips together, fast-forwarding in his mind to the breadth of punishments to be meted out by his mother. He silently plumbed his own trusted cache of white lies, stored in memory for emergencies like today's, when he needed an alternative to telling the truth.

The black detective who had run Melvyn down with a tackle at Preston's was nowhere to be seen. That means I'm in real trouble, he told himself. But he knew the drill. Keep his hands to his sides, and answer, "Yes, sir. No, sir." That's how he talked to his daddy. Like his real daddy, this detective had a whole lot of power over his fate.

"So you heard the bad news, right?" Nate went down on one knee, drumming a tree limb in front of him, stirring up the debris on the forest floor.

Melvyn nodded, blinking his eyes.

"So, why this?"

Melvyn didn't say anything, looking straight ahead, before answering, "Am I a child or an adult?"

"Well, last time I understood, you were a teenager. You got something to tell us that makes us regard you as an adult?"

Melvyn's friend, Boojay, forever seeing humor in any situation, answered, "Yeah, he takes medicine for erectile dysfunction. He a grown man, now."

His other friend, Garrett, sputtered, while Nate bowed his head, shaking it, trying to hide his laughter.

"From the mouths of babes." Nate indicated to Garret and Boojay, "You all get outta here, while I talk to Melvyn, man to man."

The three boys turned serious. "No sir, we came together, we're going back together," Garret said.

"That right?"

"Yes, sir. Those were our orders."

"Who ordered you?"

Melvyn spoke up. "I did, sir. My mother told me to always return with the people you went with."

"For protection," Garrett added.

"Well, I like that. Fair enough. Okay, you can stay, but go over there while we talk to Melvyn."

His friends looked at Melvyn for direction.

"It's all good, guys. I got this." He gave them a confident nod.

"We'll wait over here, Melvyn."

Melvyn looked straight ahead.

After Nate warmed up by asking what grade he was in, and what sport he played, he asked whether Melvyn liked Xbox or PlayStation.

"Don't play 'em. My mom wouldn't buy them for me."

Nate looked surprised. "Wow, that must suck."

"I got friends who have 'em. I could play 'em if I wanted to, but it doesn't interest me. I got my whole life to be indoors, especially when I'm your age."

Nate's eyes opened a bit wider.

Melvyn hid his smirk.

"Are you an ageist?"

"No."

"Are you sure about that? Do you know what the word means?"

"Someone who doesn't like old people, I guess."

Nate nodded. "So, are you an ageist?"

"Man, I spent my whole life with adults, sir."

"I see. You spent a lot of time at Preston's, too. What's the story over there?"

"I ain't no snitch, man."

"So you're gonna ignore your friend Sherry, who died such a horrible death, and not want to help us track down who did this to her?"

"I figure she did it to herself. She musta done something pretty bad to be dead so soon."

"I agree. So what did she do?" Nate asked him.

"I do not know. I ain't no snitch."

"Let's break those two sentences down. What don't you know not to tell me?"

Melvyn looked at him, puzzled, repeating the sentence to himself. "I don't know, and even if I did know, I ain't no snitch."

"You don't want to find the killers?"

"I want you to find them, but you gotta do the work, not me. I don't know anything."

"Have you been to Preston's house lately?"

"I plead the fifth."

Nate looked at him. "You'll do what?"

"I know nothing about nobody, and that's the way I likes it."

"How about we bring your mom and dad into the picture, again, and bring you in for an interrogation?"

That got Melvyn's attention.

"I got my lawnmower and drove it to my dad's, yesterday. I won't be doing the lawn there anymore."

"Why's that?"

"I was paid by Preston. Since he wasn't around, my momma said to stop mowing the lawn there. She didn't want me going over there anymore."

How do you know about Sherry's death?"

"Richard told me. Then I saw it online."

"When did he tell you this?"

"Yesterday."

"He's calling you up to tell you? Why? Who is Richard to you?"

"We're related."

"That right?"

"By marriage. My dad is married to his cousin. You remember, the one my momma got into the argument with? Olive."

"What does she do for a living?"

"She's a nurse."

"So Richard called you. What about Juanito. Did you hear from him?"

"He don't got my number."

"That right. He don't got your number." Nate twirled a twig as he balanced himself on his haunches. "I got your number, though."

"I didn't give it to you."

"Not that one."

"Can I be excused for a sec?" Melvyn asked.

Nate raised his eyebrows to signal his assent.

Melvyn took two steps away from Nate and turned his back to spit.

"So, all these adults wanna call a teenager to tell them about some friend's death."

"I was her friend, I guess." He wiped his mouth with his left, then right, shoulder.

"What kind of friend?"

"Just a friend. Is that a difficult word?" He looked Nate in the eye.

"You were a friend to two gay men, living in a house with a woman and a hustler."

"Hustler? Who?"

"You tell me."

"How long are you going to talk like this? I said I'm no snitch. I mowed the lawn there."

"You ever spend the night there?"

"Hell no. My momma barely likes me to stay at my dad's, let alone a bunch of white people."

"Yet she let you go over there."

"She said Whites got more green than Blacks, and that's the only color I should care about."

Nate laughed. "I'm not so sure about that. I don't see you showing any remorse. You don't seem sad to me."

"Sir, my mother told me to always show respect to a police officer, but that don't mean giving him the store. I was told if I ever got stopped by the police I should call her up and she'll come be there to talk with me."

"How about we call your daddy, instead?"

"My daddy got my back, just as good as my momma do. Sir."

Nate suddenly looked at Melvyn's ear.

"When did you get this earring?" he asked.

"I don't remember."

"Who gave it to you?"

"I don't remember."

"You mean, you ain't no snitch."

Melvyn looked straight ahead.

"Well, we got enough from you, right now. I know to look for the butler, the Hispanic dude. And Richard."

"Richard didn't give me nothing."

"Good to know. If you talk to him, tell him we're looking for him. He should turn himself in."

"Why? He didn't do nothing. He liked Sherry. He wouldn't hurt her."

"You ever hear of jealousy?"

"Yep. White people are jealous of black people, 'cuz we can tan and they can't. When they tan they look orange."

"Yeah, that may be, but whoever told you that didn't tell you the other half."

"Like what?"

"We might wanna look like you, but we sure as hell prefer to be white for everything else."

Melvyn snickered.

"That's supposed to mean what?" Nate grabbed his shoulder lightly.

"Nothing, sir. My daddy says we came up tough in this world here, but we always get the last laugh."

"You mean the ones that don't get put in prison get the last laugh."

Melvyn blinked. "So you say, sir."

"So I say. Right now, it's what I say, goes. Got it?" Like a soldier, Melvyn continued to look straight ahead. "I'll take that as a yes."

Melvyn shrugged his shoulders.

Nate threw away his stick and stood up. "Get outta here, and don't let me see you here again."

Melvyn dashed away to meet up with his boys.

Nate hollered after him. "You talk to Richard or Juanito, you tell 'em we're looking for them. Tell 'em to call us, you hear?"

"Yes, sir!" Melvyn called back, then hopped on his bike.

His friends yelled as they rode away, their voices echoing through the forest.

6:11 p.m.

By the time Lula arrived at Bebe's house, Melvyn and friends were choreographing synchronized wheelies on their bicycles. Away from the presence of his mother, he seemed more mature and self-assured, likely a product of hanging with his friends.

His front wheel in mid-air, Melvyn momentarily lost his balance and stuck his foot out to keep from falling as Lula approached slowly in her car.

He leaned forward in his banana seat to peer inside. He inched his bike forward, slowly, while Lula's automatic window rolled downward.

"Hey, Melvyn, how we doin'?"

He kept his hands on the handlebars and nodded.

"Where's your mom?" she asked.

"Traveling. I'm staying at my dad's."

Lula looked at him with suspicion.

"Why don't I believe you. I think you're home alone."

Melvyn shrugged his shoulders. "It's not a big thing. I stay home a lot. I wanted to see if I could do it. My mama always told me it was okay, as long as I went to school and called my dad to pick me up in the morning. I have food and everything."

Lula told him to wait for her to park her car.

He straddled his bike, accompanying her.

She exited the car and stood leaning against it, trying to figure out whether she should stay with him until his mother returned, or offer to take him to his father's house. She felt responsible for him.

"Look, can we go sit down somewhere?" she asked.

He nodded, turning and leading her down the terra-cotta-lined sidewalk to the side of his house. He reached the back of his yard, where long, three-tiered beds of wildflowers and cacti were showing off their colors. A patio table and chairs looked inviting, a perfect setting where she could talk with him.

She opted to say little, thinking it a better approach than interrogating him, considering that seemed to be what everyone was doing. She wondered if anyone stopped to think about his psychological state, considering Sherry's death. He'd known her, enough to flirt and joke about rubbing her feet. What was his relationship to her, and to the grown men for whom he appeared to play mascot? Lula had so many questions that she dared not ask.

She made a mental note of his cherubic face—innocent, yet so grown, so quickly. The demands placed on young black children, short-circuiting their childlike natures to ward off an expected early demise, were so unfair. Rarely could a black boy simply be a boy, anymore than a little black girl could be an innocent doll, notwithstanding rapper Lil Kim's "Black Barbie" boast.

"My mom called you?" Melvyn asked.

Lula nodded.

"I don't know why. She knows the drill." He shook his head.

"Well, maybe she's worried about you. You've gone through a lot lately."

"I'll say," he chuckled. "I can handle it. After what Preston taught me about things, I think I can hold my own. I better," he said, laughing.

"What do you mean?"

"Well, we would talk. He was kinda weird. He had some strange views."

"Like?"

"I asked him what it would take for me to become an actor. And he told me some crazy shit ... I mean, stuff."

He bent his head, looking shameful.

"Like?"

"Well, let's just say, I don't want to be an actor anymore."

"You can't do me like that, Melvyn," she laughed. "You gonna leave me hanging in suspense?"

Melvyn obviously liked his newfound role of teacher with Lula, and showed a profundity that actually surprised her. Most likely his mother thought that he was intelligent but relegated him to the periphery, seen but not heard. But with Lula, he could be candid as well as introspective, and voice his opinions about the lives of the adults around him.

It appeared to her that Melvyn had been in Preston's company enough to be able to ask him questions about just about anything. His reception to what he learned was clearly mixed. She tried to hold back her surprise at his revelations.

"He said most people were in it for the sex. Yep. That's what it's about, he told me."

Lula raised her eyebrows.

"There were too many people who wanted to be famous, he said. He said it was like a supermarket. You just pick what you want."

For young people, anybody interested in a career in Hollywood would, one way or the other, become an object of sex, in order to be a long-term player. Women had to show their bodies for auditions, engage in sexual acts, and rehearse sex scenes over and over again. And straight men had to "throw down."

"What do you mean?" Lula asked.

"He has to have sex on screen, usually within the first twenty minutes of the film. When I asked him what about black men, he told me it depended upon how desperate they were."

It wasn't the same for Blacks, apparently. For a black male to make it in the business, he had to go through his own ritual of "total emascula—I forget the word," Melvyn said.

"Like he's in a fraternity. They had to go through hazing, but not marching, like pledges do. It was kind of sexual, he said."

"Why was he telling you this, do you think?" Lula asked.

He shrugged his shoulders. "I asked him if he could get me into the business, and he said what the rules were. He said that to become famous, I'd either have to play a negative part, like a drug dealer or gay person, or I'd have to be a comedian. Comedians aren't threatening. I have to be someone white people want to hang out with, be a friend. Someone they weren't afraid of."

"And did he say anything about black women?" Lula asked.

"They have to be foreigners, like from England, or African. Or if they were from here, they have to be biracial—you know—with white features. Those kind are more acceptable to white audiences, he said."

Lula sat transfixed as Melvyn shared his insights. He talked about the hidden games that occurred underneath the American cinema-going public's eyes, where God-like producers and directors played power games to humiliate or shame actors, testing their limits for degradation.

"Preston called them slave auditions 'cuz he had the power to decide someone's career."

"Why was he sharing this with you?" Lula asked.

"I guess he was telling me what I'd have to do. He said that I could be an actor because actors were like children, but they had to do as they were told. He said I'd have to be willing to be bent, shaped, reshaped to prove that I could be someone other than who I really am. He said actors weren't all that great, really. They were one step above a writer. There was always another one in line."

Lula didn't know whether to ask the obvious. She wasn't an investigator, and didn't need to be on the witness stand, other than in her role as forensic anthropologist. She stopped there.

In fact, she was stumped, not sure what to say next. How could she engage a fourteen-year-old in questions about sex? But he seemed to want to talk.

"Did you tell this to your mom?"

He shrugged his shoulders. "Some of it."

"Your dad?"

He rolled his eyes.

"What did your dad say?"

His dad didn't like him hanging out with white people at their homes. He said they had different ways than black people did, and he didn't want Melvyn to pick up their habits. He said white people were lost ever since Blacks had been freed from slavery, because then Whites had to do and think for themselves. He wanted Melvyn to remember where he came from, and not get caught up in the values of a bunch of "rich degenerates."

"But he married a white woman, didn't he?" Lula asked.

"That's for her to say," he said.

Melvyn told her that his dad must have asked Richard to hang around more to watch over him while he was at Preston and Blaine's home. Richard had visited Preston's before Juanito was on the scene, but Richard didn't really know the men, didn't talk to them. He thought they were weird. Richard had mentioned that they knew nothing about movies—that the ones they made were usually remakes of something else. They didn't know the old classics, from back before color television, when mostly foreigners ran Hollywood, Richard had said. They had the filmmaking traditions, the ones who had escaped the Nazis. Richard loved movies.

Once Richard met Sherry, he'd asked for more work as a landscaper and maintenance man so he could be on campus more. He knew her schedule, and had told Melvyn not to tell anyone, but he had seen her at the gym and she was all that and a bag of chips. He'd told Melvyn that she was going to be his girlfriend, and they had bet $20 that he'd be taking her out within a month. He delivered on his promise. Melvyn was impressed, and called him, "Playa."

Melvyn didn't believe it when Richard came home from the university with Sherry. He hadn't been working that day, and was riding bikes with his buddies when they saw Richard's white van. Richard got out of the driver's seat and ran to the passenger side to open the door for Sherry and help her as she stepped out. Melvyn and company had started whistling.

Things started going bad when Juanito came on the scene. Richard was insanely jealous. Juanito was a wetback, he said. What right did he have to do anything in this country?

Richard started to badger Sherry about him, and they'd argue. Juanito told Richard that it was Preston's orders that Richard not come on his grounds again, and if he had to pick up Melvyn, to honk the horn from the street and Preston would send him out. Richard had cursed Preston out, calling him every bad name in the book. That's when he'd hinted that both Preston and Blaine were pedophiles. Richard had threatened to go to the newspapers, but thought Melvyn's daddy would be a better weapon.

"What did he mean by that?" Lula asked.

Melvyn looked around, scratching his arm, as if to distract himself from participating in the conversation further.

"Are you afraid of your dad?"

He shook his head several times, then moved it up and down.

"Did he ever meet Preston or Blaine?"

Melvyn's head went to the left, then right, as he sealed his lips to keep from talking.

Lula glanced at her watch. She'd have to move things along. "Could your dad have been angry at Preston and Blaine?"

"For what?"

"I don't know. You tell me."

He laughed. "Why you asking me that? I'm not a psychologist. Are you? What's the difference between a psychologist and a psychiatrist?" he asked.

"No. Well, in a way, I guess. Killing is such a permanent act ... you have to be pretty angry to do that," said Lula.

"Or you're psychotic, right?"

She looked at him. He had a healthy vocabulary.

"My mom says Daddy went off the deep end, marrying Olive." He laughed. "He told me that no killing is justified, unless it's justified, and nine times out of ten the person had it coming if the victim knew the killer. Somebody usually did somebody wrong and they were getting their—what did he call it? Up and coming."

Lula smiled at his choice of words.

"Comeuppance," she corrected him.

"I asked my daddy about the terrorist attacks of 2001; that was about two years before I was born. Did all those people in the towers deserve to die? He said that answer is a lot more complicated."

A silence hung between them.

Lula heard a buzz, and watched Melvyn take his cell phone from his pocket.

"It's Moms, texting me, asking me where I am." His thumbs deftly typed. "Mom, Dr. Lula is with me." He mouthed as he typed out the words. "Can I stay here?"

He then smiled at her reply, which he held up for Lula to see: "Ask her to take you to your daddy's. And thank her kindly."

He was absolutely fine. The recent events hadn't fazed him much, after all. This boy, raised on the Internet and technology, was impervious to any danger. People live and die, playing out their techno-lives.

Suddenly, Lula got a chill. Standing up, she told him she would take him to his dad's.

Melvyn looked at her, quizzically, his eyes slanting, still untrusting. She waited for him to say something, but he stayed silent. He seemed to be searching for the right words.

"Do you know what's going on?" he asked, letting her glimpse a vulnerability he usually kept hidden behind his seemingly effortless display of street cred.

"I'm not sure what you mean, Melvyn."

"At Preston's. What are the police doing?"

"Are you concerned?"

"Well, I did know those people."

"And?"

"I told my momma, I ain't gonna get caught for nothing."

"Have you gone back to the house since we saw you there?"

He looked down, then up, as if to argue his case. "She said that I better get anything and everything out of that house that belonged to me. So I did."

"What do you mean, Melvyn?"

"I had the key to get in. So I got my stuff out."

He seemed intent on looking down, as if to hide his face from her. Something didn't ring right. She couldn't tell if he was acting or actually feeling the puzzlement that showed on his wrinkled brow.

She reached to touch his chin, gently forcing him to look her in the eye.

His shoulders squared as he tried to match her gaze.

"What'd you take, Melvyn?"

"My dad's lawn mower. And a shirt he gave me."

"Where is the lawn mower?"

"At my dad's."

"A shirt *who* gave you?"

"Preston."

"Did you stop mowing the lawn at Preston's?"

"I guess so. I was told to just bring it back."

"Did your dad want it?"

"I forget. Maybe."

He looked down, wiping a tear from one eye, revealing the escape of another.

"I know, Melvyn. You lost a friend, didn't you? And nobody's considering that, are we? Nobody is asking you how you feel, right?"

He didn't say anything. He was breathing heavily, trying to restrain his tears.

"I know you'll miss her. Melvyn, have you any idea who would want to hurt Sherry? Or Preston?"

She watched him, but could read nothing. "I'm just trying to understand what you know. So you had keys to his home. How frequently did you visit him?"

"Every week at four o'clock, on Thursdays."

"Did he give you money for each visit?"

He nodded.

"But he didn't ask you to do anything for him, except talk to him?"

"Right."

"Did you like Preston? I mean, as a person. Did you like him, in general? You spent a lot of time with him."

"We all did, man. He was cool."

"Yeah, but after a while it was just him and you, right? He asked you to come over more regularly? How'd he do that? In front of your friends?"

"He just said, 'Come by on Thursday, Melvyn, I got a job for you.'"

"What did your friends say?"

"Nothing. They were jealous. They made fun of me. Saying I was gonna suck his ...." He stopped talking, pursing his lips together tightly, and looked away from Lula. "When I showed them the crisp fifty dollars I got, they wasn't laughin' at me anymore."

"And all he wanted to do was talk."

"That's all it was about. He wanted to talk. It's like he wanted to be young or something. Like he wanted to know what it was like being my age n'all."

"Why you?"

"I don't know."

"What do you think happened to Sherry?"

"Too many men liked her, and one of them killed her?"

"Do you have any idea who did it?"

"I don't know."

"How many boyfriends did she have?"

"I don't know. Richard said she was his girlfriend, but I always saw her with the Cuban dude."

Lula asked whether the men ever fought over Sherry.

"I don't know. I don't hang out with them all that much."

"Were you ever with Sherry and Richard together—just the three of you?"

"Sometimes he would take her to her place, too, after he took me home."

"Did they ever fight?"

"Sometimes. She would say he was a stalker."

"Why?"

"Probably 'cuz he was a stalker?" He chuckled.

"Why do you say that?"

"Because she said it—and she was pretty ... aggravated. They might have broken up their friendship that day."

"When was that?"

"They had an argument at the Hot Sauce Festival. Maybe he got his revenge."

He put his phone away and asked for five minutes to go to the bathroom and get his homework to do at his dad's house.

16

RICHARD

Juanito had cooked a patriotic Cuban meal of beans, rice, and spicy fish stew, then rested for a couple of hours.

Dressed in an expensive long-sleeved white dress shirt and a pair of black leather pants, he put on a diamond earring and black cowboy boots with an ornate design and a metal clasp hugging the back of the heel. He intended to paint the Nakadee club scene Fidel-Castro red.

Clean-shaven, he looked like a mature altar boy, the picture of innocence, which was belied hours later as he danced in the club with suggestive rhumba and electric-guitar moves.

His guilt about recent events disappeared as he danced in Club Bayou, gyrating his hips, sweating out the impurities of his thoughts.

As usual, he relished the admiring stares of the viewers, and gave them their money's worth as he pranced and preened like a stallion. If he couldn't make it to the silver screen, he'd at least make them remember him on the dance floor.

Out of the corner of his eye, he saw a pair of eyes riveted on him. When the music changed and he had waved his thanks, like *El Duque*, the Cuban League's most revered pitcher, he momentarily locked eyes with his intrepid fan while making his way over, still bopping his head to the beat of the music.

Juanito turned to a scantily clad brunette who was dancing next to him, and held his hands on her hips.

She turned around in surprise.

Quickly adjusting, she danced with him, willingly, and held her hands around his neck, leaning backwards.

He tired of her within minutes and when his pursuer nodded his head in the direction of the bar, Juanito kissed the girl on the cheek and joined the stranger who had now turned his back to order drinks.

The music was still pumping as Juanito held his new acquaintance's hand, putting it up to his chest. Whether the gesture was clinical or sexually suggestive was anybody's guess, as Juanito invited his new friend to feel the strength of his heart beating beneath his skin.

"You're a good dancer." The man patted his back, massaging, holding his hand there a bit longer than Juanito expected.

The stranger motioned the bartender over, who leaned forward as the guest asked Juanito, "What's your name?"

"Juanito."

His new mate echoed, "Juanito's having ...."

Juanito looked at the bartender. "I'll have a Hurricane."

"Give him three. Give me four. Put them over there, could you?" The man slapped a fifty-dollar bill on the counter, then nodded to Juanito. "Wanna cut another rug?"

They danced—by themselves, with each other, with other women, periodically returning to their waiting drinks, which were always replenished. They were getting more wasted with every bottoms-up. Each dance and drink was a buildup to the next.

When the music slowed, they sat at the bar again, Juanito looking his new friend in the eye. "Hey, you know my name, don't I get to know yours?"

The man took a swig, and stood up to dance again. "One for the road."

Juanito stayed seated. "Hey, mystery man. How about a name?"

"Wally."

"Was that so hard?" Juanito brushed the hair out of his eyes, examining Wally, trying to keep his head upright.

"You get high?" Wally asked.

They walked out together. Outside, the music was muffled, but people were still talking loudly, their voices reverberating against the night silence. Cars lined the streets, and inebriated couples stumbled arm-in-arm. The cool, heavy air felt like a fan against their sweaty bodies.

Wally asked where his car was located.

"There." Juanito pointed to a shiny midnight blue Mercedes Benz. "Yours?"

"Borrowed it from a friend."

"Nice. Do you turn into a pumpkin?"

"What?"

"Joking." He stood away from the car door as Juanito opened the passenger door for him. "How about the riverbank?" Wally offered.

They both got in and drove into the night, the pulsating beats of the nightclub trailing behind them.

When they reached the highway, Wally asked Juanito to pull to the side of the road.

"You do blow, right?"

Juanito looked at him. "Naw, man. You didn't hear me. I don't do none of it."

"I asked you if you got high, don't you remember?"

Juanito shook his head slowly. "Naw, man, you didn't hear me say nothin'. You're undercover. I seen you at the festival. I got nothing to do with nothin'. I used to gang-bang, but that was when I was a kid. I got plans now."

"Did they involve Sherry?"

Juanito looked him squarely in the eye. "Nope. She got into drugs. We hung together, but she's not my speed. I didn't give up the life to get involved with a druggie."

"Even though she was selling for you?"

"She needed cash. I helped her out."

"And where was your cash from?"

"My employer."

Wally looked at Juanito, and wound his hands around, telling him to spill the beans.

"We had a spending account for office supplies, gas, maintenance of the cars, you name it."

"But you couldn't get enough."

"Indeed, I could. And did."

"You're admitting you stole—"

"You're saying it. Not me. You've got nothing on me, man. I'm an immigrant. I like it here. I don't want to go back to Castro's government."

"You'd rather steal here."

"Look. I know hell. I've been there. I'm not going back there or to one of your minority prisons here."

"What about Sherry? That's no loss to you?"

"I warned her it would end badly if she didn't clean up her act."

"And you saw this coming?"

"No. I saw drug addiction as an outcome."

"When did you see her last? And be prepared to confirm it because I already know the answer."

"So, I was at the pool. Yeah, I was there. Do you see me running anyplace, or hiding out? We met there all the time to go swimming."

"Did you take separate cars?"

Juanito nodded.

"So, what happened to her car?" Wally asked.

"You're the cop. I'd like to know myself."

"Drugs?"

Juanito raised his hand, shrugging.

"It's money."

"Worth killing for?"

Juanito was almost relaxed by now. He leaned back in his seat and looked up. "Nope. She wasn't worth killing over."

"But you're okay that she's dead."

"No. But it's been some time now that I realized that life and liberty don't mean happiness. There's too much freedom here. Do whatever you want—just don't get caught. I have long since stopped trying to figure gringos out, man. Long since. I'm just ready to go. Leave this place."

"I'm afraid you can't do that, just yet. We'll be calling you in for more questioning. You got a number where I can reach you?" Wally asked.

"You gonna arrest me?"

"You said you were going somewhere."

"What are you going to tell Richard?" Juanito asked, politely. "He's going to take it hard." He laughed.

"Where can we find him?"

"If he's not at Preston's he's probably looking for Blaine."

"And what is Blaine doing with the news?"

"There's some information he doesn't want to get out, so he may be talking with his lawyers." Juanito checked his watch. "But about this time, Sherry would have been at Harry's Coffee Shop for the screenwriting classes. Preston usually does them, but Blaine is probably substituting for him."

"Drop me off there, will you?"

"I'd be happy to." Juanito said, smiling his understatement.

8:50 p.m.

"The best stories are the ones that come from the deepest recesses of the writer's life experience." Blaine crossed his arms as he leaned on the faux log table, causing it to tilt. He puckered his bottom lip, searching for just the right words to display his literary profundity.

His affectation of contemplativeness had become a signature that endeared him to his younger fans in Harry's Coffee Shop and Bakery. Although he was fifty-fold wealthier than his fawning audience around this table in the back corner, his self-deprecating nature, along with his well-worn jeans and tattered shirt, were just the right mix for the small community that had adopted him as half of its celebrity duo-in-residence.

"Whether it's fiction or non-fiction, if you look back at our literary greats, history remembers the writers whose canvas was their internal life, painted on paper, for all of us to see," he said. "Faulkner lived in New Orleans for two years, an experience that enriched his writing immeasurably."

Blaine was a poor substitute for Preston, who was AWOL. A frequent lecturer to women's organizations, Preston had basked in the local limelight. This was about as great as life could get, he had said: a river running right through the town, Harry's Coffee Shop and Bakery, family-owned shops, and no McDonald's in sight for at least ten miles. Fast-food America belonged in the relatively newer towns where Walmart reigned.

Blaine also loved his life in Nakadee, notwithstanding its constant reminder of the duplicity he'd used to reach his success. Hiding the fact that he had hailed from the grimy streets of Detroit prior to becoming a New Englander, like most self-reinventors, he preferred to put his past behind him. This was his wilderness, of sorts, away from the industrial bustle of the old and rusty motor city.

He and Preston frequented Harry's often, as did other local literary types, some quietly chatting and sipping coffee, others reading books, the *Times-Picayune*, or the *Town Crier*.

He looked out through the bay window to the diagonally parked cars and quaint Main Street. Over time, he and Preston had become such regulars that people would approach them, and thus this informal lecture series had begun.

"Williams was the same," Blaine continued. "A streetcar named 'Desire'? It really existed, ran by his house."

He raised his brows, looking at his mesmerized listeners, one or two of whom were taking notes. Another was biting his eraser.

"Great writers shape their literary world from the world they experience in reality. And when you seek to tell your inner story, well, that's when the magic really begins for the writer. Syntax, punctuation, editing, that's all fine and dandy, but the real work is the inner work. It is letting your soul breathe."

Blaine paused, leaning back in his chair, staring through a woman who was looking directly at him. His heart wasn't in it. His back hurt and the weight of the world was on his shoulders. He looked at his students and kept talking, but his mind seemed to be in another place.

He was eating minuscule portions of salmon on tortillas, with cream cheese, capers, and juicy chunks of chicken in Dijon sauce. A key-lime pie dessert beckoned him. He looked at his watch.

"What about screenwriting?"

Blaine practically jumped out of his seat. "Oh! I'm sorry. Could you repeat the question?"

His questioner was attractive, with a freshness to her skin that almost made Blaine want to reach out and stroke her face. She wore a soft pink cashmere sweater with a brown suede jacket. Textures. Blaine liked the feel of materials. He tried to focus.

"Is it the same with screenwriting? I mean, how do you take your characters and make them a part of your own history, when you're trying to write a drama about—let's say—a boy raised by wolves?"

Blaine pondered the question, this time scratching his eyebrow.

"Well, in your case, I would ask you what is it about wolves that you like? What is it about the concept of growing up with them that you like? Does that mean you like the wilderness?" He waited. "I'm asking you."

The young woman with sandy-colored hair and bright eyes was startled.

"Well," he added. "What do you like about the story—the wolf story? How do you—in creating your character, because your characters are you—how do you relate to that story?"

She answered. "Well, in my case, I grew up in an isolated community, where all we really had was each other and our dogs. And a herd of deer that fed from our farmland. I guess I relate to the solitude of not being around many people."

"Well, it also says something about your parents, doesn't it? Were they around, or were they working all the time?"

"Are you asking me again?"

He smiled. "No. I was merely showing you how the answers to those questions about yourself might inform your writing."

Richard, sitting at an adjacent table, stood up, turned his chair around, and sat down again.

A waiter deposited another beer on his table. "Thanks, man. Keep 'em comin," he said, then leaned over in his chair, shoulders resting on the high back, and spoke.

"I'd like to know how a writer can write about a totally different culture. Let's say, I'm a white boy living in Maine or New Hampshire.

How can I write a gritty urban drama like you wrote for *Words Without Thought*? Your characters—the little black kid, for instance. The wealthy boy who lives with his mother, the crack addict. Where did that story come from? I don't see any resemblance of African-American in you, man."

Blaine looked straight ahead, lips pursed, as the class chuckled. He joined them with a smile and tried to speak, first taking in some air, then nodding, with a nearly imperceptible trace of defensiveness.

"Like any good soldier, you must know the terrain. So you must also do your research."

Richard looked intently at Blaine, who was tight-jawed, tapping his face lightly with the eraser end of his pencil.

"I mean, how did you even come up with the idea of a black kid and his mother trying to cope with life? And then telling the story through the eyes of the kid?"

He raised his hands toward the heavens, dropping them to his lap with a slap. "I mean, shit, where in the hell did that come from? Where are you from, dude? You ain't from these parts, right? You a Yankee. And here you are all up in the suburbs of Louisiana, man? How did you possibly get here from there? That's where I wanna go. Take me there—show me how to do that!"

Blaine looked at his watch. "That's a question that could be asked of any hit television series. How does it happen? Well … it's alchemy, a form of chemistry, mixed in with a huge dollop of luck."

He looked out of the window as he talked. "You try to hear someone else's voice if you can't hear your own. And you listen to it … and you, well, honestly, you adapt it. And if you do your research, you'll find that most human emotions are not race- or background-specific. So you get the voice of other people, and infuse it with your own sensibilities."

Richard was leaning back in his chair. He wore jeans with two T-shirts that skirted below his waistline underneath a grubby-looking poncho with patches on it. Like Linus in *Peanuts*, this must be his security blanket, Blaine thought. Richard's almond-colored eyes were large and probing.

"Well, that sounds like stealing, to me."

Blaine stared up at him as the class gasped in surprise.

222

"How's that?" Blaine replied.

"You said you take another's voice. What's the word you said? You infuse it with your sensibilities. That means you steal it and you hide the stealth. That's what it sounds like to me."

"Not quite." Blaine glanced at the large clock sitting above the door.

"And what happens if someone believes you did steal something from them? What can they do?"

"Hire lawyers, get their day in court."

"I see," Richard said. "But there aren't any witnesses to the theft most times, right? I mean, something could happen to them, right? I remember, and this is true life: some screenwriter made an accusation of theft against some Hollywood bigwig, you know? Gone. What about that movie, 'The Player?' That dude kills the guy he stole from. Truth is stranger than fiction, isn't it? And now Sherry's dead."

Some of the group members gasped. One or two of them, Catholics, crossed themselves.

"I suspects I know who did it." Richard was gesticulating with his hand, commanding his audience's attention. "Somebody has a secret, right? Sherry knew about it. You had a good set-up, anyway, didn't you? You kept her in the family because she was helping you all with your scripts and stuff. She was ready for Hollywood. She's gonna have to be cast as a corpse now. I don't see how you can sit here and talk to these people when one of your fellow writers is dead." He glared at Blaine, waiting for a response.

"Well, that's a personal issue that I wasn't sharing with anyone."

Richard looked around at the group, his beer bottle in hand.

"Sherry. Did you all know her? She came to his classes? Lived in his house? And he didn't say anything to anyone? Hey, man, whaddup with that? Another one bites the dust? Use 'em, then leave 'em. Is that how it works?"

Blaine told his entourage, "I imagined that you would have read it in the papers already."

"Right. They'd read about it. How about that, class? How about you all write a story about a first-class jerk who doesn't have the

223

decency to let people know that your classmate is dead. You was keeping that one to yourself, right? Gonna write about it yourself. Isn't that where we get our ideas? From real life? What kind of writer are you not to share this woman's life with her colleagues? You can't even honor the dead. That explains what you do to the living, right?"

Blaine stood up. "Well, everybody knows where this is leading. We can continue this discussion at our next round table. Thanks for coming by."

His students looked perplexed.

"Don't worry. He's upset. We're friends." Blaine nodded them away. "I'll be fine. See you next week. Same time."

The students looked uncertain, timid, concerned for Blaine's safety, as they moved away.

Blaine put on a purple windbreaker with an expensive-looking logo, and motioned to Richard. "C'mon. Let's go outside."

Richard slid his chair out of the way and walked up to Blaine. Standing an arm's-length away, he said, "Never tell a man to step outside, dude. That's an invitation for a whuppin'."

"Where I come from, it just means, let's go talk outside. I don't want to make a scene. Shall we?"

Opening the door, he let Richard go out first, then waved to his departing entourage, smiling apologetically.

"Okay, let's take a little walk, shall we?" Richard put his arm around Blaine, forcing him to walk alongside.

"Honestly, I'm not in the mood right now. I have other pressures weighing on me," Blaine said, crossing his arms.

"Well, this is important," Richard said as he led him up the street in the direction of the riverfront.

It was 9:30 p.m., and the sidewalks were deserted, except for a homeless person shrouded under coats and hats, sitting erect, head bowed. Large overhanging pecan and magnolia trees threw shadows on the sidewalk.

"You see, I have a story I want to tell you, and you tell me, is this a good what-do-you-call-it?"

"A pitch. Like baseball," said Blaine.

"I didn't know you all played sports. Dude!" Richard slapped him on the back, grabbing his shoulders. "So, this ... pitch—what would you do with it? What would you and your girlfriend, Sherry, do with that story?"

"I don't have a girlfriend."

"Your boyfriend."

"Don't have one of those either. And I'm not gay," Blaine said arrogantly.

Richard snickered. "That so? Okay. So, I got a story for you about a little boy."

"That's more like it. I'm into movie themes with children." Blaine's voice was higher-pitched, now, his gaze fixed straight ahead.

Richard thrust his pelvis forward, positioning himself, planting his feet into the sloping hill.

"Okay. Well, this might work, then." He licked his lips and spread his hands dramatically. "Once upon a time, this guy, let's call him Richard, fell in love with a girl who was a student at Nakadee University. Her name was Sherry. She worked for two writers who had a production company. One of the writers was a part-time writing instructor. Let's imagine what his name is, but it's really not important. He's not very well-known in the grand scheme of things. I mean, he didn't write *Gone With the Wind* or anything like that. Oh—I forgot to add the visuals."

Blaine's jaw tightened as he kept his eyes on the riverbank while Richard spoke. He stole a glance as Richard clapped his hands like a magician, conjuring his story.

"This girlfriend of mine—I mean, of Richard's—well, she was beautiful. My fairy princess. Lady Diana didn't have nothin' on her, and Prince Charles would have left her if he had met this girl. Her name was Sherry. Richard could hang with her for years and feel like only a minute had passed. Out of respect for her, because she's a princess, I won't talk about her womanly gifts, as you might call them in fairy tales or literary circles—not you, of course, but real writers."

Chuckling, Richard scratched his head, looked toward the heavens, then sighed nostalgically, "Okay, where was I?" He looked around, snapping his fingers. "Right. She was an angel. But she was one of those angels—are they called fallen angels—are they agents of Lucifer? You wouldn't know, would you? You don't read the Bible, I'm sure of that, New or Old Testament. I don't know your religion and I ain't about to check your Johnson to find out, either."

Blaine stood stoically.

"Well, anyway, it turns out she had a secret. It wasn't a big one, because it didn't take a professor to know who was gifted and who wasn't. It was ... well, it was an obvious thing. She wasn't a writer. But she was a foil. I bet you didn't think I know'd that word, right? She was a ruse, an abstraction, a decoy, a red herring."

He looked at Blaine with disgust.

"What this producer was doing was making a movie for little kids. So, they befriended this kid. Let's say his name is Melvyn. Does that name ring a bell?"

Blaine, standing immobile, said nothing, though the color drained from his face.

"They was taking pictures of the boy and his friends, when they came over to mow the lawn or rake leaves. He was a yard boy. He even knew how to clean your pool. He spent a lot of time at your house. And you was filming it."

The river's murmur could be heard in the background as they talked. There were rocks below them. A brick wall served as a breaker that stopped at the river's edge, where the murky water undulated hypnotically.

Blaine nodded, slowly.

"Is that a good story or what? Is that gonna sell? Is somebody gonna buy that story from me?" Richard crossed his arms.

Blaine smirked imperceptibly, visibly registering only a nod, staring ahead. "Well, it depends."

"On what?"

"On who you're pitching it to."

"Or did you mean, 'to whom you are pitching it'?" Richard corrected him. "You can't even speak good grammar."

Without warning, he hit Blaine with his fist, connecting with his face.

Bright red blood spurted from Blaine's nose, but his feet didn't falter as he held his ground.

"One of those, are you?"

Blaine stared at him, face twitching as blood dripped out of his mouth. He touched his tooth and wiggled it.

"You accept your punishment?" Richard said, before hitting him in the other jaw, this time causing Blaine to stumble and adjust his balance before standing upright again.

Wally, who had been watching them for several minutes, trotted over and stepped between the two men.

"Dude, you can't hit him like that. Where do you think you are?"

Richard was still slapping at Blaine, who turned his head away but didn't raise his hands in protest.

"You like this shit, you spineless fucker. You are too vile to waste my energies on. You really want this."

Wally gripped Richard's arm, almost lifting him off the ground.

"Hey, man! Watch the arm. If you ain't police, leave me the hell alone."

Wally released his grip and Richard took two paces, then spun around, his hands on his hips.

"Well then. Whadda ya say we have a talk, copper. About my man here."

"Even if this is a lover's quarrel, I still can't let you beat up on your boyfriend."

"Man, what you talkin' about? Man, you don't want to go there with me, unless you looking for a beating yourself." Richard raised his fists, beginning to dance. "I feel like whuppin' ass today. Step in line. Come on."

Turning his back to Richard, Wally slowly retrieved an automatic hiding against his back underneath his shirt. At the toss of Wally's head, Richard understood the non-verbal cue to scram.

"Have it your way. Whoever you are. He don't need more attention, you know. He gets off on this. He's some kinda twisted sicko who likes to get beat down. Makes him feel alive. Right, Mr. Filmmaker? This is what you call child's play, right?"

"You live together?" asked Wally.

Richard laughed. "What you take me for, man? Look at this pitiful sucker. He's a grown man with the mentality of a ... what is it, dude ... fifteen- or sixteen-year-old?"

Blaine was wiping his face, still spitting blood. "Can I leave?"

Wally spoke softly. "Whadda ya say we let your friend go first. I'll escort you to your car."

Richard spoke. "Dude. He's not interested in you. You're too old. For him, you gotta be a teenager."

"Where's your car?" Wally asked Blaine.

"Land Rover. It's in front of the corner spot." Richard answered.

Wally jerked his head. "Right, then. Get to it."

"You lucky you packin', dude. I takes my orders from no one." Richard turned around, deftly sidestepping to avert tripping over a large rock embedded in the uneven grass.

Walking backwards, he raised his voice. "You'll meet Sherry in hell, you know. And if you reckon taking these licks is absolution, there's more where that came from. Clean yourself with this."

Richard raced forward toward Blaine, spitting at him.

Wally pulled Blaine back from the spit as it arced in midair.

"I wanna hear your car engine moving away from here, you hear?" Wally warned Richard.

"Sure thing. As long as you continue where I left off, man, we're cool. He's all yours, man. I'll catch him next time around. Believe that."

17

JUANITO

10:00 p.m.

Juanito parked his car a half-mile away from Preston's house and walked the rest of the way. He used his key and opened the front door, slowly.

It was time to go back to Florida. Things were getting way too hot here. If they couldn't frame little Melvyn, then it would be him next.

He looked around the room with both nostalgia and regret: nostalgia for the innocence lost, regret that he hadn't done something about it earlier.

Gringos.

His father had forewarned him. "*Hijo*, this country is for immigrants who know how to stay in their place. If you go outside the dotted lines, you'll be pulverized. You can't make it in Hollywood, no matter what you think."

His papa was right.

He took off his thin jacket and set it on top of a box in the living room, then went upstairs to his room to gather his belongings. Seeing his half-filled duffle bag, he wondered whether he should drive to Florida, or fly and let TSA go through his dirty socks and underwear.

When he heard the front-door lock turn, he rushed to extinguish the bedroom light and tiptoed to the door, almost closing it, leaving just enough space to see a shadow on the stairs. He heard footsteps that stopped in Preston's study, drawers opening and closing, and the sound of someone rifling through papers.

Then he heard voices and dropped to his knees slowly, to listen:

Male Voice: *So what's it gonna be today, Melvyn, my man. Did I say it right?*

Melvyn: *You da man, brother man.*

Male Voice: *So, I'm the man.*

Melvyn: *You got it.*

Male Voice: *I'm the man. Cool. (papers rustling).*

Melvyn: *What's all that?*

Male Voice: *Where?*

Melvyn: *All that paper. You writing about me?*

Male Voice: *Well, in a way.*

Melvyn: *You for real, man?*

Male Voice: *You don't mind, do you?*

Melvyn: *It depends. Why you writin' about me?*

Male Voice: *Writers write. I'm creating a character, you might say.*

Melvyn: *A character. Like Harry Potter. Like that?*

Male Voice: *Not quite. But a character, just the same.*

Melvyn: *What's my name gonna be?*

Male Voice: *Jamal.*

Melvyn: *Jamal? Why you gotta give me a Shaka Zulu name?*

Male Voice: *(laughs)*

Melvyn: *Why don't you call him "Melvyn," like me?*

Male Voice: *Well, because this is called fiction.*

Melvyn: *But you said it's about me, and I'm real.*

Male Voice: *How about, for the time being, we call him that, and maybe down the road we'll think about changing his name.*

Melvyn: *Call him Alvin.*

Male Voice: *Not a bad idea. I'll think about that.*

Melvyn: *Okay. So what else you wanna know?*

Male: *Well, I'd like to know about if you have any girlfriends.*

Melvyn: *Yeah, man, a whole lot of 'em. They call me 'Melvyn the Playa' at school.*

Male Voice: *The Playa? Like in Spanish? The beach?*

Melvyn: *I don't know no Spanish. Play-er.*

Male Voice: *What does that mean?*

Melvyn: *You know. I rap to them. You know, like I talk to them, and ask them for their numbers, you know. My dad taught me that. That's what they called it back in the day. Big pimpin'.*

Male Voice: *Do you call the girls up?*

Melvyn: *Naw, man. A Playa doesn't do the calling. They call me. Every night. I get about five calls a night. (laughing)*

Male Voice: *Wow! All girls?*

Melvyn: *Yeah, who else? I ain't gonna talk to no dude on the phone, am I?*

Male Voice: *I guess not. Well, when you talk to them, well, like … what do you talk about?*

Melvyn: *We talk about school. Movies. Music. Things. This 'n' that.*

Male Voice: *Like what movies?*

Melvyn: *Well, it depends on if she goes to the—(interruption) movies. I go to the movies a lot with—[unintelligible]. We go on Tuesday nights. She takes me. So I ask them if they seen such and such a movie. Heck, I don't know. I mean, what does anybody talk about on the phone? Nothing important.*

Male Voice: *What about books?*

Melvyn: *Well, we talk about* Harry Potter *and stuff like that. I just finished the* Twilight *stuff.* The Hunger Games. *We'll talk about that.*

Male Voice: *Well, do you talk about drugs or anything like that?*

Melvyn: *No man. Don't go there … I don't know anybody that does drugs. My mother would kick me up and down the State of Louisiana she hear me doin' something like that.*

Male Voice: *You've never seen a joint?*

Melvyn: *I seen 'em smoke it on the street, you know, they do like this … (hissing sound) and they hold their breath. You ever try smoking weed?*

Male Voice: *Well, yes.*

Melvyn: *It fucks up your head, don't it? My mom said she catch me with that shit, she'd slap me silly before I finish my first puff.*

Male Voice: *Your mom sounds pretty strict.*

Melvyn: *So you gonna rag on my momma now? You know you can't be doing that, right? That's the one thing I can teach you. You can't go talking about a black man's momma.*

Male Voice: *Oh. Well, I didn't mean it that way, I just … well, okay. Sorry. Forget it.*

Melvyn: *S'aright. I know. You didn't know. We cool. Can I have another one?*

Male Voice: *Sure. Take two. Go ahead. So, where's your dad?*

Melvyn: *Here. There. Everywhere. I see him on weekends. He takes me on the weekends, you know, to his house. Sometimes, I just ride my bike there.*

Male Voice: *Is he married?*

Melvyn: *Yeah.*

Male Voice: *How you feel about that?*

Melvyn: *It's cool. I guess. If he's happy, I'm happy. (quiet)*

Male Voice: *Your mood changed. You okay? (pause) You wanna talk about it?*

Melvyn: *No. I'm fine. I was just thinkin', that's all.*

Male voice: *Okay, well, let me ask you again about drugs. You don't do them, but do any of your friends do 'em?*

Melvyn: *No, not mine.*

Male voice: *Well, do you know anybody who does drugs?*

Melvyn: *Well, I know they got some potheads who hang out before school, and they be smoking and shit. But I don't go near 'em. They're bad news, Preston. They got arrested once in front of the school for smoking some weed and then going onto the school grounds, you know. They said it was a drug-free zone and they were expelled. Our school is pretty strict about drugs. Besides, what the hell are drugs good for if you gotta keep paying for them? Man, I'd rather get more Nintendo or Sega than smoke up all the money into the air. They stupid, man.*

Preston: *You're a smart kid, Melvyn. Where'd you get a name like that, anyway?*

Melvyn: *Back to that, huh? Why you so fascinated about names? You gonna pay me fifty dollars to talk about names. You must have an awful lot of money to waste time on that.*

Preston: *I guess you're right.*

Melvyn: *Oh, yeah. My mom said her mom named me after some movie star or something. Right. Anyway, she asked me to ask you if you …. (pause)*

The recording stopped. A minute later, Juanito heard the front door open, then close again. He ran his fingers through his hair, letting minutes pass before he tiptoed downstairs toward the living room. On the bottom step, he saw Mare standing behind a chair, looking at him, calmly.

"I wondered whose jacket that was on the box there. And here you are. I wasn't sure you were still staying here, now that your source of income has dried up."

He said nothing, glancing at the computer screen in the study. The video on his screen was frozen. "You look like you've seen a ghost, Juanito. So, you've been found out, have you?"

He still said nothing, but rubbed his chin, creasing his forehead. "So, what was that all about?" Her hand was outstretched toward the study. "Kiddie porn?"

"A kid with his shirt off? Since when is that pornography? I'm not a babysitter," he snapped.

"Why was it being filmed?" Mare walked toward him. "They're videos of a boy's scantily clad body! What's with the close-ups of his chest? His stomach? His arms?" She raised her voice, putting her head in her hands. "I want to vomit!"

Juanito, still puzzled, walked toward the computer. "Maybe they wanted to learn about his mannerisms, or something. What do I know? He has shorts on! Maybe it was hot? Since when is that illegal?"

"Cut the crap, Juanito."

"I'm serious. I haven't seen these before."

"You're a liar."

"Consider again who you're talking to, Miss Miriam."

"Then you're an accomplice."

233

"I wasn't here all the time, no matter what you think. I don't know anything about this." He took out a black bandana and wiped his brow. The air conditioner was off and the room was humid.

"Was this Preston's doing?"

Juanito shrugged his shoulders.

"What did he do with the little boys, Juanito—that you let happen?"

"I didn't know it was happening."

"What's 'it'?"

"Whatever you say was happening."

"Were you present in the room?"

"No."

"Then how do you know what he was doing?"

"Who said I knew?"

"Who shot it?" she demanded.

"Sorry. You'll have to pay me for my knowledge." He put his hands behind his back.

"Like hell I will. You've already ransacked Preston's accounts."

"That you gave me permission to use, or did you conveniently forget that?"

"I gave you access to one account: his house management account—which you and Sherry depleted. I didn't know Nakadee had so many limousines. What do they cost here? And who did you bribe to bill them for you? I never heard of Ricky's Limousine Service before. I looked online and didn't find anything. I asked my limousine driver, too. So that's how you siphoned his checking account? Creative billing."

"I'm sworn to secrecy. You know. Hollywood." He stared at her, his dark eyes flashing.

"Who said you were a talentless hunk? You're Hollywood all the way!" Mare was getting exasperated. She turned slowly, canvassing the room. "You know something else, Juanito? I thought it was kind of strange that I never got a call from you once you found out that Preston was missing. Blaine—well, let's just say that he lives in his own world. But you were an employee of our company."

She waited for him to respond.

Juanito rolled his eyes. "That's funny, you never talked about the company in terms of *our* before. I wasn't even here at the time to really know he was missing."

"Conveniently." Mare turned around, her lips parted, disbelief flashing across her face. "Well, you could have called to ask questions or something. It's not as if you don't know my number."

He didn't look at her.

Mare stood up and moved through the cardboard boxes stacked on top of each other in piles. She sauntered past Juanito, heading toward the mother of pearl writing secretary with the ornate feet.

He followed her, asking, "You're looking for the prenup, right?"

She rubbed her finger on the powder that had been used to lift prints, touching the ornate handles of the drawers, opening them listlessly and peering inside. They were all empty. "You two choose this together, too?" she asked about the desk. She turned to face him. "You're in my home. I was his wife. Not you."

"Here's some news, Miriam, and you might want to sit down." He pointed to an oversized chair, but she remained standing. "What if I told you that you were never even married? What then? What if he told me you were his cover, not because of his, um, sexual orientation, but because it never hurt to have a contact, meaning, *you*, with access to other agents and industry people. Do you see how hard it is to get really bad reviews when your partner has access to all the do-nothing agents in Hollywood?"

"Is that supposed to be news? We called ourselves Bill and Hillary, if you must know."

"He told me," Juanito smiled.

"And what's your point? So he loved you more? Run with it. No contest." She clapped, the sound reverberating in the high-ceilinged room. She turned toward the bookcases. "I'll keep looking."

She bit her lip, staring at him, as he continued speaking.

"Wanna know what else he told me? When you had your fake ceremony here—way before he moved here, right? It was because Louisiana doesn't recognize common-law relationships. He said that the Justice of the Peace here was one of his Mardi Gras co-sponsors, a judge who was kicked off the bench, who wasn't even allowed to perform wedding ceremonies."

She smiled knowingly. "You memorized this one, didn't you?" She laughed from a place deep within. "Was that after you killed your little girlfriend, Sherry?"

"Keep Sherry out of this. She has nothing to do with anything."

"Didn't you go to the same gym? I'd call and ask Preston where everybody was and he'd say, the young'uns are at the gym. She was killed there, wasn't she? So what's your alibi? Didn't you two usually go together? Did you leave her there? Let's talk about that, Juanito, the Marielito."

"She's none of your business."

"Like hell she isn't. All of this is business. Even Preston. But I better be quiet. You might get rid of me, too."

He took a step closer to her, putting his hands on her shoulders, glaring into her eyes.

She couldn't hide her fear.

"What did I kill him with, Miriam? Should I do the same to you?"

Mare was frozen.

"See. I'm a pretty good actor."

She smiled. "You're finished in Hollywood. You know that, right? Let me look into my crystal ball and tell you your immediate future: the closest you'll get to Hollywood will be on the streets of Hollywood and Vine, hailing down cars. But you won't get discovered there. The men looking for your kind of talent will want you to perform in an alley, and your only audition will be them asking you to open your mouth so they can look for canker sores. Your career trajectory is preordained. Oh—one more piece of advice. When your good looks fail you, after three years on the street, you'll be only a facsimile of who you are today."

Walking away from him, trying to hide her fear, she stumbled over boxes, which he easily stepped over to reach her, grabbing her by the shoulders.

"But you'll still be begging for it then, too." He pushed his body up against hers as she closed her eyes. He drew her closer. "What? That leather-faced Congressman can't do it for you?"

She opened them again as his groin pressed into hers; her face was one of both apprehension and expectation. He hung onto her neck for a few seconds, then gently stepped away.

"What? Bored already?" she scoffed.

He laughed as he stepped back, dusting his hands together. "No. I'm not gonna give you what you want."

She said nothing as he took big strides toward the stairs, his voice sounding hollow in the stairwell. "I'll get my things. I want nothing more to do with you *gringos. Madre de dios.*"

"Except Sherry. But she's not alive."

"I have my spies. You keep your secrets and I'll keep mine."

"My guess is you have been paid a nice sum to stay mum."

"Mum? I don't know that word. It's not in my Spanglish vocabulary."

"Maybe the police can make you talk."

"Yeah? The minute they question me, I'll have both you and Blaine locked up. I have no motive to get rid of Preston. You do realize that, don't you? He would do anything for me. I'm the friend he never had."

"That could be bought and sold."

"You married the gay man, Miss Miriam. I'd say you had the most to gain. Which is why you're here, right? Trying to see if he ever filed for that divorce? Why don't you pick up the phone and call the court?"

Mare glared at him.

"Right. The evidence could be used against you." He crossed his arms. "Don't let my pretty face fool you. I know you stand to inherit everything if you can save face as a widow and go through the motions of shedding crocodile tears. And if you *are* divorced, well, you still have leather-face. I'm sure he pleases you better than any young man like me ever could."

Chuckling, Juanito picked up his jacket, shook it out, put it on, then walked up the stairs.

"Hurry up. I'll be taking that key from you," she called out to him.

Leaning forward, she watched him continue up the steps to his room, then moved to the study, and began putting compact discs into her oversized black handbag. She turned to the computer and clicked on the documents icon, then waded through a morass of computer files and folders.

About ten minutes later, Juanito came back downstairs with a full duffle bag.

"Wanna inspect to make sure I'm not taking your precious belongings?"

"Just so you know—you are free to take all of my gowns."

He held a lone key in front of her and dropped it on the rug. "You won't find what you're looking for. I suppose whoever had what you're looking for is dead by now, so their secret died with them. Or, maybe I have what you're looking for—not what you want—what you need."

He leveled an imaginary gun at her and pulled the trigger. "Goodbye, Miriam. Pleasant dreams," he said and walked out of the side door into the night.

18

AMBROSE GIRABEAUX

Thursday, March 24th, 4:44 p.m.

Ambrose sat in a taxi, pondering the email message on his smartphone. His heart beat wildly. Someone was specifically conveying threats to him, first at the Hot Sauce Festival, and now in this message. The email was cryptic, telling him to go home immediately. Fearing danger, he did as he was told.

He barely let the cab stop at its destination before depositing a ten and a five in the front seat. "Receipt, please."

He snatched the white piece of paper and ran up the short steps to his three-story walk-up. The door was not locked. Good. Someone was home.

"Bela! Bela!" His housekeeper was fixing her hair when he bumped into her rounding the corner to the foyer. Her white tennis shoes were in her cloth bag and she was ready to leave.

"*Dios mio!*" She held her throat.

"Sorry to startle you."

"*Señor*, you got some flowers. They are so pretty. I put them in the living room on the coffee table. Go look. The yellow really brings out the color on the wall. You should order them all the time."

"Oh, okay. You leaving?"

"See you next week," she smiled, fussing with her trench coat and scarf.

He barely heard her as he rushed into the living room. He watched from the window as she walked down the street, then hurried over to pluck the white envelope from the plastic clasp jutting out of the purple lilies and hyacinths.

"Go online," the message commanded. "I'm waiting for you in a Motorcycles chat room on _ _ _ _ _ _ _ _ _.com. "Meet you in Motorcycles. You're COUNTDOWN. Opening line: 'I'm here looking for a Harley.'"

He raced upstairs to his study.

The Internet was a silent window on the world of its inhabitants, he knew. Over time, someone in that world might literally figure out who you really were behind your avatar. Ambrose's nemesis could not see exactly where he was in his house, but knew he'd be there, clicking his way through the Internet search engine to reach his destination. The twinkling sound came on, telling him someone wanted to chat, but it took him a minute to find his instant-message partner.

Twenty people in the room. He's looking for cover. Here goes. A bead of sweat was forming on Ambrose's brow as he typed. He clicked a button to create his chat-room name.

COUNTDOWN: *I'm here looking for a Harley.*

Ambrose hissed through his teeth. "Oh, you give me a name and I don't know yours. Brilliant. Where are you? Who are you?" He scrolled through the names of the biker enthusiasts, looking for a clue.

BJHOOKER 1244: That's what you say! LOL. I bet you didn't say that last night!

CALLMEGOOD3245: Hey, does anybody know where I can buy cheap oval alluminator billet style mirrors? Wholesale?

CARBRATER: I did. And it worked like magic. I'm telling you, that's the only way to keep her. When you coming this way, BJ? Looks like you need some coaching! LOL.

SUZYQUEUE: Anybody going to the Ride-a-thon in Marina del Rey?

There's gonna be some smoking a*$($) b$(tches there!
Like me! Be there or be a Kawasaki-Rider!

NOJOKE4456: *What kind of Harley are you looking for?*

Ambrose's heart missed a beat. Was it fear or excitement? Was that really him, or was it just someone making inquiries? How would he know who the hell it was? This was a real goose chase. Then he figured it out.

"'No Joke.' No kidding. I get it. No joke," Ambrose snickered. A bead of sweat was cresting the first fold in his wrinkled brow as he squinted. He wasn't sure what to say. He didn't know anything about Harleys. He'd never ridden a motorcycle in his life. He scrolled down through the messages, looking for other respondents. BJ and CARBRATER were old friends, it seemed. Suzy Queue was looking for fun. He scrolled some more to see if anyone else was biting.

FESTERING33: Hey, I'm going, Suzy. Wanna hook up? Meet me in New Mexico?

BJHOOKER 1244: Honestly, she did exactly what I requested. Boom. It was worth it.

Ambrose continued to look at the screen. NOJOKE was still in the chat room. He wasn't conversing with anybody else. Ambrose paused, frozen with anticipation.

NOJOKE4456: What kind of Harley are you looking for?

Typed a second time. Bingo.

SUZYQUEUE: Cool. As long as you don't mind traveling with a female gang. We're looking for cover!

BOOTYCALL21: Anybody looking for a handsome biker?

COUNTDOWN: Not sure. I was told I could buy one here, however.

NOJOKE3456: "It might cost you if you don't like THE BILL. It could be very COSTLY."

The reply was rapid.

FESTERING33: Hey, Booty, stay out my way. I'm in charge of rapping to the ladies.

COUNTDOWN: What bill?

Ambrose mouthed the words as he typed.

NOJOKE: Do you have a COPYRIGHT on your stupidity? :)

Ambrose read the message, his eyes darting to NOJOKE'S name. No time to read the other messages. This is definitely him. And he's warning me.

"Is that a kind thing to say to someone who wants to find out what you're offering?" Ambrose spoke aloud as he typed. He was going to play hardball.

NOJOKE: Well, that MARKUP in price tomorrow might be deadly if the BILL doesn't PASS. I'd do anything in my power to PAY THE BILL. Motorcycles are dangerous and delay could destroy your LIFE! You need to do your research. Cycles are dangerous instruments of death.

The Markup? Ambrose directed his attention to the screen again. PASS THE BILL. DELAY. LIFE. Certain death. He could read between the lines. He wiped his brow as if to clear his brain, while still staring at the computer.

This is about the Markup? He and Killian had not spoken since their dinner at Ambrose's home. The benefit of the bargain would be irresistible, he had been told: the as-yet-to-be-created Girabeaux-Killian amendment would throw him into a spotlight that would shine on his political fortunes down the road. He was definitely angling toward a Senate run in the next couple of years. This would get him elected, along with his wooing the female vote.

He had sure enjoyed wooing Lula.

He smiled, then frowned. Concentrate.

NOJOKE: Went to Carnival in LA. It killed me to go there. But I had to go. I'll call on you, too. Soon.

NOJOKE disappeared.

Ambrose pressed the Print icon and closed the screen, then sat, holding his head in his hands, rubbing his temples as the transcript of their conversation slid out of his multifunction printer. He went downstairs to the living room and sat on the sofa. Whatever he decided, he had about eight hours in which to do it.

He stared at the flowers.

Purple.

Death.

He thought about calling the Capitol Police, but didn't want to be trailed wherever he went in D.C. He was going back to Nakadee for meetings about the natural gas pipeline, and hoped to see Lula again.

He smiled. She was a woman he could come home to.

"Concentrate, Ambrose," He said aloud. He walked upstairs, cleared the mounds of papers from his desk, and loosened his tie as he spilled papers from his hands. They were trembling.

Surely this was a prank. Like there is really a killer on the loose, right under Congressman Ambrose Girabeaux's nose, fighting over the language of picayune laws concerning procedural etiquette for Markup sessions.

He shook his head, smiling, wanting to negate the possibility. But could he risk it?

5:17 p.m.

Lula, Devon, and Nate were greeted by a police officer standing guard and a balding forty-something year-old man in a black suit who was swaying on his feet. Nate introduced him as one of the detectives.

The victim's remains were on old man Arcenaux's land, about a half-mile away from his home, where he and his terrier, Rusty, had been walking in the forest. They were well into an area of ten-foot-tall trees.

Arcenaux's dog had run straight ahead, as if chasing something. When Arcenaux caught up, the dog was sniffing and barking at a curious-looking mound. Arcenaux immediately called the police on his cell phone.

From a distance, the dead body looked like an Impressionist painting, with colors of earthen red, white, pink, and blackish brown. Once-firm muscles were now quivering pieces of undulating slime that made their way into, out of, and around the internal organs, further exposing them to the elements. Limbs were missing, likely strewn about by the ravages of animal hunger.

The person who had once walked, talked on the telephone, and interacted with other humans was now one with nature. Steam rose from the body, generated by the metabolic heat of the thousands of maggots burrowing deep into its cavities, giving the illusion of its movement. Such a ghostly sight in a lonely forest would make anyone question what was real and what was illusory.

Nate looked ashen, but was putting up a good front. "I won't be eating pudding or Jell-O for a while. I bet you could eat right here in front of this, right?" he asked Lula.

"I wouldn't say that."

"How did it affect you, the first time you saw something like this?"

She pondered the question momentarily. "I guess I was fascinated, but I couldn't sleep well for a full month. I wasn't haunted, per se, but it was unsettling. Then I psyched myself to snap out of it. I realized that death is just a different stage of life, although perhaps not like we understand it. Corpses provide food for maggots, which actually spares the living, if you think about it. With all the people who have died, wouldn't the earth smell pretty bad if we didn't have the maggots to take care of things? But the bones, those will live for centuries, unless they're cremated. So, the more you understand what you're looking at, the more you'll be able to stomach this." She looked at him, smiling. "You're doing great."

"See anything?"

Lula decided not to respond, just yet. Several limbs were missing: a hand, the left femur, and the right foot.

"I just wonder, how do we know this isn't a suicide and that animals took the body apart afterwards?" Nate asked.

Lula pointed out a noticeable telltale feature—a slice through the skull—which she called a "perimortem trauma."

"Number one, I don't see the implement used to commit the suicide, which, if used by him or her, would likely be found at the scene, unless someone came back and took it away."

"How about someone forced him to kill himself, and then left with the weapon? Would that be a suicide, then?"

Lula wished he would shut up, but realized that he had to talk to keep from losing his cookies.

"You're steering me into legal territory now—I don't feel competent to answer those types of questions, truthfully. The police can't rule out suicide, but given where the wound is, I'd find the scenario a bit difficult to imagine. My goal as a forensic anthropologist is to figure out how the death was caused, not so much who caused it. Figure out the race and gender of the corpse, identify the cause of death, and establish what might have happened to the body in between the victim's death and when it was discovered."

She knelt at the left side of the corpse, pointing toward the back of the skull and lifted her smartphone to record: "I see a fracture line, with a relatively sharp break, at the left, at the parietal bone and extending caudally into the occipital bone."

She was mystified by the corpse's appearance. The remaining maggot activity was unlike any she had ever seen, as the larvae appeared to be five times the size of blow-fly maggots.

Still more eerie was the fact that the maggots were black, not white. Lula was struck by the patches where the maggot activity appeared to cease, leaving behind a frozen white maggot porridge. White maggots hung like icicles from an area of the skull where the victim might have been struck, as if the maggots, themselves, had been struck by something, too.

Lula surmised that the maggots had first feasted on the sliced wound to the head, then been overtaken by the new marauding black maggot species that overwhelmed them.

Even after death, there is a war over the corpse, she thought. Some larvae were grayish-white, while others were dark brown. Oddly, the larvae had no hair or spine. Whatever the war may have been between the species, the black maggots had won the battle. This was highly unusual, and she needed to make sense of it. Just when did the victim die? Was the body eaten alive?

Unsure of how long she had been poring over the body, she looked up to see Nate and Devon watching her quietly, waiting for her to speak.

"It's hard to tell what kind of fracture this is—pathological, stress fracture, fatigue fracture, or trauma," she told them.

"Let me help," Devon said. "The answer is that somebody got fucked up, real bad, Dr. Logan. That's how I'd describe it." He subsequently walked away.

"So, what are all those clear husk-like things lying around the corpse?" Nate asked, pointing. The whiteness of the skeleton contrasted with the wisps of insect puparium that lay scattered about the ground, creating a thin veil.

Lula explained that even within a couple of hours after a human's death, flies appear and lay eggs, which hatch into larvae. Those maggots or larvae will transform into pupae, and then into adult flies, which completes their life cycle.

"These are the husks of the shell that they break out of to become flies." Like wisps of caterpillar casings, the husks blew in the wind, scattering throughout the grassy area, a large birthing room for adult flies. "The maggots aid in the decomposition process by eating the body."

"So the flies in our homes are from dead bodies?" Devon asked, returning to the conversation.

"Not all of them. But flies and insects, though a nuisance to us, have a purpose. They are natural garbage disposals. Most blow fly maggots generally feed on decomposing organic matter, whether it's a human body, a dead animal, vegetables in a mulching garden, or even where pipes leak water."

She peered closely at the corpse, still keeping her distance. "I can't say it's my specialty, but these puparium husks are a bit different from what I'm used to seeing, so I'll take a sample and send it to my entomologist contact."

Nate heaved a sigh. "Poor sucker. Woman?"

"Can't tell." Lula answered.

"Looks like there's some kind of dress around it," Devon conjectured.

Nate clicked his teeth. "I sure hope this isn't somebody's mama, God bless her soul." He peered closer into the grass.

Lula put on her latex gloves. The quiet in their surroundings was broken by occasional bird cackles—crows waiting for their turn, no doubt.

"Is there anything we can do to help you, Miss Logan?" the plain-clothes detective asked.

Lula had her work face on now. "If you wouldn't mind looking for anything in the way of evidence—human remains, personal effects, beyond this perimeter, that would be great. Just be careful not to walk anywhere in a direct path to and from this site, because the perpetrator may have left tracks somewhere."

Lula moved forward, peering at the ground, as she inched toward the middle of the clearing. She saw Nate walk toward Mr. Arcenaux.

Nate heaved a sigh. "Looks like the poor sucker might have been trying to escape. With one hand, no less."

Lula looked over the terrain, where a variety of creatures had left scratchy tracks, some webbed-footed, others from four-legged visitors. Alligators were also in plentiful supply in the area, mainly on private lands for hunting purposes. The investigators would have to see if any amphibians from nearby marshes might have come to sniff out the remains.

The body lay face down a hundred yards from a large dilapidated shack whose colorings matched that of the birch trees. The shed was what remained from a fire that had ravaged the dwelling once adjacent to it.

Lula handed Nate some Vicks Vaporub to put under his nose to mask the smell, which was obviously nauseating. He took out his handkerchief and covered his nose as he followed her into the shack.

For Lula, the menthol smell would interfere with her olfactory senses, which she needed for her work.

Protein bar wrappers were strewn about, along with empty plastic water bottles. The smell coming from the mound of human excrement, covered with sawdust, in a hole dug in the corner of the room, was diminished somewhat by the ammonia used to decrease the putrid odors that assaulted their senses. A mattress lay in the middle of the room next to a metal folding chair with a cushion. There were LED lanterns hanging from hooks placed in the wood ceiling.

Nate and Lula used their flashlights to canvas the room, but didn't spend too much time inside. The crime-scene investigators needed to do their jobs.

Outside, Lula surveyed the surroundings: a verdant forest that looked more like a magical setting than the backwoods of a wealthy man's 3,000-acre back yard.

Nakadee had had centuries of plantation slave labor, now replaced by family-owned poultry and fertilizer plants throughout its fifty-five-mile perimeter. Some of its forest hadn't even been documented yet. Environmentalists hadn't sought protection for their preservation, nor had the government taken the land over through eminent domain. So it was the private landowners of Nakadee Parish, like Mr. Arceneaux, who tended the forests, which meant that the area was still wild country.

Animal sounds were beginning to herald the arrival of dusk.

They all paused again to look at the corpse. Though none of them spoke, their feelings were obvious: no human being, decent or not, should die such a hideous death.

"I'll go check things out over there." Nate walked away, slowly.

Lula raised her voice. "Can anyone remind me whether or not it's rained here since Fat Tuesday?"

The detective, who was sweating profusely, spoke. "Yes. Once. We've had dry springs for a couple of years now."

She looked at him practically dripping in his sweaty clothes, his black suit coat still buttoned.

"Could you do me a favor and stand over here? We don't want any of the scene contaminated with your DNA, just in case we have to take some samples."

"Lula!" Nate yelled. She was startled that he hadn't used her title, as was his custom. "I've found something."

She looked up toward the direction of his voice and motioned to the officers to stay put and not venture closer to the work area. She walked toward Nate, who was ten yards away, kneeling next to a tree.

"Here." He looked at her with a smile on his face.

Moving forest debris with the eraser tip of his pencil, he exposed the platinum earring of a Celtic-type design. "I've seen this before."

He yelled to Devon. "Hey, man! You seen this before?" Devon came over toward Nate carefully.

"Yep, on Melvyn," he said.

248

Nate looked at Devon, triumphantly. "And guess who was hanging around in this area yesterday with his friends?"

Friday, March 25ᵗʰ, 7:00 a.m.

After a restless night, Lula awakened with a nagging headache. She took a shower and dressed in what felt like slow motion.

Opening her front door to go to work, and blinded by the crispness of the sun's rays, she tripped over a small bouquet of flowers that lay on the doorstep.

The bouquet of purple, yellow, and red-edged freesia gave off a pungent scent. The small accompanying envelope was slightly damp with dew. There was no handwriting on the outside.

Lula placed the flowers in the crook of her arm, opened the envelope and pulled out a piece of paper. *Expect more.*

The words were handwritten.

She looked around but saw no signs of life. She heard a car door slam, and the faint sounds of children "talkin' trash," as they congregated en masse on a corner to walk the fifteen long blocks to school.

Peering down at the note, she saw that the cursive penmanship was awkward, as though written by a child. She had no clue who had sent the flowers.

Could they be from Ambrose?

Suddenly, Lula felt ill at ease. Had someone watched her while she slept last night?

Tentatively, she walked around the side of the house, stopping at her bedroom window that faced the grassy backyard. Satisfied that nobody had been peeping at her, she walked slowly to her black Lexus and climbed in, still clutching the flowers firmly. She smelled them again before putting on her seatbelt.

Those window bars might not be such a bad idea, after all. As she drove away, she glanced at the hose that she had coiled up the night before. It appeared to be untouched. She told herself to calm down.

However insecure she'd felt at home, she was fine by the time she arrived at her lab. There was no need to put a "Do Not Disturb" sign on the door. The smells that hung in the air likely would repel almost anyone with an impromptu inclination to drop by. She spent much time alone, especially during the cadaver's soft tissue removal process.

Lula had long accepted the gruesomeness of her profession, adopting a clinical approach to what her friends in Oakland considered a witch-like, ghoulish preoccupation with death. Indeed, slow-boiling a human stew to carve and dissect its bones did conjure up Macbeth's witches' brew, but she insisted that her work was vital for solving the mysteries of the unclaimed dead.

Turning on the flame under the vats, she peered inside. The powdered laundry detergent she had added to the water gave the contents a soupy, opaque appearance, much like that of a washing machine soaking dirty colored clothes. The detergent degreased the skeleton, making the bones glisten.

Inspecting the industrial-sized cooker on the left, she saw a hand jutting up from the bottom, its fingertips looking like thick, broken roots grasping the air. The hand leaned against the femur that she had earlier wrestled free from the pelvis. She had had to twist the limb gently, repeatedly, as it was tightly attached to the *os coxa*, a thin broad piece of flat bone that, if tugged at too forcefully, could break.

The limbs were cooking nicely. She looked at her clock. She didn't want to be late for her meeting with Tom-Tom.

The retired entomologist was part mentor and had become something of a father figure after her own father died during her first year at college. After her graduate studies, she and Tom-Tom worked for a forensic laboratory in the Bay Area. He was the only person toward whom she gravitated, and the two of them lunched at different gourmet restaurants each month. Maybe their age difference was the leveling factor in their friendship. Tom always supported her work; her success didn't threaten him, as it often did her peers.

The cream-colored, grits-like substance mysteriously sticking to the corpse they'd discovered yesterday was a mystery. Even more puzzling was the size of the white larvae, some as long as twenty-seven millimeters. How long did they incubate? What had caused them to harden, and was that a detail that would determine when the subject died? Answers to those questions might aid in identification, too.

Tom-Tom was always jovial, especially since his retirement. He and Lula had a tradition of prefacing their conversations with a pun on their profession. When she had first called him for advice, she started her conversation with, "I'd like to put a bug in your ear, if you don't mind."

It felt good to hear the voice of someone from back home. They bantered a bit, then arranged for Lula to drop by for a visit.

"Should I ask my wife to guess who's coming to dinner?" Tom asked, playfully.

"How about a rain check on dinner?" She glanced up at the clock. "I need to come back within four hours at the most."

"Are you a chicken-hater or a chicken-lover?" he asked.

"Well, Tom, I don't mind chickens, if that's what you want to know."

"You'll see why I asked when you get here."

Hanging up the phone, she walked toward the cooker and turned down the flame to its lowest level. She stood over the boiling brew, peering in. She could now see the gashes in the head more clearly. They were in a parallel pattern, as if someone had taken tongs and slashed the victim, creating fault lines and deep punctures.

Had the victim been tortured? Whatever the weapon was, it had a point, or some protruding object that jutted out of it. It would now simply be a matter of looking in the forensic databases to find instruments with similar dimensions, and identifying who might have them. Once found, that weapon would be the circumstantial evidence of the murder.

In the meantime, she needed to talk to Tom-Tom about those large black pesky maggots.

From the highway, it was hard to know where the boundaries of Tom-Tom's chicken farm began. There were no signs among the dense foliage and underbrush to alert a driver that there was a dwelling nearby.

His home was a quarter of a mile from the asphalt road, at the end of a narrow, meandering gravel driveway, the entrance to which was surrounded by brush.

But what the eyes couldn't see the nose could detect, as the manure had a sweet smell that was overwhelming, even in the air-conditioned car.

Lula reached a clearing and arrived at the pastel blue and beige two-story home with large wooden planks stretching across its façade. The house was surrounded on three sides by a mesh and chain-link fence erected to keep the chickens from invading the human habitat.

As Lula walked toward the front steps, Tom-Tom appeared from the side of the house, carrying two large plastic glasses with straws jutting from them.

He had put on a couple of pounds, but his white hair and beard hadn't lost their brilliance and still gave him a Santa-Claus appearance. He had taken to farm life well. He was dressed in jeans, a blue denim shirt with red suspenders, and a thick leather belt with a large brass buckle that sported a mountain motif. His once-yellow walking boots were caked in layers of dry and wet red-clay soil.

He bellowed as he held his arms out to hug her, rocking her back and forth. "I told my wife I was cheating on her, and warned her not to be surprised if a beautiful black bombshell came a-knockin' one day to take her place."

Tom-Tom was like home, and Lula relished his arms around her as he kissed her forehead, then rubbed her shoulders with his forearms, the chilled refreshments still in his hands. Releasing her from his grip, he handed her a drink.

Less than a minute after leaving her air-conditioned car, her clothes were already sticking to her. She took a long sip of the iced tea, refreshed by its sugary sweetness.

"And what does the old battle-axe say to that and everything else I say nowadays? 'You're full of chicken shit.'" He spread his arms wide. "She tells it like it is, wouldn't you say?"

He began walking, turning in mid-step to take in her ankle-high hiking boots. "Okay. You're prepared, of course. Let's take a walk."

He steered her along the gravel driveway, away from the house, opening one of the mesh metal gates and holding it for her. Lula saw two miniature red barns the size of storage sheds.

"So, last time I talked to you, you were in the midst of a big dig. Anything happening with that?" he asked.

Lula chuckled. "Well, sometimes it seems that my own big-dig research has taken third place behind teaching and this police investigation."

The farm was situated on more than thirty acres of flatlands and small hills—part grassland, part scorched earth—with plants dotting the landscape. The setting was eerie. Lula watched colorfully plumed roosters standing quietly, mechanically pecking at the ground. An occasional squawk pierced the quiet countryside; otherwise, it was silent.

Tom-Tom pulled a glass vial out of his shirt pocket. Inside it was a dead fly. He handed it to her.

"Okay. This is your heralded black soldier fly, I'm sure you know. You all took samples of it, right?" He nudged her with his elbow, playfully. "Now, before you get on a tirade about Africanized-bees and black soldier flies, I'd like you to look at them and tell me that the head doesn't look like a helmet." He pointed to the heads of the flies, which indeed resembled black helmets with long shields hanging down to cover their necks. "I would have called them the 'Darth Vader' fly or something, but the soldier appellation was coined a long time ago."

Putting the vial back in his shirt pocket, he sipped his iced tea, pointing with his drink in the direction of an imposing barn-like edifice.

Lula stared in fascination as they walked along a dirt walkway beside the large pens that gave the wandering chickens breathing room.

"Here. This is what I want to show you."

A fenced-in area under a heavy plastic canopy was protecting a huge mound of maggots feasting on chicken feces piled in a trough.

Tom-Tom picked up a shovel that was leaning against the barn wall. "Now, that's what I call a shit load of maggots. These like the ones you saw?" He held his drink aloft as a pointer.

She nodded. The maggots looked like undulating masses of white, gray, and brown fattened worms weaving through the manure.

"And the maggots you saw, were they large, white, or black, like these?" He stooped down, bending his knees outward. "Here. If you look at the maggot, you'll see hair on it."

He let the shovel fall, then reached over to grab a stick and carefully picked up a maggot with it. As he held the stick toward the top to keep it steady, they both watched the maggot wriggle along the splintered wood.

Lula glanced at the trough, where hundreds of maggots slithered about. "So they turn from white to black?"

He nodded. "It's easy to confuse them with the blow-fly maggots, which are white, too. Now, if it's got hair, it's a black soldier fly. If it's hairless, it's a blow fly. And if it's as big as these mothers, it's a black soldier fly maggot. But just so you know, it's the white maggots that are doing the eating. The black maggots are only procreating. And no jokes, please."

She smirked at him, remembering the black maggots slithering over the corpse, burrowing themselves into the ground. Their purpose was to be "born again," hatching into soldier flies that would start the egg-laying cycle all over. If the body had been outdoors for a short period of time, ordinary maggots would reveal as much. But these were a different breed of maggots altogether. Lula tried to make sense of her newfound knowledge.

"Well, how did this black soldier fly that eats human flesh end up here, and not the blow fly? Or if they did show up at the site, when did they outsmart the blow fly to take over, and why?" She looked into Tom-Tom's gray eyes, wrinkled, soft and pink around the rims.

"Where was the body found?"

"In the woods."

He put the maggot back and leaned on the stick. "That's interesting. Not quite their hangout, you might say. If you consider the black soldier fly as you would a human being, the woods to them are like a mall with no stores. There's nothing for them unless there's a dead animal or some fecal matter nearby. That's not their hangout. At least the masses of them don't hang there. But they *do* travel, as far as fifteen miles, even."

His white beard was gleaming with moisture in the muggy heat.

"Well, that's your mystery, Doctor Logan. What's the black soldier fly doing in the woods, and where did they come from to end up there?"

He tapped the side of the trough gently with his stick. "I get rid of this every couple of weeks. In fact, I'm doing a controlled experiment to see how fast they eat manure. I got a buddy toxicologist who says the soldier fly can help the environment by eating the waste and reducing the amount of natural gasses in the air."

He put his arm around her shoulder, took a sip of tea, then asked, "Whadda ya say we have a little sit down? A genuine, and I mean genuine, fresh chicken sandwich, and shoot the breeze a bit? I'd like to get the wife a bit jealous for a spell, and flaunt my black beauty in front of her. Let's go inside, and you can ask me any questions you want. And I hope you like free-range eggs, 'cuz you're taking three dozen home with you."

19

MATT KILLIAN

Friday, March 25th, 10:00 a.m.

Markup Session, Rayburn House Office Building,
Washington, D.C.

"Thanks for hanging in there, everybody, but this is what we're paid for, after all. Lots of people are waiting to see what's taken place here today. We all know this is a private session. No recorders will be present. If anybody has plans to go rogue and rush for camera time after this session, I would discourage that. We do our work here, and we leave. We have ten more minutes to go, and you have the floor, Ambrose." Congressman Killian spoke slowly, showing signs of fatigue.

After three hours of debate, harangue, and concentration, the members at the Markup voted not to take a break so that they could all have a chance to speak and still reach the noon deadline. Matt was right. They were earning their keep, going through the legislation line by line, arguing about changes to be made, with the goal of avoiding judicial challenges down the road, including accusations of vagueness in their word choices.

As he rose to speak, Ambrose looked at Matt, who met his eyes with a steel gaze.

Ambrose looked away, then back at him. He was concerned about his silent, invisible interlocutor, NOJOKE, whose five-word admonition kept playing in his mind, like a mantra: You Pass or You Pass.

Ambrose stood up slowly, taking in a deep breath as he shuffled his papers, glancing at the wall clock.

"Okay, class," he began. His introduction was met with a communal moan and several wary smirks. He clapped his hands to wake up his audience. "This is the last session, and I need you to put your thinking caps on."

12:16 p.m.

"If I had a hundred dollars for every time a young upstart tried to show off and grandstand his way to political defeat, I'd be one rich man," Matt muttered under his breath, with a taciturn glare at Ambrose as they stepped outside the floor-to-ceiling doors of a committee room.

Other legislators filed out, some talking quietly together, others strolling right past the hoard of reporters, or moving quickly down the hallway back to their offices.

"There's no dispute about your current net worth, Congressman," Ambrose replied.

The press stakeout of lobbyists, media, and other interest groups stood around patiently, recorders in hand and cameras on tripods, behind a red rope guarded by two Capitol Police. They sprang to life in search of a morsel of news.

Matt and Ambrose faced each other, profiles on display, though they kept their conversation out of earshot. Red-faced, Matt was demonstrably upset that Ambrose hadn't done his bidding to scuttle the proposed copyright legislation Markup. He was further chagrined that Ambrose was going to beat him to the punch to explain his take on why the Markup failed to move the bill forward.

"Look, I'm sorry to disappoint, but I have my reasons," Ambrose responded, "one of them being that I'd like to buck the trend of political patronage and do what my heart tells me to do. Better yet, what my constituents want me to do."

Matt placed a hand on Ambrose's shoulder, as much in admonition as a gesture of camaraderie in front of the press, already snapping pictures. "Funny, I wondered if you had the chops to be a politician, and you just answered the question for me. I have also learned that you are not a man of your word." He shook his head, still smiling in his patrician way. "You promised."

Ambrose took a step closer, turning his back on the reporters. "I promised to consider. Nothing more."

"What was the handshake on your porch that night?"

"A handshake to give it my consideration. I said I could not be bought."

"Bullshit. You've just hurt your political career, Mr. Girabeaux, and we'll do what's necessary to be sure you're defeated come election time."

Patting him on the shoulder again, Matt brushed Ambrose aside this time, and walked toward the crowd of reporters.

Ambrose watched the senior Congressman work the press. He sighed, taking mental notes as Matt spoke, gloating about the amendment's defeat.

Watching Matt try to persuade the press that the copyright amendment's failure was good for business, Ambrose felt a tinge of regret that he hadn't lived up to expectations. He had fully intended to support Matt, to scuttle the Markup.

But something had changed between discussing the controls of Ambrose's Cessna 206 on their flight to D.C. and going into the Markup session this morning. He couldn't tell Matt that he had changed his mind because his life depended upon it.

It was Ambrose's turn to speak. He approached the microphones.

"Every one of you here has a big ego."

The reporters erupted in laughter and protests.

"Now, see here, what has that got to do with anything?" Matt asked defensively.

"Now, see here, what has that got to do with anything?" Ambrose echoed.

"And your point is?" Matt asked with a raised eyebrow.

"And what is your point?" Ambrose said, mimicking Matt's face and hand gestures.

"I don't think anyone came here to listen to you mimic me."

"I don't think they came here to hear me mimic you, either." Ambrose said, staying in character.

"I guess this ends our session. He has nothing original to say." Matt grimaced, then started to turn around.

"No, this begins our session. I have something very original to say, Congressman."

"Then say it, will you? You're wasting our time."

Ambrose faced the reporters.

"Did you detect his ire when I was mimicking him? It was annoying, right?"

The reporters were transfixed. Now he had everyone's attention.

"My esteemed colleague didn't like it, did he? Here's a question to you, reporters: do you like it when someone copies your words without attribution?"

Ambrose held his lapels in his hands, as if preaching.

"That's what this bill was about. What do we do when someone takes your words and starts copying them? Well, not copying verbatim. The names might be changed. The location might be different. But the story is there. We reward the copier's creativity, instead of punishing the theft. And *that* is immoral, which is what this argument is all about."

He paused to take a deep breath as he scanned the faces of his rapt audience. "What if I told you that there are writers, male and female, who serially rape other writers? I don't mean they sequester their victim in a room, taunt them, and terrorize them, physically."

Matt raised his finger at Ambrose. "Point of order, Congressman Girabeaux. Is this about rape or is it about writing? I don't see the connection. This is going far afield."

Ambrose looked around. "They do it mentally, in a literary way. They steal with impunity."

Ambrose faced his colleague.

"Writers are raped. Every. Single. Day." He turned away to talk to the reporters. "That's my point here. We have professors, newscasters, and writers who are accused of plagiarizing someone else's work almost every month—and then it dies down, because, truly, we can't have famous people being pilloried for something everybody does, can we?"

Ambrose crossed his arms.

"This bill is about helping that rape victim. That writer whose life's work is shattered by the stealth of someone more powerful, more coveted, more beautiful than the no-name writer."

Ambrose was in the zone now, using physical gestures to make his point.

"Did you ever stop to think who these famous authors, screenwriters, playwrights, television writers were before they became famous? They were no-names. We put the famous on a pedestal that's ill-deserved. Who are they? Who are we? Who do we think we are to allow the individual efforts of a person to be sullied by the corporate entertainment elite?

"Athletes cheat all the time because they want to be stronger, and it's not fair, we say, if they're using steroids to enhance their strength. Why does this not hold for writing? Even if there is a right to copy, there should be no right to steal and hide the theft, which is what the industry allows. Every day. We must give the writers relief.

"We need to create a special court to which writers can turn to redress the theft, have it litigated before a special body, like the Chancery Court in Delaware, which is specifically charged with handling complex financial cases. Short of that, we need to pass the proposed language and put a stop to this financial and corporate fraud.

"You and I know this, but the public does not. We need to protect these writers, not ignore them.

"How does the theft occur? Let's say I'm a copyright thief. I get access to this novel, movie script, stage play, television script, whatever—it doesn't matter—and I decide that I really like it. And I decide that I can do better than this novice. I'm a superior writer who understands the foundation of a good story—the anatomy of a story, if you will. I know this writer has limitations, but it's not worth throwing the baby out with the bath water. So, what do I do? I look at the story. And I study it, carefully. And I ask myself, 'What can I do to keep this story, but change things around so it becomes *my* story?' I look at the characters' names; I'll change Mr. Blue to Mrs. Yellow, or a Mr. Green to Mr. White.

"With all due respect, copyright thieves, in the form of studios, executive producers, uninspired writers, and their evil-doing assistants should not be able to wear a cloak of immunity for their dastardly deeds. Our Supreme Court has spoken: corporations are individuals. So is talent: people whose creativity is their life's work. But others, hiding behind a corporate shell of greed, pilfer the artists' efforts. The entertainment industry is not about talent; it's about the acquisition of talent, from any source, through which one can become a multi-millionaire producer, mogul, or kingmaker. Who cares where the talent comes from? They don't. They just want it for as little as possible. Some of our most respected film-production companies, television shows, novelists, and playwrights have been involved in some of the most heinous acts of theft.

"It's fraud. Simple as that. And we should have said as much by sending the bill for a vote. No entertainment conglomerate should have a right to cry copyright infringement when their corporations consist of people engaged in repeated acts of theft with impunity. I said as much in the Markup session."

Matt, now his foe, began to speak to the media throng, which had grown to at least twenty people, including live-feed from C-Span. The man's hubris was unfathomable.

Ambrose put on his photogenic smile as one or two reporters straggled in his direction while Matt's voice boomed in the hall.

Matt spoke: "I, for one, am grateful that we have averted a catastrophe. We successfully quashed a bill that would have stifled American creativity. A couple of kook whiners, who have been shut out of the business of creative writing due to their own pitiful lack of talent, have somehow taken it upon themselves to avenge what they perceive as an injustice, and what most of us see as a need for them to work harder at their craft. Creativity cannot be legislated. I look at those of you standing before me. You're writers. You've managed to forge a career. You did your homework. We have others who don't go the distance and who, instead, wish to point fingers at those who have had the audacity to take their creativity further.

"Now, I have to run. Thank you, gentlemen—and ladies," he added hastily.

Ambrose approached the podium again as Killian was making his exit. "I'd like to ask the Congressman a question, if I may," he said.

Matt turned around as the media cameras stopped clicking.

"Can you tell us how the bill managed not to pass when the votes were actually counted, and there *were* enough to pass?"

Matt turned around to face the press. "Rules are rules, my esteemed colleague."

"Yes, but *who* is making them? I'd like for the American people to know."

"Congress did, and there's a reason."

The reporters fanned out to allow the men to debate, but Matt looked at his watch and turned around, saying, "You have the podium, now. Tell them how you want to make trial lawyers richer than they already are by clogging up the courts with useless litigation by would-be writers, jealous that their work isn't good enough to be bought."

Ambrose faced the media, who were now at rapt attention, soaking up the drama. "But it's good enough to be stolen, right, Congressman?"

A reporter jumped into the fray, seeking clarification. "Can you tell us what happened, Congressman Girabeaux? We'd like to hear your version of events."

Ambrose straightened his tie. "All I have to say is: writers need real protection, not a law that says anyone can copy their work."

Matt interrupted. "The law is simple. It says, 'Right to Copy.' Copyright is the right to copy. And we'll never inspire creativity without the dissemination of ideas."

"I believe I have the podium, Congressman." Ambrose spoke firmly. "The American people should know that this Markup was scuttled on an arcane technicality."

"That's an oversimplification, Congressman," Killian countered.

Ambrose raised a hand to quiet him. "You had your turn. Strange how your concern about time in the Markup isn't as important to you right now, Congressman Killian."

Ambrose continued to speak to his audience, raising both hands to elaborate.

"You see, this is about time. I spoke ten seconds beyond 12:01 p.m., which, according to the law, is a violation of rules. However, there's a difference of opinion as to whose clock we should have used to time the session.

"Mr. Killian was in charge of the time, so, based upon his watch, thousands of writers will not receive the protection they are due. It's a sad day for writers.

"Worse yet, it's a sad day for America, because Congressional bills that affect literally billions of dollars in intellectual property will continue to remain in the hands of those with the most resources to defend their deceptive acts."

He looked at the faces of the reporters, hoping his comments would appear in print for his stalker to hear.

He chose his words carefully. "I want to say to the American writers out there that I'm personally sorry I let you down. Sometimes, laws can be put in place to prevent passage in a fair vote. I had no clue that my esteemed colleague would resurrect a law rarely used to defeat a Markup. To those who have been contacting me to voice their concerns, I'm grateful that you've shared your insights with me. Do not be discouraged. You got my attention. It's not over yet."

4:23 p.m.

It was around noon when Nakadee police found Blaine's bloated body stuck in the Cane River where thick tree trunks that elevated the pier had trapped it.

The owner of Harry's Bakery recognized the corpse, informing police that Blaine held a class at the coffee shop and also frequented the place.

Nate watched his men hovering around the body on the stretcher. "We better notify next of kin."

One of the men zipped up the bag, as if to keep the corpse warm against the cold winds.

Nate fingered on one hand the number of victims now dead in the small parish: Preston, Sherry, and Blaine.

Who was left standing?

7:00 p.m.

Matt was in boxer shorts, tie loosened, sleeves rolled up, overcome by the humidity. The long socks and formal shoes he was still wearing made him look comical.

But neither he nor Mare was in a joking mood.

When he'd arrived at Preston's, Matt had found Mare drunk, her hair disheveled, makeup smeared by beads of sweat.

"We've searched everywhere. Where else is there to look?" he asked, exasperated.

"I don't know."

"So, remind me of the importance of these papers?" he said testily under his breath.

She stared at him. "Well, there are two issues, if you must know."

"Maybe it's best I don't know, honey. This not being my district and all."

"You're a congressman. What do you fear?" She looked incredulous.

"If you must know," Matt said, mocking her, "Ambrose asked me if I was sending him hate mail before the Markup. It was coming through his D.C. home computer, apparently. Threats."

"Well, call him. Find out if he's being harassed and followed. It'll take the heat off of us! Who runs your campaigns, Matt? Are you really so slow on the uptake?"

"I have been trying to reach him since the Markup. He's angry with me."

"Great. You're becoming less valuable to me the more we talk."

"Playing double agent, are you? Why should I help you find divorce papers? If he didn't sign them, you'll have no need for me, right?"

Mare glared at him. "There's no time for that, Matt. I've got to find those papers. He said he hadn't filed them yet, and they're nowhere to be found. Goddamn him! I should have killed him when I had the chance."

"Miriam!" he hissed.

"I'm obviously speaking rhetorically, Matt."

"You know what they say about joking. There's usually truth lying there somewhere."

A bead of perspiration dropped from his upper lip. Standing up and leaning back, he took a damp handkerchief from his back pocket and wiped the sweat from his face.

Had there really been some urgency in Ambrose's objective of recording the vote? Those black politicians. Classic orators, they were. He could almost remember, verbatim, the lecture Ambrose had given to his colleagues. While it was coherent, his quest was naive and impossible to achieve in today's business world.

Fairness. Right. Those Negroes and their Constitution.

He shook his head. They are a constant reminder of our inequities against them. Even the rich ones, like Ambrose, take sides against us, and I treated him like a son. But his treachery cost him.

He and Mare were standing in a dark corner of the study, near a bookcase that hugged the wall to the left of the ornate writing desk.

"I've been thinking ... something doesn't quite fit, Miriam. I couldn't put my finger on it until just now. Come over here." He motioned her toward him as he leaned lightly against the desk.

She stared at him in anticipation.

"None of this is news to you, is it?" he asked.

She blinked, looking up at the ceiling. "How long have you known? Did he tell you he stole the work?"

She bit her lip. "It's not that simple, Matt. The reality is that he could have gotten the original idea, you know, from something he read or even saw on television twenty years ago—any number of ways—and maybe decided that he wanted to do something similar. The law allows that."

He looked around the room, taking in the expensive furniture, the textured walls, the paintings, the statues.

"I didn't write the scripts, Matt. Preston and Blaine wrote them." She rested her hand on the secretary, staring him directly in the eyes.

"You're talking to a congressman, Miriam. I chair the sub-committee on Intellectual Property. Don't talk to me about the law. If somebody killed Preston, chances are there was a legitimate reason for the suspicion of theft. There usually is. Every time."

"And that *really* explains why you don't want to help writers. Funny. Now all of a sudden you're sympathetic. Your protestations of outrage seem a bit too unbelievable, Mr. Congressman. You gloated over getting rid of that Markup."

"Don't turn the tables on me, young lady. What you have to say doesn't come close to the issues I have with you. He stole somebody else's work, and you're sitting in this house. You know more than you're letting on." Meeting her gaze and lowering his chin for emphasis, he fingered the desk, emphatically. "And if I protest too much, maybe it's because our very lives might depend on it."

He looked away, then returned his gaze to her.

"The money always wins. You know that, Miriam. What sucker writer can successfully go after a Hollywood writer with a movie studio behind him? Who can fight that Hollywood juggernaut? I just can't believe that someone like him, with his career, would resort to stealing. He was so conscientious about everything. He was dedicated, a concerned citizen. He was so enthusiastic about my work on the Intellectual Property subcommittee." His voice trailed.

Mare finished his thought. "The Copyright Amendment." She regarded him with an expression, almost motherly and knowing, yet antagonistic at the same time.

Matt froze, hands on his hips as he studied the floor, then tilted his head toward her. They both knew what was in his thoughts.

Mare spoke, quietly. "So, now that you've brought it up—that's where you come in, isn't it? You made a deal with him, didn't you? To protect the studios."

Matt couldn't disguise his look of contrition.

"That bill. Preston was lobbying for you not to pass it, correct?"

"It wasn't just him," he said softly.

"Who else, then?"

"Let's just leave it at 'influential people in the industry.'" He stood erect, giving himself room to breathe.

Mare's eyes narrowed. "How did this bill even come into being, Matt?"

He looked helpless and vulnerable, as he tried to get a grip on events.

"When and how did this all come about?"

"I'm not quite sure. A couple of studio heads got some anonymous letters about writers getting their work stolen. The studios kept it quiet." He looked up, shrugging.

His explanation was only part of the story: he had left out the meetings at the various studios, the lunches, the invitations, the lobbying. The visits to his office. The dates he went on with some of Hollywood's glamorous actresses, even while he was cheating on his wife by dating Mare. He hadn't "slept" with them. But he did receive every other favor the definition of sex would allow.

Hollywood had lobbied him fiercely, giving him the keys to the fictional city in return—his own invisible star on the Walk of Fame in exchange for his favors.

But he hadn't known that he was helping them steal others' work.

"So, the killer's still here in Nakadee?" Mare asked.

Matt shook his head, this time giving voice to the concern in both their minds.

"Who's next? Jesus Christ. Who's next?" Mare whispered. She stared at the ground.

"I could never figure out the sequence of events until now."

Matt looked at the ground, too, as if he were hunting for something, while his mind raced.

"Remember when you asked me to marry you?" Mare asked.

"Of course, I do. I said after my divorce, however."

"Of course," Mare mimicked. "I saw you on C-Span. You announced that the Copyright Act didn't need changing. And that very day Preston told me that he would give us his blessings." She snapped her fingers. "Just like that, it was all resolved." She looked up at him. "After despising you, forever, even though he wasn't interested in me anymore, he was jealous of my relationship with you and refused to agree to a divorce."

"I'm not sure what you're getting at, Mare."

She spoke, slowly. "Preston came up to me one day, you know, after I had asked him, for a whole year, for a divorce—after he came out to me. Because before, he had kept saying no. Then, one day, he just called me up and said, 'Okay. We can divorce.' What was that about, Matt? When I asked him, he told me, 'Ask your fiancée.'"

He stared at her, his lip slightly tremulous. "Let's just say we struck a compromise so he would give you the divorce."

"Like I was a piece of meat. You bartered me like some prize heifer."

"Miriam, listen. You wanted to talk—well, I'm talking. In all truth, he had given me the impression that, as an influential Hollywood player, this was something that the industry was concerned about. He didn't want the Copyright Act amended. We made a pact. Well, more like a gentleman's agreement. He told me that was the condition, and that it was all up to me."

He pointed his finger in her face. "You knew he was stealing. You knew that he was a total fraud and you benefited from it. So don't get high and mighty on me. I told him that I was paying a ransom for your heart in doing so. I had no idea that he was stealing people's scripts and wanted to manipulate a member of Congress to retain the unfettered right to do so."

Mare spoke in a whisper. "He had given you his blessing, as long as you did that little favor for him. But Preston's been missing for some time now. What's all that about, Matt? So, you see? You're involved, too. Your selfish act contributed to a young woman being killed. She had a family who will never see her again."

Matt patted his shirt, as if looking for his keys or a pack of cigarettes. He paced slowly, leaning away from the desk.

"You said somebody else helped him write the script?" he asked.

"What?"

"So Blaine stole it, too?"

"Before, I wasn't sure. No." She shrugged.

Matt grabbed her elbow gently to walk her to the door. "I think we better stop seeing each other until this is all cleared up. And you better hire a bodyguard." He paused a moment. "You know, I never bothered to ask. But since everything is out in the open now, I will."

He walked over to an armchair to retrieve his suit jacket. "This is a Congressional-privilege situation here. You can tell me. Did *you* kill him?"

Mare broke into laughter, with an alien sound he would never have associated with her.

"Me? Kill Preston? Why? Why would I want to kill him?"

He answered in a low voice, "Your prenuptial agreement. You know, the one where you'd get absolutely nothing if you divorced."

"Oh, Matt. I would laugh at you if you weren't so absolutely pathetic."

"I'm out of here." He held the front door open. "And you, little lady, watch that pretty back of yours."

8:00 p.m.

Lula hadn't heard from Ambrose on the afternoon of the vote. He had advised her that no news would likely be good news. It meant that he would not cancel his return trip, and they would still go out for dinner at around 8:30 p.m., after his meeting at the Mayor's office.

She didn't quite understand the hullabaloo about the proposed copyright legislation. Nor did she know Ambrose's position on the vote. He said he'd been poring over it and had talked to his constituents, namely corporations that might be affected by the Act.

Lula tried to focus on the task at hand. She was going on a date with a United States Congressman, she'd told her mother.

Had she listened to her mother, she would have at least worn the maroon chenille top lying on the other side of the bed, because it was more elegant.

They had plans to dine at the restaurant where Chef Lyonnais, the only certified chef in the area, cooked, Ambrose had told her proudly when he called two days ago to suggest plans for tonight's date. When she thanked him for the flowers and the note, he hadn't really responded.

Politicians.

She continued to ruminate over her options as she put on her watch and rings, wondering if she could really make a life in

Louisiana. She was a single woman in a neighborhood of married couples with children in a town where people believed that it was not normal that she had never married. She was attractive and single—surely she should be with someone by now.

Slapping on some dark lipstick, she spritzed on perfume and tugged at her pants legs. Why was she so chipper and animated whenever she thought about that black Republican?

"You're trippin', girl," she said.

Hours later, she was angry, literally sitting by the phone, waiting for the Congressman's call.

"Like I said," she admonished herself. "You were seriously trippin'." She lay back on her bed, staring at the ceiling.

20

DEVON

Saturday, March 26th, 7:50 a.m.

Lula was startled awake by her doorbell. It better not be Ambrose at this hour. These brothers and their booty call hours. Oh, hell no.

She was lying to herself. She was *hoping* it was Ambrose. She was even rushing, which surprised her, as was her reaction to finding Devon standing at her door with a serious look on his face.

"I hate to tell you this, but I'm supposed to take you to the police station. The chief wants to see you."

Caught like a deer in headlights, Lula's reaction to the unusual request, coupled with her disappointment, was a revelation to her. She leaned her face against the door, looking at him sideways.

"Touché, Devon."

He looked away from her, sounding strange. "Right. Like I have that kind of power. No, it's for real."

She looked outside at the blue sky and green grass of her lawn, trying to gauge his demeanor. The emotional roller coaster of their recent dealings seemed devoid of any sense of their shared history—of waking up together in the morning, taking their time getting dressed, or engaging in small talk over morning coffee.

"I gotta get back to work. Please hurry." He began to walk toward his car.

"I'd prefer to take my car, Devon," she called after him.

271

"I got orders to pick you up and then bring you back home, or wherever you got plans for the day. We got a dangerous chemical thing going on or something, so you'll need to get your gear. We gotta hurry. That natural gas agreement deal was about to go down and they have a meeting on it at HQ. So, we gotta go. This ain't about you and me anymore. I've moved on. Like you."

She begged for five minutes to change her clothing, to which he reluctantly agreed.

Lula put on her no-nonsense uniform of navy-blue pantsuit, white blouse, and flat walking shoes. After locking her front door, she hurried to her car to fetch her forensic kit. She kept her car very neat, with spotless seats and vacuumed carpets, so the piece of paper on the passenger side of the front seat leapt out at her.

She reached for it and turned it over, wondering when she had written herself a note. Not bothering to look, she balled it in her fist and awkwardly reached over the front seat to pick up her gray duffle bag in the back. Its long zipper was open, and another paper was sitting—rumpled, not folded—on top.

Perplexed, she turned her head to look back at Devon's car. He was starting the engine.

She unfolded the paper on top of the bag, and then the one still in her hand. They were identical copies of neat, studied handwriting, evenly spaced in both width and height.

Dear Prof Lula,

I promise, promise, promise to God, God, God. I will not, not, not, hurt you. I am waiting in your office. Please. Be there. I will wait all day if I have to. Please come alone.

Your Maintenance Man

Which day? Yesterday or today? She quickly reviewed her schedule, trying to divine when the note had been placed in her car. As she hadn't noticed it yesterday, it had to have been put there this morning. Lula racked her brain for the names of the campus maintenance men, until Richard's face loomed in her mind's eye.

He had the keys to her office.

She looked at the note again. He had written the word "promise" three times, underlining each. God was mentioned three times, too. But whose God was he summoning to protect her, and did his God kill forensic anthropologists? Was he setting her up? Had the police given up the hunt for him? Was he even a suspect? She stalled for time, performing her actions in slow motion.

"Everything good?" Devon called out, as he stepped out of his idling car.

She remained stooped over her duffle bag, head still inside the car, trying to figure out what to do next. She glanced at her watch. It was 8:35. The police were waiting for her less than twenty yards away, and a one-time police suspect was lying in wait to see her in her office. Alone.

If it was Richard who had sent the invitation, his timing could not have been worse. She needed to meet him quickly, and here she was planning a trip that might take four to six hours of work before she returned.

Her heart was pounding as she pulled her duffle bag out and looked at Devon, who was leaning against the shiny Cadillac.

She averted her eyes. "Sorry, but I need to swing by the office. If this accident involves what I think it does, there may be some contamination, which would be quite dangerous. I'll need to get the proper protective gear. It'll take about ten minutes to locate the masks and inspect them."

Devon motioned for her to proceed to his car.

"I'm sorry for the delay," Lula added as she stepped into the car, taking note of its plush interior, and relaxed back in the seat behind Devon. As the car sped away, she looked at Pomona's vacant porch, nervously.

Devon was on the car radio, alerting someone of their detour to pick up masks. He spoke in the muffled police-speak that they used when communicating with each other. "We're taking Frank to our first destination. Frank is concerned about contamination." He listened to more mumbling, then, answered. "ETA will be twenty minutes plus, now. Frank will bring equipment. Over."

She heard Nate's voice on the other end. "Copy. About an hour and a half, then? Things are getting pretty dire. Building is emptied."

Leaning forward, Lula volunteered, "Make sure they turn off any air conditioning—or fans—or other ventilation. We don't want spores to spread."

Devon repeated Lula's admonitions, followed by "Over."

"Copy. Roger." Nate paused. "Spores?" he asked.

"Copy." Devon intoned, emphatically. "Sam-Paul-Oxford-Rabbit-Edward Sam." He turned to Lula, asking for a translation of the term.

"Airborne particles that can do serious damage. They need to keep them from circulating through the building."

Devon conveyed her concerns to Nate.

"Okay, we'll await your arrival." Nate was only faintly audible.

The red and blue police lights that Devon placed on the front dashboard helped to disperse the sparse Sunday traffic ahead of them during the fifteen-minute ride to the campus. Lula was on the verge of spilling the beans about the note before she stopped herself. She had thrown both notes into the back seat of her car. She closed her eyes, praying for divine intervention to relieve her anxiety.

When they reached her building on campus, Devon opened his door to accompany her, leaving the engine running. She walked briskly toward the lab building.

"I'll be right back down."

"Chief's orders." Devon said, continuing to walk with her.

"Well, it might take me a minute or two to find my supplies, and it'll just make me anxious and nervous. Please." She stopped, looked him firmly in the eye, and spoke with authority. "I'm a big girl, detective. I can walk without an escort. I need to concentrate."

He gave her a puzzled look. "Suit yourself. Fine." He turned on his heel and returned to the car.

Lula's eyes followed him, then glanced up at the third floor before she began her own Bataan death march, duffle bag in tow. She was plagued by "should-haves" as she continued up the steps to the entrance. Was she making a mistake?

Midway up the steps, she searched inside her duffle bag for anything she could use as a weapon in case Richard attacked her. A long-handled flashlight would have to do.

By the time she reached the top of the stairs, she was panting, wishing she had left her jacket in the car. She leaned against the handrail, catching her breath.

Once on the landing, she scanned the empty halls, then approached the lab door, which now felt like the portal to a chamber of doom. Was there a chance that she might not return? She opened the door, accepting her fate.

Standing in the entranceway, with the door closed behind her, she was grateful to find that nothing was disturbed. Taking a couple of steps, she stopped when she felt someone standing behind her.

"Don't turn around."

Lula did as instructed. "You're not going to do anything, are you?" Her voice trembled. "Please."

"You come alone?"

She nodded as she recognized Richard's voice.

"Walk forward please," he said.

She took a couple of steps, holding the duffle bag tightly.

"You got a weapon there in your hand? Put the flashlight and the bag down. The sooner you do what I say, the quicker you can get out of here."

She kept her eyes on the wall in front of her.

"I came to tell you something."

She could see him, peripherally, as he tiptoed sideways to peer out of the window. He wore blue jeans, blue deck shoes, and a dingy red-and-white-striped shirt.

"Straight ahead," he admonished her. "You say you came alone. Is that man in the Cadillac with you?"

Lula took a deep breath. "He's waiting for me."

"You told them I'm here? I asked you to come by yourself."

"I was with him when I got the note. I told him I was coming to pick up supplies. The detective wanted to come upstairs with me, but I made a fuss and lied to him. Get it? We're in this together now. I already know who you are. Remember, we met, and I can recognize your voice."

He walked in front of her, facing her.

"Who's him? Who are you talking about?"

"One of the detectives. So please, let's get this over with. I'm committing a crime by not telling them you're here."

"Fair enough." He looked at her.

She looked back at him. He had bags under his eyes, and his skin color was sallow. He looked sad and dispirited. His hair was disheveled.

"Can I relax, or should I continue to be afraid of you?"

He chuckled. "Now, you know as good as I do that I couldn't kill a fly, which is why you're here. You know that I ain't got nothin' to do with nothin' and it's purely my Boy Scout's nose for detective work that's got me into this jam."

She relaxed her shoulders. "So what am I supposed to do?"

He crossed his arms. "Tell them who the real murderer is."

"Do I know him?"

"Come over here." He led her gently by the arm, steering them both away from the large window. His hands were clammy and cold.

Lula felt repelled by his touch.

"I ain't gonna bite you. I just don't want anybody to see us here, and we're right smack dab in front of the window."

"Sherry's dead," she told him.

"I know."

"How do you know?"

He furrowed his brow as if to reprimand her. "I ain't the killer. I'm figurin' you also know that Preston Pratt is dead, too, right?"

"Is this what you called me here for?" She was suddenly angry. "Is this a game to you? Guess who's the killer?" She took a gamble, showing her ire. "The police are right downstairs, and if you called me here to play some silly head trip, you're messing with the wrong girl."

He held his hands out to calm her. "Hear me out. I didn't want to believe it either, Miss Lula, but I've had time to contemplate and use my own deductive reasoning."

She stood erect as he leaned his hands against a lab table housing several limb artifacts. "I knew they were up to something. I'm not sure, exactly, and I got no real proof, but I know they're up to something."

"Who? And what?" Lula asked, not able to hide her frustration. "Hey, for your own sake, I'd spill everything now before they come looking for me."

"Sherry and Juanito were taking money from the company accounts, and somebody found out. Or, somebodies. They're all dead, now, and guess who is left standing?"

"Richard, I haven't the foggiest idea who 'they' are, or what you're talking about."

"Sherry and the Cuban dude, Juanito, who worked with Preston, and who worked with Blaine. Preston and Sherry are dead. Now Blaine's dead. It's like a riddle."

She looked confused. "Blaine .... "

"I was there when you met him at the house."

"I must call Aggie," Lula realized aloud.

"Who's that?" Richard asked.

She took a step away from him as he continued speaking. "If three people are in a room, and only one is left standing, you can logically conclude who did the killing."

"There's nothing logical about killing, Richard. What are you saying?"

"Sherry had something to do with that dude Juanito, who also worked for them. They had a production company. Ten Fingers Productions. They were all up to no good."

"How would you know that?"

"Because she had a credit card, and it didn't have her name on it. Preston's name was on it."

"It was his company. Maybe he gave them an expense account."

"I think something started going wrong, and Sherry and Juanito panicked."

"Where's your proof?" she asked.

"Search Sherry's computer. If they got a police inventory of her apartment, they'll find something on it. I used to hang out with her, and she was always retyping the information from the damn scripts right into the computer."

"Couldn't she have been grading them?"

"I asked her about it the other day and accused her of stealing.

She got pissing angry and kicked me out of her apartment." Richard looked vulnerable.

Lula shook her head, confused.

"She and Juanito were up to something and Juanito's the last man standing. What's up with that, Dr. Lula? What did I do to be framed?"

He looked at her expectantly, then answered his own question. "I'll tell you what—because I am alone in this world. Nobody gives a damn about me if I live or die. I'm the scapegoat. I'm the one with the least to lose, going to jail."

Lula watched him.

"It ain't me. I got a problem with thievery. When somebody takes somebody you love away, or something that's yours, well, it ain't quite right. Killing another to save a life, maybe, but takin' for the hell of it—hell no. Besides, I got my reasons to stay outta jail, including that I likes women way too much to play the role of one in a cell with Bubba, the overweight lover."

Lula would have laughed had his face betrayed any sense of comedy, but he was dead serious.

"Well, how do you expect me to trust you, Richard? Sometimes killers like to be around during the aftermath of their crimes. It gives them satisfaction that nobody knows about them and they're right out in the open."

He walked over to the window and peered out, keeping his head from view. "You got a cell phone?" he asked, walking over to her.

"Yes, but it's in my car."

"Let me check. Give me your bag, since I can't trust you, n'all," he grunted. She pointed to the bag that lay on the ground near the door. He picked it up and rifled through it. "How many people in the car down there?"

"One."

"Someone's on their way, then. Did you call them?"

"I keep my cell phone in my car, Richard. You'll have to take my word for it."

He rushed toward the front door, leaning forward to listen, cupping his ear. "Somebody's coming. Shit."

Lula's desk telephone rang. She stood still, staring at it, and, on Richard's urging, walked over to answer.

"Don't tell them I'm here. Please," Richard pleaded.

Lula said firmly. "Go into the bathroom. Stay there."

His eyes pleaded with her before doing as she ordered. Lula walked after him, keeping the bathroom door open. Quickly, she turned on the fume hoods to add noise to the room, while the telephone rang a third time before she picked it up.

"Lula Logan." She said, somewhat expectantly. "Tom-Tom! Hello!" She was relieved.

Devon appeared at the door, opening it. "Everything okay?"

She smothered the telephone mouthpiece with her hand, looking in the direction of the bathroom. "I'm almost ready. I'm on the telephone." She stared at Devon firmly, then directed her attention to the phone call. "I'm actually on an emergency, but I have thirty seconds."

It was about the maggots.

"Chief's getting restless," Devon whispered, closing the door.

Lula nodded at Devon while she continued listening. "That's interesting news, Tom-Tom, and I'll look into it, and I appreciate it immensely." Then she asked, "Tom-Tom, do you remember what the weather was like around Mardi Gras?" He laughed as he told her he had fled town to get away from the debauchery.

She looked toward the door to the hallway, ready for it to open again, at any minute. "The victim was last seen on Fat Tuesday. If you have the time, can you do me a favor and look back to the weather during Mardi Gras and leave a message at my home number, or if all else fails, the Nakadee police department? I forgot my cell phone, but I'll try to reach you later, okay?"

Through her lab door, she could see Devon pacing back and forth in the hallway outside. Lula hurriedly thanked Tom-Tom, promising to talk to him soon.

The minute she hung up, Devon opened the door and walked briskly toward her.

Defensively, she stood up, opening a drawer as if looking for something. She was grateful that Richard had managed to stay still in the bathroom.

"I couldn't remember where I put my masks." She volunteered. "I'm falling apart at the seams."

She looked downward to collect herself while Devon came toward her, invading her space as if he had the right. Not anymore, he didn't.

She stepped back from him.

"Lula, I know this isn't the time, but I wanted to talk to you, alone."

"Devon. Please. Not now."

"I know what time it is. I just wish you'd listen to me. I know what I want, and nobody's getting in the way except you."

"Devon, your timing couldn't be worse. Please. Could you put your dick away for now?" She intentionally sought to provoke him to get him out of the office as she darted a look toward the front door.

Unable to hold back his frustration, he yelled. "What the hell is wrong with you? I'm trying to show you my heart, and you're talking about my dick? Forget it."

She intercepted him. "Devon. Look. There's a chemical emergency where people could be hurt, and I'm supposed to help, and all you want to do is talk about us? You will agree that I have a lot on my plate right now. A man's skull is sitting on my table over there. And a student of mine is dead. That's what you should be caring about—"

"Ain't this some—you see what you done did here? You got me all up in your business and I'm supposed to just be a statue, friggin' Drivin' Miss Daisy, like it doesn't matter? Like I don't exist. I know every inch of your body, and you can't even give me the decency ...."

Devon's jaws were working overtime. He looked like a sorry combination of angry, hurt, and upset. The room fell quiet.

"What's the deal, Devon? Why now? Why is this coming up now, Devon?" She stared at him, angrily. "Please. Go away. I'll be down in a second."

"No. I'm ordered to walk you out of here. Immediately. Come with me, now, please."

"Well, are you going to escort me to the bathroom, too?"

He raised his hands in defeat as she picked up her duffle bag where Richard had left it, handing it to Devon. "Here, take my duffle bag. I'll be right behind you." She walked to her locker, pulled out three breathing masks and handed them to him. "Could you hold these, please?"

She ducked into the bathroom, where she found Richard standing on the closed toilet seat. He stepped down as she shut the door, locking it and turning on the water.

He stood flush against the wall next to the toilet, looking at her, breathing heavily, his eyes like saucers.

She whispered. "Richard. I've got to go. So, what do you want me to do?"

"Talk to the police, Miss Lula. Tell 'em the case isn't over yet. I ain't the guy, you hear? I ain't the guy. I went to Blaine's class, hunting for Sherry, and I sat in on it at the coffee shop. She didn't know jack about movies. She doesn't know William Wellman from William Wyler from William Styron to William Shatner, from William Penn, to Penn and Teller. They are stealing other people's work, changing it around, selling the rights to real companies under his production company."

"I'm not sure I understand. I know nothing about that industry, Richard. I gotta go."

He held her elbow.

"People get greedy. Two of 'em are dead. The one left over is sitting pretty."

"Why would they kill a business partner?" Lula whispered.

"That's what the Mafia does. You start getting greedy. You make threats. Who the hell knows? Look, I'm telling you the honest-to-God truth. I seen a guy in front of the gym where Sherry was killed, and I seen him again last night, like he's following me. Maybe he's the one doing all the killing."

"They could say the same about you, Richard. Do you see why you'd be the prime suspect?"

Fear shone in Richard's eyes, and his mouth opened in amazement. Then he asked, "So why aren't you pointing the finger at Juanito? They were members of the same gym, the one she was killed in, and I've seen them in the pool together."

"It's my understanding that you thought they were a couple. Jealous?"

"I'm smarter than that, no matter how dumb I look. Come on, is that all you got?" He rasped louder but still low enough for his voice to be covered by the rush of the water flowing down the sink drain.

Lula squared her shoulders. "Look, I'm not looking anywhere except as far as I have to so I can do my job. You visited me, remember? You wanted to tell me you didn't do anything, and I'm listening."

She flushed the toilet, holding the handle so that the sound of gushing water would last longer.

"Why are you doing this?" she whispered, facing the mirror, letting water cascade over her hands. She picked up a paper towel, but did not turn off the tap.

He looked her in the eyes. "Look. I do sell drugs—the kind students need to get through school. That's it. And Sherry used the ones I gave her. Though I don't know this to be the case, but I'd bet my bottom dollar, Sherry or Juanito, or even Blaine, might have drugged Preston, and then killed him. Remember, you should know this as her teacher—she went away for a couple of weeks, and came back from vacation, looking tan an' all? As if that was her alibi? But she was there for Mardi Gras? I'll bet you all found the same drug found in Sherry was in Preston, too—if she died of an overdose like the media is saying. I know you all can do drug tests, even using their hair."

Believing he had struck a chord, he swallowed, then continued gesticulating. "I might be a jackass, sell a bit of dope—hell, call me a scoundrel, but I don't steal, and I didn't kill anybody. Tell them to look at Blaine. He knew things, and he didn't make one move to talk to anybody. Where was he? Huh? Where is he? Hiding out, that's what! He liked those boys that come over there—like Melvyn. He knew he was next." He stopped mid-sentence. A dribble of spit fell onto his bottom lip.

She caught his mistake, but didn't show it in her demeanor. *Blaine was next? How could he be next if Blaine was doing the killing?*

Maybe it was Richard who was deciding everyone's fate.

She made eye contact with him and spoke firmly: "I gotta go."

When she left the bathroom, Devon was still standing in the center of her office, impatiently. "You gonna leave the water running in there?" Devon asked, walking past her toward the bathroom just as the water turned off.

"It's an automatic faucet. It turns itself off, Devon." He stopped at the door, and Lula breathed a sigh of relief. "You said let's go, so let's go," she urged, seeming irritated.

He walked ahead of her as she took one last look around before closing the lab door.

Minutes later, Lula and Devon sat in silence, listening to the car engine humming underneath the murmurs of an FM news announcer. The familiar soundtrack introducing the news came on the radio for an instant before Devon turned it off, quickly glancing at Lula, whose head was propped against the back seat.

Lula's power nap had revived her by the time they reached the police department. Devon walked to the passenger side, opening her door.

She strode into the station while Devon trailed behind, wiping his brow.

She took a deep breath at the chief's door and stepped inside. The chief called Devon, trying to peer around Lula's frame from his desk.

"Come on in, Devon."

Chief Broussard was in full police regalia, wearing a dress-uniform jacket with American flags on both sides of the collar and a shiny badge on his chest. His somber look and demeanor added to the sense of formality.

Devon spoke up behind her. "Lula, the chief wanted to share some bad news with you, and wanted me to be here for support." He took two strides to the side of the chief's desk, his hands touching it lightly.

She was silent, gazing up at Devon, who couldn't look at her.

Chief Broussard spoke. "It's about Congressman Girabeaux. He's dead."

Lula felt light-headed. She gave the room a once-over, as if to affirm her existence. She was in the police chief's office, with various framed commendation certificates on the wall, and metal file cabinets. The chief's cap rested on top of one of them. It was 10:00 a.m. A coat rack leaned precariously like the Tower of Pisa. It held a windbreaker and a gray trench coat. The office was cluttered with stacks of papers and yellow manila folders. A cigar butt sat in a black ashtray, unlit, but its essence still permeated the room, giving out a sweetly pungent, if slightly rancid, odor.

She didn't say anything.

The chief had a phlegmatic, gravelly voice; he seemed always in need of clearing his throat. "I'd like to hire you to help us with your forensic expertise," he said softly, "for lack of a better word. This little town ain't used to this kind of intrigue. We'll likely get all kinds of federal types like the Secret Service or whatnot. I'd like to get a head start on them, at least."

"I'll have to check with the university," she spoke at last, surprised that she could find her voice without betraying her emotions. Her heart felt like a stone in her chest.

"You just tell me who you need me to convince, Dr. Lula. My administration is trying to bring some big—I mean, *big* business into this here town. It might be that someone was trying to stop that happening. We have our ideas, mind you, but I can't bring in the whole Aryan nation, if you get my drift. So, science is the way to go. We're gonna have Devon take you to the Congressman's local office, where it happened. They got a box in the mail. A dead carcass of some animal. He was gone within one hour."

Lula listened, but didn't hear him. She had never felt as caged in as she did right now. Her emotions were everywhere and nowhere, because her private life had to remain just that. With Devon taking her to the site, she'd have no time to herself. It was as if her life had stopped but nobody else knew it.

She returned her attention to the captain, who was gesticulating as he talked. She had to force herself to hear him.

"The last thing we need is fingers pointing at us, if you get my drift, and no pun is intended, considering ... so we're counting on you to help us get to the bottom of this within the next 48 hours before they come knocking with their federal badges n'all. Life in this parish will never be the same the minute the Feds show up." His lip curled in disgust. "Let's just look at the State DNA Index System, then be done with it. Button this up as soon as possible."

12:30 p.m.

The car raced along the highway that wove through wetlands. Lula's seatbelt held her firmly, though she still planted her hands on either side to steady herself. As the car hurtled along at ninety-five miles an hour, other cars slowed and moved out of the way.

Richard's information had overwhelmed her, and so did her guilt about not telling the police about her clandestine meeting with him. She was trying to sort out the logistics of whether she should say anything, and, if so, whether she could bring up the information Richard had provided without delivering his head to them on a platter.

She closed her eyes, but rest eluded her. Forty minutes later, they approached the outskirts of a burgeoning industrial wasteland of gas stations and small restaurants.

Devon turned into the driveway of a quaint-looking home that seemed out of place in the sleepy business district. Spotting other officers, Devon parked the car in the center of the street.

Nate greeted them, accompanied by men in uniform that she didn't recognize at first. An older, leather-faced officer was supervising traffic and keeping onlookers at bay, explaining that there was a threat of contamination.

Nate nodded to Lula as she stepped out of the car. She was putting on extra-long latex gloves and carried her hazmat mask, having given the others to Nate.

He instructed her about the layout of the office, information he'd received from the Congressman's secretary, who had been hospitalized. A fire engine was at the scene, with two firefighters on hand to assist.

Lula's plan was to spend no more than five minutes inside the building, if possible. With her infectious-materials bag in hand, she told the firefighters to create an area in the driveway where a fire could be built, so that the box and its contents could be destroyed immediately. If they could find a tin drum, that would be a good incinerator, she added.

Once inside, Lula rapidly canvassed the office. A large oil painting of Ambrose hung in the foyer. His winsome smile still beckoned, but she couldn't think about him now.

In the corner leading to his office was a portrait of a woman who looked mulatto. Italian cherubs smiled down from the four corners of the vintage frame. An American flag stood in a stand with brass legs, opposite a Louisiana state flag. The room was steeped in European Old-World elegance, a bit anachronistic for Lula's tastes, but a proper formal setting for a congressional office, she imagined.

It took her less than two minutes to confirm that the package delivered in a brown cardboard box had contained a dead animal carcass, with open sores that disseminated *Bacillus Anthracis* spores. Without realizing it was poisonous, the Congressman had handled it, breathed in the spores, and had immediately fallen ill.

Lula took a swab of the animal carcass for a laboratory confirmation of its poisonous properties, placing the sample in a double layer of wrapping with the appropriate "INFECTIOUS MATERIAL" label.

She hurried outside, still wearing her mask, accompanied by a firefighter. Lula confirmed with Nate that firefighters had taken photos of the box.

By now, all spectators had been told to leave the vicinity. Per her earlier instructions, the controlled environment had been created for destruction of the carcass and its container. Several firemen stood by with foam canisters to douse the flames.

Lula had known Ambrose for only a few fleeting hours, but with an intimacy that she had not known was possible with a total stranger—a Republican, no less. She had put her politics aside to get to know a man that she liked, and could possibly have grown to love.

She would never see him again. That fickle finger of fate had other plans for her. She was not meant to find luck in love. That was her curse.

Was Richard the missing link in all these unexplained deaths, and was he trying to deflect attention away to some other culprit?

Nate intruded into her thoughts by asking about Ambrose. They were standing at the back of the Congressman's office, where firemen were moving around large trash bins on wheels as they inspected them.

"How well did you know the Congressman, Dr. Lula?"

"Not well. You introduced us, if you recall."

Nate corrected her. "I thought it was the chief who did the introductions. But if I'm not mistaken, you did spend some time at his home."

"And?"

"Well, this is an investigation. I'd like to know if you saw anything unusual at his house. How many staff did he have, for instance? We'll want to question them."

"Is there a chance I might be asked in a more formal setting?" she asked.

"Outside of Detective Devon's earshot?"

"I know Devon as a professional," she said.

Nate cocked his head. "You might want to have a friend around when I am asking you questions. He's a married man, I'm sure you know, so there's nothing for me to suspect."

What was Nate trying to do to her? Because whatever it was, it was working. "Well, I'm sure you know my relationships are my concern and no one else's," she replied.

"Except when one of them ends up dead. It's a line of questioning I'd have for anyone who has crossed paths with the deceased. Trust me, I'll be easier to deal with than the Feds or the Capitol-Police types from D.C. They're not going to take this lightly. I'd like to head them off at the pass, so we can remain in control of our own town, if you know what I mean."

Nate glanced at Devon, as he came over. "Devon's cool, right Devon?"

"Like ice. Ice."

Fortified by his sidekick's tacit permission, Nate turned back to Lula. "So, do you mind?"

She sighed, feeling exposed, embarrassed. She and Richard did have something in common. They had both fallen for phantoms of their own imaginations.

Ambrose did have enemies, and she was likely going to point fingers at the one known to her: Matt Killian. The pushing and shoving that she had witnessed must have related to some life-or-death matter, for each of them. The anger had definitely been mutual. She wondered how she could disclose the content of their discussion without divulging the context in which it had occurred. What had he said that night?

She had been lying in Ambrose's arms while they talked softly. Her recall was sketchy. Her senses had been enveloped by the crisp fragrance of his cologne, his minty breath, the way her shoulder fit so snugly under his arm.

He had taken off his dinner jacket and laid it on the sofa. She'd felt in two places at once: comfortable in his light embrace, yet wondering how she got there. So soon. It was exhilarating, but risky. Her breathing had been shallow. She hadn't been that giddy since her first truly soulful kiss on prom night.

She didn't want to share those moments with anyone. To divulge this would destroy the moment that had led to their perfect night of lovemaking.

"Let's just say, my life depends upon it," she recalled hearing when the two men had argued passionately. Ambrose had mentioned a constituent.

"Well there was an argument with the other Congressman, the one with Preston's wife."

Nate's face fell. "Really."

"I remember Congressman Girabeaux saying something about his life depending on something or another."

This was all she shared. She wanted to savor that evening, which would now be a memory to take out on lonely nights.

Lying under the vaulted ceiling, she had clasped his arm as it rested around her upper body, his hand rubbing her shoulder gently. Lula always marveled at the male torso, the soft leathery texture of a man's skin, the coarse hairs of his chin as she rubbed her hand along his face, feeling the small spurs on the back of her hand.

"What are you thinking?" He'd touched her nose with the tip of his forefinger.

"How handsome you are."

"So why the sour look? Does that offend you?"

She burrowed her body into his for warmth. "I don't think so."

His eyebrow creased briefly and he leaned his head on his forearm, his hand dangling above her head. "Is that a problem?"

"Not right now, anyway."

"Why should it be? I yam what I yam."

"And you eat them, too, right?"

They both chuckled.

"Should I look like one of those intellectual black effetes? Some women like that. A strong chin is just a strong chin. You know there are some conservative brothers out there who wish they were white. They speak a certain way, spend their whole lives trying to prove that they're one of them. They use six-syllable words, and end up sounding like a bunch of white women. Well, I'm not one of them."

"Who are you, then, Mr. Republican?"

"I be what I be. That's the vernacular, right?" he raised his eyebrows suggestively.

"Hmm ... the vernacular," she groaned.

"Would you like some more vernacular?" He smiled.

"Give me some vernacular," she crowed.

They laughed together as he wrapped his arms around her, lifting her body, revealing his physical strength.

"Can I say something?"

"You have the floor," she replied.

He responded with a wink, then took a deep breath.

"I just want to say that I really enjoyed—"

She put her finger up to his lips, gently pushing against them. "Don't. Let's not ever discuss us, or anything related to us. Please. You know the song ... about the words getting in the way."

He regarded her for a long moment, then leaned to pull her forward, kissing her gently. "What radio station do you listen to? I haven't the slightest idea what you're talking about. Are those hip-hop or rap lyrics, 'cuz I can agree on that one. The words do get in the way of those songs." He had looked deep into her eyes. "Okay, all joking aside. You were saying?"

Lula didn't want to move from her place in his king-sized bed. "I was going to say that I really like eating pancakes after I make love, and wanted to make you some."

She belted out a throaty laugh.

"No, you weren't going to say that," he said.

"Then what was I going to say?"

He looked at her with faux consternation. "You were going to say that you ... like to make waffles after you make love."

He scooped his hands underneath her and her breasts brushed up against him as he shifted her on top of him.

"Come here, my black wench."

She spoke firmly under her breath: "Oh-no-he-didn't."

His agility was visible as he bounced up into a crouch, jostling her about.

"Oh, yes I did ... that's how it all began, and I'm going to keep up the tradition."

Her body stiffened as she pushed her hands against his chest. "That's not even funny."

"Are you black?"

She laughed, still holding him at bay.

"You're kidding, right?"

He threw his hands above, then behind his head. "Really? What is black?"

Lula sat on top of him. Her nakedness with him felt right. She didn't feel exposed.

"It's a race," he corrected. "No, it's a negative. Does a negative exist if it doesn't have an apposite group to which it can belong?"

"Your point?"

"Blacks in this country have white in them, yet they call themselves black, instead of white."

"It's the other way around. Black is the dominant gene, Ambrose, and it's the Whites who have us in their blood, from Lucy. Not the television show—but at the risk of boring you with anthropological theory and the like, I'll just state that I do beg to differ with you."

"I'm impressed, but not intimidated. I have a theory that blackness is a state of mind, not a state of being."

"Well, if that's the case, I doubt any one of us would opt to be in the state of mind of being black. Who wants to live a life on the defensive, looking around wherever we go, wondering when the next insult is coming? Trying to figure out how to disguise their race so they can get the job? I'd like you to run that theory by our ancestors. I don't think they had a mind to be slaves, anymore than you have to ... I dunno, compromise your values to cut a deal with the devil in Washington."

When she saw his expression change Lula realized she had made a mistake.

He fell quiet, looking through her.

She bit her lip, reproachfully. "I'm sorry."

He nodded. "No bother."

She lay on top of him, her hands brushing his chest hairs softly.

His eyes had a faraway look.

"I'm really sorry, Ambrose—I sure put my foot in that one."

"That's okay. We have to get back to reality."

She pulled the sheet over them.

"Politics," he said. "It's much more complicated than it seems, I'll have you know."

"I can't even imagine."

"Well, I have people I have to answer to, though I don't even know who they are. It could be dangerous if I disappoint them." He turned to look at her.

"Politically?"

He shook his head slowly.

"You don't really believe that, do you?"

"Somebody is trying to tell me something, if I could just figure out what it is."

"You don't suppose this person is a killer, do you?"

"I don't know."

"Are you serious?"

"No. This person is ... a nutcase."

"Making threats?"

"Well, if you call legislative Markups a life-and-death matter, I might could be in trouble."

"Might could. Sounds serious to me." She smiled.

"This person is a nutcase, but for a legitimate reason. He's communicated with us on several occasions, sometimes directly. He's not seeking media *attention. He likes to write. He's a frustrated writer communicating his angst over the copyright laws. He threatened me at the festival, the day we met. I didn't realize he was serious until later. I should have kept the paper he gave ...."*

He stopped and stared at her.

"I gave it to you," he remembered.

"What do you mean?"

"You should have it. It's the one I wrote my number on."

"I can look, although by now, it's been handled by too many people for it to have any forensic value to it." She moved to get up, but was thwarted by his two arms, which held her in place.

She raised herself onto her forearms. "Seriously—why don't I go look for it?"

He interrupted her with a firm kiss on her mouth, as if pantomiming a cinematic kiss, then rubbed her back playfully.

"End of story," he smiled.

3:30 p.m.

Nate steered Lula to the front of Girabeaux's office, where the police were still prohibiting traffic access. They spent the rest of the day working with the fire department, sanitizing the Congressman's office, pausing only for a quick dinner break.

"Dr. Logan, you're a godsend, and we won't forget what you've done for us, will we, Devon?" Nate said, finally.

Devon nodded, his face stone-like, unreadable.

"You sure I can't entice you two to an early drink?" Nate asked.

"How 'bout a rain-check?" Lula said. "I'm flying to Boston for a conference and haven't packed or prepared for my lecture yet."

"It starts on a Sunday?"

"No, but I do have a meeting, and need to prepare."

"And here I was, wanting to spend some downtime with a beautiful lady."

Lula looked away, certain her awkward feelings showed on her face.

"Well, let's wrap things up," Devon rescued her. They walked together in silence.

Lula stopped to talk with the firefighters and police, who were cordoning off the building, restricting entry, while two firefighters searched the premises for more suspicious boxes.

The anthrax was presumed to have been left on the steps of the office, like a package delivery. Lula wanted to be sure there weren't more boxes with noxious poison in them. She described what steps should be taken in the early morning.

Again, she felt her sadness rise. The memory of Ambrose lingered, his smell like incense inside her mind. She could almost feel his touch.

She turned around. Devon was tapping her shoulder.

"We gotta go, Lula. The Feds will be on this by tomorrow afternoon. We need to have a game plan, now. Chief said we should meet sometime tomorrow. I told him you were traveling. What time is your flight?"

She nodded, but heard very little.

21

OLIVE

4:30 p.m.

Richard tried not to look conspicuous as he strolled through his cousin's manicured neighborhood. Magnolia Estates had a nouveaux-riche aura that made him feel like a walking eyesore in his grungy jeans as he moved past the imported cars and lush green lawns. He zipped his windbreaker, hoping to look more respectable.

He was deep in thought, wondering what was going to happen to him. The fact that the police knew where he lived and hadn't made a move to pursue him made him crazier than not hearing from his cousin after two days of phone calls to her workplace.

When they did finally speak, she'd been none too pleased, afraid that her work phone was being tapped, as part of efforts to stem suspicious or criminal activities of hospital staff. She'd made it clear her home phone was off limits to him, and that her husband was gonna ask her questions if he kept bothering her. A childhood friend relayed messages between them.

Rounding the block for the third time, Richard decided he should hold steady and take a seat somewhere before someone decided he was canvassing the houses to rob them.

Knocking loudly on his cousin's front door, he waited for thirty seconds, then walked back down the driveway to sit on the curb.

Any Neighborhood Watch fanatics would see that he showed no ill intentions, sitting out in the open.

The last time he and his cousin Olive had seen each other was six months ago, when she gave him the bottles of Temazepam that had provided him with a healthy income, until the recent turn of events. He was feeling a bit anxious about drug dealing, had psyched himself to believe that what he had told Sherry that last time would hold true: he would go to school, make something of himself.

Richard's heart began to race when his cousin eventually rounded the corner in her red Toyota Corolla, a shiny, maroon-colored Ford Bronco trailing behind her, and another car, a faded, beige Volkswagen, bringing up the rear.

The convoy stopped in front of the house. His cousin parked in the driveway and climbed out of her car.

Richard could barely contain his enthusiasm, but, in an effort not to draw attention to himself, he stood his ground on the pavement, looking disinterested.

He watched her pull her nurse's smock aside as she dipped into her deep cleavage and removed a wad of bills. The car dealership's driver made lame protestations, refusing payment, but she reached around his flailing arms and deposited a bill securely into his front pocket, patting his chest as she thanked him.

The men nodded at Richard.

Olive motioned to Richard to join her inside, something she allowed only when no one else was home.

Once inside, they walked down a large hallway to the back of the house and into the kitchen. She reached for a bag of salted peanuts from a lower cupboard, offering him a diet soda from her refrigerator.

She hugged him, apologetically telling him she just couldn't risk "things." Her husband was doing big business now, and stood to get a hefty percentage of the pipeline's profits as a preferred shareholder. The last thing she wanted was to be caught up in any scandal.

The vacant space that a tooth had once filled held Richard's attention as Olive grinned.

She had done as he instructed, taken his money and found a used Bronco, with a 5.8-liter engine, like he asked for. He could camp in it at night, and it only had 60,000 miles.

Richard rinsed the empty soda can at the sink and placed it on the counter, then leaned against her stove, studying her profile. Her hair, with its sweet-smelling coconut pomade, was greased back tightly, making the blue veins in her skull stand out. He even noticed a faint slant in her eyes, and wondered whether she had pulled her hair too tight. In less desperate times he'd have teased her. Instead, he gently pulled her ponytail, then hugged her.

She smelled of coconut, talcum powder, and Opium perfume. He could always recognize her scents.

He held onto her tightly, then released her, silently staring at her, seeing traces of his mother in her face.

"You're all I got," he said gruffly.

"I know, Ricky. I know. But you need to lay low, you know. Just get in that truck and go take a little ride somewhere. When you settle down, let me know where you are, okay?"

He nodded.

"When you leaving?"

His eyes welled with tears, but he blinked them away.

"Tomorrow, most likely. I gotta take care of a couple of things before I leave."

"You got enough money after paying for the Bronco?"

"Yeah. You know I'm a cheap-ass bastard." He bit his lip and rubbed under his moist nose with the back of his hand. "I'm gonna miss you, cousin."

"Me, too," she said.

He pulled back, jokingly. "What? You gonna miss yo'self, too?

"You know what I mean. You know good and well what I mean, you coon-ass."

He put up his fists and lightly tapped her shoulder, ducking to the right, then left, as she walloped a fake one upside his chin, causing him to lean backwards in a pantomime of surrender.

"And you say this is the right thing to do?" Richard asked shyly.

"Yeah. There's a bit too much bad blood here, right now, Ricky. And memories, too."

"They not all bad, though. I'll remember you, but I'll be away from *ma mere*."

"Well, I got a theory about that, little Ricky. Look behind you."

He jumped, expecting to see the police, then shook his head, holding his heart.

"What you see, boy?" she asked, looking at him, holding his arm.

He put his hand to his chest, rubbed it, then, sighed. "Girl, don't do that to a man on the run."

"So what you see?"

He chuckled out his answer. "I see a fan in the breakfast room, a table, a kitchen cupboard and the sink, shelves, and some Cajun seasoning."

"Well, that's where you and I see different, I guess. You see a room with things, but I also see all our people just over your shoulder. I see MaTaunte, looking at you and smiling. Cousin James, Percy, and George. See there? Aunt Geneva. Aunt Matt. There's Aunt Grace. Aunt Nita. Your momma was my aunt, don't forget that. I loved her, too. She's always been telling me to help you out. I did, even when it jeopardized my own situation."

He put his hand on her shoulder. The print on her smock had different shapes of pasta, spoons, and bottles of olive oil. "I know that, cousin. I do. You all I got left in the world."

She glowered at him, reproachfully. "No. That ain't quite so."

He put his head down and she lifted his chin with her finger. "You got uncles, but they just in a worse position than you. You the smartest of all of us. You just got a bum deal in life."

His nose was burning. He cursed himself for getting emotional.

"You scared?" she asked.

"No. Just feeling stupid, I guess. Looks like your job got you somewhere in life. My job didn't get me nothing but trouble. I fell for the wrong chick. She's dead. It was all a mirage."

"We all make mistakes, *cherie*."

"Yep. We all makes mistakes," he echoed.

"But as long as we alive, we're doing fine. Give me a hug, Ricky."

He put his arms around her, their heads touching while she held his right arm.

He held onto her, muffling his response in her neck. "You gonna watch the house for me?"

"Yes, sir."

"Don't go selling it and all, you hear?"

"Okay."

"I mean it. Promise."

"I promise. Remember, I was a Scout, too."

"Okay, then. How 'bout those keys? And a commode?"

"Yeah, you better go, baby boy. Little Bubba's boy is coming to stay with us. His Daddy don't wanna see no man in my house, even if we is cousins."

"You're right about that. Which toilet?"

"The one down there, near the garage." She motioned with her chin.

"I'll say goodbye then, Olive. Don't walk me out. I'll be in touch."

"Send me a postcard, okay? That way I know you all right. Don't put no name or return address on it or nothing, okay?"

"Okeydokey."

"I'm gonna go upstairs and change."

He reached his house in twenty minutes and was taking out his old scanner to put in the new truck when he heard his name and his old vehicle's description on his police scanner. In connection with Blaine's death. His heart nearly leapt out of his shirt.

Nakadee police couldn't arrest him without extraditing him back to Nakadee, so he'd high-tail it beyond the parish limits. He'd give 'em the ride of their lives.

Sherry was a distant memory now.

22

WALLY

Remnants of beignets, bagels, and donuts covered the table, next to a tray of coffee, tea, and condiments. Lula was about to lament the lack of herbal teas when she realized that she could use some caffeine.

In all the bustling activity in the room, the meeting was never really called to order. Nate took a seat next to Chief Broussard. Devon leaned against the wall in a chair beside the door, which he closed.

The voice on the police intercom surprised everyone but Lula when it announced a call for Dr. Logan from someone named "Tom-Tom."

Chief Broussard picked up a cordless receiver from the conference phone on the table, pushed a button, and handed the phone to her. Lula walked outside as she addressed her friend.

"Tom-Tom. I'm in a meeting. Can you give me the Cliff Notes version?"

"Long story short—I looked up the weather during Carnival and learned that about four days after Fat Tuesday there was an unusual cold spell for three or four days. Temperatures were in the mid-thirties at night, and it was pretty overcast during the day. If your victim was killed sometime during Mardi Gras, his body was exposed just long enough for the maggots to appear. But they were probably killed once the cold front came in."

"Are you saying that maggots could have returned when the weather thawed?" Lula asked.

"Yeah. It's called re-colonization. Like they get back to work when the weather's hospitable. Now, it doesn't tell us how he died, but that information about the maggots might help you sort that out. But based upon what you explained to me, and the photos you sent, it looks as though two species of flies were fighting over the banquet. Why do I know this? Well, because the maggots were two different colors."

"Really." Neither a question nor a statement, but Tom-Tom didn't notice.

"You got the black soldier fly—those are the dark maggots that seem to have overtaken the first blow flies scoping out the corpse. So here's what you gotta figure out: where did the soldier flies come from, because they don't feast on carcasses; they just find places to procreate, as it were. So that's your mystery number one, and, number two, you'll need to count how many days the first maggots feasted, before the cold came in, so you can get an approximate date of death. Now, here's the linchpin: it takes two days for maggots to appear if a body is exposed outside, you know—in day heat n'all. So, I've got my calendar here. Mardi Gras was on a Tuesday, but it doesn't look like the person was dead until almost a week later, because the cold spell happened on the 20th. Are you following me?"

"So far, so good," Lula said.

"Okay, good. So, I'm cogitatin' that the poor chap found outdoors was alive up until the 18th. That was a Friday. I would list the death at sometime on the 18th of March, when the corpse was exposed to normal Louisiana heat."

"Friday the 18th," Lula confirmed. "Over a week after Mardi Gras."

"That's it, for what it's worth. I'll let you cogitate on my cogitation, and let me know if we ever cohabit the same thoughts."

Lula thanked him and hung up, then walked back into the conference room just as Devon's head peeked out the door, looking for her.

"Lula. The chief wants to talk to you," he announced.

She couldn't read the expression on his face as one of either caring or concern until she saw his jaw tighten. "Be strong," he whispered.

She looked at him quizzically and followed him into the room.

She was about to share Tom-Tom's explanation but was cut short by Chief Broussard.

"Dr. Lula Logan. I'm concerned that you may have been sitting on some information that you did not disclose to detectives here. Do you care to explain why you did not tell anyone about Richard?"

She looked puzzled. "Richard? I know no Richard."

"That's not what the surveillance pictures show."

"Surveillance?"

"We were doing it for your safety, but it turns out it helped us solve the case. We found the perpetrator."

"Excuse me?"

"The case is solved, no thanks to you."

"How can you even say the case is closed, when you haven't heard my scientific conclusions on the matter?"

That's when the chief introduced Wally, who was sitting at the table. "He saw you with Richard in your office, before you went to the Congressman's office today."

"With *me*? What do you mean, with me?" she asked.

"We've been tracking him. Well, Wally has. He saw him go to your house, write something and put it in your car, and followed him to your office. We never saw him come out. Devon mentioned that he was most likely in your bathroom. The water was running while you were talking, and it turned off by itself after you left the room."

Lula couldn't take it anymore.

"So, why in the Sam Hill would I be helping Richard out, pray tell?"

"Well, we're not quite sure, but it's not like you told us about him."

"He's a part-time janitor on campus and odd-jobs man. I had no idea it was he who left the note. When I got to my office, Richard was explaining to me that he felt he was being set up as the killer. He wanted me to know in case something happened to him."

"Did he say who was out to get him?"

"No, he just wanted me to be aware of it. Probably for the very reason that I'm sitting here now, defending him."

"Well, that's the problem, Dr. Lula. You cannot aid a suspect."

Frustrated, she looked up at the ceiling. "Let me count the reasons why you're wrong here."

"Doctor, whatever you say, the facts on the ground show differently."

"I am not privy to all of your investigations, gentlemen. I've assisted where you needed me, but I'm not sure whom you suspect. So all I can tell you is that, genuinely, he was not a suspect to me. He was a janitor who had delusions of importance. I didn't really take him seriously. He seemed kind of on the fringe of things, more like a bystander."

Nate asked: "Well, how did he know to seek you out?"

"I was there, if you recall, during your visit to the home of the producers. Richard was there—let me rephrase that—everyone was there. I'm on the campus, too, and he's a part-time janitor there. His girlfriend, Sherry, was my student. Moreover, let's not forget that I'm in the phone book."

"According to Wally here, Richard is far from innocent. He's potentially responsible for at least two of the murders."

"Surely you jest." She looked at her new acquaintance, who sat in a swivel chair, moving slowly from side to side. "Which ones?" she asked.

"Hell, maybe all three," Wally smirked.

Lula sat down, put her elbows on the table and massaged her temples as she closed her eyes.

"He said this would happen."

"What?"

"This. He said he was being set up."

Nate spoke up. "He was seen harassing Blaine two days ago. In the evening."

"Who was the witness?"

Nate moved his head toward Wally.

Since when had she become someone to watch over? At what point had Wally started trailing her?

"Do you wanna see the statement? Will that make you feel better? Give her the statement. We're using it to swear out a search warrant for Preston's and Blaine's homes. There may be evidence there that might will give us clues," Nate said.

Lula felt very distrustful. Was her investigation merely to dot the i's and cross the t's so they could say they had performed their due diligence? Why were they so interested in a man whose only crime was being lonely? Sure, Richard was everywhere and nowhere, forgotten by most. Could they have planted or were they going to plant the evidence? After the notorious police bungling in the now legendary O.J. Simpson murder investigation, when police had chosen their culprit but performed an untold number of procedural errors that actually acquitted him instead—anything was possible.

Could she even trust Devon to do the right thing in this investigation?

Nate put his chest out a bit further. "We have some leverage in the matter. We're taking his cousin, Olive, into custody for some petty drug dealing she's been doing. She might be able to spill the beans on her cousin."

Lula looked perplexed.

"Olive? Melvyn's father's wife?"

"Dr. Lula—everybody, and I mean *everybody*, is related here, in some form or fashion. You know the 'Know your Customer' rule in banking? Well, in Louisiana, we have a 'Know your Cousin' rule, before you register for a marriage license. It's against the law here to marry your cousin, not that it's stopped anybody."

Lula knew she was treading on thin ice, and realized that a change of tone from accusatory to inquisitive might uncover their underlying obsession with Richard.

Everyone she met felt like a suspect. Was that a factor of small-town life, that it was the collective that was innocent or guilty?

"Have you figured out Richard's motive?" she asked.

Nate spoke up. "Well, not yet. He and Melvyn were up to something. "If you recall, they are related, too—by marriage. It might be that Richard knows something that we don't and he was avenging something the filmmakers might have done to the boy."

Lula listened quietly while Nate continued, confident in his authority.

"Wally has been undercover for us since the beginning of our investigation. He was at the Hot Sauce Festival, and took videos when Melvyn and the SwampBoyz were performing their rap ditty. Tell us what you think of this."

He moved to clear table space for Wally, who, reaching down by his side, pulled out a laptop from a dark knapsack.

"Put it here so all of us can see." Nate instructed. He studied the laptop's screen as he continued, "We aren't sure about Melvyn, but I definitely want to speak to him or his parents before we make any arrests."

Wally sat back down, pushing his chair away from the table, angling the laptop to get a better view.

"Can everyone see it? It's keyed up, right?" Nate asked. He got up from his seat and stood at the foot of the table to get a clear vantage point.

Lula asked Devon to cut the lights.

"Yessiree," he responded, his tone taunting. She wanted to pummel him for divulging the situation in the bathroom. After all he had done to her, he had the nerve to distrust *her*?

As they watched, the laptop screen showed three preteens dressed in LSU basketball jerseys, starched white T-shirts and long jeans. All of them wore purple baseball caps with "SwampBoyz" emblazoned in fluorescent gold lettering. They were typical teenagers, living out their fantasy of premature rapper rock-star fame, holding their hands close to their genitals. Whistles and catcalls sounded as beats streamed from the speakers, chants of "Go SwampBoyz, Go SwampBoyz."

"Fast forward past the banshee stuff." Nate said contemptuously.

Wally stopped on a dime at the beginning lyrics, where Richard could be seen in the foreground of the crowd, dancing gracefully, his whole body in syncopation. At one point he had his hands in the air, pointing downward to someone, as if featuring someone else's dancing. But Richard was the only one visible in the throng.

Nate nodded to Wally to pause the viewing. "Of what importance is the rap song to Richard? Is he their manager or something?" he asked, looking at Lula.

Nate seemed to feel perfectly fine asking her about rap, making his big assumption about Blacks and music.

She decided to go along. "I'd say that's some pretty good rapping, if you must know. But if you're looking into it for a message, you obviously don't know his mother. She'd ground him for life if he were even *thinking* of getting involved in a crime. She's got a tight rein on him."

Nate stared back, incredulously.

Lula shrugged. "It's a rap song. That's what they do."

"But words have consequences, too," Nate insisted. "Look where Tupac and Fattie, Big—or whatever his name was—are now. Dead as doorknobs."

"Because their fear of the other took hold of each of them and got out of hand. They were fast buddies before the madness."

She decided to try to make her case for science. "Now, would you like to hear something related to forensics, or is that not so important, now?"

Nate nodded for her to go ahead.

"An entomologist has given me information about the maggots we found on the body."

Nate's expression was blank. "And ...."

She took a breath. "I'm still thinking it through. Can you give me a calendar, please?"

Nate nodded at Devon to retrieve one, but Devon didn't move.

"It would appear that there were two waves of maggot activity, the first most likely closely after Mardi Gras. If you recall, we had a three-day cold spell immediately afterwards," Lula described.

Nate looked at Devon for confirmation, who responded with a shrug.

"I say the victim was tied up in the shack and tried to escape, but had a heart attack," said Lula.

Nate's voice rose in disbelief. "A heart attack? Are you trying to give me one? You mean to tell me this poor sucker wasn't murdered?"

The chief looked at Nate pointedly. "Well, if that's the case, this is a federal matter. He could've been kidnapped, but the felony murder rule will kick in and we lose jurisdiction."

Nate grunted. "That corpse out there was chopped to pieces, with the fingers practically used as door stops, and you wanna tell me he died of natural causes?" Nate wasn't exactly red-faced, but his neck was crimson right above his shirt collar. He was wearing a suit and tie instead of his usual polo shirt.

"What I'm saying is that the death most likely came a week after he was kidnapped, but he was being tortured in the meantime. Perhaps he escaped. He was bludgeoned after he died."

"What was he hit with, then? What cracked the back of his skull? Was he just tanning out there, in the sun?"

"Well, Detective, you're stealing my thunder. There is a chance that the sun, which was in full force after that cold spell, and has been ever since, could actually have an impact on the wear and tear, and even cracking of the skull. I haven't been able to find any implement that fits the shape of the cracks. I've searched a lot of databases but can't find anything that fits those markings."

"Devon," Nate looked frustrated, "do you want to have a talk with the doctor here, about what she's saying?"

"You doin' fine, Detective."

"Science doesn't take sides. It can only reveal what's true." Lula said.

Lula's respect for Devon sank even lower, as he pretended to rub his head, took a couple of small steps, then retreated.

"I want to talk to Aggie Sheaf. Immediately," Nate demanded. "Wally, go track down her number for me. Let's call her in here."

Wally barely moved other than to uncross his feet as he leaned back in his chair.

Lula spoke softly. "You can arrest half the town, but until all the evidence is examined, all you'll have is crowded court dockets while your suspects are free on bail because you're nowhere closer to getting the culprit today than you were yesterday. You have to let me do my job."

"Who's stopping you?"

"You're not serious, are you? From the day I came on board, you had me playing Mammy to your targets more than allowing me to do my job as a scientist."

"You're kidding me. Mammy?"

"You will admit that I've been pretty occupied on a daily basis, helping your investigation beyond what any FA should be asked to do, really."

He looked slightly pained at her accusation. "You didn't say anything."

"I didn't mind, for the most part, but it did keep me away from my tasks. Between the hospital, classes, and helping your department, I have barely gotten any sleep since I came on this case."

"You got some sleep, Dr. Lula. We know that you did."

Lula looked at Nate while Devon's arms, unfolded, were at his side, as if he might need them to prevent the verbal combatants from breaking into a physical fight.

"Just what do you mean by that, Detective? Because I see a million-dollar settlement coming out of the sexual harassment case I'll file the minute I return from Boston."

She knew her expression was goading him to "go there."

Rather than escalate the situation, she turned away from Nate, who asked Wally whether he wanted to say anything.

Wally shook his head.

"Where's Melvyn's mother?" Lula demanded.

Devon spoke this time. "After that argument they had here in the office, we thought it would be easier to approach his dad for questioning."

"If I were handling this, I'd call his mother first. I spent some time with her. She's smart. She can handle anything you throw at her."

Lula wondered how many times black women were ignored because it was easier for Whites to deal with black men?

"If you want to come along, sure," Nate offered.

"I'm sorry, but I have work to do. I'm going to get you your information before I catch my plane."

Lula couldn't help but delight in Nate's ironic predicament of needing her help while simultaneously trying to undermine her professionalism.

"It's highly inappropriate that his mother wouldn't be called, especially with charges like these. You should probably have her cell phone number. Why don't you let me call her and you can talk to her, at least?" Lula said.

"We need you as a witness at trial, Dr. Lula—as an expert, not a friend of the family. We'll call up Tyrell and ask to meet him at his plant. We'll take a statement there."

Lula persevered, explaining that if they didn't contact Melvyn's mother, she'd be wondering what happened. And if Tyrell or his wife were arrested, by chance, Melvyn would have no place to go until his grandmother came to get him.

Much as they wanted to ignore her, they knew Lula had a point, so they finally opted to call Bebe to ask her to come pick up her son.

Lula dialed on the speakerphone, hoping that her participation would put Bebe at ease. She let Nate do the talking after he introduced the names of those present.

On the other end, Bebe was as collected as a judge, as the police notified her that Richard and her son were involved in some way in the disappearance and murder of Preston Pratt. Then Nate mentioned the rap song, asking her if she was aware of it.

"Look, I know my son. He's smart, even precocious, but he's got nothing to do with nothing. He's a kid. If you could prosecute for words spoken or written, there would be no rap industry. Or heavy metal, which is even more violent—and outright demonic, if you ask me."

"What about Richard?"

"Richard is a petty nuisance. I don't know how much he knew those people. I'd have him pick up Melvyn sometimes, or Melvyn had to go somewhere before I got home. Richard practically lives in his car. I gave him something to do. He's the better half of the family he belongs to. If anything, you need to check out my ex-husband's wife. She's the criminal among all of them." She laughed. "I shouldn't do that. I don't know a thing about her except what I learned when my husband left me."

Bebe asked questions about the evidence linking her son to any of the suspects. She acknowledged that her son might dress like a rapper, but never missed a day of school, and could usually be accounted for at night, at least the nights that he was with her. She couldn't talk about when he was with her ex-husband and his wife. Her son visited the film people once a week to mow their lawn, riding his bike there from school. When asked if Tyrell approved of this arrangement, she tittered.

"Tyrell has no say in the matter. My son was learning how to be responsible. We both learned from the ground up how to build his business. He learned how to operate the lawn mower, ride it to and fro, without incident—and he brought all his own equipment, like a real landscaper. He learned the value of work. Hard work. Something a lot of people don't believe in doing, nowadays. They paid him well."

"Is Tyrell aware of the extent of Melvyn's access to the home, his having keys to water the indoor plants, etcetera?" Nate asked.

"My son knows to talk to me. We might speak in code, but he knows he can come to me about anything. He's going to college."

There was a pause, then Nate asked: "Did Melvyn ever tell you that the filmmakers used to film him?"

"Come again?"

"Film him. Like interview him on camera."

"No. I didn't know that."

"Did you know that one of the filmmakers was gay and the other was a possible pedophile? We believe the pedophile may have committed suicide as we were closing in on him."

"Last time I checked, being gay was not a criminal act, in most parts of the country."

Nate looked at the chief, then stammered, "Well, some beg to differ, but ... well, what the hell ... they can marry now, so where's the crime?"

Bebe interrupted him. "Melvyn told me about the gay man, but that didn't bother me none. Gays are the new Black, aren't they?" She chuckled. "He sees 'em up in church all the time. But he didn't tell me that they filmed him. I find that a bit troublesome. Now, if his daddy knows that, then you might want to investigate. He would definitely want to murder someone over that. But he's not going to do anything too stupid, what with him about to become a millionaire, I hear tell, if the pipeline comes through. God knows he bragged about it enough, and we don't really even speak to each other unless we have to."

Nate's voice was firm. "Well, what time will you be able to meet with us, Mrs. Armstrong? We can wait for you, if you want."

"I'm about forty miles from Nakadee. I'll come as soon as I can, but it's still going to take me an hour in traffic. Go to my house and wait there. I'll call Tyrell to be there to pick up Melvyn. I'd allow Dr.

Logan to go with you, if she can. Melvyn is comfortable with her. But don't give me any speeding tickets while I'm rushing back." She laughed. "My license plate is BTD 528." She hung up.

Lula was impressed at Bebe's level of cooperation, considering the last dealings she had witnessed between Bebe and the police. Perhaps because her son's welfare was hanging in the balance she felt a need to be more congenial.

Nate told Wally, "You better be right about all this. We got a whole department that will be discredited if you're barking up the wrong tree. Go swear out some warrants: the filmmakers' homes, Tyrell's, and Richard's."

"What about the boy's home?" Wally asked.

"We'll get permission from the mother. She needs to be there. I don't want some motion filed that says we handled it wrong. We'll wait for her, to witness everything. Devon, can you go pick the kid up and bring him to the Hollykook house?"

Lula cut in, "We have to make a detour, if I'm supposed to be with you when you find Melvyn." She explained that she needed Devon to take her home so she could go back to her office and gather her reports before the police did "anything reckless." She told him she would retrieve her car, do her tasks, and meet them wherever they were if her services were needed. She saw Nate and Devon silently communicating with each other before Nate walked away to confer with Wally.

"Let's sit tight for a while," Devon said.

She looked at him, surprised. "What was all that about? So I'm a suspect now?"

"Not quite, but you're not exactly in the clear, either."

"And who is doing the suspecting? You, the tattler, or your boss man?"

"I called it as I saw it, Dr. Logan. You were harboring a fugitive."

"Whatever, Devon. But until you put the cuffs on me, I'd like to do my job. Do you have a copy of the forensic pathology report?"

Devon, jaw taut, looked away from her.

"Can I make a phone call?" Lula asked. "Mine's in my car. Or didn't Wally find that out when he was snooping?"

Devon handed her his cell phone.

Aggie answered immediately. Lula updated her a little, then asked whether there was anything in the remains that suggested that the victim had suffered a heart attack. With the body so ravaged by maggots, it might be hard to discern if the victim had had a pulmonary embolism.

They were also waiting for Preston Pratt's primary physician's medical records from Cedars Sinai Hospital, in Los Angeles.

Aggie was frustrated. "Those friggin' television shows make it impossible for us to do our jobs. All we know is that somebody bludgeoned him with a weapon, on a date uncertain, after he died of a heart attack on another date uncertain. Will that help any of us feel more secure?"

Aggie was probably right. No matter the theory of the murder or murders, no one would feel any sense of relief if the evildoer were still at large.

Lula's fatigue was kicking in as she pondered what more she could accomplish in the limited time left before she had to leave for the airport.

She knew, as a black woman, she'd need allies if her opinion was to be respected. Regardless of her position, those with less aptitude would always question her intelligence. Even the first black President had little credibility in the eyes of his detractors, notwithstanding his Christian faith, his middle-of-the-road, bipartisan attempts to be there for all Americans, his Ivy League credentials. Race was always under the surface in the country's body politic, and it looked like the white officers here would have the last word on who was guilty or not. She was determined to use forensics to prevent that.

Nate returned from his huddle with Wally and suggested that Devon and Lula pick up Melvyn and bring him to Preston's house, while Wally retrieved the search warrants to enter the home.

Lula protested, reminding them that they were supposed to wait for Bebe's arrival.

"And that's why you're not part of the police department, Dr. Logan," Devon said as they walked to the car.

"We got some questions for him. Better he can answer at the scene."

This man beside her, that she'd slept with regularly, now felt like a calculating symbol of authority who could bully others at will because he carried a gun. She felt powerless in his company.

He looked at her, opening his passenger door.

She stepped inside.

***

This time Melvyn did not run as the car approached his home. He set his bike down, waving away his friends, then walked to the passenger side to explain that his mother wasn't there.

Melvyn's somber look spoke volumes to Lula. He was overwhelmed and in need of understanding about what was going on with all these people dying. And everyone expected answers from him.

Lula didn't dare say anything.

Devon spoke firmly. "Get in the car, boy. We'll bring you back 'fore your mother gets here. We just got some questions we might have to ask you at Mr. Preston's, and want you on the scene. You know the place pretty well, right?"

"I guess," Melvyn said from the back seat. Lula could see him through the passenger side mirror. He was gazing out the window.

Lula was running on empty, her emotions jumbled, torn, and conflicted. Everything felt upended, from her research to her relationships.

Did she even have any friends? Was Bebe someone she could confide in?

She didn't want to be here, was counting the hours till her flight. Then she thought about Ambrose. Her heart felt like lead.

***

As Devon's car approached the property, the Hollykook house seemed a ghastly, lifeless relic now, uninhabited, its lawn overgrown.

"Looks like they could use your services," Devon said jovially, glancing in the rear-view mirror.

Melvyn said nothing. If he had any emotions, Lula knew they were buried deep. On the surface, he showed only boredom and listlessness. He'd already crossed that threshold between being a child who could display his emotions freely and a teenager who must keep them in check, a defense trait worn like armor on black youth nowadays. She wondered if there was any safe place for him to show his angst.

A black boy's identity was always wrapped up in how others reacted to him. She knew this double consciousness was what kept Blacks alive in this country, not knowing who was friend or foe—and never letting their guard down. The result was often realizing that they had no friends, except the always-evolving relationships they created for, with, and against each other, plotting for survival.

Lula pondered the irony of returning to the scene where she had first met Melvyn, weeks ago, and wondered whether Devon's objective today had been the same then: to catch a suspect that was now within arm's reach. She also wondered how Bebe felt about her son's situation, entangled in the lives of two white men who were now dead. Did any of this faze him?

As the three of them walked to the side entrance, Devon asked Melvyn, "Where are your keys?"

"I threw them away."

"What? *Why*?" Devon demanded.

"I didn't need them anymore."

"Why did you need them in the first place?"

"I didn't," Melvyn said, firmly.

"So why'd he give 'em to you?"

"Who knows?"

"Then why'd you take them?" Devon sneered.

"Because I thought he'd feel bad if I didn't. We was buddies. I couldn't diss him."

"And you never used them?"

"To do what?"

Lula watched Devon shake his head in faux exasperation. This boy was no dummy. Melvyn was goading them to come right out and say what they wanted him to confess: that he was involved in the murders of Preston Pratt, Blaine, or both.

They were approaching the side entrance, when Melvyn volunteered an answer: "I threw them away after I got my stuff back."

"When was that?" Devon asked.

"Man, I told you all. When I took the mower home."

"And that was when?"

"I don't remember."

"You either know or you don't. Was it daytime? Nighttime? You too young to have memory loss, brother. Or maybe it's selective memory loss." Devon grunted.

"I'm not gonna say anything until I have a lawyer. I know that much."

"Nobody is calling you a suspect."

"Yet." Melvyn mumbled under his breath while following them into Preston's study. Nate was already in the living room, talking with Seng, the crime-scene photographer.

Melvyn stood with his hands in his pants pockets, looking glum.

Nate led them all into the center of the living room while Melvyn looked around as though he were in a stranger's home.

Lula watched Nate, who was putting on surgical gloves. His eyes were focused on Melvyn. She saw what Nate likely saw: a kid at a stage of development who, despite his posturing, was unconscious of his handsome features, and possessed an honest vulnerability that made him approachable by men like Preston and Blaine. That vulnerability was hidden today behind an emotionless mask.

Nate began walking around the periphery of the room, pretending to be looking, absentmindedly, at different artifacts. Occasionally, he glanced at Melvyn as the boy continued to stand with his hands in the pockets of his baggy shorts. He ducked his head a bit, sucking on his lip. He didn't look comfortable.

Lula watched Seng observing Melvyn, too, as Seng also explored the room. He then paused to admire a writing secretary with intricate legs.

"Hey, Doctor Lula?" he called her over. "Do you remember this desk I was talking about?"

Seng seemed alert and convivial, a direct contrast to everyone else in the room. "This is like the one my father had in Kampuchea—or

Cambodia—as you call it. Count how many drawers are in it." He motioned with his hand. "Go ahead, count."

Besides babysitting Melvyn, Lula wasn't sure she had a place in the investigation anymore as she moved to look at the desk.

Seng next motioned to Nate. "Hey, Nate. Are you a betting man? Can I prove to you that I am a magician?"

"I'm not sure we have time for that, Seng," Nate said, dryly.

"This is part of the investigation, Nate. We have a warrant to search the house, right?"

"Yeah, but we're also on the clock."

"This is part of the house, you will agree?"

Nate looked at Melvyn. "You know about this, Melvyn? This magic desk?"

Melvyn stood as if suspended in space, careful not to look anywhere in particular. Lula figured he was taking the Fifth, as he stayed put where he was.

Seng placed his hands on his hips, triumphantly, as Nate approached him.

"Count the drawers," Seng urged.

Nate walked to the desk and began opening them slowly, bending over to peer into the interior.

"Dr. Lula?" Seng invited cordially. "How many?"

"Ten?" She shrugged.

"Nate?"

"Well, I'm not going to say ten, because then we'll both be wrong." He stepped away from the secretary.

"I asked how many drawers do you see. You can't cheat on this one."

"No, Seng. You asked me to bet you. How fair is that if you know the answer?" Nate walked away. "I'm not playing your games."

"Okay, fine then. I will show Dr. Lula." Seng motioned her toward the back of the secretary, which showed the same intricate mother-of-pearl inlay as the rest of the desk.

Seng's touch of a hidden lever at the bottom of the desk made the whole back spring open, revealing beneath the drawers a false bottom that was three-quarters the width and length of the desk's writing surface.

"Eleven," Lula proclaimed.

"I told you." Seng leaned over and peaked inside, taking digital photos. "Magic."

"What's there?" Lula asked.

"Some documents. Keys. Digital tape cassettes, a thick notebook or something, without a binder. The papers fastened together."

"That's it?" Lula asked.

Melvyn came closer as they were speaking.

Seng stepped aside for him to see the contents.

"Oh wow." Melvyn covered his mouth. "That's sick," he exclaimed.

Seng began taking photos from different angles, then let Lula have a look. "No more fingers," Seng volunteered.

Nate was pacing around the room, looking detached.

"Take your inventory, Seng, and we'll let the crime scene investigators look for prints."

Seng put the contents of the hidden drawer on top of the secretary, setting up the process for taking pictures of each item for inventory. "I might need some help. I don't have the English vocabulary for this one."

"What does it say?" Lula asked, walking back to the secretary where Seng was bent over, taking pictures of what looked to be a typewritten manuscript with handwritten notes, pinned together by brads. There were two titles on the cover page. The first was, *Think Before You Speak*. Those words had been crossed out and replaced by, *Words without Thought*.

"What?" Melvyn exclaimed. His look of recognition was too obvious for him to recover, or hide whatever information he was trying to keep from them. He shook his head. "Wow."

Nate looked at him. "You wanna tell us something, Melvyn?"

"I was just thinking, that's all. I mean, I never thought I would see the ... connection."

"Connection?" Seng asked.

Melvyn tried to recover. "You know, he wrote. You know, he said he wrote it, but I never saw him writing. He was always talking about writing. I never saw the end of it."

"The finished product?" Lula suggested.

"Yeah. He said he was a writer, but I never saw him do it. I know he made money. I could see that. I just thought he was kind of a joke. He was so ec-eccen—"

"Eccentric," Nate finished for him.

"Right." Melvyn shook his head. "That's what kinda kept me comin' over here, I guess."

"Did you like him, Melvyn?" Nate asked.

Melvyn fell quiet, scratching his ear. "Man, you never knew what he was gonna talk about. Every time I came over, he cooked me some kinda meal and we would eat it together. I guess he thought I was from the projects or something, even though we lived down the way and my daddy got plenty bank."

"Did you like his cooking?"

"It was okay. Not as good as my momma. He let me help him choose the menu and the wine for the meal. He said Europeans drink it all the time. My moms don't know that part."

"How many times did he give you alcohol?"

"Who's counting? But each time he only gave me half a glass. It was kinda bitter, to me. He said it was—how did he say it? An acquired taste. He said there were lots of things that I wouldn't like now that I'd like later."

Nate walked toward him slowly with his hands in his pocket.

"Are there other things your mom doesn't know?"

"No," Melvyn said, looking at the floor, then around the room.

"Did you ever ask him why he wanted to hang out with you so much?" Before giving Melvyn a chance to respond he added, "He never touched you, right? In a wrong kind of way."

"Hell no! He tried to touch my head once or twice, and I told him, 'Hey, man, don't touch my stuff.'"

"What did he do?"

"He laughed. And wrote something down. He took notes sometimes."

Nate gave him a gentle nod, then asked quietly, "Did you know he was gay, Melvyn?"

"No. I kinda figured it out, though. He got a lot of telephone calls, and sometimes his voice would change. Like a sissy, or something. But he was funny, too, so I'm not sure whether he was just putting on an act."

"What about visitors? Did people come over when you were here?"

"No. Well, not a lot, anyway."

"Did you recognize anybody in particular, like someone who came over regularly?"

"The Cuban dude. And Sherry." He looked downcast.

"I'd like to know what you saw the night you last saw Preston," Nate said.

"I didn't see sh—anything."

"When?"

"Fat Tuesday."

"Sounds like you disobeyed your momma's orders."

"Is she gonna find out?"

"Well, we're waiting for her. What will she say if she finds out?"

Melvyn looked worried. "What you gonna tell her, Dr. Lula?" he asked anxiously. "He invited me over."

"So you stayed home, or did you go?"

"I don't want to discriminate myself." He scratched his head. "Is that the word?"

No one corrected him.

"Let's just say ... well, there are two of me," Melvyn said. "When I do something good, there's only one of me. But if I do something bad, then that's another me."

Everyone was quiet.

Nate spoke softly. "So, you managed to sneak in here, right?"

Melvyn nodded.

"Technically, no. I was in the front of the house, looking in from the window."

"Were you with anybody?"

"No."

"Did anybody see you?"

"Doubt it."

"What makes you say that?"

"I was just on my bike, by the side of the house, looking in—the party was inside."

"What about helpers? Were there caterers?"

"I wasn't paying them any attention. They were all toward the back of the house, near the kitchen and dining room."

"How many?"

"About five of them—man." He shrugged. "I don't know. I'm guessing. This feels like school, like I gotta know the answer."

Nate asked suddenly, "Did you go to Mass at midnight?"

"No, man. I was home, coppin' some serious Zzs by then. I was still tired from our trip to Brazil, and I knew I had to mow the lawn the next day, so I left. I just wanted to check out the party."

"How long were you in Brazil?

"Ten days."

"Who did the lawn while you were away?"

"Richard."

Lula's mind traveled back to when she had first seen the house. There had been no women present. No dogs. Grown men and a teenager who mowed the lawn. She froze, cocking her head to the side.

"Is there a laptop around that I can borrow?" she asked.

"There's a computer in the study," Melvyn said.

Nate glanced at him, then nodded to Lula, "Seng carries a tablet. Can you get it for her, Seng?"

Nate told Devon to set Lula up in the study, then asked Melvyn to have a seat on a couch.

Nate joined them in the study. Seng switched on his tablet for Lula, then walked off to take more photos.

Lula opened a web browser and typed the words, "lawn mower blades."

Nate looked at Devon, who put his fingers to his lips, pointing to the next room where Melvyn was sitting.

Scrolling up and down the screen, Lula studied the photos that came up for display. She noticed a series of blades with three jutting indentations in the metal—for mulching, the description explained. One blade would probably weigh about two pounds, slightly heavy in her hands. The blade's slender beveled edges, in a large mower, would trim grass at a fast rotating clip, and could surely slice into someone's skull if wielded with force.

Looking over Lula's shoulder at the screen, Nate leaned in to speak close to her, in a low voice, whispering, "So, you think the kid could have done it?"

Devon, well within earshot, watched them.

"I'm not sure—not sure he has the muscle strength to do it." Lula answered.

"Lemme see," Devon said, striding off into the living room, with Nate close behind. Lula heard him say, "Stand up, li'l man. How tall are you, boy?"

"I dunno."

"You five feet yet?"

"That's 'bout right." The boy nodded, looking down.

"Yeah, wait fifteen more years, when every man says he's six feet, brother. For real. Let me see. Stand up."

Lula walked into the living room, tablet in hand. Melvyn was standing, looking uncomfortable.

"You shoot hoops?" Nate asked.

"Naw. I shoot *hoop*."

Nate looked at Devon for clarification.

"Only white boys say *hoops*, man." Devon laughed.

"Did you bring me here to chat about basketball? My daddy's supposed to come get me."

Devon answered. "Your momma has veto power. We'll get you there. Okay, you don't shoot hoop. You play soccer?"

"You ought to know."

"How is that?" Devon asked.

"You got a taste of my twitch muscle when we met."

"Right. When you was runnin' like a jackrabbit?" Devon nodded his respect. "Kissadee forest don't got no soccer field on it. Why I always see you on bikes, far away from home?"

"I'm an explorer."

"You were exploring—out near where Preston's body was found."

"Whatever."

"Your buddy's dead, and all you can say is, *whatever*."

"Can somebody tell me why I'm here or is this a kidnapping?"

"Hold your diapers. We'll get you to your daddy in a sec."

Nate motioned them to follow him into the study, where Lula resumed viewing the lawnmower blade images on Seng's tablet.

"Pratt was approximately 5'9," she said.

"They seem so much bigger in the newspapers and TV, don't they? The little runts," Nate chuckled.

"Do you see three teeth that jut out? It's that part of the blade that could have caused the blunt-force trauma to the skull." She touched the screen with her index finger, sliding it along the beveled edge of the blade on the screen. "The curve of the blade, which is unique, fits the shape of the fracture line."

Next, Lula pantomimed Melvyn lifting the blade. "The blade would've dug into his fingers. He wouldn't be able to hold it. Take a look at his hands."

Devon walked back out into the living room again. "What you up to, there?" He spoke gruffly, then returned. "His hands aren't big or strong enough, 'specially if he plays soccer. They don't have strong grips if they play a lot of soccer, you know. They don't use their hands. He's too scrawny, still."

Nate looked at him, questioningly.

Devon whispered to them both, "No boy Melvyn's size would have the necessary force to strike a man with the blade without signs of it somewhere."

"Unless he had gloves on when he did it."

Lula put the debate to rest. "This was an exacting, precise cut to the head, made by someone with calm precision."

"A kid couldn't drug him, either," Devon volunteered.

"But the drugs could definitely be gotten from Melvyn's father's home, and used by his father," Nate spoke.

"To do what?" asked Devon.

"Avenge whatever wrongs these guys might have done to the boy, whether real or imagined."

The two men gaped at each other for a few seconds.

"Let's go," Nate said. "*Now.*"

23

TYRELL

Nate's car was approaching the poultry plant from the rear, driving up a narrow gravel lane about a quarter of a mile from the road. Devon, who was driving, stopped, at Lula's urging.

To their left was a massive structure made of concrete blocks with a large sign that read, "Caution: Rendering Area," with a hand-drawn skull and crossbones on either side.

The building blocked their view of whatever was on the other side. A familiar stench met Lula's nostrils: animals were decomposing nearby.

"I'm gonna get out and I'd like you to move up a ways. There may be anthrax spores around here. I'd stay in the car till you get closer to the plant," she told Devon.

She reached into her duffle bag, grateful that she was still wearing her ankle boots, and pulled out her hazmat mask, checked it carefully, and put it on.

She set off, approaching the area with fast, purposeful steps until she reached the front of the cement building. The stalls were covered by sloping planks that provided cover for mounds of dead animal meat stewing in heaps encased in concrete. She counted seven stalls, a field day for flesh- and dung-eating black soldier fly maggots.

It was beginning to make sense now. Only someone with access to these carcasses would know the danger of disease that they carried. Someone like Tyrell.

Lula walked for three minutes along the dirt road to the poultry plant before taking off her mask.

Catching sight of her expression, Nate radioed for patrol cars to fan out and prevent entry and exit from the plant. He also called for a police escort to bring Chief Broussard in to handle Tyrell.

Fifteen minutes later, seated in his office at a large mahogany desk, Tyrell looked up, startled, as Nate, Lula, and the police entourage walked in.

"We holding a service here today? Can I assume you have some good news for me?" he asked. "Did we get a green light?"

Nate looked to the chief, who shook his head, slowly. "I'm afraid it's not that kind of visit. My detectives have some questions for you, Mr. Armstrong."

"Oh, it's 'Mr. Armstrong' now, is it?" Tyrell had a vacant look in his eyes. There was split-second tension in which it felt as though, at any moment, things could turn ugly.

Events in the nation's past and present proved that it was never a cakewalk arresting a black man, however armed an officer might be. The likelihood that he would put up a protest and make it more troublesome to interrogate or haul him in created too many episodes of tragedy for all parties concerned.

Tyrell stood. He was dressed in khaki pants, a tucked-in blue denim shirt, and a belt with a large buckle, looking more like a decoy than a criminal suspect.

The décor in Tyrell's office had the hallmarks of an important businessman: dark wood wall panels and brown leather furniture. It looked more like a lawyer's smoking lounge than an office in a poultry plant. Framed portraits of Martin Luther King and Abraham Lincoln hung on either side of the door facing his desk.

"Tyrell, there's an accumulation of evidence that suggests that you have some involvement in at least two murders," Chief Broussard said.

"Two who? Accumulation of what?" Tyrell exclaimed, with a look of defiance. "Let me make this clear. For your information, I do not have a Ford Bronco, and whatever car I do drive, it's not white."

His reference to the O.J. Simpson police chase was not lost on the contingent of law enforcement assembled.

"I guess it was bound to happen sooner or later, so it might as well be now, right?" Tyrell returned to his seat and spread his hands for all to see. "I was gonna be bringing in millions of dollars to this town. And I open the papers to see that a Congressman I was working with is dead—a *brother*, let me add. And *I'm* being hauled in? Whatever you think, I can tell you: you got the wrong guy. It is I, as in *me*, who would like to get to the bottom of this." He shook his head slowly in disbelief. "So, this is how you do it. Get me arrested and scuttle my involvement in the pipeline project? That's what this is really about, right?"

His quiet outrage hung over the room, along with a tinge of discomfort and guilt.

"We'd like to take a look at your garage and your house," the chief said finally.

"What's in my garage?" Tyrell's voice rose in pitch.

"We'd like to look at your lawn mower."

Tyrell stared at the chief. "You've got to be kidding." He began to laugh, shaking his head. "My lawnmower." He looked at his audience, who did not appear to find this humorous. Shrugging, he held out his palms in supplication.

"My wife—my ex-wife—has it. My son uses it."

Lula looked at Nate, who spoke up. "What kind of lawnmower is it?'

"Man, I don't know the name. I bought it at Sears. It's not like it's manufactured here, right?" Flummoxed, he picked up the telephone, then set it down, his hand still gripping the receiver. "Look, man, I need to check up on Melvyn, first. He's supposed to stay at our house for a couple of days, but he's at his home, playing with his friends. Can we make a pit stop so I can take care of that? Otherwise, I'll have to call my wife and have her make some other arrangements for him."

"Melvyn's outside," Nate told him.

Tyrell's face fell. He slowly balled his hands into fists, then leaned against them as if he were going to lift himself up. "When did these murders take place?"

"Respectfully, Ty, we'll do the questioning."

"I have a right to know of what I'm being accused, so please—cooperate with me. Tell me when I murdered these people?"

"Don't you want to know who they are?" Chief Broussard asked.

Tyrell leaned his head back slowly, his mouth open, as if catching air.

"Don't you even care who we're talking about, Ty? A college girl, with a whole future ahead of her. And your son's employer, a Hollywood writer and producer?"

Lula found it interesting that Blaine's murder wasn't mentioned, and only two murders were being pinned on Tyrell.

"Do you want an attorney?" Broussard asked.

"Hell no, I don't need an attorney. If you think I don't know what's going on, you're dumber than you look. I got my own spies, Chief, and they work for the local papers. I know a couple of things you don't want me to know."

"This isn't about me, Ty—

"The hell it isn't! I got the minority certification to put this on a fast track. You think I'm just going to hand it over to you to take the spoils, after you get rid of me? Not gonna happen." His hands were on his hips now.

There was a quiet standoff, as no one moved, though the law-enforcement entourage collectively braced itself.

"Aren't you going to ask me where I was the night or day in question? Or is my statement already written out to use after one of your goons throws me in the river, too?"

"If I may, Chief?" Lula asked.

Broussard nodded his assent.

"Aspects of your defense and claims will bear out with the science, Mr. Armstrong," she told Tyrell.

"Science doesn't explain motive, Dr. Lula. What in the hell motive would I have to destroy my life at the expense of everything dear to me?"

Lula's heart felt heavy. She wanted to take a deep breath but feared it would convey too much. She breathed out slowly.

Chief Broussard rescued her. "Precisely because of those you hold dear. This has nothing to do with the natural gas pipeline, Ty.

It's about you, your son, and his relationship to a gay man and a suspected pedophile." He spoke calmly, adding that they might be able to resolve this issue within a couple of minutes if Tyrell would take them to his home, where the evidence, or lack thereof, would speak for itself.

Outside the plant, Melvyn ran to his father, who hugged him tightly, kissing his forehead.

No one said anything, or hurried either of them.

Melvyn licked his dry lips repeatedly as he looked up at Tyrell, his arm still around his father's waist.

"Where's your lip grease, boy?" Tyrell scolded him.

Melvyn shrugged, looking up at him as if for forgiveness.

"Where we goin'?"

"Home," Tyrell said, hugging his son.

Twenty or so minutes later, outside Tyrell's, Melvyn sat in the police car parked farthest from the house.

Lula, Nate, and Devon stood in Tyrell's garage, where seemingly unbeknownst to him his lawnmower sat next to the trash cans.

With Seng's help, it took a half-hour for them to slide the lower deck from under the frame and turn it over to look underneath.

Everything looked new, including the blades and the mounting bolt that kept them secure. Lula suspected they all hoped Seng would come up empty-handed when he performed the luminol tracing, but under the purple-ish light, florescent bloodstains appeared in crevasses of the spindle shaft.

Tyrell looked shocked, his mouth hanging open. Both the chief and Nate held him up as he stumbled backwards.

Lula wasn't as affected by the sight of a man crying while they read him his Miranda rights as she knew Melvyn would be. She was relieved he wasn't around.

She inadvertently distracted attention away from Tyrell by asking Seng for a close-up look at the blade, which he had removed to photograph.

Lula donned gloves, then fingered the nodules on each side of the blade. Sure enough, the distance between them appeared to fit the pattern of the wound in the skull on her lab table.

They asked Tyrell where they would find drugs in the house. He gave them noncommittal permission to search.

When the bottle of Temazepam was found in the medicine cabinet of the downstairs bathroom, Tyrell insisted he neither knew what it was or why it was there, and asserted his ignorance of the meaning or significance of the drug, but to no avail.

"Who uses that bathroom?" Nate asked.

"Guests." Tyrell answered.

"Do you have many?"

"Melvyn, Richard, when I'm not around."

Nate began asking questions about Tyrell's comings and goings during Mardi Gras.

Tyrell was emphatic that he had been on a business trip to Brazil at the time.

"We had some last-minute negotiations, so they asked me to stay an extra two days."

"We'll do a Customs check on that." Nate nodded at him. "What airlines?"

Tyrell shook his head, slowly. "I was on a private plane. They chartered—a damn jet." He looked at them angrily, as he realized the bind he was in, and the lengthy investigation that would tie him up for some time.

Like a burst of wind, he renewed his defense. "Why would I do this?" he asked the walls above the heads of the small group staring at him.

"Why does anybody kill, Tyrell?" Nate said. "We got the maggots from your workplace. They could only have come from your plant, right, Dr. Logan?"

"What the hell do maggots have to do with anything? How far away was the body from my plant?"

"About seven miles, and according to Dr. Logan, that's close enough, right?" Nate turned, looking for confirmation from Lula.

Everyone was staring at her. This was not where she wanted to be—in the middle of an investigation that relied on her skills to help put away a black man. She was a scientist, not a sociologist, yet she was being called upon to use both skills to put a black man behind bars—and to reveal his "guilt" in front of him.

"So far as we know, only black soldier flies procreate on corpses *and* manure, and in general, Louisiana isn't their habitat. So, the only way they'd be near a body in this area is because they were already nearby. The body found in the forest was close enough to the rendering area of the plant where the black soldier flies congregate."

"What does that tell us about when he was killed?" asked Nate.

"It doesn't tell us the exact date, but it was sometime around the next week after Mardi Gras, maybe Thursday or Friday. I'm not an entomologist, but my source confirms that the first wave of maggots found on the body were killed prematurely by the cold spell, which lasted until a thaw several days later. The newer batch of soldier flies laid eggs, too, accounting for the second colonization."

"Thanks for that." Tyrell pointed his finger up into the air to ask a Socratic question. "Since you know so much, please educate me on this one issue: what was my motive?"

Nate walked past him, pondering the floor. "We'll find that out with further investigation."

"Translated: you're not even sure. So you're going to arrest everybody who is remotely associated with this case, then? The girl you talk about? I don't even know who she is. Why would I kill a college student?"

"I understand, Tyrell, but honestly, we can't have you out on the loose while we're trying to sort it out."

Tyrell, looking shell-shocked, stood quiet for several moments. Then he asked, "So, is Melvyn off the hook, then?"

Nate looked at the chief, who spoke up: "Interesting segue. Give us permission to ask him some questions on video, and we'll have an answer for you, immediately. But if you're trying to protect someone, I'd say it's time to come clean."

Chief Broussard led them all out of the garage.

Lula glanced at her watch as they walked behind Tyrell and quietly told Devon that she had a plane to catch and needed to leave.

Devon nodded, not really paying attention, as he followed Chief Broussard out to the police cars. Instead, Devon took out a smartphone and turned it on, touching the screen several times.

Melvyn was sitting listlessly with one knee propping open the back passenger door, wearing a perturbed expression until he saw his father approaching. His face lit up as he bounded out of the back seat to run toward Tyrell.

"Am I in trouble, Daddy?"

Tyrell bent over to hold his son, comforting him.

The sight of affection moved Lula. Then she remembered how compartmentalized a mind could be, that it could destroy one life and nurture another in quick succession.

"You're okay, Melvyn. You're okay. I'm gonna call your mother, though, and let her know you're going to your grandmother's. You can stay with her for a while—we got some questions to ask you, okay?"

Chief Broussard nodded at Nate, who retrieved a micro-cassette tape recorder from a police officer. By now, four patrol cars were parked along the curb. Nate opened the front passenger door of the car, motioning to the driver to turn off the engine.

Melvyn sat up, putting his feet on the curb.

Devon held his smartphone in his hand to record the proceeding.

"Melvyn, you're aware that we have interviewed you to discuss the circumstances surrounding the death of Preston Pratt, right? Do you remember that occasion?" Nate began.

"Yes, sir. I do."

The boy looked to his father, who crouched on his haunches beside his son, a protective hand on the boy's shoulder. It was obvious that Melvyn worshipped his father and would do anything for his approval.

"I have a couple of questions to ask you again about your relationship with Preston."

"He was my friend, that was all. I told you I don't do that stuff he does. Did, I mean."

"I know. I know, man. You like girls," Nate said. "Good choice." Nate held his hand out to pat palm against palm.

The boy smiled an infectious grin at having reached a milestone of approval by another man.

"We don't think anything happened between you two, okay, Melvyn? So there's nobody in this room that thinks he did anything to you, except record you, and then pay you money. That's what he did, right?"

"Yeah. That was it."

"But did you know it was happening?"

"No. I just learned about the videotape. I knew he was tape recording me, but not filming me."

"How do you feel about that?"

Melvyn spoke slowly. "Sounds kinda creepy to me."

Nate nodded to a police officer, who handed him a micro-cassette player. "I'd like you to listen to something, okay?" Nate started the tape recorder:

> Male Voice: *So what's it gonna be today, Melvyn, my man. Did I say it right?*
>
> Melvyn: *You da man, brother man.*
>
> Male Voice: *So, I'm the man.*
>
> Melvyn: *You got it.*
>
> Male Voice: *I'm the man. Cool. (papers rustling).*
>
> Melvyn: *What's all that?*
>
> Male Voice: *Where?*
>
> Melvyn: *All that paper. You writing about me?*
>
> Male Voice: *In a way.*
>
> Melvyn: *You for real, man?*
>
> Male Voice: *You don't mind, do you?*
>
> Melvyn: *It depends. Why you writin' about me?*
>
> Male Voice: *Writers write. I'm creating a character, you might say.*
>
> Melvyn: *A character. Like Harry Potter. Like that?*
>
> Male Voice: *Not quite. But a character, just the same.*
>
> Melvyn: *What's my name gonna be?*
>
> Male Voice: *Jamal.*
>
> Melvyn: *Jamal? Why you gotta give me a Shaka Zulu name?*
>
> Male Voice: *(laughs)*
>
> Melvyn: *Why don't you call him Melvyn, like me?*

Male Voice: *Well, because this is called fiction.*

Melvyn: *But you said it's about me, and I'm real.*

Male Voice: *How about, for the time being, we call him that, and maybe down the road we'll think about changing his name for the series.*

Melvyn: *Call him Alvin.*

Male Voice: *Not a bad idea. I'll think about that.*

Melvyn: *Okay. So what else you wanna know?*

Male: *I'd like to know if you have any girlfriends.*

Melvyn: *Yeah, man, a whole lot of 'em. They call me Melvyn the Playa at school.*

Melvyn looked at his father out of the corner of his eyes. Tyrell's hands slapped him gently upside his head. "What you know about mackin' boy? You too young for that."

Nate gave Tyrell a remonstrative look, and they continued listening.

Male Voice: *The Playa? Like in Spanish. The beach?*

Melvyn: *I don't know no Spanish. Play-er.*

Male Voice: *What does that mean?*

Melvyn: *You know. I rap to them. Hard. You know, like I talk to them, and ask them for their numbers. My dad taught me that. Mackin'. That's what they called it back in the day. Big pimpin'.* Male Voice: *Do you call the girls?*

Melvyn: *Naw, man. A Playa doesn't do the calling. They call me. Every night. I get about five calls a night. (laughing)*

Male Voice: *Wow! All girls?*

Melvyn: *Yeah, who else? I ain't gonna talk to no dude on the phone, am I?*

Male Voice: *I guess not. Well, when you talk to them, well, like ... what do you talk about?*

Melvyn: *We talk about school. Movies. Music. Things. This'n that.*

Male Voice: *Like, what movies?*

Melvyn: *Well, it depends on if she goes to the–(interruption) movies. I go to the movies a lot with–[unintelligible]. We go on Tuesday nights. She takes me. So I ask them if they seen such-and-such a movie. Heck, I don't know. I mean, what does anybody talk about on the phone? Nothing important.*

Male Voice: *What about books?*

Melvyn: *Well, we talk about* Harry Potter *and stuff like that. I just finished the* Twilight *stuff.* The Hunger Games. *We'll talk about that.*

Male Voice: *Do you talk about drugs or anything like that?*

Melvyn: *No man. Don't go there ... I don't know anybody that does drugs. My mother would kick me up and down the State of Louisiana she hear me doin' something like that.*

Male Voice: *You've never seen a joint?*

Melvyn: *I seen 'em smoke it on the street, you know, they do like this ... (hissing sound) and they hold their breath. You ever try smoking weed?*

Male Voice: *Well ... yes.*

Melvyn: *It fucks up your head, don't it? My mom said she catch me with that shit, she'd slap me silly before I finish my first puff.*

Male Voice: *Your mom sounds pretty strict.*

Melvyn: *So you gonna rag on my momma now? You know you can't be doing that, right? That's the one thing I can teach you. You can't go talking about a black man's momma.*

Male Voice: *Oh. Well, I didn't mean it that way, I just ... well, okay. Sorry. Forget it.*

Melvyn: *S'aright. I know. You didn't know. We cool. Can I have another one?*

Male Voice: *Sure. Take two. Go ahead. So, where's your dad?*

Melvyn: *Here. There. Everywhere. I see him on weekends. He takes me on the weekends, you know, to his house. Sometimes, I just ride my bike there.*

Male Voice: *Is he married?*

Melvyn: *Yeah.*

Male Voice: *How you feel about that?*

Melvyn: *It's cool. I guess. If he's happy, I'm happy. (quiet)*

Male Voice: *Your mood changed. You okay? (pause) You wanna talk about it?*

Melvyn: *No. I'm fine. I was just thinkin', that's all.*

Tyrell stared at the machine with a look of recognition.

Lula checked her watch again. She couldn't stay much longer if she was going to get to the airport in time.

Male voice: *Okay, well, let me ask you again about drugs. You don't do them, but do any of your friends do 'em?*

Melvyn: *No, not mine.*

Male voice: *Do you know anybody who does drugs?*

Melvyn: *Well, I know they got some potheads who hang out before school, and they be smoking and shit. But I don't go near 'em. They're bad news, Preston. They got arrested once in front of the school for smoking some weed and then going onto the school grounds, you know. They said it was a drug-free zone and they were expelled. Our school is pretty strict about drugs. Besides, what the hell are drugs good for if you gotta keep paying for them? Man, I'd rather get more Nintendo or Sega than smoke up all the money into the air. They stupid, man.*

Preston: *You're a smart kid, Melvyn. Where'd you get a name like that, anyway?*

Melvyn: *Back to that, huh? Why you so fascinated about names? You gonna pay me fifty dollars to talk about names. You must have an awful lot of money to waste time on that.*

Preston: *I guess you're right.*

Melvyn: *My mom said her mom named me after some movie star or something. Anyway, she asked me to ask you if you–*

"Hold it a sec." Tyrell's hand waved at the recorder, which Nate turned off quickly.

"Can we step aside for a minute? He doesn't need to hear what I have to say here."

Tyrell stood up, and took several steps away.

Nate followed.

Tyrell could barely contain his anger.

"What the hell is this supposed to be?" he hissed. "Are you trying to embarrass my son? Why are you putting him through this?"

Nate explained, "We didn't know what your boy's relationship with the man was and wanted to get your take on it. We also wanted to get some answers from your son about what happened at this man's house."

Chief Broussard interjected. "We have reason to believe that one of the men was a pedophile. We were closing in on him and he committed suicide, jumping into the river downtown. So that's one line of inquiry closed. By getting your son's reactions, we could tell what, if anything, Melvyn had to do with the murders."

"I thought *I* was the target?" Tyrell asked.

"Well, you might or might not be, but we think your son has something to do with the whole thing." Nate said.

"I'm trying to get rich, man! What the hell would I be doing killing people?"

"Maybe because they get in your way?" Chief Broussard looked at Tyrell, his eyes steely.

"And the proof?"

"Anthrax."

"Ant who?"

"Don't pretend that you don't know what anthrax is, Tyrell. You're a chemical engineer."

"What anthrax? Where is it? Where do I keep such a toxic substance? What did I do with the anthrax?"

"Your rendering area. Aren't animal carcasses disposed of there?"

Tyrell touched his forehead, then started laughing. "Oh, wait a minute. So I killed the Congressman, who was going to make it all happen for me? That's weak, man. I'm just glad it wasn't you hunting for Osama bin Laden, 'cuz you'd still be chasing bogus leads."

"Do you want to call a lawyer?" Nate asked, handing the tape recorder to the police officer.

"Hell, no. You ain't got nothing on me, or my son. I'm not one of those okeydokey Negroes you all might be used to; I'm from the South, but I'm the free South, now, ya hear? My family built this business, sold it, and I'm about to embark on something much bigger. And, contrary to what you might be thinking, you're not going to get in the way of it. I will not be going to jail. Hell no." He wagged his finger at Broussard. "You're going to regret this, Chief."

"I'll have to take my chances, Ty."

Tyrell held his hands over his face, entreating the heavens. Then he called out to his son, "Melvyn, will you dial your mother's phone number for me?"

Melvyn pulled his cell from his pocket and dialed. The digital voicemail could be heard on speakerphone.

The men returned to Melvyn's side.

"Do you remember what you were talking about with Preston when we turned off the tape?" Nate asked.

"I can't remember everything we talked about. That's why he had the tape. He couldn't remember either."

Trying to hide his frustration, Nate changed his approach. "I'm gonna play the tape for you and when it goes off, I want you to remember what you were telling him, if you can."

"Well, I can try."

"That's the sport. Just try to remember back to where you were and what you said when he turned it off." Nate instructed the officer. "Rewind it about fifteen seconds, will you?"

Nate looked at Melvyn.

"There."

The tape played and Melvyn's voice rang out clearly:

> *Oh, yeah. My mom said her mom named me after some movie star or something. Right. Anyway, she asked me to ask you if you–*

"Do you remember what you said here?" Nate asked.

Tyrell was standing, looking down at his feet. He stroked his mustache, his other arm hugging his waist.

Melvyn glanced up, looking confused. "What did I say, again?"

"Replay it, please," Chief Broussard directed.

Melvyn listened to his voice. He looked lost. Or, he was a good actor, Lula thought.

"Let's continue." Nate looked at his watch. "I want to be sure of this." He nodded to the officer, who resumed playing the tape.

> Preston: *Okay, that ends this session. Here's your money. A clean bill, like you like them. I want to thank you very much, Mr. Douglas.*
> Melvyn: *Mr. Who? Sure. What do you want me to tell my mom?*

The machine stopped.

"Why were you asking him questions about your mother?" Nate asked.

Melvyn furrowed his brow, putting his thumbnail in his mouth. "Oh, Yeah. I remember now. Momma wanted to know if he was ever going to give her script back to her."

Lula looked at Nate.

"Your mother is a writer," she said slowly, each word feeling heavy. She stood frozen as she spoke.

"Your mother is a writer, Melvyn? Is that right?"

"Yeah, she wrote this idea for a series. She's a good writer, too. I told him one day, and he said he'd read what she wrote. So I gave it to him. She wanted it back."

"Do you remember what he said?"

"He said to tell her that he accidentally lost it."

Devon interrupted him. "What was that you said when we found that manuscript hidden in the desk?"

"I didn't mean anything."

"I'm not buying it, Melvyn."

"I got nothin' to sell," the boy countered.

Devon walked up, towering over him. "You know that's bullshit. You recognized something. What was the name of your Momma's book?"

Melvyn pantomimed zipping his lip and looked at Devon defiantly.

"Let's get phone records. Let's go, guys," said Nate. "Mr. Armstrong, we can get a warrant or you can give us permission to conduct a search of your home."

As his eyes moved to Melvyn, Lula decided to run interference. "You have your headphones for your cell? Why don't you sit and listen to music for a bit, okay, Melvyn?"

She returned to the men who had moved back toward Tyrell's house again, out of earshot, and were standing in the driveway.

"Okay, let's hear it, Dr. Lula," Nate said.

"My ex-wife? Is a suspect? Of what?" Tyrell asked.

Nate spoke. "Any clue as to what she wrote about that would have pissed her off so much that she would kill other people?

"*Kill?*" Tyrell's tone showed his disbelief.

"Time is of the essence—do you have any idea of where she's traveling, Tyrell?"

Tyrell seemed dumbfounded, said nothing.

The chief appealed to Lula. "Does it really fit, Dr. Lula?"

Nate interrupted. "Well, not so fast. She would have had to

kidnap him. Could she have done it alone? Somebody would have had to help her."

"She'd have to have been at his ball, too." Chief Broussard said. "We need to find out where she was on Mardi Gras."

Lula was speechless. So, this was how it was done. Just make up your mind on the spot, before the evidence is gathered? She needed to say something, as they rushed to judgment. She was about to speak when Devon did it for her.

"Everybody is everywhere on Mardi Gras! You mean, if she showed up for a party, she's the killer?"

Nate had just put a stick of gum in his mouth. "Well, she's a mother. And Tyrell here is the father. If you thought someone was taking advantage of your child, wouldn't you move heaven and earth to protect him?"

Devon's glance at Lula spoke volumes. To her, anyway. "I'm just saying, we gotta slow down, think things through, calmly," he said. "This could be a conspiracy among several people, for all we know."

Every man present looked at Devon. With distrust. He was speaking up for a black woman and no one knew why. Even Nate stopped chewing his gum, probably surprised that Devon, who mostly took a back seat, was asserting himself now.

"I'm just saying—everyone was wearing masks. Anybody could have shown up. Those parties end up open-door, especially out here, where everybody knows everybody. What did she do? Pick him up and carry him around over her shoulder?"

"Okay, so we'll look for more evidence of who was at his ball. Do we have a full inventory of Sherry's computer, phone, and digital photos, Wally?" Nate asked.

There he was again, invisible, but always visible. Lula had no idea who Wally was in relation to the detectives. Was he "the fixer" or was he a "finder?"

Lula said, "If the evidence shows that Preston Pratt was killed on the same day that we found the first two fingers, then there's a complication."

The men all stopped to listen.

"I was with Melvyn's mother that night. Do you remember that I drove Melvyn home?"

Nate nodded.

"Well, she invited me in for dinner and the three of us were at her home the whole evening. Melvyn was performing at the festival the next day. I spent the night at her place. I'd had too much to drink."

Nate's face fell. "Your point is ... what? You've taken sides now?"

Devon held his hands out. "Hold it, Nate. I take offense to that. So, now we have to stop talking because we're trying to save a suspect because she's black?"

"Look. I'm not gonna have that in my department," said the chief. "We deal in facts, not factions." He gave Wally a quick glance. "So, Dr. Lula, tell us where you're going with this information."

Lula tried not to sound as defensive as she probably looked with her arms folded in front of her.

"I'm trying to fill out the picture, gentlemen, so I'm sharing information that you might not know, that hasn't been relevant, until now. At this stage, the case isn't solved, unless we confirm that the victim had a heart attack and was dismembered afterwards. So, the nature of who did what changes. It would appear that we have kidnapping charges that could stick, as he was kept in that shack for a week. We have a crime, because his fingers were cut off. The question is, who had the physical force to accomplish that against a male weighing 140-plus pounds?"

"That puts you in the crosshairs, Tyrell. Here's your chance." Nate took two steps back, as if signaling the wider berth Tyrell was being given to free himself from suspicion and make the case against his ex-wife.

"I don't wanna believe it, but it looks like she set me up. I dunno, man. But I'm being set up." Tyrell hung his head. "She hated me more than I thought, I guess. We just didn't have much to say to each other, anymore. When we divorced, she shook my hand, and said, 'What you do with your Johnson is your business, but it's mine when my son is affected.'"

"Anything else you want to tell us, Mr. Armstrong?" Nate asked.

"It just seems like you're looking at everybody related to me, and not other people that might be up to something." Tyrell said. "It's a set up—blame it on the black man. I was waiting for something like this to happen."

A silence hung in the air.

Chief Broussard looked at Lula. "Let's see what Melvyn says, and we can take it from there."

When they returned to the car, Melvyn walked toward his father, but Chief Broussard put out a hand to stop him. "Just stay here for now, okay, Melvyn? We want to ask you some more questions."

"Why? I didn't do anything!" The boy exclaimed. "Damn!"

"I know, son. They're just looking for some evidence, Melvyn," Tyrell told him.

"Why they comin' to me?"

Tyrell looked for permission to speak.

"They think your momma might know something about this matter. Maybe she was trying to protect you, or something. What do you think?"

"I think she knows white people, after all. She said that they'd try to frame me."

"Do you know why she thought that?" Lula asked. Devon was looking at her intently.

"She says that's what they do when they can't find somebody. They go arrest the nearest black man. I told her I'm just a kid, but she said that didn't matter. To them, I'm a grown man, she said."

Melvyn looked up at his father. "You think that's right? They think I'm a man?"

"Did Preston give that earring to you?" Nate asked.

"No. Juanito did. He said Preston gave it to him, but he didn't want it anymore."

"Damn it. I'm getting a migraine." Nate was exasperated.

Chief Broussard instructed Tyrell to stay with Melvyn and not go anywhere. Everyone else walked up the sidewalk toward Tyrell's home.

Chief Broussard asked Nate, "What about that nuisance who was always hanging around? Richard?"

Lula answered. "When he was in my lab office, he was angry about the producers. He said they didn't know anything about film. They were frauds. Richard thought he was the better writer."

"But why would he kill anyone?" Nate asked.

"Well, he was angry with Juanito," Lula reminded him.

"Then why would he kill Sherry?"

"I don't think he killed anybody. But I think he might know more than we suspect, might be involved in some way. Maybe he helped Sherry and Juanito, and wanted a piece of the action. Who knows? But whatever you do, I don't think it's wise to rush."

"I told Juanito he can't leave until we clear him." Nate said. "We can find Richard pretty easily—he has nowhere to go. He'll end up back at his house, eventually. We can get some information from him. He knows Melvyn's family pretty well, I imagine."

"We haven't even talked about Ambrose Girabeaux," Lula said.

The men were quiet. "That was out of deference to you, Dr. Lula," said Devon.

After a pause, she told Devon, "I'm not so sure we can make judgments about who is the better suspect without all of the facts. You're probably privy to other information that I don't have, and I have information from my own forensic work that has to be factored in. I'll have the report finished when I return, but my plane is leaving soon, gentlemen. I'll be back in two days—you can text me if you need me. Devon has the number."

She scanned their expressions.

"Let me add something, for the record. I've befriended Bebe, but our discussions revolved around her concern for Melvyn. I don't know her well enough to vouch for her one way or the other, but I was at her home on the very night that Preston was supposed to have died. There are two people not being talked about who are still alive, who each have a connection to the victims: Preston's wife, Mare, and Juanito."

Nate nodded to Devon. "Get them down to the department. Now. Doctor Lula, we will welcome your report upon your return."

24

LULA

Lula turned up the air conditioner in her car to keep her awake as she drove to Dallas/Fort Worth International Airport. She'd gone close to twenty-four hours with barely any sleep, and was taking her life into her hands by driving at all.

Her reflection in the rear-view mirror showed eyes that were haggard and puffy. Her mind was restless and overwhelmed with disparate thoughts, all vying for attention. She thought about Ambrose, Melvyn, and wondered how Bebe would survive the drama.

She, who had studied the history of slavery and its violent consequences, might have implicated a black woman in a murder.

Every Black American she knew always felt a sense of loss when one of their own was involved in a crime. Outnumbered by a majority of Whites who already distrusted them, they knew that one misstep by one Black, in the eyes of the uninformed majority, was a step toward undoing Blacks' slow, incremental progress toward acceptance.

As the air-conditioning blasted into the car, she turned it off, instantly feeling the humidity that enveloped her.

She couldn't wait to get out of this furnace of a place, get a good night's sleep in the hotel, and get ready for her preliminary meeting tomorrow.

10:00 p.m.

The sky was dark except for the garish yellow lights that illuminated the airport terminals, which turned the blonde streaks in Bebe's brunette wig a sickly green. Her navy-blue Jones New York pantsuit and Italian walking shoes gave her the sophisticated look of a cosmopolitan traveler, or a flight attendant navigating her way through the airport between flights. She was able to hide right out in the open, rather than furtively, like the fugitive she was.

Her disguise proved foolproof as she approached a black female attendant who, without hesitation, pointed her in the direction of a VIP lounge. Feigning inability to reach her money, she opened her wallet and asked the attendant to take out a crisp ten-dollar bill for a tip. No skin would pass between them.

The empty executive lounge was spacious, with televisions in each corner, couches and chairs, footrests, low coffee tables, and a wide window overlooking a busy tarmac.

The bathroom, with shower, was also vacant, piped-in music playing a Muzack rendition of an old Destiny's Child hit.

Bebe changed clothes, put her suit in a plastic bag, and dumped it at the bottom of a trash bin. With several yanks at the dispenser, she ensured that the bin filled up with paper towels. She figured VIP bathrooms were monitored for cleanliness more often, and trash would likely be emptied soon. She checked her rolling luggage, glancing at her new passport, and reminded herself to use her maiden name. With one last look in the mirror, she admired her brown Jones suit, an exact replica of the blue one she had just discarded.

Luggage in tow, Bebe headed to Terminal E to make an appearance for a domestic flight, in order to confuse her eventual pursuers if they used airport cameras to track her whereabouts. She'd have to high-tail it via taxi to Terminal A afterward, to board her international flight.

Despite the hour, the airport was alive with activity. Most of the check-in counters were busy. She stepped into the long line, her sunglasses giving her a sense of being curtained off from her surroundings. She opened her purse, and, without looking, rummaged inside for her ticket. Then she took the purse from her shoulder and opened its side compartment.

Empty.

In any crime, there is the likelihood of a perpetrator making a fatal mistake.

She shook her head. *Here's my mistake.*

She peeked behind her, then got out of line and retraced her steps to the VIP bathroom. The attendant she'd seen earlier recognized her, and asked, "Did you forget something?" Bebe responded with an apologetic nod.

The bathroom was now filled with three women gabbing about nothing, their chatter increasing her anxiety and clouding her thoughts.

Think! Think!

She opened and entered one of the stalls, but did not stoop to sit, waiting until the bathroom was quiet. Minutes later she exited, washed her hands, and grabbed a paper towel.

A toilet flushed. She looked up, surprised. An attractive Japanese-looking woman with silky black hair walked toward her, sullenly ignoring her existence.

The clock was ticking. She had forty minutes before they closed the ticket counter. She glanced at the ring on her finger, and got an idea. Wiping her hands, she dropped the towel, and her ring, into the bin.

"Oh my God. You idiot!" she exclaimed loudly, bending over the bin to dig for her ring, the whole time feeling for her ticket.

"What happened?" the Asian woman asked.

"My ring. I dropped it in here, like a moron."

"Oh, wow. That's terrible. You want me to call the guy to have them unlock the door so you can open it? It'll be easier."

"I don't think it dropped too far. I hope. I think I'm okay."

The woman walked to the other side of the sink, washing her hands and pulling a paper towel from a dispenser.

"Sure?"

"I think I'm okay. Thanks a lot."

"Good luck!" The svelte woman walked out, taking one last glance at herself in the mirror.

Bebe looked up to check the mirror. The bathroom was now vacant.

Turning back to her task, she dug deep down into the metal trash receptacle built into the wall. By now there were several dozen pieces of trash on the floor. She bent forward, searching for the plastic bag with her discarded clothes, and found it.

Clasping the black bag, she yanked it out. Misshapen and smashed, the bag was moist from the still-damp towels that dozens of women had added to the bin since Bebe had stashed her discarded clothes. She scurried to the bathroom stall again to sift through the contents.

The ticket wasn't there.

She finally faced what she'd hoped to avoid: the possibility that the ticket was still in her rental car. She'd seen her purse contents tumble over when she made a turn, but thought she'd retrieved everything.

Now she had to attempt the impossible: get back to the Terminal E parking garage to retrieve her ticket, then race to Terminal A to check in and board her international flight.

Bebe did everything with precision. She had patrolled Nakadee, ostensibly while carrying out her pharmaceutical sales, when she was actually shadowing her nemeses. She knew their comings and goings like clockwork, and during the evenings kept her son occupied with homework and television while she ran brief "errands."

She had timed her departure from Nakadee so as not to give police enough time to catch up with her before her flight departed.

Now, she was in a panic, although there was little chance that the Dallas/Fort Worth police would intercept her. She had deliberately left a clue to throw them off: a flight itinerary crumbled on the floor of her personal car's front seat, showing that she was flying out of nearby Shreveport's smaller airport.

She walked briskly, the sound of her luggage wheels reverberating off the concrete along with the hollow click of her high heels. She contemplated abandoning her burden to make a break for the parking garage, but needed her luggage as a prop.

Sweat was beading on her brow as she entered the Terminal E garage. She only needed five extra minutes—that she didn't have.

As Lula hurried into the terminal, the black woman's blonde-streaked tresses stood out in the sea of white faces.

When she looked up again, the woman had disappeared down a corridor. Lula tried to shake off the common misperception black middle-class women have that someone looks familiar, and focused on her mission of reaching her gate in time.

When she looked up again, the black woman was a distant blur on the horizon until she turned around to look back—and their eyes met.

Lula slowed, pretending to stop and read a map on the wall, while trying to use her peripheral vision. She saw Bebe surreptitiously peep back at her again.

Lula's eyes scanned around for a police officer. Seeing none in sight, she continued, following Bebe.

When her quarry turned a corner, Lula ran, racing to catch up and keep her in view. Rounding the same bend, Lula reached three doors, one of which appeared to be a locked utility closet. The other two doors, one on her left, the other on her right, were closing at the same time. One led to a women's bathroom, the other exited to the parking garage at Terminal E.

Lula did not take the bait, and headed out to the garage, straining to see Bebe's blonde hair above the heads and shoulders she was bumping into in her hurry.

"Hey, lady, we have a plane to catch, too!" Angry expletives trailed her as she ran. Several yards into the garage, she stood still, listening for the sound of hurried feet.

Bebe took off her shoes and stood frozen in place, hunched over beside a car, and listened. She heard footsteps. Then a voice.

"Bebe!"

Bebe made a mad dash for her rental car and took the keys from her pocket, thanking her stars that she hadn't thrown them away yet. She had had every intention of depositing them into the bathroom garbage bin with her change of clothes, but her instincts had told her that she should discard them only once she had boarded the plane.

She opened the car door, leaned over, and saw the ticket partially hidden under the passenger seat.

"Did you see a black woman with blonde hair come this way?" Lula's query only produced see-through stares, until a bearded, longhaired young man with multiple piercings replied. "Was she wearing a brown suit?"

Lula nodded.

"I think she went thataway."

She smiled her thanks.

Lula spied movement in that direction and took off her shoes, clutching them in her hand.

A part of her wanted to believe that everyone was wrong about Bebe, that she was yet one more black woman being scapegoated.

"Bebe! I need to talk to you!" Lula's voice echoed off the concrete walls.

The garage was dark, with only small streaks of artificial light illuminating the dust wafting in a hazy mist. Lula glanced at the stairwells on opposite ends of the garage, and ran to the nearest one.

She opened the heavy door to the stairwell, peeked inside and— was felled, like a branch off a tree, collapsing to the ground in a heap. She felt a heavy thud against her shoulder as her head hit the pavement.

"You gonna give a sister up? You gonna give a sister up?" Bebe hissed. "If I go down, you're going with me, bitch."

Lula groaned, dazed. She tried to raise her arms to her head to protect herself, but her shoulder was caught under the weight of a female defensive tackle, whose shoulders pressed into her side.

"You think you got something on me? Why you coming after me, bitch? Who's going after *them*? Tell me that! Who's going after *them*?" She pushed into Lula with each word, as Lula lay frozen, immobile against the weight of her attacker.

346

"What ... what are you doing, Bebe?"

Breathing heavily, Bebe pushed against her, propping herself on one knee.

"Stand up. You're gonna stand up and shut the fuck up while I decide what to do with you, you hear?"

Lula moved slowly, her head throbbing. "They know it's you," she panted. They were each breathing heavily. "It's over, Bebe."

"No, that's where you're wrong, Miss Lula. I'm schooling *you*, now. It's not over. It has just begun! I'm going to get on an airplane and you are going to let me, and my son will be joining me once I get settled."

Bebe's jacket was crumpled and askew, uncharacteristic for someone so polished. Her eyes were fixed on Lula.

"You're helping the wrong people, Lula. You're helping the wrong people. You and I both know it. Those people conspired. Together. They could've bought the idea from me. Instead, they leave me on the road for dead. How they like me now? 'The people of the land have used oppression, and exercised robbery, and have vexed the poor and needy: yea, they have oppressed the stranger wrongfully.' Ezekiel 22:29. It's payback time."

Lula could almost feel her skin move where her heart was pounding. She was in the fight of her life—for her life—with only words as her weapon. She needed to use them carefully now, to appeal to an intelligent woman who appeared to have lost her mind.

"So you're going to kill people up and down the State of Louisiana to avenge a wrong?"

Expecting another blow, Lula flinched, but Bebe took a step back. Even a man would have felt menaced by the look on her face as she looked up at the ceiling.

It was then that Lula made her move. The two women grunted, one trying to escape, the other lunging after her, grabbing her leg with one hand, trying to pull her down from the stairs.

Lula tried to kick her assailant in the face, but Bebe grabbed her other foot as if palming a baseball. Her balance compromised, Lula grabbed the stair rail, holding on for dear life.

"A tiger, huh!" Bebe laughed. "The little investigator's a tiger! Well, you're in *my* jungle now, bitch. I don't want to have to kill you, but if I do, just know that I killed because they killed me first! I'm just retaliating! They reap what they damn sowed."

"Well ... let ... me help you. Please! Not like this." Lula didn't know whose words came out of her mouth, but regretted them instantly. She felt her arm being tugged, her body pulled upward and spun around, like a rag doll, her neck in the vise of a very strong arm. Bebe could give any man a run for his money. The thought that she could have picked Pratt up and killed him with her bare hands was now conceivable.

"What did they do to you, Bebe?" she asked, plaintively.

Bebe slowly walked backward against the wall, as Lula felt her assailant's warm breath on her neck, with small sprays of saliva as Bebe hissed: "They stole my soul."

She clinched Lula closer in her headlock, her breasts against Lula's back, seeming to protect her like a young cub, until the menace of Bebe's tone quickly dispelled that wishful thinking.

"Do you hear me? They took my private thoughts, my words, my feelings. About my beautiful son. About my story. *My* history. *My* essence. That maggot-infested motherfucker mixed them up, jumbled them around to tell his own story, using what was *mine*. Then he probably got some hungry black Uncle Tom to fill in the blanks, make it sound ethnic. Why didn't he tell a story about Tyrell's white drug-dealing wife? These white people and their drugs—and they're so worried about crack?"

Mirroring her assailant's movements to show her understanding, Lula first bobbed her head up and down, then tried to interrupt Bebe by shaking it from side to side.

"That shit was way too easy. I got the drugs and used them on everybody, including you." Bebe chuckled. "That hangover on the morning of the festival was no hangover, sweetie. You were out in seconds."

"You drugged me?"

"That's right. I needed a way to get out of the house to check up on my captive. He tried to escape. Can you believe the fucker had the nerve to die without me being there? Had a friggin' heart attack. He managed to get outside—where he died just yards from his hell-hole."

"You didn't kill him?"

"Not technically. But close enough. I whacked him a couple of times. He had half a brain as it was. Now he's on your examining table. Ha!" She sounded gleeful, though her eyes were steely.

Unsure what to do, Lula stalled for time. "What about Sherry?"

"You think you're gonna live to tell someone, don't you? My son told me where she went to the gym, so I joined it. I'd go there every now and then. She was a swimmer. I was lucky. They leave their keys in a basket at the front desk. I figured out which were hers and took them, drove her car around the corner, then walked back into the gym. I got to talking with her, offered her a cold drink. She was high already, tell the truth. She said something about swimming with a buzz—it brightened her experience. I knocked her out, like I'm about to do *you*, and left my calling card. She was helping Pratt. And she baked like a turkey for it," Bebe laughed. "I know it's not funny, but revenge is sweet. I didn't do half of what I intended, but God helped me mete out justice. That's right. And it isn't a white man's god, either."

"Bebe. They can try, but you can't steal a soul. It is *their* souls that are condemned. Think about it. Every time they take credit for someone else's work, whether they're successful or not, that's *your* work up there, and they know it. In their own way, they've created their own hell. They're slaves to someone else's ideas and thoughts that were better than their own. They're not writers. They're copiers. That's not the same thing, is it? Why not look at it that way?"

For an instant, Bebe's face relaxed, showing an understanding. "But they did it with malice, and criminal intent. Ain't nobody going after them. Those cops aren't going after those criminals. They're coming after me." Her face softened for an instant.

"Do you know what it's like to listen to a radio station and hear your own voice in someone else's? To hear your words, with their changes made to them?"

Bebe held Lula's torso tightly, pulling her closer. "I killed—to be heard. They're fucking impostors."

Lula managed to eke out, "Hell ... hell," she was breathing with difficulty, "hath no fury, like a black female writer scorned."

Bebe loosened her hold on Lula, though her arm still gripped her shoulder tightly.

"That's right. I did it, and I'm glad I did. Drug him. Drive your victim to a secluded wooded area. And read to him. Show him how shallow his words ring when they belong to someone else. Then go in for the kill. Excrement should not have a long shelf life. Let him starve while you feed him his drivel. Then walk on and don't look back.

"I wanted Pratt to die anonymously, like my script did, when it was pilfered, pored over, studied, and reshaped into the television series. Nobody knew it was a stolen work. That the man masquerading as a writer was a white-collar criminal." She squared her shoulders. "This is the Land of the Free. Land of the free to steal." Bebe's chuckle was a sinister gurgle. "Those fuckers paid for their crimes."

Lula whispered. "I think it's *you* who's paying for it."

Bebe looked around, frantically.

"Whatever. Look, sister girl. I need about a half hour to do what I have to do. Let me get on that plane, and you can keep your life. Either you let me go now, or I'm going to have to strangle you right here. Take your pick."

"Look, you're twice my size, and I can't beat you up. I can't let you go, though." Lula tried to reason with her.

"You scream, you're dead. You gonna die for these fuckers, too?"

"You can't run from your crimes, Bebe."

"And who the hell says I can't? *They* do it all the time. *They* steal, and let the law reward them for it. The Congress, the Senate, the courts that rubber-stamp their crimes—the producers, the writers, the actors. They all say, 'Hey, we have the right! The right to steal another person's efforts, their labor, their experiences. Their *lives*. And let's all go for a swim, afterwards.'"

Bebe hit her chest with her free hand.

"They go to award ceremonies, and get trophies for *my* work. Who says I can't kill them, like they killed my characters?"

She turned toward Lula, who tried to meet her gaze.

"Look at it this way," Lula said. "Every time they see their characters, they know they're looking at yours. If you steal a car, you know it's not yours for long. Worse yet, for them, they will forever doubt their own imaginations."

Bebe snorted. "Yeah. I see 'em all the time, trying harder and harder to do it better. But they never do. They write articles and shit, and tell the world what they did, as if it were done honestly, but nobody reads between the lines."

"Right. They can never purge their guilt." Lula said.

"That's not enough for me."

Lula tried to think fast, and talked even faster. "When did it happen, Bebe? When did he take your work?"

"I wrote it four years ago."

"I beg of you. Let me help the innocent people who are accused of the murders, Bebe."

Lula saw pain, terror, and fear in her captor's eyes—not of Lula, but of what she intended to do.

"What about Juanito and Richard? And Tyrell?" asked Lula.

Bebe was alarmed. "Tyrell? That's what the dumbass gets for marrying a whore. Juanito was all a part of the conspiracy. He gets no help. I'd have tried to get him, too, but he's too strong."

"And Melvyn? What about your son?"

"Don't you worry about him. I told Tyrell a long time ago to send my son to my mother to raise if anything happened to me. I'll see him again, soon enough. Don't you worry about him."

Lula took a step backward while Bebe, as if dancing a tango with her, took a corresponding step forward.

"Did you ever talk to Pratt on the phone about the script?"

"No. When I found out Melvyn had given it to them, I told Melvyn I wanted the script back, or at least some opinion about what I'd written. He never brought it back—the fucker said he had lost it. Then I saw my shit on screen. My characters. My dialogue. He rewrote it and baited me with the title 'Words without Thought.' Guess what my title was? 'Think Before You Speak'. He changed everything around. So I turned his life around, and now he's dead."

She laughed, then, as if reminding herself of the urgency, looked abruptly at Lula. "So what we gonna do here, Missy? You coming with me, or am I leaving you here? I gots to go, and I don't want to hurt a sister."

"But you did kill a brother."

"He didn't pass the copyright amendment to protect writers like me. I warned him." A pensive look crossed Bebe's face. "You pass or you pass. I doubt the Uncle Tom even bothered to read the bill."

"He was black. And innocent."

Bebe stared, a flash of alarm on her face. "Yeah, well so are a whole lot of brothers who are spending the rest of their lives in jail. You win some, you lose some."

She looked around, as if bored. "I'm leaving now. You done good, sister. You have done your race proud. Go ahead, Ms. Forensic Anthropologist. Now you've discovered me. Try discovering them. Try discovering the law—the laws that were made not for you and me, but against you and me. Who's there to defend me, sister? Tell me that. Why didn't anybody come to help me. They stole my son. *I* created him! Lawyers denied me, said it would cost me too much and they wouldn't take it on contingency. They all help their own."

"So why not find a black attorney?"

"Black attorneys help Whites, not Blacks, except to take their money.

"Nobody's thinking about you, or me, from the time they brought us over here. As an anthropologist, you know that. Who came to the rescue when our people were enslaved and made to come here? Who rescued us when our people toiled in the fields? Who came to our rescue? Even the abolitionist states benefited from slavery. *You* can claim this country. I'm out of here."

"What about Blaine?"

"What about him? I don't claim him, although he got what he deserved. Somebody got to him before me. He was a pedophile, like most of 'em. They wanna stay young but they do it on the backs of little children. If someone makes an accusation against those thieves, you better trust him."

Lula's breathing had calmed, though her head was throbbing, likely concussed.

"Yet you let Melvyn go over to Preston's every week."

Lula wondered whether what she heard was her scream or the slap that produced it reverberating through the stairwell. Instinctively, Lula ran, but was soon backed into a corner by her assailant.

"Teaching my son how to make money is not exploiting him."

The slap smarted, but it was Lula's heart that hurt more—for a woman whose anger had destroyed her life, and the lives of the ones she loved.

"So this is how it is," Lula whispered. Her eyes filled with tears. "Killing? Over a ... copyright?"

"And what the hell is the Bible, Miss Lula? We been killing over the written word forever and ever. Open up those pretty eyes of yours, Lula. You done drank the Kool-Aid, too?"

Bebe raised her hand, covering Lula's face.

"Now, close your eyes, Miss Thing, and turn around and face the corner like a good little dunce girl who is stupid enough to do the white man's business—to put Black-Africans away, when its 'dem who should be in jail."

She looked almost philosophical, casually discussing her views. "You were rooting for the wrong side, so you, my dear, are a casualty. When it's all said and done, there's only one right we have on this miserable earth, Miss Logan. Miss Louise G. Logan, who lives at 348 Buford Street, Social Security number 081-22-00_4. Your God-Bless-America bullshit about patriotism and doing right. It's all bullshit. Only one thing you have—that any of us African mother fuckers has—we got one right in this country from the time we were brought here." Bebe held her finger in the air while Lula tried hard not to flinch. "Whether it comes sooner or later, we got one right. No matter what any white man tells us—do this, but you can't do that—you can't steal ... but we can."

Bebe was breathing heavily, now, and there was no life in her eyes. "We all got one right. *To die.*"

She leaned into Lula, close enough to kiss her cheek, and whispered. "I knew you'd be on my trail sooner or later, and it'd be you to solve the mystery. Congrats. *Tag*, girl. You're it." Bebe brushed her clothing off and stood over Lula. "Now, I wanna hear you loud and clear. Keep forward, and don't turn around. Start counting."

"One .... two .... three," Lula said quietly.

"Yeah, like that."

Lula kept her eyes closed, kept counting, her voice no longer trembling. Involuntarily, her eyes opened for a brief instant, and turned around just as Bebe rushed her.

Their eyes met.

"Four .... five—"

A huge blow connected with Lula's temple, and she collapsed to the floor in a heap.

Bebe opened the metal door and calmly strolled out of the stairwell with her luggage to Terminal A to catch her flight.

Epilogue

Lula was found lying unconscious where her assailant had left her. She will return to Oakland, California to recover from her injuries and to contemplate her future—until her services are needed again, this time, in a manhunt for an elusive fugitive.

sciunt bene qui sint

M

J

B W

T

S

L

A

C

R

CPSIA information can be obtained at www.ICGtesting.com
Printed in the USA
BVOW08s0752010216

434990BV00002B/2/P